# GROWING PAINS

He didn't notice when he first heard the slithering sound, a soft rustle followed by a dry whispering crackling noise, as if paper had fallen—or leaves. Then he felt something slide across the toe of his boot and curl to brush his pant leg, and as he turned back to the cave entrance, he saw that a thick net of greenery had replaced what he had hacked away a bare hour before. He tried to kick off the vines clinging to him, succeeding only in embedding the thorns deeper into his ankles.

Feeling an edge of panic, he jumped, hopped, and ran, hacking as he went. He never saw the root looping down from the ceiling to lash itself around his throat while another knocked him to the floor.

By Anne McCaffrey and Elizabeth Ann Scarborough
*Published by Ballantine Books:*

POWERS THAT BE
POWER LINES
POWER PLAY

Other titles by Anne McCaffrey
*Published by Ballantine Books:*

DECISION AT DOONA
DINOSAUR PLANET
DINOSAUR PLANET SURVIVORS
GET OFF THE UNICORN
THE LADY
PEGASUS IN FLIGHT
RESTOREE
THE SHIP WHO SANG
TO RIDE PEGASUS

**THE CRYSTAL SINGER BOOKS**
CRYSTAL SINGER
KILLASHANDRA
CRYSTAL LINE

**THE DRAGONRIDERS OF PERN®**
DRAGONFLIGHT
DRAGONQUEST
THE WHITE DRAGON
MORETA: DRAGONLADY OF PERN
NERILKA'S STORY
DRAGONSDAWN
THE RENEGADES OF PERN
ALL THE WEYRS OF PERN
THE CHRONICLES OF PERN: FIRST FALL
THE DOLPHINS OF PERN

*With Jodi-Lynn Nye:*
THE DRAGONLOVER'S GUIDE TO PERN

*Edited by Anne McCaffrey:*
ALCHEMY AND ACADEME

# POWER
# LINES

## Anne McCaffrey
## Elizabeth Ann Scarborough

A Del Rey® Book
BALLANTINE BOOKS • NEW YORK

A Del Rey® Book
Published by Ballantine Books

Library of Congress Catalog Card Number: 94-6631

ISBN 0-345-38780-5

Manufactured in the United States of America

First Hardcover Edition: July 1994
First Mass Market Edition: July 1995

10  9  8  7  6  5  4  3  2  1

This is for two fur gentlemen of great dignity and
courage who have meant
a great deal to both of us in their separate ways
and on different continents:
Mr. Peaches & Simon Big-Paws

# 1

SpaceBase occasionally still rumbled underfoot, as if to remind everyone that Petaybee planet was by no means pacified. The riders from Kilcoole village had kept well to the wooded trails farthest from the steaming, freshly thawed river, now merely rimmed with ice like a frosting of salt along the top of a glass. Several times on their journey, the planet shook and shifted, as if telling them of the urgency of their mission, but by now the Petaybeans calmly accepted the planet's new mood.

Major Yanaba Maddock, Intergal Company Corps, Retired—well, mostly retired, anyway—looked around at the faces of her lover and her new friends and neighbors. Their own mood was both happy and expectant as they dismounted in front of the SpaceBase headquarters building. Clodagh Senungatuk, Kilcoole's healer and one-woman information center, dusted her divided skirts while her curly-coated horse gazed impassively as flurries of its freshly shed hairs floated on the unseasonably warm air.

Sinead Shongili, Yana's own beloved Sean's sister, assisted Aisling, Clodagh's sister, from the saddle while Buneka Rourke held the reins of her Uncle Seamus's and Aunt Moira's horses as they dismounted. The churned mud that formed the roads at SpaceBase was dotted with stones and boards and pieces of metal to be used as steps. Hopping from one of these to the next, the party of Petaybeans made their way into the building.

They all had such high hopes for this meeting, Yana thought, almost with irritation. Personally, she hated meetings. Always had. Most of them provided no more input than could be contained in a two-second burst on a comm link. Waste of time, ordinarily. She took a deep breath and neatly tucked in the shirttails of the uniform blouse that Dr. Whittaker Fiske had suggested might be the politically tactful costume for the occasion. Partisan as she was, she was the most neutral person attending the meeting. While the company she kept announced her leanings, the uniform would remind the bosses of her long-standing affiliation with Intergal.

Sean Shongili, sensing her tension, reached up briefly to knead the back of her neck, and she gave him a nervous smile. As the chief geneticist for this area of the planet, Sean was a key member of the Petaybean delegation. He and the others seemed to think that it was predestined that the company men would see reason and accede to the requirements of their planet and its people. Sean, who despite his profession was no more experienced at being a prospective parent than she was, had already suggested that her premeeting trepidation was in part at least a hormonally stimulated response. He was wrong, but as he had been born and bred on the planet, she could hardly expect him to understand.

Petaybeans gathered only to entertain themselves and each other or to discuss a problem and arrive at a consensus for solution. Company meetings were far more often power plays where the issue was secondary to whose view prevailed. But then, Yana had never before been to any meeting where the issue was the survival of a sentient planet and its people.

Two deep breaths, and she followed Sean into the building and on into the conference room. As the Petaybeans and Yana entered, Dr. Whittaker Fiske stood, forcing the other dignitaries to do likewise. Here most of the cracks from the earthquakes had been sealed. The screens along the walls were still slightly askew on their brackets but functional. There wasn't enough seating for all the Petaybeans who had been invited, but the major players ringed the beautiful table, handcrafted from native Petaybean woods.

As nominal chairperson, Whittaker Fiske sat in the center with his son, Captain Torkel Fiske. Yana, Sean Shongili, Clodagh, and the Petaybean survivors of the last ill-fated exploratory mission sat to the left of the Fiskes; Francisco and Diego Metaxos and Steve Margolies were placed to the right, along with various other company dignitaries. The latter looked considerably more confused than the Petaybean group, who were, to a person, optimistically resolute.

A bare half hour later, when the comm link with Intergal Earth had been established, the optimism on many faces had been replaced with disgust and dismay at the unreasonableness of certain officials.

"And you actually have the unmitigated gall ..." declared the occupant of the main screen, Farringer Ball, the secretary-general of Intergal's Board of Directors, "to tell me that the planet is making these demands on us?" His round, fleshy face had taken on a reddish orange hue.

Yana thought some of that color had to be generated by the faulty connection or the disrupted innards of the comm screen. No human flesh could turn such a shade.

"Yes, Farrie, that's what I'm saying," Whittaker Fiske replied, smiling gently as a fond parent might to an erring child. "And I've proof enough that I haven't lost my marbles or melted my circuits or any damned thing else you can think up to account for such a—" Whittaker Fiske paused and grinned before he added, "delusion. Delusion it isn't!" He said that with no smile whatever and a very solemn expression. "We may not have encountered such a phenomenon before, Farrie, but we have now, and I don't need my nose rubbed in it any more than it has been. So let's get on with—"

"We'll get on with nothing, Fiske," Farringer Ball said explosively, and a thick finger rose from the bottom of the screen, followed by a hand that was shaking with anger. "I'm sending a relief company down immediately, with a squad of medics to check out every single—"

"Just be sure none of the company or the medics happen to have Petaybee as their planet of origin," Torkel interrupted.

"Huh? What's that, Captain?" The secretary-general shifted his scowl slightly to Torkel.

"It'll be hard to do, Secretary Ball, since most of your best men and women come from this planet."

"I don't believe what I'm hearing." Farringer turned away from the camera to address others on his end of the communications channel. "We've got a planet issuing orders, respected scientists gone barmy, and now captains telling secretary-generals how to choose reinforcements! This situation is now Class Four!"

"You never were reasonable, Farrie," Whittaker Fiske remarked in an amiably placatory tone, "when you come up against something remotely unusual."

"Remotely? Unusual?"

"Like I said . . ." Whittaker glanced around the screens at the other people who were attending the conference from a distance. "You can't handle what isn't in the book. This isn't. I came here myself to sort out what looked like a minor glitch. And it's the majorest one I've ever encountered. However, keeping both mind and options open, I'd still like to get on with the substance of this conference. Take a trank, Farrie, and listen, will ya? I'll explain if you stop interrupting me."

"We do owe Whittaker the courtesy of hearing him out, Farringer," said one of the other board members, a woman of elegant bearing and composure. She had a beautiful countenance, sculpted on classic lines that owed nothing to surgical skills. Her black hair waved back to frame her heart-shaped face; even the harsh colors of the comm unit could not hide the porcelain fairness of her complexion, or the clear, bright blue of her eyes. Her makeup was discreet, and the only hint of her high rank was the exotically set firestones that she wore as earrings. Marmion de Revers Algemeine had made several fortunes on "hearing people out." "I rather fancy the idea of a planet knowing what it wants, and doesn't want! Sentience on a vast scale." She leaned forward, elbows on the surface in front of her, and rested her chin on her fists. "Besides, Whittaker never gives boring reports."

She flicked her glance sideways, but as the speakers were in different offices, at widely separated locations, it was impossible to tell if she was looking at someone in her vicinity or one of the other attendees.

"This won't be the least bit boring, Marmie," Whittaker said, grinning. "Torkel sent me an urgent call that there was a breakdown in the terraforming on this planet—we used Terraform B, the Whittaker Effect, which has never before broken down—so I figured that a simple adjustment would suffice, but I certainly wanted to be on hand . . ."

"Yes, yes, we know your grandfather developed that program," Ball said testily, flicking his fingers impatiently.

"The point, then, my impatient friend, is that no breakdown has occurred. Unless one counts evolutionary development of a quite extraordinary nature as breakdown." Whittaker said the last triumphantly, and Yana saw some of the Petaybean contingent nodding in agreement and looking relieved.

"Am I missing something here?" Ball demanded. "Have you found a way to extract the minerals we require after all? Or located the missing members of the teams?"

"No, but one surviving team member, who has made quite a spectacular recovery, is sitting here in this room. Dr. Metaxos?"

"Secretary-General Ball." Francisco Metaxos nodded to the screen. Metaxos's hair was now spectacularly white, but otherwise he looked much younger than he had when he was first found, closer to his true age of forty-some-odd years. When Yana had first seen him, she'd thought him a man of seventy or so. The only change that hadn't reversed was the hair. It had been, when he landed, as black as his son's, or so Diego had said.

Marmion Algemeine suddenly smiled. "Frank! We heard you were . . ."

"I was," Metaxos said, returning her smile. "But as happens with many maladies, once the cause of mine was made clear, the appropriate treatment was administered and I'm fine now."

"Why is everybody talking in riddles?" Ball asked, almost plaintively.

"If you'll allow me, sir," Torkel cut in, "I think I have the explanation. It seems that all of us, myself included, have been under some sort of massively induced hypnotic illusion. It is quite strong, quite real-seeming. Under this illusion, one becomes *certain* that this terraformed rock on which we stand is actually a sentient being. That is, of course, impossible, a bit of superstitious nonsense, but I assure you the quality of the illusion is exceptional. I feel that it is induced primarily through two of the inhabitants of this area, the woman called Clodagh and this man, Dr. Sean Shongili. Even our own Intergal agent, Major Maddock here, has fallen under their influence and—"

"None so blind as the man who will not see, son," Whittaker Fiske said sadly.

"Even my father has been taken in, sir."

"Excuse me," Yana said. "I thought we were here to present evidence, to talk over solutions. There is the evidence of Lavelle Maloney. The autopsy report is objective enough. There were physiological changes in Lavelle's body that the doctors couldn't explain. Dr. Shongili here can. Whether or not the company accepts the explanation is another matter, but you should at least hear Dr. Shongili out."

Ball waved a dismissive hand. "We've seen the reports and the treatise he sent in with its highly imaginative explanation of Petaybean adaptation. Still smacks of obstructionism. Besides, Shongili is one of the ringleaders down there, if certain parties are to be believed."

The Petaybeans cast resentful eyes on Torkel Fiske, who smiled, a wronged man vindicated.

The elegant Marmion spoke again in her slow, considered way. "Tell me, Doctor Shongili, Ms. Senungatuk, are your perceptions that the planet is sentient shared by other Petaybeans, planetwide?"

Clodagh nodded, but Sean looked dubious. "We aren't in direct contact with the southern landmass," he said.

"Not directly," Clodagh said, shrugging. "But they know."

"You seem so sure."

"How could they not know a thing like that?" Clodagh asked. Yana had the distinct impression that Clodagh was hedging, unwilling, for some good reason, to divulge more just then. Knowing Clodagh, that would not be out of character. The woman was like the planet: round, subtly active, and full of mysteries. In Yana's experience, they were mostly comfortable, benign mysteries, but mysterious nonetheless.

Marmion let that drop for the moment, but another member of the committee, whose balding, ponytailed head had been turned to the comm screen, turned to face them. His eyes were a beautiful celestial blue, but his mouth was a thin hard line, the upper lip beaking over the lower like a snapping turtle's.

"We must ask them, certainly," he said. "We must conduct a survey all over TBeta and inquire of its inhabitants what their beliefs are concerning the planet and what experiences they have had there. It is a study long overdue." His speech contained a slight lisp and an odd intonation, an accent perhaps, mostly erased.

Yana thought Marmion and Whittaker Fiske might find support in the man's suggestion, but instead, Whittaker visibly scooted his chair farther from the table and the comm screen, and Marmion let the tip of her tongue show against her upper lip before answering carefully. "An excellent suggestion, Vice-Chair Luzon. I shall go personally."

"And I, as well, will go, Madame Marmion," Luzon

said. "I am most interested in the belief patterns and customs of colonial peoples, especially those who have been without the benefit of extensive company contact over the years."

"I'm sure you'll find Petaybee a fountain of information, Matthew," Whittaker Fiske said with a somewhat strained attempt at his customary amiability.

Matthew Luzon. Yana had heard the name often before, she realized suddenly—and not in a positive light.

"Your investigations and attempts to correct the thinking of colonists are well known, if not widely appreciated," Whittaker said. "But I think an actual fact-finding expedition, led by Marmion here, is in order now. Her delegation could take advantage of the warm weather to use audiovisual recording equipment generally too sensitive for the climate on this planet. I think the more subjective material could wait until later."

Luzon allowed the corners of his mouth to curl in his version of a smile. "Oh, no. I think my presence will be of great assistance. Come, come, Dr. Fiske. I do not take up so much room. I will accompany Madame Marmion."

The floor trembled beneath their feet and the screen wobbled on its brackets for a few moments. Yana glanced at Clodagh and saw that the big woman was watching the image of Matthew Luzon with a certain studied wariness that Yana had never seen on her face before. It wasn't fear exactly; dread, perhaps. That was when it hit Yana who Luzon was. And she was instantly appalled to learn that he had risen to such prominence in the company.

Luzon was trained in cultural anthropology, a discipline that should have made him more broad-minded and accepting of others. Instead he had the reputation of using his eminence to condemn the "less civilized" or "unenlightened" peoples, using their cultural differences as cause to withdraw or withhold company support or cooperation. Saved the company a lot of money, she supposed. His name had been bandied about when the inhabitants of the central continent of a world called Mandella had been herded into tenements so the jungles and bogs they had formerly inhabited could be tapped for fossil fuels. The tenements had not been well built, and the reeducation program had not included instruction in the use of the modern implements in the new homes, including the sanitation devices. Those Mandellans not killed in the great fire that raged through the tenements died of the communicable diseases that swept through later. Luzon's reports had been what allowed the company to sidestep its responsibility when dealing with the Universal Court. In fact, Yana thought she recalled hearing something once about Luzon being under consideration as a judge for the court.

And now the man was proposing to come looking down his nose at Petaybee!

"Well, I'm not coming down there," Farringer Ball was saying. "Lot of damned nonsense. I have a company to run here. Can't go traipsing around to every backwater bush planet whose colonists get a little peculiar. Hell, if they weren't peculiar, they'd be in the corps or out in space."

Marmion raised an eyebrow and he desisted. "Anyway, I can't and won't interrupt my work to go. But Matthew's done some crack investigating before, and Marmie will bring back the goods. I'll be guided by their evidence."

"That's a relief," Whit snapped. "You sure as hell haven't shown any inclination to be guided by mine, or that of Metaxos and Margolies."

"Of course I have. I read the reports and I haven't evacuated the place and stripped it back to rock yet, have I?"

"Sir," Torkel Fiske said. "What about the additional troops? And I insist that Major Maddock face an official inquiry and possible court-martial for her actions."

"We're already talking about an official inquiry, Captain, or hadn't you been paying attention? If the inquiry determines that there's been subversion or sabotage, I doubt Maddock will have gone far, and she may be able to assist the investigators. Now then. There'll be an escort with Madame Marmion and Dr. Luzon, of course, and additional technical personnel. If we decide to evacuate, we'll call in more then. Meanwhile, you've got enough manpower on hand already, I should think. It's not like an army's going to be any help stopping earthquakes and volcanoes. This meeting is concluded."

Goat-dung knew that she was evil, willful, spiteful, malicious, and would someday, if she didn't mend her wicked ways, be prey for the creature from the bowels of the planet. She had been told so often enough, as the welts from the Instrument of Goodness impressed the lessons on her backside.

For her crimes, she usually got the hardest, dirtiest work to do of any girls her age; but when the warming came, melting the ice falls on the sides of the cliffs and turning the floor of the Vale into a great lake, the rest of the community joined her in scrabbling up the sides of the Vale to higher ground, carrying with them the teachings of the Shepherd Howling and all of his sacred implements, plus what food, clothing, and housing materials they could salvage. All of the greenhouse gardens were lost and many of the animals had drowned.

For days the waters rose up the icy walls of the Vale, creating slush and even mud underfoot and also a steaming mist that made it impossible to see. Goat-dung and the other children, packs strapped to their backs, climbed the walls of the canyon and carried dripping parcels to the adults, then splashed back down in the bright cold water to try to retrieve other articles.

Bad as she was, even Goat-dung was so used to obeying the will of the community, the will of the Shepherd Howling, that she failed to see the possibilities for escape in the situation.

She'd just climbed up again after falling three times back into the water. Shivering with cold, muddy, scraped and bruised, half-naked, she huddled by the fire and ate the bowl of thin soup she had at last been permitted to ladle out for herself. The soup was mostly cold, and the fire, a pitiful stinking thing of still-damp animal dung, was nothing but a slightly sultry draft that failed to chase the ache and chill. It didn't banish the goose bumps, never mind the frigidity in her bones.

For once, no one else was better off than she, however. The one hundred or so followers of the Shepherd huddled along the rim of the steaming Vale of Tears, their lives and homes inundated by the Great Flood the Shepherd claimed had been sent to try them.

"The monster seeks to subjugate us to its will in this fashion," the Shepherd said over and over again. "We shall not succumb. When the waters subside, we'll return to our Vale and continue to defy that which would corrupt us."

The Shepherd, instead of staying within his offices and superior quarters, was now among the flock organizing, counseling, exhorting—and observing. Feeling the disapproving eyes of the rest of the flock on her was bad enough, but twice Goat-dung looked up from her misery to see the Shepherd himself watching her, and his regard made her colder than the waters in the Vale.

She rested from her last climb, as the short day drew to a close and the mists from the Vale crept up over the edge of the encampment. She heard soft footsteps approach and Concepcion, her belly as flat as it had been before the Shepherd married her and her name was still Swill, squatted beside her.

"Good news, little sister," she said.

Goat-dung said nothing. Until she knew what Concepcion wanted, silence was safest.

The other girl, a bare four years older than Goat-dung, held forth a piece of metal. "You've been chosen," she said simply, and rose to go.

Goat-dung stared at the piece in her hand. It was cut into the shape of a heart. The Shepherd had chosen her to be his wife.

"What? When?" she called after Concepcion.

"Tonight," the older girl called back and was lost in the mist.

And that was when she did the worst thing she had ever done in all of her wicked days. She ran.

The mist covered her trail and the slush muffled the sound of her steps. She ran as hard and as long as her exhausted, undernourished body could. She had no idea where she was going. She had known no other people but her own, though sometimes the Shepherd made allusions to others, outsiders, those who had fallen into error. They were horrible people, the Shepherd said, who would sacrifice girls like her to the Great Monster.

Better that than be a dutiful wife to the Shepherd, like Swill-Concepcion and Nightsoil, now known as Assumpta. Wives of the Shepherd, though they were no older than children, were given adult names, usually related to the Teaching.

Assumpta, once a rosy-cheeked, titian-haired angel of a girl, full of childish agility and grace, was now old at thirteen. She had lost four children to a bleeding disease and had been beaten after losing each one. She no longer walked very well.

Concepcion, on the other hand, was still barren at fifteen, and she was beaten for that, as well. Their own mother, Ascencion, was another of the wives, and supervised the beatings herself.

Goat-dung's mother had also been the Shepherd's wife, although Goat-dung was not one of his own lambs. One reason she was so wicked, the others told her, was that her parents had been outsiders. She had been too small when her mother died to realize it, but it was said that her mother had been an extremely unrepentant outsider who had not wanted to be the Shepherd's wife and had been prevailed upon to accept the blessings of union with him only through the firm kindliness of the flock. No one among them had met Goat-dung's father, who had died in ignorance and error and slavery to the Great Monster.

Goat-dung ran and ran, splashing through slush, hot with her effort as long as light remained in the sky, then ran to keep from freezing as the night swallowed the planet. The moons came up and she stumbled on by their light. She ran on and on, down and down, as if into another Vale. Looking back, by the moonlight, she saw the peaks of the mountains behind and above her: the monster's back, its snout, its teeth.

She dragged herself farther. Down here the slush gave way to mud in places, and a stream ribboning down the mountain steamed just as the water in the valley floor did. As she drew near it, it gave forth warmth, and when she touched it, it was as hot as if it had been heated in a pan and only cooled slightly.

She eased her way into it. It was deeper than it looked and had quite a current. It buffeted her along, lapping her with warmth, until it ran into a kind of tunnel, carrying her with it.

She was too tired, too full of lassitude from the water, to avoid being swept into the side of the mountain, and remembered, just before she hit her head on a rock and all became blackness, that the Shepherd taught that this was the very sort of place never to be caught.

# 2

"Well?" Bunny Rourke asked breathlessly as the elders and the company friends of the Petaybeans filed out of the building. She handed the reins of the curlies to each rider. "How'd it go?"

Clodagh shrugged. "Like usual. They pretended we weren't there, and if we were, that we'd nothin' sensible to say. They're sendin' down more investigators."

Yana sighed. She'd known it wouldn't be easy, but something else was disturbing her. As they rode back through the woods to Kilcoole, she asked, "I don't get it. Torkel was with us. He felt the planet, too. He knows about it. If he had really rejected it, he'd be like Frank Metaxos was."

"Denial," Diego said, drawing on his own counseling experience. "He knows, okay, he just can't stand to admit it. He's not a complete creep, after all. You and he used to be friends, didn't you, Yana?"

"Friendly, at least," Yana said. "Or I thought so. But he's been so unreasonable . . ."

"Maybe irrational's a better word," Sean said. "He might not have had the reaction Frank did, but it strikes me that Fiske isn't sledding on both runners anymore, if he ever was. Maybe his unwilling contact with the planet has done him more harm than shows on the surface."

"At least it's that lady coming to investigate," Moira Rourke said with some relief.

"Yes, but I don't like the look of that bald fella," Clodagh said.

"Nor do I," Yana agreed. "At the risk of sounding like the conspirator Torkel thinks me to be, I suggest that all of you avoid any direct contact with Luzon and save your explanations strictly for Madame Marmion. He is known to . . . twist . . . anything he's told."

As they neared the village, they were met by a pride of cats, all of them striped bright rusty orange and all of them meowing and purring and twining dangerously around the large snowshoe-sized hooves of the shaggy, curly-coated horses.

"What a welcoming committee!" Yana said as Marduk, or at least she assumed it was he, hopped up behind her and rubbed his head against her back briefly before hopping down again. "Did you call them, Clodagh?"

Clodagh shook her head. "No, but I was worried, before we left, about how committed the other villages were to the planet. So far the PTBs have only questioned us, but I figured they'd get around to asking some of the others sometime soon. These little ones scattered as soon as we left, and here they are back again." She tilted her head as she looked down at the cats.

"What's got 'em so antsy?" Bunny asked.

Clodagh reined her curly-coat to a halt. Immediately the cats converged on her, stropping the legs of the pony, who regarded this activity with mild surprise and didn't so much as twitch a muscle.

"You'll get muddy doing that," she told the cats, since the pony was coated up to and including his belly with good Petaybean wet earth. With a groan, she heaved one leg over the saddle and dismounted, ignoring the fact that her skirts immediately became as dirty as the pony's legs. "Now, what's all this?" she asked, hands on her hips, looking from one upturned cat face to the next.

Clodagh's special relationship with her cats was known—or at least suspected—by everyone in Kilcoole. So the other villagers, except for Sean, Bunny, and Yana, rode politely around the cats and pretended not to notice anything more than a woman being greeted by overly fond pets.

Frank Metaxos, in whose healing process the cats had had a rather unusual role, remained behind, too, along with his son Diego. The two were returning to Kilcoole without Frank's partner, Steve Margolies, who, still on the company's payroll, had stayed on at SpaceBase.

Both cats and Clodagh waited for the rest of the village to parade past before the mewing and chirruping began.

Ordinarily the cats would have sat down to impart what was evidently a long story, but the mud offended their dignity. So they prowled around her, twitching their tails high, as they communicated their messages. The humans waited patiently.

Sparks of uncharacteristic anger flickered in Clodagh's eyes as she looked up at Sean and Yana. "We got all kinds of trouble now." She gave a disgusted snort. "Seems like some villages want Intergal to come down and mine, while the mining's good and they can get paid for working."

Sean frowned and Yana told her heart to stop racing. "How many dissidents?" she asked.

"Four towns that the cats know of." Clodagh's usually merry face was solemn.

"Which ones?"

"Deadhorse, McGee's Pass, Wellington, and Savoy."

Sean let out a burst of sour laughter. "That figures." Clodagh had named villages which in recent years spurned contact with the others. He sighed deeply. "Have the cats any good news?"

"Yes, but the bad news is they haven't had a chance to check everyone out. If four villages oppose us . . ."

"How many more might be disaffected and looking to please Intergal for the sake of wampum?" Sean asked.

"So, the good news?" Yana prompted with a sigh.

"Well, we do have at least twelve communities behind us solid. Tanana Bay, Shannonmouth, New Barrow, Twin Moon Village, Little Dublin, Oslo Inlet, Harrison's Fjord,

Kabul, Bogota, Machu Picchu, Kathmandu, and Sierra Padre."

"Most of the closest ones," Sinead said, looking encouraged.

"And the ones," Clodagh went on with a pessimistic expression, "that have the most Petaybean boys and girls in company service."

"What bothers you about that?" Yana asked. "Wouldn't they be on their folks' side in this?"

"Might be, if they weren't required to lean on their folks to do what the company asks," Clodagh said gloomily.

"Oh!" Yana sighed. Dirty tricks department. Farringer Ball and Matthew Luzon would pull every one they needed out of storage to see that their interpretation became the official one. "Could you be wrong about which side of the blanket the Petaybean troops would fall on? The pilots, O'Shay and Greene in particular, gave us some support during the volcanic crisis."

Clodagh shrugged her broad shoulders. "You can always be wrong about anything. Sure, I think a lot of them would feel loyalty for us and for the planet. But they've been out there"—she nodded toward the heavens—"for a long time. They're used to the kind of stuff you're used to. Some of 'em have prob'ly forgot how to cook, too, like you, and how to hunt. How to take care of themselves. And if the company decided to punish them and us by dumping them here and pulling out support, well, that'd be pretty hard on them, pretty hard on us, and pretty hard on the planet. I figure if all the Petaybee troops still working for Intergal got sent back here, it'd triple our population. At the least! I don't know how many kids those troops have had. Course, they'd be welcome and the planet would provide, but it might be as hard on it as some kinds of mining operations."

Frank cleared his throat. "The ecosystem in these icy regions is quite fragile."

"You know it and I know it, but Intergal seems oblivious to the fact," Sean said.

"Are those villages one hundred percent in favor of selling out?" Yana asked.

Clodagh smiled patiently. "Now, Yana. You've been around the universe a few times. When did you ever meet any group of people who were one hundred percent in favor of anything?"

"Exactly. So presumably there are some people there who aren't in favor of the mining. And probably, in the remaining villages, a few who are. I think we need to know who's fer us and who's agin us, as they say in the Wild West vids, and maybe try to convert some of the unaffiliated. I thought everybody had the relationship with the planet you do."

Clodagh shook her head. "Not everybody wants to. Those who have enough respect to follow the rules and live wisely survive better though, so even if they don't acknowledge the presence of the planet, they get by as long as they keep out of the special places. The others, the foolish ones, don't live so well or so long. Those people would much rather try to please the bosses than forces they don't *want* to understand. Fortunately though, around here there's not much to do except pay attention, so the planet gets through to most folks."

"Well, sounds to me like we need to do a little campaigning," Yana said.

"We will make them songs so they understand," Clodagh said.

"Cool," Diego said. "Just like the old radical songs from Earth. Ah, if only I had a guitar."

"What's that?" Bunny asked.

"A musical instrument. All of the old protest singers had them. There's some wonderful mining songs in the memory banks back—back at my old place."

"I wish you had one then," Bunny said loyally.

"Me, too. Except I don't know how to play."

"I bet you could learn," Bunny told him. "You make better songs than some people who've made them all their lives."

"Bunka," Clodagh said sharply. "Each song is a good song if it says what the singer means it to say."

"Course it is, Clodagh. I know that. But Diego's sound better. He says what he means to say so everybody can understand it. That's all I meant."

Clodagh smiled, a slightly bawdy smile, with a wink to Sean and Yana. "That's all right then, alannah. He does make good songs."

In the short distance to Clodagh's house, they discussed the finer points of what needed to be said to the villages, both those which dissented and those which Clodagh felt sure could be counted upon to support the planet.

When they reached Clodagh's, what seemed to be the entire village was waiting outside in her yard. Yana found, looking at the yard, that she missed the snow. The village looked like a garbage dump, with its stores of winter provisions half-thawed in the snow, the trash that had been buried, the salvaged equipment lying around the yard, all of the items that had been lost throughout the long winter. Not to mention the leavings of the various dogs and cats and horses housed in the village. Also, without the snow, the roofs of the houses looked patchy, the siding worn despite its gay pastel colors. And everything and everyone was smeared and splattered with mud.

This dreary aspect didn't seem to lessen their regard for each other in the slightest, however, and the villagers crowded as cheerfully as ever into Clodagh's tiny house and began discussing what was to be done.

"We need to have another latchkay," Eamon Intiak said. "We should have one and invite the people who don't understand. Petaybee would speak to them and then they'd know."

"You'd think they'd know already by now," Sinead Shongili said.

"Now, Sinead," her partner Aisling said reasonably, "such things take some folks longer. Their worries about the everyday things in their lives get in the way of understanding what's here."

"We'll each go away and think about these things and make songs," Clodagh said. "Then we'll go talk to the other people. Sinead, you and Sean and the Maloneys must go the farthest because you're the best travelers. I would like to send Frank with you, Sinead, and young Diego with Liam. Yana, you go with Sean. We need you people who know about the company to make talk with the neighbors who are taken in by the promises, too."

With that, everyone began to leave. Yana was ready to leave, too. She was tired. She wanted to rest and eat and bathe in the hot springs and make love to Sean, not necessarily in that order. But Sean laid a restraining hand on her arm and lingered a moment.

"And how about the other pole, Clodagh?" Sean asked gently. "How do we reach those people?"

"Can *you* not do it, Sean?" Clodagh asked.

"Sure, I could, but it'd be a long journey no matter how fast I went. The PTBs would already have been there and found out what we need to know. Besides, I hate to leave Yanaba for so long at a time like this."

"What do you mean, Sean?" Yana asked. "I'm barely a month along. I wouldn't even know I was pregnant if you hadn't found out via your hot line to the planet. Other women have had babies before . . ."

"Not," Sean said significantly, "*my* babies. If only my sister and Rourke had been able to map that passage."

"Sinead?"

"No. Our sister Aoifa and her husband, Bunny's parents. They were trying to map some of the planet's inner passages. Bunny was barely eighteen months old—"

"And that Aoifa was pregnant again!" Clodagh said fondly. "They hadn't been married long, but that girl was a real Shongili. Not even pregnancy hampered that one, and her as curious as one of the cats!"

"What happened?" Yana asked.

Sean shrugged. "We don't know."

"Couldn't you find out? From the planet, I mean?"

"You've been with it. The information you get isn't usually that specific. And Aoifa and Mala had this theory that some of the special places that lead from one river and lake to the next here on the land lead under the sea in the same way. I searched but I never found them. Never even got a glimmer."

Clodagh made a sound like "Yuh." Then she said, "They must have gone very far. Much farther than anyone has ever gone."

"On foot or by sled or horse maybe," Yana said. "But there are other ways to travel and other ways to get to the south, if the planet doesn't mind the intrusion too much. If I can reach Captain Greene or that O'Shay fellow, maybe they can give us a lift."

"Ah, you spoiled modern woman," Sean said with a kiss to her cheek. "I love you."

"I know it's not the Petaybean way, Shongili, but until you come up with a mutant bird to match your cats and horses, we have to make do with what poor mechanical means I can muster."

"I'm workin' on it, Yana. I am. But until then, you're quite right. We'll have to use company equipment to fight its masters. Now then, what say we go meditate at the hot spring and come up with something to say to these people once you finesse the pilots into transporting us?"

"I thought you'd never ask," she said.

It was small; it was warm and wet and its pelt was of a most extraordinarily tattered nature, fine flapping threads and matted bits interspersed in an unkempt coat. It smelled like food, but not the superior sort.

It leaked savory blood into the water sloshing around it. The water was the problem. In order to reach the little morsel, one would have to get wet. Of course, one could reach down from the ledge with one's claws, and if one stretched—stretched—stretched—ah! One caught a piece of the pelt and could heft it to where one could support the weight of the rest in one's jaws and—ah—it moved. Still alive then. Good. Fresh meat was best. All it would take was biting down a bit on the neck, under the mane, and the kill would be clean, the meat fresh. There would be no necessity for leaving the relative shelter of the ledge.

One leaned forward, resting on one's chest, and extended one's neck to meet the bit rising on claw tip and—it slipped! It was trying to get away! The other paw lashed forward, claws extended, to help the first, and one instinctively leaned forward, one's jaws coming into play to assist one's claws and—and—the thing slipped again before one could sink a tooth into it. The pelt was flimsy stuff and tore out of the claws just as the other paw grabbed the morsel in a second place. The morsel let out a terrified squeal, rather like a rabbit. One was about to smack it to silence and lean forward for the fatal chomp.

Then the cave shook, the ledge broke under one's overbalanced weight, and one tumbled tail over nose into the pool, relinquishing the morsel, which yelped again. Inconvenient and embarrassing to be so indisposed in front of the food. One climbed out of the pool and shook the water from one's coat and began to wash before one's meal.

The morsel began to flail frantically toward the den's entrance. One padded nonchalantly after. The cave, the ground, the world, shook again. One knew when one was being addressed. One sat on one's haunches and perceived.

The morsel was also arrested in midflight. "Did you—d-do that?" it asked. "Are—are you the G-Great Monster?"

One yawned.

The world shook again and one realized that one had understood the speech of the morsel. One also understood that it was a youngling, and female.

One waded forward while the youngling waded backward, outlined in the dusk outside the mouth of the cave. One's paws dripped water, albeit warm water. One lapped a bit. The youngling stood still.

"You're not so terrible," it said. "You're nothing but a big cat."

One had one's dignity to maintain. One lashed one's beautifully and delicately marked tail and growled.

And from beneath one's sodden paws, the world growled back at one and bucked, sending a wave of water to swamp one, knocking one onto one's back, causing one to drink more deeply of the spring than one cared to, paws over head, and be propelled backward, away from the youngling.

When one got to one's feet, one saw that the youngling—it no longer seemed safe to think of it, no, *her* as a morsel—had not used the opportunity to run away. Indeed, it, too, was just arising from the water, sputtering and snorting. Ah, good. It had not seen one's discomfiture. Dignity was preserved.

"I'm not afraid of you," the youngling declared as one advanced—claws sheathed, teeth safely contained within one's lips, growl little more than a polite, enquiring rumble in one's throat. A mere purr, actually, one corrected, as the waters bubbled and sloshed ominously. "I used to know a cat. A little one. I was a baby then. Shepherd Howling made my mother kill my cat. He—he tried to, anyway. He—she wouldn't and—and . . ." Something odd was happening to the youngling now. It began leaking again, saltiness into the fresh sulfurous water covering it. "My mother was not like Ascencion. She was brave. The Shepherd punished her for disobedience and both she and my cat went away. So—so I'm not afraid of you. You live where the Great Monster is supposed to dwell and lie in wait for the foolish superstitious minds of the flock to be warped and maddened into everlasting wickedness while our bodies are tormented by the great fires from within. But you're not the Great Monster—you couldn't be. Are you—are you the Guardian of the Underworld?"

One was so disgusted by her ignorance and silly misapprehension of one's self and one's relationship to one's Home that one was startled into answering, *I am Coaxtl! That is enough.*

"I am Goat-dung, Coaxtl," the youngling said with the cunning of her race. She knew, one saw, the power of names. She had one's name, one had hers. She could not be food.

But one's Home had already decreed that she could not be food, which was what Home meant with the rumbling of the ground and the raising of the waters. One knew what was done and what was not done.

*Very well, Goat-dung,* one said. *Goat-dung is not food, but undoubtedly she eats. Therefore we must leave the Home and hunt.*

# 3

With the river flowing freely, close to flooding, the people of Kilcoole had more water at their disposal than they were used to. Normally, even in the height of summer, the channel remained frozen at the deeper levels. Now the planet had cut additional channels from new, warmer tributaries, and there was sufficient water to drink, to wash, to bathe in if you didn't mind a little sediment.

Since so much water was close to hand and the hot springs were a distance from town, Yana and Sean had the place to themselves.

As they rode through the brush, which was beginning to leaf out, Yana smiled at the wildflowers that peeked up from the less sodden places where they'd been buried under the snow all winter.

The hot springs were where she and Sean had first come together, where she had first had an inkling of his other nature, and where they had first made love. Beneath the waterfall was the secret subterranean chamber where the villagers gathered during the latchkay night chants to communicate directly with the planet. The mere sight of the slipping silvery waters, steaming only slightly in the warmer air, and the sweet rippling peal of the falls and streams were miraculous enough for Yana.

In this warmer weather, undressing did not have to be so hastily done. She and Sean took their time—time to undress each other, time for a kiss and a caress—before entering the waters, he with a muscular dive, she with a slow sliding from the bank, feeling the waters rise up the length of her until she stooped and allowed the liquid to cover her head. The water shut out the sounds of the birds and insects, the small animals scrabbling in the bushes, the stamping and champing of the curly-coats, and filled her ears with its own music.

Then a wet, warm silky form twisted about her and broached the surface of the water, silver eyes gleaming at her with a challenge and a sensuousness that were so perfectly "Sean" that even his selkie form did not dismay her.

"Oh you!" she said, laughing and splashing water at him. "Do you automatically change the minute you hit water?"

A pleased murmur came from the throat of Sean-Selkie as he continued to weave against her body, his furry touch arousing unusual sensations in her.

"Oh, is that all you can say?" Then Yana gave a ki-yi of amusement. "You can't talk as a selkie?" She chortled and, using both hands, sent a wave to flood him.

He dove, not to get away from the water, but to caress her where she least expected it. Startled, she tried to maneuver away from him, but his sinuous form made evasion impossible. *He* was the swimmer, she the paddler.

But she caught him firmly by a fold of silky wet skin and pulled him to the surface.

"Look, mate, I don't mind what form you take. I don't even mind what you do in that form . . ." Sean-Selkie made a pleased purring sound, the silver eyes dancing, as she went on: "But listen up! It's the man I want, not the seal. And we do have things to talk about. So, if you can't talk in this form . . . especially if you can't . . . well, you know what I mean . . . change back."

The selkie nudged her, in a rather sweetly apologetic way, toward the falls, and swam sinuously alongside as she began to swim, feeling very ungraceful beside him, in the direction he indicated. He obviously restrained himself to keep pace with her. He was so graceful, so powerful, and the touch of his fine fur against her was unfairly sensual.

She increased the speed of her own stroke. She couldn't wait to get to the privacy of the place behind the falls: she couldn't wait to get him back into a *useful* form.

He dove under the falls and she followed, escaping the battering of the water. They surfaced together but Sean-Selkie seemed to ooze up the bank and stood there, proud in his altered form, so that she could admire him. All of him. Then he shook himself and the transformation she had seen once before, near the cave where they had taken refuge from the volcano, began.

"I get it, Sean," she murmured, a trifle apologetic. "You wanted me to see you in all your glory. And you are glorious," she added, smiling as the man emerged. She went to him, stroking skin instead of fur, and twining herself around him as his selkie self had done to her in the water.

"Give me a moment to adjust, will you?" he said, laughing, holding her tightly against his wet skin.

Yana gave a sniff. "As far as I'm concerned, you are adjusted." She glanced down significantly.

"Ah, but a selkie makes love differently than a man," he said, murmuring into her ear and nibbling her throat.

"How differently? I'm game."

It *was* decidedly different, wildly sensual, and extremely satisfying, and took rather more time than she had assumed, knowing something of "animal" behavior. She hadn't known nearly enough to prepare her for all of the loving possibilities of Sean's dual nature, both animal and man, but he understood himself thoroughly and was most adept at using all of his resources to guide her into uncharted channels of pleasure. It took her a *long* time to slow her pulse and heart rate and come, slightly unwillingly, back to the other reason they had gone off.

"We have to do our part in this scheme, you know," she said, looking up at Sean's face. They were still interlocked; it was comforting and comfortable and she didn't really want to break the mood, but the dutiful part of her character prodded her into "active duty" now that the R&R was over.

"Which scheme?" he asked, smiling lasciviously down at

her. "All right, all right," he said, easily warding off the fist she shot up at him. His hands were very strong. "First we have to find out where Johnny Greene and Rick O'Shay are. Would Fiske Junior have it in for them for their part in seeing you all got into the special place?"

She sighed. "That's what we have to find out. If Adak'll let me use the comm unit, I can probably roust them out of wherever they are—BOQ on SpaceBase, probably."

"Both Johnny and Rick *believe* in Petaybee," Sean said, musing aloud, his fingers playing an idle tattoo on her shoulder, "or they wouldn't have helped us then. So, perhaps they'll help us again. How hard would it be for them to abscond with a copter or two?"

Yana shrugged. "Both struck me as pretty clever. Copter pilots tend to be a tad devious. If they could stash enough fuel in a cache somewhere, they could help us and still appear to be on duty at the base. No matter how you slice it, it's going to take a few days for Marmion and that bald buzzard to organize themselves and their escort, so we have a few days. Unless Torkel clamps down on all SpaceBase activity."

"How can he do that when the place is in such a mess? They've still got folks to rescue from mudslides and stuff."

"Good point, Sean, so the sooner we get in touch with Johnny and Rick, the better. We can provide for *our* expeditions before Torkel knows we're setting them up."

"Fiske Junior doesn't strike me as a forgetful man. Would he have thought of that, and slapped a hold on all unauthorized copter runs?"

Yana thought. "If he has, Whittaker still carries more clout than Junior. I know Whittaker will help as much as he can." Then she laughed, her chest heaving against his. "Junior! Don't ever call Torkel that in his hearing, Sean."

Sean's eyes sparkled with malice. "No? When we need every advantage we've got?"

The expression on his face, her current position, and the word "advantage" warned Yana that she'd better curtail this session right now or they'd lose a lot more time. She hoped they hadn't dallied too long already. But it had been . . . remarkable. Resolutely she pushed him away and got to her feet.

"Adak is our first stop, Sean," she said in a don't-contradict-me tone.

"Yes, ma'am, no, ma'am. As you say, ma'am."

She gave him one long look in her sternest mode before she realized that this respite might have to last both of them a long time.

She went into his arms. "Oh, Sean Shongili Selkie, I do love you so much!"

"I, you, alannah," he said softly and kissed her. But it was a kiss of exceeding gentleness and no passion whatsoever. He, too, accepted the inevitable.

"We can do a lot together," she offered as a token apology.

"We already have," he said, laughing. But his hand on her back guided her firmly out of their private retreat.

Coaxtl must be a very bad animal, Goat-dung realized, or he would have devoured such a wicked person as herself instead of sharing his catch of small game with her as if she were a cub. Maybe Coaxtl wasn't male. Goat-dung sneaked a look. It was hard to tell. The cat was extremely furry, with extra tufts on the ears and a thick, bushy tail. Its coat was dense and very soft-looking; the coloring white with large spots of different sizes, according to the muscle they were on: long rectangular ones on the neck, big circular ones on the shoulders, smaller, more regular ones on the abdomen, all shaded from gray to black, blurred and clouded by the length and thickness of the fur. The paws were also extremely large, though the face was sweet, with large golden eyes and a black nose and black-lipped mouth that seemed to be perpetually smiling. The cat *looked* female enough to Goat-dung, and there was nothing obvious showing under the belly to convince her otherwise, so she decided that she knew the reason why the cat hadn't eaten her. It was because Coaxtl was a *mother* cat, and probably she had lost her kittens and was willing to accept Goat-dung as a substitute. That must be why. The cat certainly showed no compunction about killing anything else.

With a mighty leap and a swipe of a muscular foreleg, a deft hook of the paw and a single economical crunch, the cat had bagged each victim—three snow geese and a brace of rabbits. When the final kill was made, Coaxtl sat with the rabbits at her feet and looked expectantly at Goat-dung, who took it she was being invited to partake.

"I—I can't eat raw meat," she said. Even hungry as she was, she really didn't think she could. Life was hard in the flock, but they plucked their birds and skinned their animals before cooking. She looked around at the awful openness of the mountain meadows and thought of the Shepherd Howling and the beating she would get if she was found—and, worse, having to be the Shepherd's wife and all that meant. "Besides, I don't want to be in the open. Can't we go back to the cave?"

Coaxtl gave her a long golden-eyed stare. Goat-dung wished the cat would speak to her again—not that the beast spoke actual words out loud. But Goat-dung *heard* words in her mind, and while the big cat's conversation was terse, it was conversation, and it was not angry or accusatory, which was the sort Goat-dung was used to. It wasn't that the cat *liked* her precisely, but Coaxtl did not so far appear to *dis*-like her. Of course, people in the flock never said that they disliked her. On the contrary, they all claimed to love her and said they were pointing out the error of her ways so that she would not become a victim to the evils of the world, but they did indicate, by deed and word, that they thought the task of trying to save her was quite hopeless.

She followed the cat back along the swollen streambed to the cavern. The snow had not all melted by any means, and now, suddenly, the air was colder, and the light drizzle that had been falling throughout the day turned to sleet, then snow. Only partially dressed in wet rags, Goat-dung began shivering so hard that she had difficulty walking.

The cave was warmer, perhaps warmed by the water

pooling in its center. But it was not warm enough to combat the temperature dropping as night approached. She needed a fire to keep her from freezing as well as to cook her food.

Coaxtl took the rabbits in her mouth and hopped lightly onto the ledge, looking down at Goat-dung, who stood knee deep in the pool on the floor. The birds were clutched in her hand.

Coaxtl had already torn the head off one of the rabbits. Goat-dung looked back up defiantly.

"Well, I'm sorry, cat, but this water leaves me no place to stand and no place to eat the birds even if I wanted to eat them uncooked with all the feathers on. I know I'm spoiled and selfish, but I'm also cold, and I think if I don't have a fire I really will die."

This time the cat did speak. *Youngling—I will not call you Goat-dung if you are in my charge. That is no fit name for a cub. Names are important and having yours, I am charged not to eat you, but really, who would want to eat someone named Goat-dung anyway? You must choose another name. I digress . . . Youngling, you seem to have trouble making up your mind what will kill you. Out on the plains you feared the openness. In here you say you are cold and cannot take the water. Probably beyond in the cave it is warmer. You could explore, like any other cub, and leave me in peace to finish the meal I have so graciously provided.*

"Beyond lies the Great Monster," Goat-dung said, and then realized that she didn't care. "Very well, I will go alone, but it is dark back there and I may become lost and die, as well."

*You are inconveniently frail,* the cat growled, abandoning the bird to hop down from the ledge with a splash. *Follow me. I will not endure this string of constant complaints.*

Goat-dung knew she was disgusting and whining and weak, but at least Coaxtl had not yet cuffed her, even with sheathed claws, much less bitten or clawed her. That was an improvement over the Shepherd and his flock.

The cat padded rapidly ahead, and for a time Goat-dung could follow by the splashing of the big paws in the pool; but then her own, now bare, feet touched dryness, and the cat's pads were nothing but a whisper that soon disappeared. "Coaxtl! Where are you?" she called. "I can't see you."

*Can you not? Silly cub. I'm right in front of your eyes.*

"Yes, but I can't see in the dark."

*Can you not?* the cat asked, her voice in Goat-dung's head genuinely surprised. *No fur, a stupid name, no claws, puny teeth that can't bite through feathers, and half-blind as well. You would have been better off if I'd eaten you, child.*

"I—I suppose so," Goat-dung said. "I know I'm a terrific bother but if you *are* going to help me, and you don't know how stupid and weak I really am, then I thought you wouldn't know how . . ." She floundered, at a loss for words, realizing she didn't deserve help, that she should have gratefully accepted any tiny thing the cat offered her, and that all of her talk only proved that what the flock said about her was absolutely right. But really, she had no idea at all what to do with the birds, and the Shepherd had always been very specific about the dangers of eating uncooked meats.

*There's no help for it then,* the cat said. *Take hold of my tail, but don't pull, or I may kill you without thinking about it.*

Goat-dung groped with outstretched hands and felt a brush of air go by her twice before her palm encountered a sturdy furred appendage, less like the flexible tail of a smaller beast and more like a child's arm in a fur coat. She gently took hold of the end of it, and the cat proceeded at a slower pace.

How long they walked, she had no idea. They descended, twisted in the corridors, and climbed, only to descend again on the uneven flooring. Several times she bumped into large columns, some coming up from the floor, some hanging low enough to bang her head, and she cried out for the cat to stop. In order to keep from pulling the tail, she had to let go of it.

*Those are the teeth of the cave,* the cat explained. *They rise up from the bottom or clamp down from the top. Fortunately, the cave bites very, very slowly and we moving creatures are quite fast by comparison, so we never get eaten.*

"Never?"

*Not in my lifetime anyway, or that of my mother or my mother's mother or in her memory.*

"Then you know that the cave is a Great Monster, too?"

*The cave and all caves are Home,* the cat said simply. *And Home has what one needs. If we keep looking, we will find what you need here, too.*

And much later, Coaxtl sat down and said, *Ah.* When the cat sat down, Goat-dung was forced to drop the tail, but that didn't matter then, because the cave was filled with a light of its own, and a warmth as well, that seemed to emanate from fissures in the wall.

Goat-dung recoiled and the cat turned and glared at her with eyes bright and hot as fires, shining like the jewels the Shepherd adorned himself with on his birthday. Coaxtl looked extremely fierce then, but all she said was, *If you're not going to cook those birds after all this, then give them to me and I will eat them.*

"No, I will eat them, once I cook them," Goat-dung said, clasping the geese to her and turning slightly so the cat couldn't swipe them away with one big paw.

Despite her fears, despite her sure knowledge that she was in the belly of the Great Monster, Goat-dung felt less afraid than she had before. Here it was warm and light with a soft glow. A small circle of rock in the center of the floor kindled briefly into a true flame. Maybe it would open beneath her feet and devour her. Perhaps it was a trap, but it reminded her of the cookfires and that she was truly very hungry indeed, and tired, as well. She walked to it, sat down, and began plucking the geese, while Coaxtl fell asleep beside the fire, her breath rumbling contentedly.

Goat-dung gutted and roasted the bird on the rocks beside the fire. Looking down into it, she could see no coals, no bottom to the hole in fact, and that frightened her; but the rock was very warm by the fire, and the bird cooked slowly, so she ate the outer bits a little at a time. Then she crawled over to the cat and fell asleep, dreaming the sweetest dreams she could remember having: of her mother and of her father's voice and another cave.

She dreamed on and on, almost fearing to wake, until the soft furry support beside her was withdrawn and she slipped back against the cave floor with a thump. When she sat up, she realized that Coaxtl, too, was sitting up, listening to the voices that seemed to emanate from the walls of the cave.

# 4

Mud is a great leveler and, although the military had put down plastic boardwalks so people could get around the muddy streets of Kilcoole, mud did provide a disguise of sorts. One mud-spattered person looked like any other, local or imported. As plastered with this camouflage as everyone else, Yana and Sean had no trouble reaching Adak's snocle shed. His precious vehicles were now in the loft, and one battered antique 4×4 was parked outside.

"It's not an official one," Yana said, peering at the sides for any SpaceBase markings.

"It's Adak's, all right. I hate to think when they last made those, or what Adak traded to get a hold of one, but somehow he keeps it running," Sean said, and, his hand on her back again, he propelled her quickly toward the mechanic's crawl-through set in the main door. He paused only briefly, listening. The only voice within earshot was Adak's, so they pushed through and into the smell, now redolent with oil and fuel and mud.

Adak turned from his comm station to see who his visitors were and his face lit up.

"Yessir, I got the message. Only official communications. Right ye be! Over." He lifted the earpiece and rubbed exaggeratedly. "My, that man does go on. Sláinte, Sean, Yana. Good to see you; what can I do to help?" He glanced down at the comm unit and sniffed expressively.

"Thanks, Adak," Sean said, grinning as he recognized

the man's tacit willingness to disobey the orders he had just been given.

"We need to get in touch with Johnny Greene and Rick O'Shay."

"They're airborne," Adak said. "Special missions."

Sean and Yana exchanged glances.

"What frequency are they on?" Yana asked.

Adak grinned more broadly. "Happen I just got word of 'em." He settled the earpiece again and held his finger over the keyboard. "Who'll I get ya first? Johnny or Rick?"

"I'd say Rick," Sean replied.

Yana and Sean took turns explaining to Rick what was going down, what they wanted him to do, and how they thought he could accomplish it. Rick had already heard enough rumors to know almost as much as they did—and he was willing to help.

"Hell, all I'm doing right now is figuring out what roads are passable. A lot of equipment might need to be moved," he said, his voice taking on a gloomy tone. "Johnny's up and doing the same thing to the west. We've both had to swear allegiance and die-for-it oaths to Intergal, but shit, we crossed everything we could while taking it." The customary lilt was back in Rick's voice. "Lemme get Johnny in on this where there aren't any ears to hear us."

"They've been monitoring you, then?" Yana asked, not too surprised.

"Not on this frequency, and I did a little twiddling with the bug they put in the cabin so you don't have to worry. Soon's Adak came on, I disconnected a wire. Shouldn't leave it loose much longer. But I'll leave word with Adak when Johnny and I've done what's needful. Might even get in one trip tonight if I can finagle it."

"You're top of the finaglers at SpaceBase," Adak said approvingly. "Code it?"

"Better. When I come on, ask me the mud level on the road to Tanana Bay. If I say it's ankle deep, that means Yana and Sean can meet me where Uncle Seamus collects water. If I say it's knee high, I'm having trouble. I'll get back to you soon's I can. Over and out."

"Hell," Adak said, rubbing his ear thoughtfully, "it's more than ankle deep and knee high everywhere. And I don't mean just the mud."

"Keep yourself out of trouble if you can, Adak. We need you at the comm unit," Sean said.

Adak laughed. "Those new guys don't know doodly about *this* here comm unit. It don't take kindly to rough hands and always goes all static and wheeing." He grinned. "Only old Adak knows its ways."

"We'll stop in at Clodagh's now, if you should need us," Sean said, guiding Yana toward the back exit.

The less-frequented paths actually showed some sturdy grass growth as they made their way behind houses and detoured back into the forest to avoid the new Intergal housing. One of the cats met them halfway to Clodagh's, and the tone of its greeting suggested that it was pleased to see them.

"No trouble?" Yana asked, not quite sure she was interpreting the creature accurately.

Sean grinned, but he kept looking at the ground as they went from mud to snow to the new grass. "No, no trouble. Except . . ." He frowned. "We might just have the longest growing season ever and we've got to plan, also, to take advantage of that! It could prove crucial."

Yana felt a shiver up her spine and agreed with him wholeheartedly at the word "crucial," knowing that Sean and the others were concerned about what would happen if Intergal cut the planet off from outside supply lines entirely. Though Petaybee was largely self-sufficient, the growing season usually was too short to provide enough fruits and vegetables and other plant-derived products. A longer growing season would mean less reliance on outside sources— and yes, that certainly *could* be crucial.

Evening was closing in as they approached Clodagh's house. They could hear banging and pounding and the sound of boards being shifted, and Yana grinned: someone

was doing some of the much-needed repairs of a structure
that had been held together by ice in the winter but needed
nails and mortar now that the weather was warmer. All
over the village people were engaged in similar pursuits.
Yana peered around the corner of the house where all the
banging was, to tell Clodagh they were there, but as Sean
opened the door, she saw that Clodagh was inside. From
the look of the interior, the big woman had also been thinking along the same lines as Sean.

The kitchen was even more filled than usual with good
smells, but these did not emanate from the pot that normally sat simmering on her stove. Instead, the earthy odors
came from tiers of warming trays raised above the stove
and stacked with stones. On the trays were tiny clay pots
holding shoots of greenery, and it was from these the smells
came. The kitchen table was also covered with little pots
and soil and bundles of dried flowers and piles of seeds.

"Sláinte, Sean, Yana," she said, looking up from where
she sat spread-legged on the floor, her skirts hiked up above
her moon-shaped pale white knees and colorful hand-knit
stockings. Between her knees and her feet and all around
her were more pots, more seed packets, and trays of potting
compost. Inspecting with critical sniffs all the interesting
items laid out to be worked on were various members of
the orange-marmalade cat battalion. Two had curled up to
sleep in one potting tray not quite large enough for their
bulk: they spilled over like immense orange alien plant-
forms. "Did you two think of any songs?"

"Quite a few," Sean said, fondly leering at Yana.

"Nothing we could repeat in polite company though,"
Yana said. "How about you?"

"I got a couple. Mostly though, I thought I ought to
make these plants ready to send out to the other villages,
and see if while we're sendin' folk around, they could collect starts from other places."

"I was just commenting that we'll have a longer than
usual growing season," Sean said.

"Prob'ly," Clodagh said. "Unless Petaybee has other ideas."

Bunny poked her head in the door. "Sláinte, Uncle Sean. Sláinte, Yana and Clodagh. For cat's sakes, Clodagh, don't most people garden outside?"

"Only some of this is for my garden, Bunka. The rest will be presents. But right now, help me clean this up or there won't be room for anybody to stand when the rest of the village gets here."

"Okay. C'mon, Diego," the girl said. Diego stepped shyly inside. In one hand was a piece of wood, in the other a knife. He closed and pocketed the knife and set the billet down by the door.

"It's very considerate of you to bring your own firewood, lad, but I'm not usin' so much these days as to need it."

"That's going to be his guitar," Bunny said.

"Oh, really?" Clodagh asked, widening her eyes in mild query.

"Only part of it," Diego said. At sixteen, he was a shy dark boy with beautiful eyes and an unruly lock of black hair that kept falling over them. When he had first come to Petaybee, he'd suffered from the skin blemishes common to young adolescents, but the planet's dry air had cleared them up. His voice had already changed to a most satisfactory baritone, and he was rapidly becoming gorgeous. "This wood—Uncle Seamus said it was well-seasoned cedar—probably will be good for the neck. I haven't found anything for the body, but ..."

"The planet will come up with something, don't you worry," Clodagh told him, beaming up at him with that wide sunny smile that, along with the cascade of wavy black hair now tied back with a thong, was her other greatest beauty. "Come now, give me a hand."

From the doorway came another familiar voice. "I can take some of those outside for you now, Clodagh, if you're ready."

Yana turned to see the eminent Dr. Whittaker Fiske, major company stockholder and board member, sticking a hammer back in the heavy webbed belt he wore strapped over dark gray fatigue pants. Clodagh's bone-knit medicine and the modern ministrations available to company elite had, in the last six weeks, largely healed his broken arm and injured leg: now he merely wore a light bandage for support and walked with the slightest of limps. He wore a navy blue rib-knit sweater and a matching light stocking cap rather rakishly perched over one ear and stood with his hands on his hips, grinning widely and looking immensely pleased with himself.

"Dr. Fiske!" Yana exclaimed. "How'd you get here?"

"Walked," he said. "Great therapy, walking. I used to walk the hills around Trondheim all the time when I was stationed back on Earth. Takes years off you."

Sean cast a sidelong glance at Fiske, though his own smile didn't leave his face. He knew the doctor well enough to know he was on the side of Petaybee, but Whit Fiske was, nevertheless, an outsider in the employ of the opposition. If Clodagh had no problem with him, Yana hardly thought anyone else would object, but there was tension in the air that hadn't been present before.

"Dr. Fiske," Yana said, taking his arm, "I had no idea you were so handy."

"We world builders are versatile men," he said.

"There was a little matter I wanted to discuss with you privately," she said.

"After the meeting then," he told her, rather to her surprise. He patted her hand and disengaged her arm. "Clodagh asked me particularly to stay. If I am going to represent the company interest in utilizing Petaybee's assets to the fullest while maintaining the integrity of the planet and the autonomy of the inhabitants, then I need to be working with the locals on every aspect of the operation."

"Well, if Clodagh feels that it's a good idea and you don't think it's a conflict of interests . . ." Yana said. "In that case, can you help secure enough fuel to get a plane to the southern pole?"

"I think I could do that, yes," he said, with a wink over

his shoulder as he went to give Clodagh a hand to get to her feet.

Bunny and Diego cleared all the seedlings to the sides of the room just before people began steadily to arrive and crowd into Clodagh's tiny house, twenty squeezing into a space that would comfortably accommodate about a dozen. Clodagh explained to the villagers what the cats had imparted to her. Nobody questioned her, being accustomed to Clodagh and knowing that her information tended to be reliable, however she got it.

"So," she said. "I think maybe it would be good if we started off in big groups together. Then folks can break off as we reach the villages they want to get to. When we've done what we've set out to do, we can join up again on the way back. That way if anybody gets lost or gets into some kind of trouble, there'll be somebody to notice."

The crowd voiced assent.

Sinead said, "Aisling and I will take Shannonmouth, since there's trading we want to do there anyway."

"I can't believe McGee's Pass is going against us," Bunny said. "Remember how grateful the Connellys were to you, Clodagh, when you sent them that medicine for their dogs? After the dogs got well, they drove all the way up here to bring you that parka Iva Connelly made for you."

"That was a few years ago, Bunka, back before they got the new shanachie," Clodagh reminded her.

"That shouldn't change gratitude any! I promise I'll be very respectful of the new shanachie, just like I was with old McConachie. I'd like Diego to meet the Connellys and, anyway, they'd be the best ones in McGee's Pass to tell us what's going on."

Clodagh paused. Sending youngsters to one of the trouble spots worried her until Sean said, "Yana and I will go with them and then on to Harrison's Fjord. I'd like Buneka to join us there, so she can see the place where Aoifa and Mala began their expedition."

"Good."

The other assignments were made. Liam Maloney agreed to go to Deadhorse, then chanted a new song about the death of his mother while she was away from the planet being questioned by Intergal.

*"Dog-woman, snow-woman, run-with-the-wind-woman*
*Mother-woman with the steaming springs*
*Streaming in her veins*
*Woman to whom the birds sang*
*Woman whose voice was soft with snow*
*Woman so warm, so warm*
*No ice could freeze her*
*No avalanche stop her breath.*

*"Her feet were stilled when they left the ground.*
*Her breath was stopped in closed rooms*
*Where the wind never blows*
*She turned cold in hot rooms*
*Her steaming blood all bubbled away*
*Her voice stilled where no birds sang*
*Only the croaking of carrion-crows.*
*Aijijai."*

During the recital Liam had looked straight ahead, his eyes closed, his mouth twisting around the words with a mixture of tenderness and bitterness. When he finished his song and his eyes opened, they were full of pain and defiance, and when his mouth closed, his jaw set tightly.

Diego glanced down and away, and Yana saw that Bunny was holding his hand in a fierce, comforting grip. One of Lavelle's last guide jobs, the one she was being questioned about when she died, had been to rescue Diego and his father from a blizzard. Diego had become very close to Lavelle during the trip and resented her unnecessary death almost as much as her family did.

"That is a good song, Liam," Eamon Intiak said. "I have one I'm making to sing to everyone about how the company men snatched us up from the Earth and put us on

Petaybee because they wanted our lands on Earth and now they want to take Petaybee."

"Wait a minute, son," Whit Fiske said, standing apart from Clodagh for a moment. His chin was raised a little defensively as he spoke, although his tone was as genial as ever. "I think most of you know me and know that I have a lot of feeling for what you folks are up against. But the company is a fact of life here, and let's not make it worse than it is already."

"You just say that because your granddad put us here!" Liam accused.

"No, son, I don't."

"I'm not your son. Your people killed my mother."

"His name is Liam Maloney, Whit," Clodagh said.

"Thanks, Clodagh. No offense intended, Mr. Maloney. You're partly right. My grandfather was partially responsible for choosing Petaybee to terraform, and for the process that made the planet fit to live on, but he didn't actually *put* anybody here. The resettling was done by another branch of the company. And yes, they had certain ulterior motives: at the time, those lands on Earth were very much prime real estate. But there were other reasons, too. So, before you folks decide the company is responsible for *all* your troubles, I think a little reminder of historical fact is needed. Does anybody have any idea what I'm talking about?"

Yana groaned inwardly. Fiske, with what she was sure were good intentions, had put his foot squarely in his mouth. For a diplomatic man, he had lousy timing. People here didn't read and write, and their songs tended to be about personal events or about the conditions they survived on the planet: at least, she'd never heard any historical ballads. Should she speak up and give Fiske some support? Would it do any good? She wasn't a native Petaybean, either.

"You're talking about the War for Unification, Whit?" Sean asked.

"Among others," Whittaker answered, trying not to show how relieved he was. "Half the ancestors of those here in

Kilcoole would have died if we hadn't evacuated to Petaybee the faction they were part of—the ones who were getting their asses kicked."

"And those doing the kicking?" Bunny asked, cocking her head in a semicritical fashion.

"Went to other habitable planets. We weren't about to settle ancestral enemies together," Whittaker said with a snort. "The company figured that, with warring factions split up, enough new land to go around, and no traditional enemies to fight, their energies would be put to good use and there'd be enough of them left to hand down the good traits they had submerged to fight. Then the company could restore the fought-over and very battered real estate on Earth. Everyone would end up with more than they would have had otherwise. Most importantly, they'd end up alive."

"Ah, sure and I'm moved to tears, Doctor darlin', to hear how kind you've been to us poor savages," Adak surprised Yana by saying with his brogue-deepened sarcasm.

"I'm not trying to whitewash the company or its decisions," Whittaker said. "But there *were* some altruistic and ethnic preserving reasons operating at the time. Company people aren't all bad, any more than everyone on this planet is all good. The sociologists who designed the population balance tried not only to mix people used to cold weather with those who weren't, but also to mix groups who might get along with each other and share characteristics that would make for a more successful adjustment to the environment."

"Yes, and we turned out very well, Whit, thank you," Clodagh said, and tugged on his webbed belt for him to return to her side, exhibiting her approval of what he had explained. "It was a good point to make. What we want to do is to stand together and tell the company what we want, what Petaybee wants. Just makin' somebody else to blame isn't gonna help the planet. We got to get people to understand, and you can't do that while you're shoutin'. Now then, Eamon, why don't you go speak to the folks up at New Barrow?"

When everyone had a destination, Clodagh handed out the seedlings, goodwill gifts for the hoped-for long growing season. Some people were using the trips as an excuse to visit relatives they hadn't seen in a while, and by the time everyone left, the venture had lost its bitter edge and was infused with something of a holiday spirit.

# 5

*Merde alors!* thought Marmion de Revers Algemeine as she looked out the shuttle window at a piebald landscape covered half with mud, half with dirty ice and snow. What have I gotten myself into this time? Oh, well, I promised Whit! No one in their right mind would want Mad Matt to make a unilateral decision on anything, up to and including when people should be allowed to use the sanitary facilities.

Vice-Chairman Matthew Luzon had already started his "program," Marmion suspected, when he insisted that the shuttle pilot divert to the site of "this so-called" volcano the planet was supposed to have—extruded? No, the word was erupted. They were also to swing past the area where Whittaker Fiske and everyone were supposed to have had their senses taken over by this soi-disant "sentient" planet. Marmion rather liked the notion of a planet with a mind of its own. So few people could boast that sort of decisiveness. Especially Mad Matt. She chided herself for using that term: who knew when she might tactlessly blurt it out by mistake? Her tongue sometimes didn't wait for mental censorship anymore. Did that show she was getting some sense? Or losing what she had?

No, she wasn't losing an iota of her good sense, she told herself firmly, remembering the fiscal coup she had just contrived with three supposedly moribund technical companies. They'd each had something the others needed, and none of their CEOs had had the sense to compromise an inch in a takeover, hostile or friendly. So, last year, she'd instructed one of her holding companies to buy out all three. Banging the right heads together and leaving the sensible ones in charge had resulted in such a whopping great net profit after taxes that she'd soon have to form yet another holding company to hide *that* financial triumph. No matter how Mad Matt—no, no, no, Matthew—boasted of his own recent successes, she'd done better than he had by several billions. But she wasn't one to brag.

"You can't really deny that that's one of the shapes volcanoes assume," she said, having heard what Matthew was muttering to one of his numerous assistants.

"And, my dear, how ever did you know there are various types of volcanoes?" Matthew asked in that smarmy voice of his. His assistants smiled fatuously at him and superciliously at her.

"Because I have a master's degree in geology," she said, smiling sweetly at all of them.

"But it's not doing *anything* now," Matthew remarked, and pointed out the square window that gave a good view of the "dimple" of the cone as the shuttle circled. Not so much as a wisp of smoke or a belch of ash was visible, but for kilometers around the land was shades of gray from cooling lava or wet, mud-streaked ash.

"If you've seen enough, Dr. Luzon," the pilot said over the intercom, "I'll proceed to the cave-site coordinates."

Matthew flicked a hand at one of his assistants, who immediately issued the actual order.

"Are we going to land and investigate the cave, Matthew?" Marmion asked ingenuously.

"I just wanted to orient myself for the purpose of further on-the-spot investigations."

"Wise."

He made a big show of peering down at the site when they reached it minutes later. Marmion needed only to confirm that the rocky upthrust of the cliff was visibly a limestone formation and most certainly riddled with caves. Since Whittaker Fiske was unlikely to fall for illusions, much less *de*lusions, she'd take the rest of his report as valid until she had substantial reason to doubt it. Whit was not one to jeopardize either his position with Intergal or his reputation with wild and unprovable statements.

"This is the right place?" Matthew asked, his expression bland, but Marmion knew not to trust that.

"We're right over the coordinates I was given, Dr. Luzon," the pilot said. "The stream is visible and the ledge, and my scanner's picking up the copter footprints on the nearest possible landing surface. Several footprints, and different size copters."

"Can't deny the evidence, can we?" Matthew said. "All right. Proceed for an aerial pass over that town that young Fiske mentioned. Kil . . . something."

"Kilcoole, Matthew," Marmion said helpfully, as if aiding someone with a faulty memory. There was not a thing wrong with Luzon's memory: it had proved far too accurate too often. Perhaps not honest, or properly evaluating the memories, but the details were always indisputably proffered. Details were Matthew's chief weapons—the details that others might forget or misremember. Then he'd pounce with that deadly and devious accuracy of his.

Kilcoole, as seen through the shuttle windows, was a hodgepodge of widely spaced roofs, some merely darker patches under well-branched trees, with narrow brown tracks, bordered by muddied boardwalks. Not many people were about, though she saw some industrious souls making repairs, and a few others digging up garden-size squares behind their houses. She approved of such occupations. She enjoyed taking care of the extraterrestrial flowers and plants she nurtured in a cleverly connected succession of domes, set at the required temperatures, gravities, and air mixtures that the exotics required. She had fond memories of once being able to get hands and nails dirty, mucking in the small garden of the first house she and Ulgar Algemeine had bought. How young they had been!

She mentally shook those fond memories away and listened to what Matthew was saying.

"Crude in the extreme. How long has this—this *place*," he asked, managing to pour a great deal of contempt into the one word, "been established—if you can possibly call that huddle of huts 'established'?" His assistants did not answer and Marmion had no intention of interrupting him. "And this . . . *place* harbors the dissidents? Kilcoole, indeed. Kill cool is what we shall do to such pretensions."

"Are you sure of that?" Marmion asked in a languid tone. "I feel we are perhaps a tad overcivilized at times, Matt, dear. We've lost the common touch—"

"Thank God," Matthew said explosively.

"—that would permit us to evaluate the struggle against climate and conditions. I do find it appealing that amid all the snow and mud, they're already starting gardens!"

Matthew snorted. "Gardens? More than square-meter plots are required to adequately feed even this indolent population. They can't expect Intergal to continue to support them with expensive importations of subsistence rations."

Marmion raised one hand in a gesture of indolent appeal. "I don't believe rations are imported to Petaybee, Matthew. Do check, one of you," she said, flicking her fingers at his assistants, "because I have the oddest recollection that they are actually self-sufficient."

"Not with the quantities of fuel and—"

"Fuel is for vehicles, not humans, Matthew. Haven't you got those figures for me yet?" Her attitude remained indifferent, but the slight edge to her tone made the skinny one of Matthew's sycophants tap with greater rapidity at his notepad.

"No, sir, ma'am, no rations are imported for the indigenous population." Then he gulped, his Adam's apple bobbling up and down.

Marmion had to look away. The poor dear: Matthew would probably taunt him about that when he was in one of his moods. And the other young men—Matthew only had young men as assistants, which rather gave away something, at least to Marmion, that Matthew would probably rather not have known—were all reasonably attractive and looked fit and able for anything physically taxing. Trust Matthew to make the most of comparisons.

"Thank you, dear," Marmion said to the skinny lad. "And do tell me your name again . . . my memory, you know."

In point of fact, Matthew had not bothered to introduce any of the assistants, although she had pointedly introduced Sally Point-Jefferson, her personal secretary; Millard Ephiasos, her research assistant; and Faber Nike, whose position on her staff she had not designated. Too many people presumed that Faber's large muscular frame and quiet deference marked a deficient intelligence and lack of personality. Too many people were wrong. Especially those who thought Faber was a bedmate. Marmion made a habit of hiring versatile, multitalented people. It saved money and engendered loyalty and discretion.

"My name is Braddock Makem, madam," was the reply, couched in the lowest possible audible tone.

"Thank you, Mr. Makem." She smiled. It never hurt, and for all she knew it might gain her a discreet ally on Matthew's staff.

"Stop trying to charm my staff," Matthew said testily, giving Makem a piercing glare. Makem's apple did an unhappy series of perpendicular maneuvers.

"I've given up on that score long ago, Matthew," she lied shamelessly. "You really do know how to incur loyalty among your staff. I could use a little of that genius." Then, because she was near to laughter at the expression on all those startled earnest faces, she abruptly focused her eyes on the passing landscape. "Ah, the river that suddenly de-iced itself. My, it is turbulent," she said. "And overrunning its banks, too. Flood control apparently is another local lack. But, oh, glance over toward the clear fields, Matthew. Someone's out there doing something to the ground. Plowing? Is that what you call it? And what on earth would you call the beasts they have harnessed to that queer device?" She had everyone on her side of the shuttle to see this archaic activity. "Well, isn't that nice, Matthew. They heard you."

Matthew favored her with a sour glare. She could almost see the phrase "they'll hear me loud and clear" coming out in a bubble from his tightly shut lips. Certainly that was the expression evident in his glare.

A little noise, like a suppressed cough, issued from the seats behind her. Faber, more than likely, she thought. He'd never said as much, of course, but she knew he despised Matthew Luzon. Almost as much as she did, and Sally and Millard for that matter. She'd chosen this team very well indeed.

Then the shuttle was within sight of SpaceBase and its ridiculously colored auxiliary buildings. Who had the taste-lessness to use such awful colors? Marmion wondered. Probably every color of paint rejected throughout Intergal had ended up here, on the walls of this eyesore.

She did not, however, as Matthew did at length, com-ment on the condition of the landing field, with its craters and cracks and the blocks of plascrete that had been ele-vated by the seismic activity. As they seemed localized on the field, Marmion was quite charmed by the notion of a sentient planet that could so specialize its internal effects to cause the most discomfort to the inhabitants it did not wish to remain on its surface. A most considerate friend and for-midable enemy, such an entity would be, if it was possible.

And who was to say it was not? Marmion shrugged. She had a fondness for mysteries in this overanalyzed universe in which she lived. Enigmas attracted her curiosity, and solving them gave her a chance to stretch her mind and re-sources. How wonderful if this truly proved to be the enor-mous and complex puzzle the report promised! Whether it was quite what the locals claimed or not, however, there had to be more here than the prosaic scene below, or the of-ficial explanations of the uncanny events detailed in the re-ports, no matter how disparaging the "logical" explanation. Or accurately detailed. She was quite delighted she had come, and should this planet prove to be a sentient entity, she would be even more delighted to make its acquaintance. She hoped, rather whimsically, that the planet would respond as well to her and not judge her too harshly by the company she kept.

There was, of course, much fanfare as the shuttle landed on one of the few level portions of the field. A proper welcoming committee was there, and if no red carpet had been spread, the plascrete had obviously been scrubbed clean of the mud and goo that was smeared over most of the rest of the landing area. The ground vehicles gleamed with a high wax finish in the clear sunlight.

Her lungs took in the spring-crisp air in great gulps. She was almost dizzy with the intoxication of undeniably *fresh* air.

"Oh, my word, air! Give me air like this wherever I go," she said dramatically, one hand on her heaving chest.

Matthew shot her a disgusted glance. "Marmion, the air may appear to be fresh, but you cannot be sure it isn't filled with bacteria and microbes that will have a deleterious effect on your health. Which we must preserve!" he added with that dreadful smile he affected when he was pretending to be solicitous while really hoping the person he was talking to would fall over dead.

By quickly linking her arm in Faber's, she neatly avoided contact as Matthew held out a hand to help her down the scrupulously clean stairs. Faber escorted her deftly to the ground, but Sally and Millard had to wait until Matthew and his minions had disembarked. Maybe Sally would be able to make some sort of impression on one of the handsome, physically fit young assistants. She usually managed. She'd have to be very clever with Matthew's boys, but that's what Sally was: clever, astute, discreet, and exceedingly intelligent.

Once more into the fray, dear friends, Marmion thought as she observed Captain Torkel Fiske in full flash uniform, standing just slightly ahead of his father—rather naughty of Torkel, she thought. Whittaker was dressed far more casually, but she'd never seen him look so fit and happy. Happy, she thought, wondering that that adjective should spring to mind. Who had time to be "happy" in the Intergalactic society of which she, Whittaker, and Matthew were part? In any event, she smiled at Whittaker, as he neatly elbowed his son out of the way to be first to greet her.

"Is your arm all healed? And the leg wound?" she asked solicitously as they embraced. He wore a support bandage on his arm and she'd noticed just the faintest hint of a limp as he moved.

"Of course, Marmie. You can't keep an old dog like me down. I not only had Intergal's best medicos working on me, but the best immediate and convalescent medical care available here. I'll say that for this planet—good for your health," Whittaker said. Releasing her—a trifle reluctantly, she felt—he turned to shake hands, showing just the right deference and enthusiasm, with Matthew. "You are welcome, Matthew. Your input will be invaluable."

Liar, Marmion thought, but she smiled vacuously as the two men went through the courtesies.

Matthew introduced his gaggle of ganders to Whittaker, adding the provenance of each and their area of expertise. That is, he introduced all but poor Adam's Apple.

"And this is Braddock Makem," she said, smiling brightly first at Matthew, then at Whit, and finally at poor startled Makem. "You remember Sally, I'm sure, Whit. And Millard and Faber, who are my staunch henchmen."

Whit shook hands with her assistants and then waved everyone to the waiting vehicles. The travel bags had already been unloaded and were on their way to whatever accommodations this depressing place might have for people of her and Matthew's prestige.

"We've laid on a fine meal for you, Marmie," Whit said, making sure he sat beside her in the large personnel transport. Its seats, hard as they were, had been re-covered with rather fine furs.

"How kind of you," Marmion replied, and then, feeling the soft texture of the covers, she said, "And are these locally produced?" She did not have to pretend her enthusiasm, for she had seldom felt such beautifully cured natural pelts.

"Yes," Torkel Fiske answered from the double seat behind her. "It's the one thing they do very well here."

"Really?" she asked, managing to keep the irony out of her rejoinder. "How int'rusting! You must show me more," she said languidly. "I really could use some new stoles. Maybe a muff or two for when I have to stand in freezing airlocks and transfer stations."

"Better let young Fiske buy for you, Marmion," Matthew said. "The moment they heard your offworld accent, they'd quadruple the price."

"No, *we* do that," Whittaker said at his drollest.

Marmion snuggled against him, wrapping her fingers about his arm and squeezing them slightly. "It's *so* good to see you, Whit! Whatever's been going on down here, it's really brightened you up. I do believe you were getting office-bound."

Whittaker chuckled and jerked his head at the very upright, disapproving back of Matthew Luzon sitting in front of them.

Marmion squeezed his arm again. "A field trip is what we've all needed to get the juices flowing and the lungs filling with good clean air." Luzon's shoulders twitched, and Marmion felt Whittaker's ribs moving in silent laughter. "We'll all put our minds to this little problem and sort it out in next to no time. Won't we, Matthew?"

His terse answer was lost in a screech of badly worn brake pads, as the carrier halted in front of a building, freshly painted in an aggressively bright yellow.

"Sorry about the color, Marmion," Whittaker said when he saw her wince. "All that's left in Stores, but at least it's clean and bright."

This time Matthew's snort of disgust was plainly audible. As he walked to the door, his body language spoke of displeasure, resentment, and aggravation.

"Oh, dear, we're in for it," Marmion murmured so that only Whittaker heard her.

"I believe we are," he responded as quietly.

"Forewarned is forearmed," she added, and then rose to walk as gracefully as ever down the aisle and up the steps and into the incredibly yellow building.

# 6

The long multisegmented caravan divided, then subdivided, and subdivided again. The first to leave were Sinead and Aisling, who went visiting Shannonmouth, closest to Kilcoole of the three villages on the route. Although Sinead could ride all day, Aisling did not travel as well, especially on horseback. Most of the time she preferred to walk and lead her curly-horse, chatting to the mare as frequently as she addressed Sinead, Sean, Yana, Bunny, or Diego. The mare seemed oblivious to the burdens she carried: bundles of blankets, sewing things, and decorating materials, as well as a backpack and a bale of finely tanned furs from Sinead's winter hunt.

Bunny thought it was aces traveling with this particular group. She was so used to Diego now, she'd be lost without his company, and she had liked Yana Maddock since Day One and looked forward to having her as an auntie when she and Sean got hitched. And both Sinead and Sean knew all sorts of special places where they could sleep under cover. With the people traveled Alice B, Sinead and Aisling's lead dog; Nanook, one of the track-cats who lived out at Sean's lab; and Dinah, the Maloneys' lead dog, who had taken such a shine to Diego that she preferred his company to Liam's. She also liked Bunny: when Bunny stroked her, she could even receive Dinah's somewhat frenetic communications.

After leaving Sinead and Aisling in Shannonmouth, the

group continued on, following the river that snaked uphill past McGee's Pass. There the river was joined by the Iffy, so called because it was iffy if it ran or not, depending on the season, and how frozen it was or how dry the weather had been. The Iffy was in full spate now, pouring its glacial white waters into the clear Shannon; the two mingled murkily all the way to Harrison's Fjord.

As Bunny and Diego parted from Sean and Yana, Sean said, "Listen, you two. By all means, visit the Connellys and, if you can do so, find out what's going on. But, if feeling is very strong in favor of the mines, *leave* and come find us, and we'll all do it together. I want you to meet us at Harrison's Fjord in three days' time. It's only a day to the fjord, so that gives you two days to suss things out. Okay? I'd like to have more time, but with the PTBs arriving soon, Yana and I have got to catch a ride down under as soon as we've finished our business and Johnny or Rick are free."

"Can we go down under, too?" Bunny asked.

"I doubt if the aircraft will be big enough to hold four passengers," Yana said. "Using one of the smaller copters is wisest. Now, get going so you'll reach the Connellys in time to be invited for supper. Sean and I have a ways to go yet."

Later, when the adults disappeared around the base of the next hill and Bunny and Diego steered their curlies toward the pass, Bunny said, "Did you hear? They didn't say no! We might get to go down under, Diego!"

"What's it like?" he asked.

"I don't know. Never been. Different from here though, I think. I've never heard of anyone coming up from the southern pole. You have to cross a whole big ocean, and that just isn't smart to do in our little boats. I guess they don't have any bigger ones down there or we'd see more of them up here. My parents were trying to prove a theory about an undersea passage from the caves near Harrison's Fjord when they disappeared. Hey! What if they got through and the passage—you know, something went wrong with it, so they couldn't come home, but when we get down there we'll *find* them?"

"I wouldn't get my hopes up," Diego said. "It's been how many years now?"

"I dunno. Over ten. I was real little when they left."

"I'd think in all that time they'd have found *some*body to bring word back, knowing how worried everybody would be. Of course, if it was my mom," he added, his tone turning wry, "she'd get so involved with her work she'd never notice she forgot to bring me with her, but you people aren't like that."

"Well, thanks a lot. But I prefer to hope, if it's all the same to you. Or isn't anybody else supposed to? You got *your* father back. I guess that's all that matters."

"I didn't mean for you to take it that way, Bunny. I wouldn't have got my dad back if it wasn't for you and Clodagh and everybody, and sure I *hope* there's people who will help your folks down under. I'd just hate to see you get all excited and be disappointed."

"I'll be excited if I want to," she said tartly. "And I've been disappointed before."

Diego didn't say anything, and Bunny regretted being so sharp with him. He was probably just showing how much he cared about her, as Aisling would say. But he was only two years older than she was, and he shouldn't treat her like a kid.

So after that, they rode in silence until they rounded the bend at the foot of the pass and were greeted by a roaring wind funneling through the cleft and almost blowing them back down to the Shannon.

Flattening themselves against the necks of the curlies, they trudged up the trail, which was somewhat less muddy than the flatlands. The air was also noticeably chillier. Dinah dropped behind the horses and padded along in the shelter of their sturdy bodies.

McGee's Pass wasn't very big. Not even as big as Kilcoole, Bunny thought with surprise as they rode between the first pair of houses. There were only about eight houses, situated fairly close together, lining the wide spot in the trail that passed for a road. The road was heavily churned up and tracked into ruts, ridges, and pockmarks lightly covered with a recent sprinkling of snow, making the footing extremely slippery and uneven.

The houses were unimproved original company issue, shored up with pieces of timber, stones, mud bricks, plascrete, hides, and whatever else was handy. As in Kilcoole, the ground was littered with the refuse of many long winters and warm seasons not quite warm enough to melt the snows.

"Everybody must be inside having lunch," Bunny said of the deserted streets.

But that didn't explain the quiet. She saw no dogs, no curlies, nothing except one lone marmalade cat trying to catch what warmth it could on a plascrete roof.

Dinah wandered from house to house, object to object, sniffing and whining, barking once or twice, and sniffing and whining some more. At one place, she paused to urinate near a doorstep.

The cat looked down at her as if considering jumping on her back for a ride. Dinah jumped up, pawing the house, and barked sharply. The cat rose and stretched itself, and jumped lightly down from the roof onto a barrel and then to the ground.

After a mutual sniff, the cat sauntered up the street, its tail describing arches in the air above its back, while Dinah struggled not to run over the creature in her haste to go wherever the cat was going.

Bunny and Diego followed the dog. The cat walked out of town, which wasn't all that far to go, and up toward the pass, and then abruptly disappeared into a bush beside the trail.

Bunny and Diego dismounted. A voice came from behind the bush, then suddenly, many voices, and then the bush moved aside and a person appeared in what turned out to be the entrance to a cave.

The person, a man who looked a bit like Bunny's uncle

Adak, seemed startled to see them. "Who are you? What are you doing here? What do you want?" he demanded, blocking the entrance to the cave.

"Sláinte," Bunny said as normally as possible. After all, if these people were supporting the company instead of the planet, she wasn't surprised that they might be a little defensive. "I was looking for the Connelly family. I thought they lived around here."

"Who is it askin' after the Connellys?" a woman's voice asked from behind the man. "Krilerneg O'Malley, will you move your ass so the rest of us can get out?"

"Is that you, Iva?" Bunny asked. As O'Malley did as he was bid, she saw that it was indeed Iva Connelly, or someone who looked very much like her, coming out into the daylight.

Unlike the unmannerly O'Malley, the woman cleared the doorway and came over to the horses, allowing a stream of men, women, and children to emerge behind her.

"What is it, Ma?" a boy asked. He was a tall boy, not dark like most of the people Bunny knew, but fair-haired and blue-eyed.

The woman looked puzzled herself, and for a moment Bunny was afraid she'd got the wrong person.

"Sláinte, dama," she said again. "I don't know if you remember me or not, but I'm Buneka Rourke, the snocle driver from Kilcoole. This is my friend Diego Metaxos."

"That's not a Kilcoole name," the boy said in a suspicious mutter.

"Never mind that, Krisuk," the woman said. "You've had a long journey, Bunka. You must be tired and hungry."

The people parted in front of another man now, this one dressed in skins and furs, all ornamented with beads the way Aisling did the latchkay blouses. More striking than his clothing, however, was his physical appearance. He was a very large man and very handsome, his hair worn in a black mane, with a trim black beard covering his chin and a heavy black mustache guarding his mouth.

The others not only let him pass but actually shrank from

him. He carried a staff with the skull of some small animal—a squirrel perhaps, although it looked more like . . . No, it couldn't be a cat's skull! Nobody would do anything so gruesome as to display the skull of a cat.

She did notice, however, that the marmalade cat, who had been there a moment before, had completely disappeared.

"Iva, my child, of course this lovely creature and her friend are tired and hungry. You must bring them to my house to eat and rest." He turned to Bunny and gave her a smile that invited her to admire him, and extended his hand less to shake hers than to sign a blessing at her. "I am Satok, the shanachie. Welcome to my village."

"Sláinte, Satok," Bunny said. "And thanks for the invitation. I just came bringing greetings to the Connellys from our healer, Clodagh Senungatuk, but she has spoken of you and I know she will be glad to hear that I met you."

Iva Connelly spoke to the shanachie, and Bunny thought her manner unusually timorous for someone speaking to the town's rememberer and chief singer and storyteller. "Bunka is an important woman in Kilcoole, shanachie. She is one of two people permitted to drive the company's snocles. On her mother's side she is descended from the Shongili scientists. Her uncle is Sean himself, and she was all but raised by Clodagh, the healer."

The speech would normally have embarrassed Bunny, except that she had the oddest feeling that Iva was presenting her credentials, to show that Bunny was a person worthy of respect and under the protection of important and powerful people. Satok, apparently, took the speech as an advertisement for her—her charms? He was looking at her in the way of men who were courting, except more boldly and without deference.

"Fine recommendations indeed," he said, grasping her hand. "I am so honored that you have come to my village."

"We—uh—we brought a song to the Connellys from their friends in Kilcoole," Diego said rather sharply. "Come on, Bunny. Maybe we can visit the shanachie later, if there's time. We're on kind of a tight schedule. We're being expected soon, elsewhere."

Bunny, uneasy at the burning look she was getting from the shanachie, did not mind Diego intervening in her affairs this time. Iva Connelly shot them a relieved glance and one that was apologetic to the shanachie before she hustled them, the boy, and a passel of other relatives back to a house no bigger than Clodagh's.

Iva, her husband Miuk, and their grown children and grandchildren, including the blond-haired boy, all lived under this roof. It smelled musky, of closeness and constant occupation. Except for six beds and a table, the furnishings were few and the food stores did not appear to be many.

"We brought our own supplies," Bunny told Iva. "And some seedlings from Clodagh. She and Sean both think this will be an unusually long growing season."

Iva did not respond to her remark at once. "Niambh," she said to one of the granddaughters. "Put the kettle on for our guests."

She sat herself down on one bed and motioned to Diego and Bunny to sit on another. The rest of the Connellys surrounded them closely. The youngest ones had to be deflected from the saddlebags, which intrigued them.

"That was kind of Clodagh, but I doubt we'll plant much this year," Miuk said. "We'll be busy helping Intergal at the new mine sites."

Bunny tried not to act surprised. The cats' information, after all, was accurate. That marmalade rascal who had led them to the meeting cave was no doubt a useful informant.

Diego surprised her. He usually hung back in discussions, but now he leaned forward and gave Iva a penetrating look.

"And how," he asked, "does your shanachie feel about the possibility of newly opened mine sites?"

"Why, he thinks it's about time, of course. He says the planet is very offended that we refuse to accept all of its gifts. That's why the planet won't communicate with any of us anymore, but speaks only to Satok."

*"What?"* Bunny cried.

"Just as she says, girl, are you deaf?" Miuk said. "The planet now communicates its needs and we communicate ours to it only through Satok."

"Why? Isn't the planet 'mad' at him, too?" Diego asked, just managing not to sneer.

"You don't understand," Iva said. "You've had Clodagh to guide you, to keep you whole. But McConachie was old and not right in the head for a long time before he died. And no one else came forward for years. We—we lost touch. We misinterpreted things. We did wrong things. Offensive things. Until Satok came to interpret, everything got harder and harder for us. Animals didn't come to the dying places. The river didn't thaw for three summers. We couldn't grow gardens. Not until Satok came did we know what the problem was. We had angered the planet by not cooperating with the company when it wished our help to make its explorations."

"Which explorations?" Bunny asked. She wasn't aware that help had been recruited further afield than Kilcoole.

"There was one last year. Some fellas came looking for guides. They landed in a shuttle. I don't think they even went to SpaceBase. They said there was some kinda special minerals we were supposed to have here that they were lookin' for."

"There were others, too," Miuk said. "Ask Clodagh. Sometimes if what the company wanted was near Shannonmouth, people from Kilcoole would just send them on, or bring them this far and no farther. My brother Upik guided one group, but we never saw him again."

"I went out with my father and Lavelle Maloney with a group," Diego said in a quiet, intense voice. "We got into a whiteout. But we took refuge inside the planet. My father . . . well, he was bad for a while and almost died from the shock, but Clodagh and Bunny and the others helped him and now he's better. That sort of thing seems to happen to a lot of company teams."

Iva shook her head. "They did not ask permission then.

As Satok says, we used to do it all wrong. He says that Miuk's brother and our other folks killed the company teams and the planet punished them—and us—because of it."

"Why does he tell you such lies?" Bunny asked. She had restrained herself long enough. Now she was really mad.

"He doesn't lie. As long as we've done what he says, made the payments he wants, things have been better."

"Payments?" Diego asked incredulously, sticking his jaw out.

"Just little things. Food, furs, some sewing for him, the best pups from the litters, and the best lead dog to train them."

"Oh, that sort of payments," Diego said in a tone of voice that Bunny had never heard him use. But she knew what he was leading up to. "And all your troubles have disappeared with his help?"

Universally solemn nods answered the query.

"And the planet doesn't mind you digging hard down into itself"—Diego made a savage downward thrust with his hand, then gave a mean twist to his imaginary tool as it threw its imaginary contents onto the floor—"and making big sores on its surface?"

There was a stunned rumble at his harsh words.

"You, young Diego, are a stranger, not of this planet. How can you pretend to know its wishes? How can you pretend to know our needs? You have no understanding of the planet, of us, or of how it is at Shannonmouth," Miuk said sternly, shifting his legs into an aggressive stance.

"Quite possibly I don't," Diego said, staring back at him, so unafraid that Bunny was as proud of him as she was scared. "But I have a song to sing . . ."

Bunny breathed a secret sigh of relief. Diego was sure catching on fast. Out of inbred courtesy, everyone in the tiny house relaxed just that little bit that showed they would be receptive to a *song*, but not to more words that went against their shanachie. Of all the tense faces, Bunny noticed only one, that of the light-haired boy, Krisuk, that did not wear the same defensive, half-frightened look. She had mistaken Krisuk's expression for sullenness at first, but as Diego talked, the other boy's face relaxed and she saw that he was angry—and not at them.

Diego, as if he'd been doing it all his life instead of just the past few months, lifted his head, half closed his eyes, and sang the song he had composed for the Kilcoole latchkay.

"I am new come, in storm, here.
A storm of heart and mind and soul.
I sought and found storm with Lavelle.
She saved me when the sled crashed down.
With the heat of her body she saved me.
With the wit of her mind she saved my father, too.
Saved me to see the cavern that all say I didn't see.

"But I saw the caverns and the water and the carving
Of wind and water.
I saw the gleaming snow, like jeweled cloth.
I saw the branches waving, the water talking.
The ice answering, the snow laughing. I saw
The animals of water and earth and they were
Talking, too.
They were kind to me and answered all my
Questions
But I do not know what questions I asked.
I do not know what answers I heard.
I know the cavern, the branches, the talking water.
The speaking ice and the laughing snow. I know
That you know it, too. So hear my song
And believe me. For I have seen what you have seen.
And I am changed. Hear my song. Believe me."

"Diego is no stranger to Petaybee. The planet has spoken to him," Bunny said quietly in the respectful silence that followed a true song. For she could see by their reception that the Connellys could recognize the song for what it was.

"The planet speaks to few," Iva said, nodding her head.

"But here," Miuk said in a harsh voice, "the planet speaks to Satok and none other, and it is he we must obey in the name of the planet."

"Well spoken, Miuk." There were gasps of astonishment as Satok stuck his head through a carefully opened window. "Well sung, young traveler."

Iva quickly rose and opened the door. She was red with the embarrassment at the shanachie having to listen through a window to hear something going on in her house.

Immediately it occurred to Bunny that that might be how he knew so much of what went on in his village. Inside, he made straight for the bed on which Bunny and Diego sat. But Diego, acting quickly, shifted so that Satok would have to sit next to him instead of Bunny, as had been his very obvious intention.

"Then, young traveler, do you think the planet says one thing for one town and something else for another?" Satok asked, his eyes glistening, his mouth set at a derisive slant.

"Your town is near mines, Kilcoole is not."

"But Lavelle was searching for mines, was she not, when your group became lost in whiteout?"

"We were, but well east of Kilcoole and well north of here," Diego answered calmly. Bunny thought he was much cleverer than the shanachie, who was obviously trying to catch him out.

"What else did the planet say to you that you made such a song?"

Diego looked up at the intimidating face of Satok. "The planet gave me words to sing, which I have sung. Now my mouth is dry, and we have come a long way to see Iva Connelly and thank her for gifts, bringing gifts in return."

"Bah!" Satok said with a scornful glance at the seedlings. "There will be no time for growing things when the company sends orders."

"There is time now," Bunny said, encouraged by Diego's attitude. "The days grow long enough and the soil here will soon be as ready as it is in Kilcoole. It takes nothing from the company to supply fresh food. The company only gives cans and dried stuff. Our people need fresh food."

Satok jumped to his feet. "I will tell what is good for *my* people, not you strangers." He whirled on Iva. "You will not accept these gifts." Iva's expression was terrified and shocked, but he ignored her. "When the planet feels that you are worthy of them, the planet will provide." Then, at his full and imposing height, he glared down at Diego and Bunny. "You were not invited." His thick forefinger pointed ominously at Diego. "You come here and try to tell my people what is proper." He pointed at Bunny, and a most curiously avid expression fleeted across his face. "The planet speaks through me, and *I* am the best judge of who and what is good for these people. I will decide which gifts are acceptable for this portion of the planet. Your shanachie means well, but she is ignorant of our true needs. I will instruct you tomorrow, when you have rested."

With that he stalked out of the little house, pausing briefly to eye the curlies, leaving everyone nervous, staring at nothing, or actively trembling. Bunny shook with fury, and Diego had clamped his teeth down on his lip to keep from speaking. He gave Bunny one long look, and his shoulders sagged just like everyone else's did.

Iva could barely manage to be civil after that. She had been embarrassed in front of them by the shanachie's behavior, and embarrassed in front of the shanachie by theirs. She was furious with her husband, as well. She did not, however, refuse the provisions Bunny and Diego had brought in their saddlebags to augment the evening meal.

Bunny had little appetite. She was angry and, actually, somewhat shocked. She had never been so rudely treated in her life—not even by her nasty cousins. She had certainly never thought she'd see Clodagh's careful gifts spurned.

Diego was as silent and ate as little as she, and his eyes had a wary quality to them.

They bedded down that night on the floor, between the two bunks farthest from the fire. They were cold, since they had not brought their warmest winter gear with them. Back in Kilcoole, where it was so unseasonably warm, they had been unable to imagine it being quite so cold here.

Diego shivered, hugging himself and managing to look resentful as he did it.

The blond boy, Krisuk, was in one of the beds beside them, and he threw a quilt down to Diego. "Here you go," he whispered.

"Don't you need it?"

"I can put on my parka. I just wanted to tell you, it was great hearing you tell off that blowhard."

"You mean you don't think he's the heart and soul of the planet like everybody else here seems to?" Bunny whispered.

Krisuk made a rude sound, but quietly.

Just then, from outside the cabin, came a series of furious barks.

"Dinah!" Diego said, sitting straight up.

Iva and Miuk looked up, then pointedly rolled back over to sleep; the children other than Krisuk pulled their quilts up over their head. Soon the barking was replaced by scratching at the door and whining.

"She can't come in," Krisuk said. "His Highness has decreed that animals aren't allowed in the house with people."

But Diego was already at the door, unlatching it and bending over the agitated dog. Bunny rose, too, with Krisuk stealing softly behind her. Since the dog could not come in, Bunny and Krisuk joined Diego outside, where he was rubbing her fur and talking to her.

"She's trying to tell me something. I know she is," Diego said. "But she's so excited it's all scrambled."

"Darby and Cisco!" Bunny said, remembering the curlies.

"What?"

"Where are they?"

"I—oh, shit!" he said.

Krisuk made a face. "At least he left the dog."

"Who?"

"You know—him," Krisuk said, pointing his chin up past

where the houses ended. "He thinks anything worth having belongs to him. Besides, I saw the way he was looking at yer woman here." He nodded to Bunny. "I think he means to keep *you* here, as well as have the horses."

"He'll keep nothing," Bunny spat. "Including the hold he has over this village. I don't know how he's managed to do it, but I know that, if he's the only one who communicates with the planet here, there's something seriously wrong."

Diego said cautiously, "We did promise if we had cause to think this might get dangerous, we'd go meet Sean and the major first."

"Well, we can't very well go without the horses now, can we? Not and make it there in good time. We'd be sitting ducks for that—that—witch doctor!" She used the term she had heard some of the company men apply to Clodagh sometimes.

"Your horses are gone," Krisuk said in a hard, practical voice. "No one can have back what Satok has claimed."

Bunny put on the voice she had heard Aunt Moira use with recalcitrant children and puppies. "Don't be daft. Satok is just a man—a greedy one at that."

"Everyone says he's the voice of Petaybee."

"Everyone's gone bloody deaf then," Bunny said. "No one creature is the voice of Petaybee. In Kilcoole, anybody who wants to speaks with Petaybee. This planet is perfectly capable of making itself understood to anyone who cares to listen."

"Then why does it only speak to us through him? I hate him, but the only time anyone hears from the planet, or anything good comes to McGee's Pass, is when we go to the summonings in the cave up there."

"The one where we met you and your mother first?" Bunny asked.

"The same."

"Well, let's go back there then. I'm on good terms with the planet. I'm quite sure it won't refuse to speak to me. And besides, he might have hidden the curlies there."

"No, the horses will be up there," Krisuk said, gesturing

with short jabs of his fingers, "at his house, on top of the cave, on the meadow above the ridge."

Dinah whined softly, and Diego stroked her. "You know, Bunny, I think the horses would follow Dinah, if they're not tied too tightly."

"He'd take your dog as well, or kill her."

"We'll see," Bunny said. Her chin jutted forward and her fists clenched as she marched up the road to the cave mouth. The wind was loud tonight, howling along the tree-tops and roofs, rattling doors and windows, picking up any-thing loose and banging it around. It occurred to Bunny that the planet was already speaking, if people would only lis-ten, and the message was loud and clear. It was not pleased. Not pleased at all.

"Bunka, wait!" Krisuk whispered urgently. He grabbed her arm as he caught up with her.

Diego was at her other side. "We can't wait any longer. This guy already stole our horses. Who knows what he'll do next?"

"That's what I'm trying to tell you. She"—Krisuk nod-ded to Bunny—"especially shouldn't go."

"Why not?"

"You didn't meet my older sister, Luka," he said. His tone was so angry and anguished that it stopped both Bunny and Diego in their tracks. They were just beyond the last house now, about two hundred paces from the cave mouth. "She got sent over to Deadhorse by Satok. But be-fore that, he took her."

"What do you mean he took her?" Bunny asked. "You mean *raped* her?"

"No. Not at first, anyway. At first, he was such an im-portant man, she was thrilled that he had chosen her. Why shouldn't he have? Even though I say it as her brother, she was the prettiest girl in the village, and a smart, hard worker, too. When she was younger, it was thought she might be a healer like Clodagh. She was always singing, al-ways talked to everything in the friendliest fashion. She got kinda funny when she became a woman though. I think maybe people made too much of how pretty she was and what a good catch she would make. And the local fellows—well, there weren't many in her age group, and none of them were quite right. When Satok came, he flattered her with his attention, not just because she was pretty, but he played on her shaman powers too, how close she had always been to Petaybee. If I didn't hate him so much, I guess I would have to say he's not bad-looking. He seems—bigger—than the other fellows here. She was very excited. Thought she had met her match. My parents thought she would marry him, but he just moved her up there with him, not that there was that much to move."

Slowly now, and more cautiously, they were walking against the wind, their heads bent together, their hair flying in each others' faces to hear what Krisuk was so urgently trying to tell them. As they reached the cave mouth and Krisuk thrust aside the bush that guarded it, the wind quieted as if it had suddenly been extinguished. Bending low, the three of them stepped inside.

# 7

"Coaxtl, wake up. I think they've found me," Goat-dung said into the wispy fur of the cat's left ear.

Coaxtl stretched and yawned. *Who has found us, youngling?*

"The Shepherd Howling and the flock. They're coming to take me back."

Coaxtl rolled over and sat up on her haunches, front feet propping her erect as she listened to the low voices speaking in words that were not quite intelligible. After listening for a moment, the cat lay back down again.

*Fear not, child, it is nothing but the voice of Home.*

The Shepherd Howling had spoken of the Great Monster, who seemed to be the same being the cat called Home, and how the monster had a voice, though the Shepherd always described it as a growl or a roar or a gnashing of teeth or spewing of spittle or something equally nasty. He said the Great Monster had its counterpart in all of the tales of Earth, of the underworld guarded by the bones of dead men and of terrible devouring fires and tortures. When he had her or any of the other members of the flock punished, he reminded them that if they didn't mend their ways, the Great Monster would do much worse to them when they died still in sin and error, uncorrected by his teachings.

Horrible serpents and worms and flame-belching beasts were supposed to guard the Great Monster, or be aspects of it. The underworld held all of these bad things, according to the Shepherd. Goat-dung wondered if she would see them. So far, she had only met Coaxtl.

The cat's unconcern should have lulled her back into exhausted relaxation from her adventures of the past two days. But she found that the voices—and the possibility of returning to the flock—had frightened her so much that she couldn't sleep.

"Did you ever hear," she asked the cat idly, "what it used to be like on Earth back in the olden days, before we were moved for our heinous crimes and sins to this cold place and put at the mercy of the Great Monster?"

Goat-dung awaited the cat's answer with sleepy anticipation, for in spite of all of the things that she had hated about living in the Vale of Tears, and as much as she had feared the Shepherd Howling, she liked the stories that he and everyone else told constantly. They told stories of why it was good to cook one way and not another. Stories of why a house should be built in one way and not another. Stories of how horrible it had been in their homes before they came to the Vale of Tears. Stories of how they had first met the Shepherd. Although some of the stories were frightening and the pictures they made in her head filled her with revulsion, she missed the stories. She missed having them told to her. The stories were a respite from beatings and made work go faster. A lot of them were ones like those she had just been remembering, about how the Great Monster devoured people and twisted their lives, but some were nice, about the olden days on Earth. These were told mostly to make everybody feel sad for how much they had lost through their sins, but Goat-dung liked hearing them anyway.

*Oh yes,* the cat said. *My granddam told my dam and said the tale was passed to her by an old, old male who was passing through on his way to die. But I don't think such stories are fit for cubs myself.*

"What do you mean?"

*The olden days were bad ones. First all of the things that make life good went away. Then for a time everything was sterile and made of not-real materials. Trees had leaves on them that were not alive and bark on them that was not alive, and they did not grow from the ground, for it was not alive either. Underfoot was hard and unyielding stuff, and between one and the sky were barriers. At first, some real air was allowed to pass through them but later, only light, and sometimes that light was not real, either. This was bad enough while it was clean and free of any tiny living things, but in time, the Earth became filthy, as well as dead. Finally, one of our kind had the sense to make certain that she and a male of her acquaintance were included in the manifest when creatures were chosen from our lands.*

"What an odd story," Goat-dung said, and added severely, as the women did to her when she told them something they thought to be a lie, "That is *not* how the Shepherd Howling talks of old Earth."

*The Shepherd Howling,* the cat said, washing her long sharp claws one by one, *eats his young.*

Goat-dung considered this for a moment. "True. Go on. Did the old male give your ancestress any details at all?"

*Yes. I will tell it to you as it was told to her.* Coaxtl gave a slight cough that was half a growl and began.

*Long ago, in the time when our ancestors wore tawny coats, we lived in the mountains, not mountains like these, all jagged and icy cold, but smooth mountains with hot and fragrant jungles most of the way up their ridges. In that time, the skies were filled with layers of leaves and fronds in which to hide.*

"What's a jungle?" Goat-dung asked.

*A place of great heat and many trees, sometimes much rain and bright flowers.*

"Like summer in the lowlands?"

*No, for this is much hotter and lasts year-round. You would not be able to stand such heat and neither would I. Many kinds of animals and plants existed then that no longer exist, at least not here. Not yet.*

"What do you mean, not yet?"

*Our Home,* the cat said, *has plans.*

* * *

"What's the matter, Sean?" Yana asked about the fifth time she caught Sean looking back over his shoulder. Nanook had done so twice, as well.

"I dunno," he replied, shrugging his shoulders and giving her a sheepish grin. "They should be safe enough with the Connellys. And we'd better get moving if we want to sleep warm tonight." His grin broadened. "Air's cooler up here than it is down below. I'd forgot that not everywhere would be enjoying the unseasonable warmth that Kilcoole is."

Once out of the forest and on slopes covered with lichenlike plants and mosses, they had to dismount and lead the ponies over several stretches where the narrow pathway daunted Yana, even habituated to rough going as she had been prior to her injury at Bremport. The curly-coats seemed oblivious to any danger, though it gave her some comfort to note that their ears wigwagged constantly, their tails sometimes acted like propellers—for balance, the way Nanook used his—and they snorted frequently, as if exchanging information.

They got over the rocky tor and down into forest again by the time it was full dark. The forest was denser than the one around Kilcoole, and the trees larger, with thicker trunks. The branches dripped constantly from the melting snow, so that it might as well have been raining. Yana was very tired, so Sean made her tend the little fire he started while he saw to the horses and then skinned the rabbits Nanook caught. The cat ate his raw, but with such relish that Yana could barely wait till theirs was cooked. At last, with Sean on one side of her and Nanook on the other, she slept warmly and dreamlessly. She awakened the next morning to the smell of coffee under her nose and the sight of a cup with its handle turned toward her. Sean slipped back into the bag, grinning at her, and they both suppressed chuckles at Nanook's soft snores.

The morning was well advanced when, abruptly, they reached the plateau that tilted toward the other half to the fjord. It was as if a giant axe had neatly bisected the cliff to allow the waters through a narrowing cut to the main body of the continent. The split sloped abruptly down, where a river ended its path to the sea and tumbled in a graceful, medium-sized waterfall into the end of Harrison's Fjord.

"Who was Harrison?" Yana asked as they made their way down the incline toward smoke that rose from unseen chimneys, Nanook bounding on ahead.

"Harrison? He was one of grandfather's old buddies. Retired here from the Dear knows where," Sean said. "He had a droll sense of humor and loved early space adventure stories."

"Oh?"

"The name of the place," Sean explained, looking over his shoulder as if Yana should instantly comprehend his reference. When she obviously didn't, he shrugged and continued his briefing. "Folks are mainly Eskirish—fishermen and boat builders."

"Boat builders?" Yana was amazed: they'd left the forested slopes behind when they'd crossed over the pass from McGee's and the other side of the fjord was just as bare as this one. Builders of anything would have to go miles for timber.

"More than wood makes good boats," he said.

"By the way, Sean love," Yana began, taking her opportunity while she had it, "how many people know you're a selkie?"

"As few as possible." But he grinned at her. "Many people have *seen* a selkie. It can't always have been *me*, because I know I wasn't anywhere near there at that particular point in time, and so far as I know nobody else has my—er—versatility. Some Petaybeans have great imaginations."

"I'd noticed."

"I thought you might. We can ride now, and I'd rather we made the last leg of our journey before we lose the good light."

They mounted and proceeded at the marvelously easy pacing gait the curly-coats did so effortlessly at various speeds. Yana's little mare kept her nose right against Sean's gelding's tail. The pace was rather breathtaking, but she wasn't as nervous about this as she had been on the narrow uphill climb.

Curly-coats could also stop—like right now! Only the bunching of the forehand muscles under her legs gave her warning enough to tighten her hold on the thick mane. One moment they'd been flying along—the next, dead stop! Yana measured the length of her torso on the mare's neck before she struggled upright. Then she dismounted when she saw that Sean had . . . and was leading his pony right over the edge? No, she realized as she caught her breath. Nanook's head was just visible to the right, and Sean was turning in that direction, too, and the trio proceeded down.

Sighing at a reluctance to repeat *down* what she had only recently gone *up*, Yana was agreeably surprised to find a broad, rutted grassy road leading down in an easy gradient, switching back and forth down the side of the cliff to the village that was Harrison's Fjord. This trail had to have been man-made. Nanook, tail tip idly twitching, padded on ahead of them, acting advance guard as usual.

"Harrison," Sean said. "He hated climbing, had problems with balance. I don't know who he bribed of the original TerraB group, but he got the road done and the village settled, the harbor carved the way he wanted it."

"Where did your sister and her husband enter caves—" Yana broke off, seeing that the rock formation along the roadside did not lend itself to caves.

As Sean pointed toward the waterfall, Yana was surprised to see Nanook look in the direction he was pointing and sneeze. "Near that, slightly to the left on the far side, is where the fjord cave opens."

Suddenly dogs began to bark and, while Yana made a private bet with herself, several orange cats wandered up to greet them, lifting themselves to their hind legs to exchange sniffs, nose to nose. She won. The cats immediately moved on to greet the travelers, who had undoubtedly been vouched for by Nanook.

"Wherever we go?" she asked Sean, who was bending to run a hand down an orange back. Yana could hear the purr from where she was, seven paces behind.

"Not everywhere," Sean said, lightly stressing the first word, "but they get about." He stroked another one and then fondled the ears of a shaggy black dog, with light brown and white face markings, who presented itself for similar attentions.

Going from purr to full voice, the first cat stropped itself about Yana's ankles, and she had the oddest feeling that she was welcomed for herself and not just as Sean's companion. She bent to scratch the cat under the chin and heard the vibrations of a renewed purr. More barking dogs came trotting up to greet them, weaving an adroit and skillful way among the cats.

"Who comes?" called a rasping bass voice.

"Sean Shongili and Yanaba Maddock!" Sean shouted back.

"Sean, is it? And his lady, no less? Thrice welcome! Hurry on down! A glass of the warm awaits you!"

There was no way to "hurry" down, with cats and dogs insisting on sniffing, receiving caresses, and generally impeding their progress. Nanook had leapt down and disappeared, a movement that caused Yana to scrutinize the odd arrangement of the houses: each of the twelve or fourteen had been carefully inserted on an earthen terrace, with the cliff for a back wall, and the terrace jutting out far enough to provide a small garden or yard complete with benches. The houses were perched on each side of the road as it ribboned down to the final broad terrace, which was wharf, as well—and high above the fjord water. Boats were neatly propped up on racks; nets hung from racks of high poles, drying in the last of the sun. At the farthest end of this wide terrace there was a large wooden hall where, Yana supposed, boats could be built. But the water looked an awfully long way down to make Harrison's Fjord a practical fishing port.

"Low tide," Sean said to her when he heard her exclamation of surprise. "When the tide turns, the water comes up here like a herd of running moose. Everything had better be stored high, dry, and safe. Ah, Fingaard, good to see you!" And suddenly Sean, who was no small man, was engulfed in the embrace of one of the largest men Yana had seen on this planet.

"And I, you, Shongili!" the man replied, grinning over Sean's shoulder at Yana. "This is your woman?" And he swung away, to advance on Yana. She held her ground but had to keep looking up and up as the giant approached, until she was in danger of falling backward.

Suddenly he bent his knees so his face was on her level and placed pitchfork-sized hands on her shoulders with remarkable gentleness. He peered into her eyes, with as kindly and searching a gaze as Clodagh's, and smiled. "Ah, yes, of course."

With one movement, he had taken the reins of the curly-coat from her, and placed his huge hand on her back like a prop against which she could safely lean during the rest of the switchback way to the village.

By then, others had emerged from their houses. Every house seemed to have its own set of stairs to reach the roadway, and another, she discovered, to get down to the next level.

"We heard you'd be coming," Fingaard said jovially. "You can tell us how to help Petaybee?"

"Fingaaaaaard, where are your manners, you great oaf?" A woman, nearly the size of him, clambered up to the roadway, smiling at Yana before she continued to berate her husband. "Drink, first; eat, second; and you've all the night to talk and get the needful done. Don't mind him, missus. He means well." This was directed at Yana. A hand, not quite as large as Fingaard's, was shoved at Yana, who gripped it, steeling herself for a viselike crush; but the fingers only pressed gently and withdrew. "I'm Ardis Sounik, and wife to Fingaard. Welcome, Yanaba Maddock."

It was no surprise to Yana to see the cats clustering around Ardis's feet, somehow avoiding being trampled on or swept away by the leather skirts the woman wore. They were beautifully tooled with remarkable patterns, all interlinked in a way that looked so familiar to Yana that she tried to remember what the design was called.

She didn't have much time for coherent thought after that, because the rest of the village—and there seemed to be far more people than twelve, fourteen, or even forty houses could accommodate comfortably—gathered about them. The ponies were led away, while the dogs and cats disposed themselves in places particular to them under benches, and on ledges. Sean and Yana were seated on the longest bench and given a cup of the "warm" to drink.

Her first surreptitious sniff told her this was nonalcoholic, and not at all similar to Clodagh's "blurry." Her first sip filled her mouth with flavor so skillfully blended that she couldn't name any one taste, but the overall effect made for one of the most satisfying drinks she had ever drunk. She sipped as Sean did, sipped and savored, and tried to remember the names of the folk introduced to her. They were so *glad* to have visitors, so glad it was the Shongili himself who had come to tell them how to help in this emergency, for even here the planet had told them that their help was needed and they would be shown what could be done.

Yana cast a sly glance at Sean to see how he was taking that news, but he nodded as wisely as if he had been well briefed. Probably he had. So she kept on sipping.

Then there was eating. Trestle tables appeared like magic, and torches were set around so that even as daylight faded, the hastily prepared banquet remained well lit. Yana had never seen so many ways to prepare fish: poached, grilled, spread with spicy sauces, deep fried with a coating that was seasoned to perfection, pickled in a sharp liquid, a chowder with potatoes and vegetables—"the last of dried from the year gone out but well kept." And then sweets—made of fish jelly and flavored by herbs—and a funny, thick paste that dissolved in the mouth. And more "warm" drink.

Singing began, and before she had a chance to dread it,

Yana was asked to sing her song of the debacle of Bremport, for one of the boys from Harrison's Fjord had been there, too. Whether it was all the "warm" or not, Yana just lifted her head and sang her song, and this time she had no trouble meeting the eyes of the parents of the lad lost when she had nearly died, too. This time she knew she eased their hearts, and that eased hers, too. Maybe there would come a day when the awful nightmare of Bremport would be no more than the words of a heart-sung song.

Eventually, torches lit their way to their accommodation. Yana was so weary, it took her two attempts to get one boot off. Sean's chuckle and her immediate supine posture told her that he would take care of her, so she helped as much as she could as he undressed her, and shoved her under warmed fur robes. The last thing she felt was his arms pulling her against him.

She had dreams that night, of wandering amid teeth, down tongues that were white, through bones that were like rib cages, yet she wasn't afraid in that dream, merely curious as to what she would see next. And throughout the sequence, which repeated, she kept hearing murmurous voices, like singers distant and unintelligible. Yet she knew that the song was joyful and the tune uplifting, with the odd descant of what sounded very much like a purr.

As they entered the cavern, Bunny said to Krisuk, "So this is the place where Satok speaks to the planet."

"No. This is the place where he tells us what the planet says."

"But he doesn't give anyone else a chance to talk to Petaybee?"

"Oh no," Krisuk said bitterly. "He wouldn't do that."

"What I don't understand is why, if your people have been in communication with Petaybee all their lives, this guy can suddenly come and shut them up," Diego said. "I mean, so maybe he gets his bluff in on the people 'cause they don't get around much and he's a smooth talker—

okay, I can accept that. But how does he shut the planet up?"

Bunny scarcely heard his last words. As she picked her way forward in echoing darkness, she suddenly felt as if she couldn't draw a breath, as if something inside her, a presence that she always had with her, was walled away from her, withering. The sudden terrible loneliness of being without that presence was crushing. She backed away, stumbling toward the sound of Diego's voice.

He was still talking when she reeled against him, clutching at his jacket. "Bunny? Bunny! What's wrong?"

"Dead," she said. "It's—dead. Out—gotta get—out!"

Alarmed, the boys helped her out of the cave. She sat down on the path, gulping to get air in her lungs. After a dozen deep inhalations of the cold wind she looked up at Krisuk.

"How can your people stand to go *in* there?" she demanded.

"Why? What's wrong?"

"It's dead, that's what! Somehow that bastard has *killed* part of the planet."

"How could he do that?" Diego asked.

"I don't know."

"I don't much like the place," Krisuk said, "and everybody else is uncomfortable there, too. I hear the songs about the joys of singing with Petaybee, and I remember when I used to love to come here, and I don't understand it. I sort of put it down to Satok's charming personality."

Bunny shook her head. "It's more than that. I'm surprised you didn't feel it, too. Diego, did you?"

"Maybe," he said, frowning thoughtfully. "When I was a kid one time, a ship hauled a derelict back to our station. They put it in the cargo bay. I wanted to see what it was like and I snuck in. I couldn't get out of there fast enough. Was that what you felt?"

"I don't know. Maybe." Having escaped the suffocating sensation in the cave, she was too drained to describe it properly. The wind and icy rain were oddly comforting.

"I'm going back in there," Diego said suddenly. "Krisuk, maybe you should stay with Bunny."

"No," the boy said. "I'll go, too. It's forbidden for any of us to go in without Satok's say-so. Some who have disobeyed have never been heard from again. But if there's any kind of proof in there that Satok's not who he says he is, then my word will carry more weight than an outsider's. I don't think my folks would give up a second kid to that creep as easy as they let Luka go."

"Will you be okay, Bunny?"

Dinah chose that moment to press her wet nose against Bunny's ear and lick it.

"Yeah," Bunny said slowly. "Maybe I could even go back in now that it wouldn't take me so much by surprise."

"I don't think that's such a good idea," Diego said, eyeing Bunny's pale face and eyes staring wide with shock and grief. "Besides, somebody should stand guard. I wish we had a light, though."

"Oh, there's lamps in there," Krisuk said. "Come, I'll show you."

Bunny heard their voices grow fainter as they penetrated farther into the cave. Her fingers folded Dinah's fur and stroked her soft, pointed ears. Dinah whined and laid her head in Bunny's lap. Bunny felt like whining herself.

The little lamp threw the boys' shadows into grotesque skeleton dances around the smooth walls of the cave room. It was a large room, but it stopped abruptly about forty feet from the entrance. "Has it always been this small?" Diego asked.

"No. There was this accident, oh, a couple of days before Satok came. It was the first latchkay we'd had here since old McConachie died. People were goin' back into the place like we'd always gone, when all of a sudden there was what sounded like an explosion, and showers of rock and dust came spewin' out after us. We all ran, but the first few people, McConachie's family, his apprentice, they were all killed. I remember my da and the other men diggin' for bodies. I was just a little kid then. I couldn't understand where my friend Inny McConachie had gone. That was old Mac's grandson, a good mate of mine."

"That's rough," Diego said, feeling along the walls. "I lost a friend not too long ago, too."

"The woman in the song?"

"Yeah. Wait a minute. What's this?"

"What?"

Diego's fingers dipped into a notch and a panel slid open; reaching out, his hands touched only empty space.

"How long did it take them to clean up the cave-in?"

"They didn't. Nobody wanted to. When Satok came, he pretended to be real sympathetic and went in to look for bodies. He brought out a couple of pieces of clothing and insisted we all go back into the cave to give a proper memorial service. I don't know why people went along with it. Guess everybody was kind of in shock. It's got to be about the worst thing that ever happened here."

"Not quite," Diego muttered under his breath. "Bring the light over here."

Krisuk did. The fumes from the mare's-milk lamp stank, but the acrid odor was almost welcome in the sterility of the cave. As Krisuk raised the little lamp, it illuminated an area of clean stone floor and clean stone walls.

"There may've been a cave-in here," Diego said with a snort, "but someone worked real hard to tidy it all away."

"It can't be!" Krisuk said. "The cave's been blocked off for years. Nobody comes in here except with Satok. Everybody's sort of afraid of the place."

"That's too bad," Diego mumbled, the thought coming to him like a stray line of poetry. "It should be the other way around."

"What?"

"Seems like the place had more reason to be afraid of the people—"

"What's that supposed to mean?"

"I dunno. It just popped into my head."

"Look, my people may be mistakenly following a

sleazebag but I still don't like them being insulted by an outsider . . ."

"Okay, okay. I didn't mean anything by it. Come on, let's see the rest."

"There's more?" Krisuk held the light up head high, advanced a step inside the new opening, and emitted a low whistle. "There sure is."

Even in the weak light of the lamp they could see that a good-sized tunnel had been cleared through the cave-in. The floor still was mainly stone overlain with dust, but the walls and ceiling had an odd white sheen. Krisuk ran his fingers over it and sniffed. "No smell."

Diego leaned in closer and dragged his fingernails down the wall, leaving not so much as a scratch in their wake. "No, there wouldn't be. It's bonded with Petraseal."

"What's that?"

"It's what they use in mines these days to prevent cave-ins. They bond the rock surfaces to each other with this stuff. It's very strong. Nothing gets through. I wonder where Satok got it in this quantity."

"You think he did this?"

"Who else?"

The other boy gave a quavering groan. "Oh, no. I can't believe he did this."

"What?" Diego asked, peering in the direction Krisuk was looking with a transfixed stare. Then he saw the outlines of skulls, large and small, and all sizes and lengths of bones, jumbled in with the rock, like so many fossils.

"Bastard! He could have brought them out for a decent burial!" Krisuk said.

"Looks like they're still half-crushed by the rocks," Diego said fairly. "Maybe he couldn't get them out without bringing down another cave-in. So he just sealed them up."

"Without even a proper song?"

"You did say there was a memorial service for them in the cave."

"Yes, but . . ."

"Look, I'm not trying to defend the guy, but the bonding

wasn't put on until they were already skeletons. My guess is that it took him a while to dig this out and seal it up. Would have had to. Come on, let's see how far this goes."

"I was only a tad, mind you," Krisuk said, swallowing convulsively, "but it seems to me like the cave was really long. The floor sloped down because it was a hard walk up when we came back out: Mum used to have to carry me. I also remember that the cave used to have little teeth farther on." Krisuk pointed to the darkness ahead, beyond the reach of the light.

"You mean stalactites and stalagmites?" Diego asked. "Pointy things dripping down from the ceiling or sticking up from the floor like anthills?"

"Yeah. I never saw an anthill like them, but you got the idea."

They walked back farther, their footsteps at first scuffing on the grit across the floor, then sounding with a ringing echo as the floor, too, became coated with the Petraseal and metal grates had been placed along the corridor. For a time the floor sloped down, as Krisuk had remembered, but then another corridor, of fresh, jagged rock, still sharp through the sealant, branched off and twisted upward.

"That wasn't there before!" Krisuk said and turned into the new passage.

Diego followed him up for a few feet, enough to see that the Petraseal covered the floor and from the ceiling dangled the roots of trees and bushes, preserved for all time in death-glossy bones.

Diego shuddered, in spite of himself. "This probably leads to Satok's place, if he lives above the cave, like you said."

"He did *all* this stuff?" Krisuk asked. "How could he?"

Diego shrugged. "It's not that hard with the right tools. I just wonder where he got them. Come on. I'll bet if we look further we'll find out why he's doing all this."

They didn't find out why, but they did find out what it was he was doing when they took the descending path into the lower cavern Krisuk remembered.

Lower, farther from the entrance, everything was not covered with the stone bonder. But where the stalactites and stalagmites had been were only round craters, and sometimes small tunnels, like the holes of giant snakes, burrowed deep into the rock walls.

When she was finally able to retire from the elaborate welcoming dinner Torkel Fiske had arranged, Marmion asked Faber to arrange transport for her the next morning to see Kilcoole from ground level.

"Ask Sally and Millard to see what they can hear round and about, too, would you, dear Faber?" she added, allowing herself the luxury of a yawn she didn't have to stifle.

"Shall I pull rank if I run into obstruction?" Faber asked. He was a bird colonel, currently detached to her service on a long loan basis.

"Hmmm, I'd rather you saved that for later, if at all possible. Torkel did mention somewhere in the gabble at dinner that we could make use of any facilities we needed in our investigations. So we will."

She was up and out at what would have been considered by many of her peers an obscenely early hour. She wasn't as surprised to see Whittaker Fiske as he was to see her emerging from her apartment.

"Why, Whit, what on earth are you doing up at this hour?"

He chortled. "The question applies more to you than me, Marmie." He bowed gracefully over her hand with a real skin-touching kiss. "Early birding?"

She smiled, and the arrival of Faber driving the antiquated rattletrap 4x4 vehicle spared her the necessity of replying to the obvious.

"Can we give you a lift?" she asked.

"Depends on where you're bound."

"Kilcoole. Didn't see very much from the air yesterday, and it seems the best place to start."

Whit cocked his head at her, laugh lines crinkling at the corners of his amused eyes.

"It's safe today," he said, handing her up the first high step to the passenger seat.

"Oh, your leg!" Marmion said, starting to get down.

"Don't mind me." Opening the rear door, he agilely swung himself into the back.

"What'd you mean by 'it's safe today,' Whit, dear?" Marmion asked as she snapped on her seat belt and Faber pulled the vehicle away.

The ride was going to be bumpy over the mangled plascrete, but later she would have exchanged that for the slip and slide of the mud-track to Kilcoole.

"Ah, well, Matt had his boys up before breakfast, scurrying about the place, accessing all kinds of records and reports so he'd 'have the overall picture and the demographic levels' and stuff like that." Whittaker snorted. "No chance of your running into him today out at Kilcoole."

Marmion smiled. She had hoped to do *her* research first without stumbling over those physically fit types. As the vehicle hit a particularly large bump, she clung to the handle above her head. She could feel Whittaker taking a firm grip on the back of her seat.

"Should still be able to use snockles this time of year," Faber said. "Thaw caught everyone off guard."

"So much so," Whit said with a chuckle, "that no one came close to winning the Pool."

"The Pool?" Marmion asked, clinging tightly to her handle.

"The betting pool the locals have on when the river breaks up. The thaw was so early this year it took everyone by surprise. See?" he said, pointing to the river at their left, where soldiers were working at the water's edge. "Still retrieving sunk snockles from their watery grave."

From what Marmion could see as they drove by, the soldiers were having trouble: the tires of the tow truck were slipping on the muddy bank, unable to find enough traction to pull the vehicle on the end of its cable out of the fast-running river.

"Faber," Whit said, leaning forward to point over the

driver's shoulder to the woods, "see that opening? I'd take that route were I you. Make much better time. I usually walk."

Both Marmion and Faber were happy they'd taken his advice, for the narrow track gave a much smoother ride than the churned mud by the river.

"Oh, it is pretty here," Marmion said, breathing in the rich damp-earth smells. "Trees are budding out!" she added in exclamation. "Almost overnight it seems."

"I don't think Petaybee's keeping to schedule this year," Whittaker said, sounding enormously pleased with himself. "I'd advise you to do the same, Marmie. You'll get where you're going faster."

"Then where do you advise I go first, Whit?"

"Where I am," he said, sitting back. "Just keep on this track, Faber, and when you reach the town, hang a right."

Kilcoole, despite its mountains of once-snow-covered paraphernalia, had an air of desertion. Marmion remarked on it, nobly refraining from commenting on its appearance.

"Oh, a lot of folks have taken advantage of the thaw to visit relatives and exchange garden plants."

"How wise. They're ahead of schedule, too?"

"They did get the hint. And don't be misled by all the stuff you see outside, Marmie. No one throws anything away that might be useful." He pointed to several lads who were carefully moving machinery parts in the side yard of one house, obviously looking for a particular one.

Marmie caught their running commentary as the vehicle rolled by: "I know it was here 'fore the first snow. And I know it was at this end." "Well, my father was looking for stuff, and he might have just pulled the pile to pieces looking. You know how he is." "Then try *underneath*."

Faber braked suddenly as a trio of orange-striped cats jumped out in the middle of the road just ahead of them.

"My word, do they often commit suicide that way?"

"My fault," Whit said sheepishly. "Shoulda told you to stop at that house on the left. That's where I'm working and where you should start."

"But if you're working there, Whit, I don't want to intrude . . ."

"I'm working *outside*, Marmie," Whittaker said, opening the door of the vehicle. The cats emerged from under the ancient 4x4, *prrrow*ing to him; two of them propped front paws up on his knees to be petted. The third spoke to him, then turned to wait at the passenger door. "You're invited inside," he added. "That's good, believe me."

"I'm always agreeable to invitations," Marmion replied, signaling for Faber to descend, as well. "What a marvelous shade of orange," she said directly to the cat. When it turned, tail tip idly swaying high above its body, she followed. "Mirandabelle Turvey-West would give her eyeteeth for a hair dye that shade, just wouldn't she!" she murmured under her breath.

The cat shot up the muddy steps. Marmion, eschewing Faber's outheld hand, managed to place her booted feet carefully in the drier spots.

The door opened as they reached the porch and one of the largest, most impressive-looking women Marmion had ever seen, with a complexion to die for and a smile that was the most beautiful thing so far about Kilcoole, stood in the opening.

"Sláinte, Whittaker, Miz Algemeine, Colonel Nike, grand morning for a ride, is it not? I'm Clodagh Senungatuk. I'm that pleased to meet you. Come in. I've fresh coffee and some decent baking just out of the oven."

Warmed by the welcome, Marmion held out her hand, to have it briefly but kindly shaken and given back, slightly floured. Then Faber was met with the same cordial treatment.

"The new shingles got here first light, Whit," Clodagh said, "but you've time for a bite and a sup first."

"Hey, that's good," Whit said with more enthusiasm than Marmion remembered him showing. "I can probably finish the roof today. Maybe I'll just get started, Clodagh, and grab a bite later."

With a nod to the other two, he tramped to the edge of

the porch and hopped off. A brief explosive exhalation reached the others.

"Leg's not good enough yet to be jarred by leaping as if he was young again," Clodagh said, tsking-tsking as she shooed her bemused guests inside.

Marmion's first shock at the interior dissolved with the scent of spicy warm bread and her instant realization that this small home—and *home* it definitely was—was actually highly organized and astonishingly neat if you looked past what might be cursorily dismissed as "clutter." There were, however, more cats inside who, one after the other, strolled over to make personal evaluations of the newcomers.

"Did we pass?" Marmion asked as Clodagh gestured her to the rocking chair and motioned Faber to a sturdy bench.

Clodagh delayed answering until she had served her guests coffee and freshly baked hot cinnamon rolls, and placed a pitcher of milk and a huge bowl of sweetener before them. Refilling her own cup, she sat across from Marmion, her elbows on the table, placidly smiling.

"I've always had a lot of cats around," she began.

"All of them orange?" Marmion asked. "Or are they a singularly unique Petaybean breed?"

"You could definitely say that."

"I just did. My, these rolls are delicious," Marmion said, lightly changing topics. "And thank goodness you know how to make proper coffee. Doesn't she, Faber?"

"Yes, indeed, you do, Miz Senungatuk," Faber said, smiling in that unexpectedly charming fashion that had disarmed many folk more worldly than Clodagh. Clodagh grinned and winked at him for his accurate pronunciation of her last name. That was another trait Marmion admired in Faber Nike. "Are you able to get regular supplies?"

Clodagh grunted. "Whit got this batch. Said it was a bleeding shame what SpaceBase did to unprotected coffee beans." She nodded to a corner of her crowded workspace. "I grind them myself when I need them, and keep them frozen till I do."

"Wouldn't that be a bit difficult to do right now?" Marmion asked delicately.

"Nah. Even the thaw doesn't affect the permafrost cache much."

"Ah, yes!" Marmion said. "I have read, of course, of the permafrost layer that is so like frozen rock, but I had not appreciated until now its practical applications."

"Well, usually we only use it in summer," Clodagh said.

"So then good coffee is as much a treat for you as it is for us," Marmion said and took another grateful sip. The milk in the pitcher had been fresh, too, cream rising to the top. Judging by various-sized lumps, the sweetener had also been home-ground.

"That it is," Clodagh said.

Marmion felt something press against her lower leg and dropped one hand to touch a furry skull, which she obediently scratched.

"Your cats survive the extremes of Petaybee's temperatures?"

"Bred for it. A course, they're smart to begin with, and they use their instincts, too."

"As do most of you living here on Petaybee, I'd say," Marmion remarked, getting closer to the purpose of her visit.

Clodagh folded her arms in front of her and said emphatically, "We've learned to live here. I wouldn't much want to live anywhere else."

As shrewd a woman as she'd ever encountered, Marmion decided approvingly.

"I shouldn't like to see you anywhere else but here in your home, dispensing superb hospitality to those lucky enough to find their way here, Miz Senungatuk," Marmion went on. "It's so rare these days to find people content with what they are and where they are."

Clodagh regarded her for one long moment, taking in Marmion's practical but elegant outfit, as well as her expressive face.

"Not knowing who you are or where you belong can

cause a person a lot of problems. This planet's not an easy place to live, but it's what we're all used to and we manage fine."

Hovering in the air were the unspoken words: *when we're left alone to get on with our lives as we want to live them.*

"Would you have enough coffee left in the pot for me to have another half cup, Miz Senungatuk?" Marmion asked, fingers laced about her cup so she wouldn't appear to *expect* the extra indulgence.

Clodagh's face lost the tension it had been displaying and suddenly softened into a smile. "Please call me Clodagh. I'm more used to it."

"Marmion is what my friends call me. Even Marmie's allowed." And the very wealthy, very clever Dame Algemeine held her cup out as unassumingly as any supplicant.

"You, too, Faber Nike?" Clodagh asked when she had filled Marmion more than halfway.

"Don't mind if I do ... Clodagh."

Clodagh poured him some more coffee, then passed the rolls around again.

"I had hoped to meet more of the people of Kilcoole, Clodagh," Marmion said, her tone brisker now. "I'm here, as I believe Whit will have told you, to investigate the unusual events which the planet seems to be taking the blame for."

"Planet's not taking any blame, Marmion," Clodagh said with a grin and a dismissive wave of her hand. "Planet's doing what's needful, too. Showing folks what it will and will not allow done to it. Same's you wouldn't want a lot of holes dug in your front yard or pieces of your garden blown up. Whittaker got that message loud and clear, but that son of his didn't. Nor some others—but the ones who did understood real well."

"You *know* the planet did this on its own cognizance?" Faber asked, his voice gentle, the way he spoke when he didn't want to scare misinformation out of people.

"If you mean did the planet do it without us helping it, yes. Not that anybody could *help* a planet if it's got its own mind made up and is perfectly capable of making *that* known."

"The problem we face," Faber went on, "is establishing that the *planet* is the source of the unusual occurrences."

Clodagh gave him a momentary blank stare. "And what else could be doing such amazing things? Do you know how long it takes to melt a pail of ice over a fire? Do you think *we*"—her unusually graceful hand circled an area over the table that signified Kilcoole—"could have caused the melt so early? Or pushed up a volcano? Or shaken the land as I would crumbs from this table?" Her tone was not argumentative; it sounded slightly surprised at such thick-wittedness from an apparently intelligent man. She shook her head. "No, the planet decided all by itself that there had been too many diggings of holes and plantings of explosives and such, and it wants those stopped."

"The planet is, in your opinion, sentient?" Marmion asked.

"The planet is itself, alive, and," Clodagh said, turning to Faber with mischief in her eyes, "totally cognizant of what it's doing."

Marmion rested her head against her propped arm and, with her free hand, turned the coffee cup around and around by its handle, absorbing this message. Frankly, she was now far more worried for Clodagh's sake than the planet's. The woman truly believed it—Marmion was half-way to believing it herself—and Matthew Luzon would make mincemeat of her.

"Is there any chance that the planet's intelligence can be *proved*? Without scientific doubt?"

"Early spring, volcanoes, and earthquakes aren't proof enough?" Clodagh asked.

"I am not the only person investigating the unusual occurrences on Petaybee, Clodagh," Marmion began slowly. "Is there someplace, someone you could visit, somewhere inaccessible? For a week or so?"

"What for?" Clodagh stared at Marmion as if she'd lost her mind, then rose indignantly half out of her seat. "Why should I leave? When Kilcoole needs me the most it's ever?" She plumped down again, her jaw set, spreading her fingers possessively and protectively on the table's surface. "No, ma'am. I stay! I stay *here*! No one's moving me from *my* home!"

"No, I don't guess that would be easy, Clodagh, but impossible it is not, I fear." Marmion leaned across the table to the healer. "If somehow, I could . . . experience . . . the planet myself . . ."

"Like Whit and the others did in the cave?" Clodagh asked, relaxing a bit more but crossing her arms firmly across her formidable bosom.

"Yes, something subjective so that I can come down as heavily on your side as possible."

"Ah!" Clodagh said. "So you can stand for us against whatsisname, the one Yana calls the buzzard."

"His name's Matthew Luzon, Clodagh," Whittaker Fiske said with a not-quite-reproving grin as he appeared in the doorway. He paused to wipe the clods of mud off his boots, mopping his sweaty forehead as well, before he entered. "Do I smell cinnamon buns? I do." Snaking a cup from the many hanging underneath the wall cabinet, he sat down at the table, angling the chair so he didn't have his back to Faber. He poured coffee and took two big bites out of the cinnamon roll from the plate Clodagh passed him. "We're lucky you decided to come, Marmie. You've got more common sense in one strand of your hair than Luzon has in that egg head of his, *but*—" and Whit emphasized that with a pound of his fist on the table.

Marmion noted the crumbs jumping on the surface. How *would* a planet do such a thing on a larger scale? Shift tectonic plates? But those shifts were minute and occurred under specific conditions . . . She turned her attention back to Whit.

"*But* . . . the one we have to contend with is Matthew Luzon, and you know what he's like. He's never been one to let the truth, even if his nose is rubbed in it, stand in the way of his preconceived notions. If you hadn't come, Marmie, I'd've—no, by God, I *wouldn't* have left Petaybee." The fist came down again.

"If, however, Whit, we—Faber and I, plus Sally and Millard—can be convinced, we are a united force on *your* side."

Whit inhaled deeply, obviously mulling over the arguments for and against. "They'd say you'd flipped, Marmie."

"Ha! I've too many PIHP—that stands for persons in high places, Clodagh—for even Matthew to succeed . . . But it is *he* who has to be convinced."

"Convincing *that* man will take considerable effort, time, and probably a miracle, although we've had the next best thing to one, and that doesn't seem to have impressed him either." Whit paused, his shoulders slumping in momentary defeat. He saw Clodagh's eyes on him and straightened up, his attitude once more decisive. "We'll just have to outwit him."

"Or," Faber put in, turning to Clodagh, "let the planet do it?"

She pulled at her lower lip. "A man doesn't hear what he doesn't want to hear. Your son's like that, too, Whit, sorry as I am to say it to your face."

"I'm sorry, as well, Clodagh, but for your sake, not mine."

"Matthew's not begun his investigations," Marmion said, breaking off pieces of another cinnamon bun and chewing to aid her thoughts, "so we've a little time in hand. He loves to have plenty of hard copy to support his claims even before he makes them. He's got all those physically fit young men running about SpaceBase. I wonder . . ." She turned to Faber. "I wonder if *they'd* be the place to start. And as soon as possible. We'll leave Braddock Makem till last. I thought at first I might win him over, but since then I've noticed that he apparently rather relishes Matthew's brand of management, instead of resenting it as one would expect. Indeed, of all of the minions, he appears to be the most in accord with Matthew and the least open-minded. Doing the others first will slow Matthew down to a crawl." She began to smile at everyone around the table as she popped the last of her roll into her mouth and happily chewed it down. "Well, let's get started. Clodagh?"

# 8

Dinah heard the noise before Bunny, footsteps coming down from the hill above. The dog strained forward, listening, doing the whine-yip, whine-yip that preceded her full-throated "woo-wooing" cry.

Bunny, still feeling queasy from her experience in the cave, held on to a handful of brush to pull herself to her feet. She heard Dinah scrabbling up the path, icy rock slipping under her paws.

"What is it, girl?" Bunny began, turning toward the sound of the dog. But about then, Dinah yipped and fell silent.

"Dinah?" Bunny whispered into the dense shadows, reaching for the comforting warmth of the dog's coarse thick fur. "Dinah?"

Her outstretched hand was suddenly clasped in a vise and Satok stepped out of the shadows.

"Sláinte, pretty Shongili snocle driver. How sweet of you to come and meet me. Where's your boyfriend?"

"What have you done to Dinah?" she hollered at him. "Let go of my hand."

Instead, he captured the other one. "The dog? I knocked her fraggin' skull shut. She should know better than to bark at the shanachie. The other dogs learned. Go ahead, scream. I'm waiting for your boyfriend to come to the rescue, and then I can send him to keep his dog company."

Bunny did scream, and kicked, and hollered, but the

whole time he dragged her up the path to his house, no lamps lit in the darkness of the village below, no faces peered out windows or doors to see what the commotion was about. Not at the Connellys', nor anywhere else.

As he dragged her away, her hand brushed against Dinah's still warm fur, sticky with what could only be the faithful dog's blood.

But the boys must have heard her. They must have.

Once, she thought she saw the shine of coppery eyes from one of the surrounding rocks, but otherwise, there was no witness to her abduction at all.

When they were well above the village and beyond the cave mouth and no help appeared, she decided to save her strength for later, and allowed herself to be led with only token resistance to the man's house.

Several outbuildings dotted the rocky mountain meadow where the sturdy stone house stood. It was the finest Bunny had ever seen, without a bit of scavenged material in its makeup. Thick stone walls, a roof of some sturdy material Bunny recognized from her trips to SpaceBase as similar to the stuff on the barracks buildings, and real windows of thick plasglas, heavily draped.

A high corral fence contained many curlies, among them Diego's Cisco and Bunny's Darby. A team of dogs, snarling and snapping and for all their red fur as unlike the gentle and intelligent foxhounds of Kilcoole as they were unlike caribou, were tied in the open, a short distance from the house. She could smell the filth of their leavings even through the icy wind.

Satok misinterpreted her lack of struggle and perusal of his holdings.

"Ah, so you're impressed, eh? Well, girl, all this comfort and luxury can be at your disposal if you're nice and do as you're told. Come in now, while the night is still young."

She tried to struggle again, but he was very much stronger and she was in the wrong position. She knew that once he got her indoors, her chances of escape and her danger from him were much greater, but she also thought that perhaps the secret of his hold over these people who wouldn't come help a girl when she was screaming bloody murder was inside this fine house.

She was surprised at herself, at how analytical and calculating she was being. Her anger at what he had done to Dinah, to the planet, and to these people had turned to cold calmness, as cold as the profound loneliness she had felt in the cave. It was even lonelier here, with a man who had to be crazy to even attempt to do this to the planet. Bunny knew that she needed to keep her wits about her, if she was going to learn what she needed to and keep him from killing Diego and Krisuk as ruthlessly as he had murdered Dinah.

He hauled her indoors. She didn't give up all show of reluctance, feeling that that would alert him, and indeed, she had trouble suppressing the panic she felt at being alone with him in his house.

The first thing she thought was it was no wonder he wanted a woman there. The place was a mess. The second thought she had was that it was an interesting mess. She hadn't known there was this much technical gear on Petaybee outside of SpaceBase and, maybe, Sean's lab.

Two computers and a vast array of hand tools, scales, and rock samples were interspersed with bones, a couple of small skulls, feathers, and desiccated bits of animals. She noted that there was a wide choice of objects that would make good weapons.

The tools were spread across several makeshift tables, but there was no proper eating table, and no chairs, though there were cooking facilities—greasy and covered with dirty utensils—and a large mattress spread on the floor.

Once inside, Satok released her and she edged as far away from that mattress as possible, though she'd had enough run-ins with her pubescent cousins to know that a mattress was not strictly required for her to be in deep dogshit.

Before he could say anything, she decided how to act in the same deliberate way she decided what to do when she was stranded on her snocle, or she and her dogs were attacked by a moose. She wouldn't provoke him until necessary. In fact, if he thought she was stupid just because she was a girl, she was prepared to let him go on thinking that for a while.

"Wow!" she said, with a nervous giggle she hoped didn't sound too forced. "What a place!"

"What's the matter, little Dama Shongili? Not good enough for you?" he sneered, setting his staff by the door and shedding a couple of layers of clothing.

"No, it's *great*," she said, ignoring the fact that he wasn't calling her by her own name. She wasn't sure she wanted her name in his filthy mouth, much less any of the rest of her. "I've never been anywhere except SpaceBase where they had *two* computers. Are they both yours?"

"Yeah," he said.

"Gosh, where'd you get them?"

"They were part of my retirement benefits," he said and started for her, but she danced away and picked up another piece of equipment. It was fairly heavy and made of steel.

"What's this?" she asked.

"Come off it. You're not interested in that stuff. I got something to show you over here," he said, and grabbed his crotch.

She pretended not to notice while she was examining the heavy object more closely. "I am too interested in this stuff. I take mining expeditions out all the time and they always have the most interesting stuff. Usually they disappear before I get to see it work, though."

"Don't worry, baby, I'm not about to disappear. I know this planet's ways, and I'm way too smart to fall into its traps."

He started walking toward her and she put one of the many workbenches, little more than two sawhorses and a flat piece of junk, between her and the self-proclaimed shanachie.

"How do you do that, really?" she asked, casually, though the very thought of what he could have possibly done to the cave made her furious. But not afraid. She couldn't afford to be afraid. "You're not from around here, are you?"

"I was born on this planet, if that's what you mean," he said. "I know about the caves. I also know that's the easiest access to the goodies Intergal and other companies are ready to pay big dinero for."

"Looks like you know all about how to get those goodies too, huh?" Bunny asked with her impression of girlish enthusiasm, an imitation of her boy-crazy cousin Nuala. The technique featured opening her eyes very wide and looking a little like a rabbit that'd been suddenly blinded by the lights of an oncoming snocle. "How'd you learn to do something like that if you're from Petaybee?"

"In the company corps, how else?" he said. "I did the standard hitch until I got in trouble. Lucky for me I managed to find more lucrative employment before my court-martial."

"Here, you mean?"

"No, this came later, when I was ready to settle down with a good woman."

Bunny made something that she hoped could be construed as a cooing noise. She thought it was very strange that he hadn't found this at odds with her struggle on the way up here, but she did know that where girls were concerned, some fellows didn't consider that logic or even thinking entered into their behavior. He probably thought she had been protesting out of form, but now that she was here she was as overwhelmed by all this stuff and his manly charms as she pretended to be.

She gave him Nuala's one-shouldered shrug and asked hesitantly, "Well, yeah, but where then?"

"Intergal's not the only one who can do business, baby. I joined up with an independent firm engaged in the import–export business. Ever heard of—Onidi Louchard?"

Bunny shrugged again. As long as she could keep him talking, maybe he'd say something useful. The conversation also gave her a chance to tuck something as pointed as an ice pick into the back of the band of her pants.

"Maybe," she said in a semi-interested tone of voice to keep him talking. "I think maybe some of the soldiers mentioned that name—not a businessman though . . ."

He laughed, showing a lot of his yellowed teeth—kept strong and even by company dentistry, no doubt.

"Ah, but that's where you're wrong, baby. Onidi knows supply and demand like no woman in the world."

He seemed to be drifting off into a reverie of his own. Bunny noticed that, oddly enough, there was a rug spread across a small area of the unswept desolation of the house's floor.

"Ah!" Bunny said. "Yeah, I remember now. She's sort of a pirate, isn't she . . . a black marketeer? Didn't they say she'd supplied the gas and the arms to the rebels at Bremport?"

He seemed pleased at the recognition. "That's her, okay."

"Wow, you worked with *her*? That must have been so exciting. I've never been off—this planet—myself," she said, managing to sound regretful.

"Oh, that can be arranged, baby. I'll teach you a few things. Then I know lotsa people who'd be glad to show a cute little thing like you around."

"What's it like—out there?" she asked wistfully.

She thought she could hear sounds beneath the floor, fortunately muffled and indistinct, for Satok didn't seem to hear them.

He picked up a bottle; not Petaybean blurry like Clodagh made, but off-planet stuff that Bunny could smell clear across the room. He locked the front door from the inside, something she had never seen anyone do before except herself when she'd had to barricade herself against her cousins. He settled down on the mattress alone with the bottle.

"You wouldn't appreciate most of it," he said with a lewd grin, then shrugged and gave her a hideous wink. "Or who knows, by the time I'm finished with you, maybe you will."

Bunny suppressed a shudder and continued to inspect his tools and computer screen while he told her about whorehouses on planets in several different galaxies, not excluding the impressive tricks he'd seen performed by humanoid alien exotic entertainers with a wide variety of sex organs and practices.

The subject made her a little queasy, especially the lip-licking relish with which he related it and the way he kept eyeing her as if she were already undressed. She realized he was in no hurry at all. In fact, he seemed to be relating these stories with the expectation that she might want to try some of the things he was talking about. They did give her a good excuse to make loud, shocked exclamations, which covered up the noises coming from beneath the rug. Still trying to appear fascinated, she worked her way backward while he swigged from his bottle until she shoved a corner of the rug back with her foot. A rectangular trapdoor was concealed beneath it.

Maybe the lout would drink himself to sleep.

No such luck though. Having exhausted the topic, he kept patting the mattress, then hoisted himself up, his expression growing ugly again.

"So," Bunny said quickly. "What made you decide to give up something as glamorous as shipping with Onidi Louchard to come back to Petaybee?"

He was less steady on his feet now than he had been, and his next words were slurred. "When my shipmates found out I was from Petaybee, they told me what idiots we all were to be sitting on the biggest cache of raw ores in the known universe and pretending it wasn't there. I told 'em the company kept us all barefoot and pregnant, so to speak, which is what I heard all the time I was growing up here. Then I realized I'd bought into the whole Petaybee trip ever since I was a kid: how the planet doesn't want us to take this and the planet doesn't want us to take that." His voice slipped into a mocking whine. "So I thought, screw the planet. The company's going to do it sooner or later, so how about me? I knew how the planet and the people get around the company, and how the company could get around the planet and the people if it had the balls to come down and take what it wants, so I 'borrowed' a little company technology, showed up in one village or another on foot, parking my shuttle out on the tundra, looking wise and finding out who might be in need of a shaman. McGee's Pass had come in for a few of the planet's less benign tricks and they had no shaman. I did a little recon, set up my base, and arranged for a disaster in the local communing place."

Bunny strove to keep her voice steady and sound shocked instead of simply furious as she asked, "W-why? Why did you do that?"

"Because, the first time I saw the way raw ore looks before it comes out of the ground, I realized I'd seen it back when I was a kid and the planet was scaring the shit out of me for not being real interested in all the little mind tricks it plays on people around here. Don't you get it? There's a good reason your so-called elders feed you all this bunk about the communing places that makes you scared to go in there without them."

Bunny thought he must have had a much different elder than Clodagh to think that anyone was barred from talking to Petaybee any time they felt like it, but most times people just got by on what was offered on the surface until it was time for everybody to go visiting.

"The communing places are also the entryway to the planet's goodies. Frag it, girl, you don't even have to dig very deep or blast your own tunnel in the surface. Ore's right there staring at you every time you go talk to the rocks."

"Really?" she asked. But she was running out of things she wanted to know and trying to think of what to ask next to keep him talking. "Well, I've got another question. Why take me? Aren't there local girls . . ."

"That's just the problem. They're local. You're from a powerful family in Kilcoole, and they think you're special because you drive a snocle. Your family and friends in

Kilcoole shoot their mouths off a lot about how mines are so evil for the planet. Maybe if they know mining the planet is in *your* best interests, they'll be a little quieter. Really," he said. "It's been real nice chatting with you, baby, but now that we know each other better, I want to get to know you *real* well. So are you going to come over here to me, or are you going to tempt me to get a little rough? Both ways are fine with me."

Bunny backed away from him, and he rose and lunged across the table she'd been using as a shield.

She dodged and ran, but was as trapped as she'd ever been. She knew she couldn't elude his grasp forever, and even though she had the weapon, he was bigger and stronger than she and not much out of shape either. She knew she had no chance against him in a fight, but she could keep out of his way as long as possible. She jumped back to where the trapdoor was and risked slowing long enough to pull at the ring. She pulled the door partially open, hoping against hope that she could slide down into it before he caught her.

The door was heavier than she thought, and he was quicker. He grabbed her hair and jerked her across the open door, as she screamed and beat at him with one hand while reaching for the ice pick with her other.

The planet had not been Petrasealed to death in the lower cavern, but it had been gouged and blasted. There was a pool there, too, foul from chemicals and dense with residue from the damage that had been done.

Diego touched the scars and felt as if he were seeing the wreck his father had been all over again: he was so full of sadness and pain.

Krisuk, who had grown up with this particular place, but grown gradually accustomed to its death through Satok's machinations over the years, touched the blasted areas once and reeled back as if he'd been punched.

Both boys stood at the juncture to the corridor, shaking. "How could you let him do that?" Diego accused.

"We didn't know he was doing anything in here!" Krisuk said. "We thought it was all buried, like he said. You forget there's a wall between this and the outer cave, and a lot of tunnel between. There's got to be. We feel the mountain shake sometimes, but it's not like you *hear* anything."

The truth of the last statement was sharply illustrated for the boys as they stepped from the Petrasealed inner cave into the meeting room and through the bush, out into the cold wind whipping down the pass. The rock Bunny had been sitting on was empty.

"Bunny?" Diego asked. "Dinah?"

A whimper rode down the wind from the path above them.

Diego scrambled up the path, almost tripping over Dinah's prostrate form. He began feeling the dog all over, which was difficult because there was a lot of blood. She was terribly still when he first began, but her respirations picked up a bit as he handled her.

Then he called for Bunny and called again, but he didn't see her. Meanwhile, Krisuk ran back down the hill to his own house and flung the door open.

Diego picked Dinah up in his arms and stumbled down the hill after him. Krisuk had a lamp lit. The family was not in bed but hunched together around the table, staring guiltily toward the door.

Diego entered the house and carried Dinah's body to the table. He knew from the expressions of the Connellys that they knew exactly what had happened to the horses, the dog, and Bunny.

"What kind of people *are* you anyway?"

"Don't ask them anything," Krisuk said disgustedly. "She's at Satok's. You can bet on it. He took her."

"Then I'm going to get her," Diego said.

"You can't!" Iva said. "He can kill you—kill us all—he might turn the planet against us again, make it swallow us up. He's too powerful for any of us to fight."

"He sure is if you just sit there," Diego said. "And the

planet has no reason at all to like him. If you looked a few yards beyond the ends of your noses, you'd know that."

"You're not going alone," Krisuk said.

"No?"

"No. Come on, Da, Mother. You kids," Krisuk added, addressing his younger brothers and sisters. "You go wake the neighbors. Bring them to the meeting cave." His siblings looked up at him as if they'd been stunned, unmoving till his five-year-old sister, Maire, jumped to her feet.

"I'll go!"

"Me, too," one of the younger brothers said.

Diego had stripped one of the quilts from the beds to cover Dinah, while one of the older sisters began cleaning the dog's wound.

Seeing that the dog was in good hands, Diego grabbed a knife from its hook above the stove and ran out the door again and up the path.

"Wait!" Krisuk said. "Diego, not that way. You'll be too good a target."

"I'm not going to just let him have her because you're all scared of him," Diego shouted back, never shortening his stride though the wind battered him. He didn't hear what Krisuk said in response.

Diego was about to pass the cave entrance when Krisuk caught up with him and pulled him back.

"Look, you can't just go confront him," he hollered above the wind. "But remember the upper passage? I'll bet it leads up to his house."

Diego paused for a moment. He had read a lot of hard-copy books, and many of his favorites had secret passages and tunnels in them, something he had previously related only to the ventilation systems in ships and space stations. "Maybe so," he said. "But if it doesn't, we lose a lot of time. We don't know how much we've lost already."

Krisuk said, "According to Da, they heard Bunny hollering about an hour ago. Look, I can get them to follow me into the cave. I want to show them what Satok's done. But they're too scared to go to his house. It's a strong house and he's armed."

Diego shook his arm loose. "If you want to go that way, then you go that way. I'm going straight to the house. I'm not going to risk Bunny's life again because your folks don't want me to stand up to Satok."

"Okay then, *I'll* try the cave and if it doesn't work out, I'll come up and help you, so take it easy, okay? Unless you see he's actually—well, unless she really needs you right then, don't jump in until I get there."

Diego was already striding forward. "I'll handle it," he said, and began to climb up the hill leading to Satok's.

The house was visible from the top of the path, a stone building about a half a mile away set back in a meadow. The windows were lit, and as Diego approached, a banshee chorus of howls heralded his arrival.

Satok pinned Bunny to the mattress and snatched at the band of her trousers. She tried to kick him, but he'd pinned one of her knees down with one of his own. Her right arm, stuck between her back and the mattress, groped for her weapon, which was digging into her hip.

All of a sudden the dogs began to howl. Satok swore and rose, grabbing a weapon as he turned toward the door. Almost as an afterthought, he turned on Bunny. As he struck her openhanded across the face, her teeth bit into her cheeks with an explosion of pain.

"Don't move," he said, waggling his finger with mock playfulness.

Of course, she did move the moment he threw the bolt on the door. It was hopeless to dart past him into the night, and the trapdoor was too far away, but at least she was able to pull out her ice pick.

"Shut up, you lazy pack of mutts, or you don't eat for another week!" he bellowed out the door. The howling quieted to a whine. He took a long look around, then turned back to Bunny.

Fresh out of more subtle tricks, she jumped up and ran

back to the trapdoor. She was smart enough not to show her weapon.

"Don't you touch me again, mister," she said, lisping a little through her cut lip.

The dogs began howling again, but this time Satok refused to be diverted. He reached Bunny in two seconds flat, and Bunny, backing up, found she was against a wall with nowhere to run, not a good position for any animal to be in. Furthermore, Satok was standing on the trapdoor as he closed in on her, his hands going for her throat.

The front door slammed open, flooding the room with strong icy wind.

Bunny punched upward with her ice pick and felt the pointed tip sink into meat. Satok's grip on her loosened, but he had twisted away from her to face the front door and her weapon didn't make the lethal strike she intended. She was trying to loosen her neck from his arm and her weapon from his wound when another body crashed into them, almost strangling her as the impact drove Satok's arm against her windpipe.

As Satok whirled to meet the new attacker, Bunny dove out of the way, searching for another weapon.

Diego was riding the big man's back, punching at him with a dagger, but Satok reached back and wrested the dagger from the boy's hand as if he were taking a rattle from a baby. Bunny groaned. Diego was good with books and computers—he wasn't a fighter.

She picked up a wrench and danced around the two of them, trying to get in a lick here and there, but she was afraid of hitting Diego.

Satok looked annoyed, but hardly worried. Still standing on the trapdoor, he reached back and grabbed Diego's head in both hands and started pulling him over his shoulder.

Bunny dropped to her knees, threw herself forward, and whacked the big man hard with the wrench, first on the knees, then the shins. He whirled around, still holding Diego's head in a vise, and she slammed the wrench against the backs of his knees. He fell to the ground with a crash that swept Diego's legs against the computer table and toppled the machine to the floor.

But when he and Diego fell forward, they cleared the trapdoor, and the pounding under the door that had been obscured by the sounds of the fight became clear. Bunny crawled to the door and pulled up the ring. Through the widening crack, Krisuk's arms and head appeared, and with a shove he pushed the door back across Satok's calves.

Satok was slamming Diego's head against the floor.

Gaining confidence at the sight of Krisuk climbing out of the hole, followed closely by his father, Bunny dove toward Satok's head and brought her wrench down over it. Again, the man twisted at a crucial point, and Bunny's wrench only tore loose the back of his ear just as a third person emerged from the secret passage.

Satok grabbed the injured ear, staggered to his feet, and ran, Krisuk and the others after him.

Bunny knelt beside Diego. "Are you okay?" she asked.

He blinked at her twice, rubbed the back of his head, and said ruefully, "I came to your rescue."

She kissed him, bloody nose and all. "You sure did. Are you hurt bad?"

His hand came away bloody. "Not bad, I think. My dad always said my skull was the hardest part of me."

Iva was kneeling beside them now. "Come on and I'll bandage that for you," she said. "We've seen what Satok did to the planet. Some talk *he* had! The others will catch him and he'll tell his lies no more."

"No," Diego said. "We've got to get to Sean and Yana and tell them what Satok's done."

"How did *you* know he was a pirate?" Bunny said.

"If we go back through the cave, you'll—" Diego stopped and stared at her. "What do you mean, pirate? As in *pirate* pirate?"

"He's one of Onidi Louchard's shipmates," Bunny said. "I think he's still working with them to loot Petaybee."

"Frag! We gotta warn the others!"

"Shh," Iva Connelly said. "You're not going anyplace till I bandage your wounds. You, too, young lady."

Diego and Bunny insisted on leading the curlies back down to the village. Meanwhile Krisuk and some of the others returned, empty-handed.

"Satok got away. Kev Nyukchuk and his sons are trying to trace Satok by the tracks and blood in the dark," Krisuk told them.

"Where's your father?" Iva asked.

"He stayed to feed the dogs. You remember Satok taking Tarka's pups?"

"Yes."

"They're half-starved and mean now, but Da recognized them and he's going to try to tame them again. The curlies were in bad shape, too, and we found more cat skulls . . ."

The next morning at first light, Bunny and Diego, carrying a carefully bandaged and bundled Dinah, were back out on the trail away from the river, the Petaybean wind at their backs, pushing them toward the fjord.

Matthew Luzon was as amused as he was capable of being that Marmion Algemeine thought she was controlling him by contradicting his theories, cultivating the enemies of the company, and trying to seduce his staff away from him. Of course, she was incapable of understanding a man like him. She was nothing but an overaged debutante whose inherited greed made her good at acquiring more wealth. She couldn't begin to understand someone like him, someone motivated not by money or personal aggrandizement, but by a strong, totally altruistic commitment to truth and the scientific process.

Others laughed when he called himself a scientist, but Matthew was devoted to science in a way that few were. A literal-minded man, he was nevertheless fascinated by the lies people were fond of telling themselves about the universe in which they lived, despite all of the evidence pointing to the fact that the average human being was powered by electrochemical impulses in the same way that computers were powered by electronic ones, and the universe itself was a large, marvelous accident.

Most of the scientists and troops within the company believed as Matthew did, but few had his zeal not only for believing the truth, but for exposing the lies and self-deceptions that weakened the sentient mind, every inhabited sector of the universe, and the company, as well.

There was a sort of brain fever that people contracted once they left civilization. Matthew had seen it again and again, not just among the inhabitants of colonial outposts like this, but also on space stations and ships too long away from port. People encountered a few mysteries that had not yet been properly investigated, and they suddenly decided that even the things they understood had some sort of strange causation. They started believing in myths, anthropomorphized machinery, and nonsentient life-forms; they talked to plants and animals. Ridiculous, but there it was. Matthew considered himself to be something of a deprogrammer/reformer/reformationist.

Usually, he had found, there was a ringleader, or maybe more accurately, an opinion maker, generally someone suffering from the borderline schizophrenia that passed for "creativity." These people had to be stabilized and adjusted, or eliminated. Elimination was not the preferred option, simply because one such person would invariably be replaced by another leader, whereas if one used the power they had already built up among their fellows for one's own purposes, results were much quicker.

As an anthropologist, he had made a particular study of the sort of beliefs people were apt to indulge in, and from what he'd heard of Petaybee, their mass illusion was not an especially unusual one.

They thought their planet was sentient. Quite likely all these seemingly remarkable incidents of meteorological and geological shifting were merely coincidental, possibly a delayed reaction to the TerraB process—and he faulted Whittaker Fiske for not remarking on that probability. Certainly these natural occurrences should not be attributed to some gigantic powers or some sort of immense alien life-form, dabbling in so-called adaptive changes.

He was no fool. He had studied the autopsies and all of the Kilcoole group's other "evidence." He was more inclined to think that the claims were more in the nature of a local belief than a planetwide one. The "adaptive changes," which bordered on extremes, were no doubt mutations from some latent toxins contained by this world which had previously gone undetected. They would, of course, need to be eliminated—or the inhabitants removed, which would suit Intergal's purposes quite well.

But the commission wouldn't do so on his unsupported opinion. His wisest course was to find other opinion leaders who held beliefs different from those of the people in Kilcoole, to demonstrate to the commission that local superstition on the part of one group should not be allowed to be taken as a planetwide condition.

To that end, he ordered a helicopter for his own use while Marmion was out and busy charming the locals. He was told that a pilot named Greene could be made available to him.

"Destination, sir?"

"I wish to travel to the settlements on the *southern* hemisphere," Matthew said. "I will need transport and accommodations for myself and three assistants."

"I'm sorry, sir," the woman said with an apologetic wince. "The only craft now available has room for the pilot and two other people. That's all."

"Then make another craft available. Do you think my work is so trivial it can be performed unaided?"

"You said that, sir, not me."

"What is your name?" Matthew sputtered.

"Rhys-Hall, sir. Captain Neva M. Rhys-Hall, communications officer. No offense intended, sir. If it's the pilot's name you're wanting, sir, it's John Greene. He's scheduled for Harrison's Fjord anyway at 1220 hours, can refuel there and take you southward. If you can be ready and at the field by then, you'll save time and be there before dark."

"And accommodations?"

"You're on your own there, sir. Up till recently, the company never considered this planet worth *two* depots and command centers. I'd take a sleeping bag and a survival tent, if I were you."

"Thank you for the advice, Captain. I will not forget it." Or you, you impertinent bitch, he told himself.

One assistant, then? The decision was not difficult to make. Braddock Makem, a man who thought much as Matthew himself did, was the most trusted and resourceful of his assistants. He found Braddock in his spartan quarters, studying the various reports, and told him what was required of him, in perfect confidence that the gear and Braddock would be ready at the appointed time.

# 9

When Marmion arrived at the building—which was painted a really awful murky dark green—where Matthew Luzon had set up his office, she found only his five minions, all industriously tapping out commands while their screens showed curves and graphs and columns of figures. She didn't approve of statistics of any kind: they only proved what the statistician wished them to. Credit reports and prospectuses were, of course, in an entirely different category.

They had the good manners to stand when she entered the room, so she smiled at them while she made a show of peering about.

"I don't see Dr. Luzon, and I did so wish to have a word with him," she said, beaming at the nearest of the lot. "You are . . ." She struggled to remember Sally's tips on how to distinguish them one from another. "Ivan, aren't you?"

"Yes'm."

"And where is Dr. Luzon?" Marmion noted the absence of one—Braddock Makem—and began to realize she might have underestimated Matthew's devious zealotry. How embarrassing. "Has he gone off into the wilds on adventure and left you here, slogging away at the tedious details?"

One after another of the physically fit young men cleared their throats.

"Ah, I see that he has, and it's very much too bad of him, as I'd arranged for Captain O'Shay to take *all* of us to that so-mysterious cave for an on-site investigation. Matthew's so keen to do on-sites," she put in, managing a little moue of disappointment, "and this is one of the most important ones, so Whittaker Fiske assured me." She paused to consider her disappointment. Then, brightly, she smiled around at them. "But that doesn't mean that *you* can't come with me, since it's so *hard* to get a big enough copter to take us all. In fact, just us will take up all the room. So, come on, now. Save those important programs, laddie bucks, grab your anoraks and let's be off . . ." When another of them—ah, yes, the very blond one was Hans— started to object, she said, "Now, now, I won't hear any excuses from you, Hans. This is as important as all those figures, because it's *sub*jective, not *ob*jective, and it will certainly show the commission how diligent you are in examining every facet of this investigation."

Sally and Millard had deftly slipped in behind her and were handing out outerwear to the men, who were so accustomed to obeying authority that they automatically complied. They were out the door and in the personnel transport and on their bumping way across to the big copter before they knew what had happened.

Rick O'Shay hurried them aboard, directing the seating in order to balance the load. "Real glad you fellows could make the time for this side trip, because you don't see much from a shuttle. Blink your eyes and you're past the interesting points. Miz Algemeine, you're up front . . . Hey, where's Dr. Luzon?" Rick looked around, surprise and disappointment on his face. "I thought he was the one wanted so much to come."

Marmion could have kissed the young man—he was very attractive, anyway—because Ivan and Hans were obviously having second thoughts about the advisability of this sojourn.

"Hell's bells." Rick shook his head, a lugubrious expression on his face. Then he brightened up and took a deep breath. "Well, you guys can give him a full report on what he's missing. That's it, now buckle up."

The big copter swung up and headed north by east, barely troubled by the turbulence.

Sally was wedged between Hans and Marcel, with Millard at the window and facing Ivan, George, Jack, and Seamus Rourke, whom Marmion had introduced as their expedition guide. Seamus had been Clodagh's suggestion. "He's as good, bar Sean or myself, as you'd want or need," Clodagh had assured her.

"You've often been to this cave site, Mr. Rourke?" Sally asked conversationally when she saw the first hint of "should we really be here?" anxiety on Jack's well-tanned, handsome face. With Marmion out of earshot in the front, Sally felt responsible for keeping things running smoothly in back.

"Not this particular one, Miz Sally," Seamus said affably, twiddling his thumbs: sitting down, doing nothing while traveling a long distance was new to him. "Been in most on the east coast, whenever the folk there invite us to a latchkay. We exchange hospitality like, us in Kilcoole and them on the coast, once a year. Good things, latchkays," he went on when he saw her look of inquiry. "Gets folks from nearby and as far away as the weather permits figurin' out how to solve any problems that've come up since the last one. And we get some fine singing done. Too bad you weren't all here for the last one we had. *Fine* songs from Major Maddock and young Diego. Kind of songs that ease the heart and mellow the soul. Maybe we could fix it that we have another one, sort of to welcome you all to Petaybee," he added. "What with the early thaw, we couldn't've planned another short of June, but I don't see why we can't show you lads a bit of Petaybean hospitality while you're here. You do like dancing, don't you?" He asked that with such skepticism that one of Luzon's men had to reply.

"I think we all do, sir," Hans told him.

"We wouldn't expect you to sing a' course, unless," Seamus hastily added, not wishing to insult anyone, "you had a song you wanted to share with us."

Luzon's men looked totally out of their depth. Sally and Millard managed to keep their expressions merely receptive, but they dared not look at each other.

"Ah well, you can always listen," Seamus said, "and eat some real good chow, and a' course, Clodagh makes the best blurry on Petaybee."

"Blurry?" Hans jumped on the word.

Everyone turned toward Seamus.

"Blurry's a tradition here," Seamus said, warming to his subject. "Drink it cold, warm, hot, and it soothes the cockles of the heart. Doesn't take a man's senses from him like al-ki-hall-ics do—" He frowned. "—and no one's ever had a hangover like the SpaceBasers get from that rotgut they drink. You could say . . ." He considered his next words carefully. ". . . that it's a tonic for what ails you. Give it to the kids when they're feeling puny, and next day they're up and out again. 'Bout the only thing it can't cure is frostbite, but I wouldn't be surprised if Clodagh'll figure out how to do that soon, too."

Sally and Millard exchanged significant glances. Marmion Algemeine would have to hear every detail of this.

"Is this blurry of yours good for indigestion?" Sally asked, seizing on the common complaint as the safest.

"Sure it is, and as good for labor pains as it is for flatulence, heartburn, and yer all-purpose bellyache," Seamus assured her, turning his face toward her so that she alone saw the broad wink.

"Do you use many . . . local remedies here, Mr. Rourke?" Ivan asked, his eyes sharp on the old man's face.

"We've not much else to use, laddie," Seamus said, hitching his hands up under the slight sag of his belly on his thighs. "And I'm not criticizing SpaceBase folk if they keep their own medicine for their own people. We got ours and it works for us. Petaybee takes care of us real well, you know."

"That's exactly what we're here to decide," Hans said, setting his jaw at an obstinate angle.

Inwardly Sally groaned. Maybe kidnapping these young

men out from under Matthew's rigid authority had not been such a good idea after all. Certainly having Seamus Rourke as a guide was turning disastrous, since he had already implied the existence of one questionable substance in the "blurry." The wink had indicated that perhaps he was simply having a joke on them, but people like Matthew Luzon had no sense of humor, and Sally knew that Luzon would be delighted to learn of blurry's "miraculous" properties and suggest the possibility of "drug-induced hallucinations." First thing she would do when they returned to SpaceBase would be to get herself some blurry and run it through exhaustive tests, just to be safe. Sometimes even innocuous elements, when combined, produced potent, if not lethal, results.

A glance at Millard told her he was thinking the same thing.

Fortunately, before any other dangerous subjects could be raised, the helicopter went into hover mode and began its descent. The cliff loomed over them higher and higher, rock crags like upturned claws avoided by inches as Rick Arnaluk O'Shay neatly put the skids in the footprint of his previous landing.

There was the bustle of disembarkation, with Rick and Millard distributing hand torches, a blanket—"to sit on during the show"—and a packet of rations, so that Sally didn't have a chance to report to Marmion. When Seamus enthusiastically urged them to follow him into the cave, there was no option to refuse or hang back, especially with Rick acting as rear guard.

One of Luzon's lads was talking into a handheld recorder, but when Sally got close enough to hear him, he was merely mumbling about the composition of the rock surfaces and reminding himself to look up examples of luminescent rock types.

Suddenly they were in a cavern that stretched incredibly far in all directions, with Seamus chivying them to find themselves a comfortable spot, in case they had to wait a bit.

"What? No blurry?" one of the lads murmured.

"You don't need no blurry in a cave, boy," Seamus said severely. With a sniff of disgust, he found himself a comfortable knob to settle on.

"What's this 'blurry'?" Marmion asked Sally.

"It's a native drink," Sally began. Then she noticed the mist rising from the water, and started taking note of their surroundings. "Why, Marmion, this is just like—"

Marmion's hand on her arm stopped her surprised exclamation. "Exactly what Whittaker Fiske *and* that doubting Thomas of a son of his reported . . . We'll talk later."

Marmion always sat upright and managed to do so even on the hard surface of the cave, crossing her legs and resting her hands lightly on her knees. Sally felt that the ancient meditational position was quite suitable and copied it as the mist began to thicken and swirl around them.

She remembered sniffing deeply, wondering if there was some sort of hallucinogenic in the very air they were breathing, but if there was, it was nothing she had ever encountered anywhere. And she had been just about everywhere Intergal went.

Everyone heard the *thwump-thwump* of the copter echoing back and forth across the fjord. Yana rushed out of the kitchen where she'd been helping cut veg for the evening meal. Shielding her eyes against the westering sun, she saw the flash of sunlight off the rotors.

Fingaard and some of the other men were rushing down the switchback road to the wide terrace of the wharf area. Sean had gone out with the fishermen that morning. Turning her back on the incoming copter, Yana looked down the long high-walled fjord for a glimpse of returning fishing boats. She'd been appalled when she'd seen how insubstantial the curraghs were: no more than hides bound to a larchwood framework with a wide slat, bored through the center so a slim mast could be stepped into the hole and a small sail attached. The current carried them out with the tide and in with the tide; otherwise it was a long, hard paddle up the fjord unless the wind was just right to use the sail.

She breathed a sigh of relief to see black blobs on the horizon raise small white triangles of sails as they made their way up the fjord. Then she turned again to head in the direction of the approaching copter. She had her foot on the first step when Nanook casually barred her way.

"C'mon now, I need a word with Johnny, Nanook!"

From the big black-and-white cat issued a noise that was half snarl, half voice command. Bunny had said Nanook could speak to those he chose to have listen to him. This comment didn't need words. Nanook's warning was too clear.

"Something's wrong with the copter, Nanook?" Yana asked.

Nanook sneezed and sat down, barring her way up the steps.

She peered more intently and saw two men in the front of the copter. And only one of them was someone she wanted to see.

"Ooops!" She turned and hurried back into the house. Nanook followed. That *did* surprise her. "I won't go out if you don't want me to," she told him.

He sneezed again and settled himself by the hearth.

"Ardis, is there any way you can hint to Johnny Greene that I'm here, and Sean's out with the curraghs? They're on their way in."

"Sure, if that's what's needed," Ardis said, grinning as she hauled off her apron. "Johnny might just have a letter for me from my sister up New Barrow way. She's expecting—again."

The last cat in McGee's Pass was named Shush, because in her youth she had been a noisy kitten. Those days were long past. Shush was not the last cat left in the pass because she lacked discretion. She was silent as smoke, quick as a spark, and very, very discreet. She had learned discretion shortly after Satok came to live among the people. The skull on his staff had once graced her father's shoulders.

It was she who had sent word to the Kilcoole cats that the people of McGee's Pass would vote to mine, as Satok had been urging them to do. Frankly, she didn't know if they would or not, but saying so could have brought someone to challenge Satok. Stupid cats of Kilcoole to send only two half-grown kittens! And now Satok had taken one of them. Perhaps soon her skull would be an ornament for him, as well.

Shush's family had been murdered. More critically from her viewpoint, all the toms had been murdered. She had gone through heat after heat alone, risking death in the woods to keep her cries from reaching the ears of Satok. Krisuk Connelly commiserated with her occasionally, but everyone else had been told the cats were spies; which, of course, they were, since it was only natural to lurk and spy and satisfy one's curiosity.

Until she had heard from the Kilcoole cats, in fact, she had imagined herself the last cat on Petaybee.

Well, the last *proper* cat anyway. There were lynxes, of course, and bobcats, and she had once or twice heard the hunting cry of a track-cat, but her mother had told her that those sorts of creatures, if you caught them on a bad day or when they had nothing in particular to socialize about, would eat you as soon as look at you.

So Shush stayed solitary for years, living off her wits, spying on the village and making herself invisible whenever Satok was around. It had taken a great deal for her to lead the Kilcoole cats' people to the cave, but she had in mind that somehow, being from elsewhere, these ones might not succumb to Satok.

When the girl was taken there was no one to cry to. The dog lay stricken, as Shush's own family had been stricken, by Satok's cruel staff. Krisuk and the Kilcoole boy were in the dead place. Not even to save a litter of her own would Shush brave that place.

Instead she bounded off in the opposite direction, down

the road and out of town, backtracking the hoofprints of the big horses, already nearly lost in the snow. When she was tired, she rested, licked the snow from her feet, and thought. The Kilcoole cats had contacted her, but she didn't know how they had done it. She had been trying to flush out a rabbit at the time, pawing at the half-thawed ground, when a voice spoke to her in her own tongue, within her mind. She asked the voice who it was, thinking it was perhaps the ghost of one of her relatives, asking if it was safe to spend another life there, but the voice replied that although it was, like herself, a cat, it was from the village of Kilcoole.

The voice belonged to a tom. She was sure of that. The question was not highly detailed. It wanted to know if the people of McGee's Pass would mine for the company or not. She said they would if they were told to, which had been her experience of them. They weren't bad people, but Satok had taken away their partnership with the planet and creatures like herself and turned it to his own purposes and against them.

The tom had said nothing about people coming, but Shush sensed that there would be visitors. They had come! And now Satok was dividing them and destroying them as he had so much in the village.

So Shush left, having nothing more to wait for. She leaped from one horse track to another. She sniffed when the track disappeared; she felt the howling wind roughing her fur the wrong way.

Late that night she found where the horse and dog tracks met with other tracks, including those that made her lift her lips in recognition. A track-cat, quite likely a Kilcoole cat, since the people had come from Kilcoole. A large one. And more horse tracks, like those of the people. She clawed at the cat tracks, rubbed her head against them, marked them with her scent. From the other scents mingled with the big cat's, he had been among others of her kind and probably was unlikely to eat her.

Thinking that these new folk might be camped just

ahead, she followed the tracks. But she was small and the trail was long, and Satok had won again. She yowled for the Kilcoole cats to answer her, but none did.

Finally, at daybreak, she slept for a few hours, then began moving again, though the tracks were older and much harder to follow. What other choice did she have?

Matthew Luzon felt aggrieved and aggravated by the pilot's attitude. He had felt from the first that this Captain Greene did not take him and his mission with sufficient gravity. He did not exude a positive attitude. He also appeared to be an uncommonly bad driver, hitting every pocket of turbulence no matter which altitude he attained, flying far too close to mountaintops at times and into cloud banks at others.

And that was *after* they were finally on their way. The man had dawdled an unconscionably long time loading various items into the cargo net behind the seats. In fact, the copter would have been quite large enough for all of Matthew's assistants, had it not been for this cargo.

"Here, can't you leave that behind?" he'd demanded at one point when his patience was strained, but the pilot just smiled and said, "No can do, sir. The villagers at the fjord need this stuff. Be with you in a jiff."

Then had come the dreadful flight and Braddock regurgitating all over the floor, so they'd had to smell it during the entire first leg of the trip.

When they landed at Harrison's Fjord, a pretty little place, he disembarked from the aircraft to allow Braddock to clean up his mess and found himself a boulder to occupy upwind, where he could continue his annotations. The pilot opened all the windows and doors to flush out the rest of the stench.

"Gotta unload, Dr. Luzon," the man said, although Matthew had assumed an attitude that few would have bothered to interrupt. "And refuel. Might as well take on some grub now." Then he lowered his voice so that his words would not carry to Braddock, lying on a mossy stretch of ground, legs drawn up to his aching belly. "They do good fish fries." Matthew waved his hand dismissively at the mention of such greasy fare. "And," the pilot went on, indicating Braddock, "get him an airsickness pill. He ought to have mentioned the problem before we took off."

Matthew nodded, wondering why the pilot had not had the courtesy to inquire before they took off from SpaceBase. Then the village folk arrived to help unload, and the pilot turned to greet the one woman in the group. She was a slightly different rustic type from those Matthew had seen in Kilcoole. She chatted affably with the pilot as he and some of the men unloaded the helicopter. Matthew wrote down the iniquities of the flight he had just endured to be sure they were entered onto the pilot's record. He noticed that someone had given Braddock a blanket to keep off the chill of wind stirred by the idly rotating propeller blades.

Scanning the village, Matthew assumed that the chief industry was fishing. No doubt this would present a fruitful subculture to study, since coastal peoples occupying somewhat more temperate areas undoubtedly had customs, mores, and folkways that differed from those in the interior. He made a note, since Braddock was in no position to take dictation, to return for a proper investigation later.

When he made one more sweeping scan of the village before reboarding the newly lightened copter, he was surprised to notice, sunning itself in the doorway, a very large cat. About the size of a panther, he supposed, except that it did not have the conformation of one of those sleek, predatory, and now almost extinct beasts. Though large, it was more like an immense domestic feline, with rather common black and white markings. Possibly one of the track-cats he had heard so much about: one of the miraculous beasts said to have aided in the rescue of the Fiskes and to have been instrumental in the healing of Frank Metaxos.

He stood up, closing his notepad and wondering if it was wise to approach the beast. It did not seem to be under anyone's control. If it happened to be a stray, perhaps he could acquire it for the laboratory and extensive examination. He was about to order the pilot to have the beast caged until he could return for it when the pilot beckoned urgently to him and unceremoniously boosted him back aboard. Braddock was already belted in, thankfully looking more sleepy than nauseated. Before Matthew could mention the cat or protest their precipitous departure, the rotors were whirling and the aircraft was up over the deep waters of the fjord, well above the masts of some primitive sailing craft.

Oddly, the flight to the southern continent was markedly absent of the turbulence they had encountered over land. Matthew attempted to shout over the noise in the cabin, a query about the village they had just left. He finally resorted to touching Greene's shoulder to get his attention. The man merely smiled affably, tapping his earphones, and shrugged. Matthew subsided in his seat and tightened his seat belt—then had to loosen it slightly or risk cutting off the circulation in his torso. He did not like being isolated by the exigencies of travel and wondered why there was only one headset. So he made a tremendous effort to contain himself during what was likely to be a very dull and long journey. Fortunately the cold air and the smells of machine oil covered the faint residue of Braddock's indiscretion.

Every time Matthew flew in one of these vehicles, he resolved to take flying lessons, for the procedures seemed ridiculously simple, but he never seemed to find the time for the formal course. Once, a long-gone member of his bevy of assistants, a perhaps too easily influenced young man, had showed an aptitude for flying. Unfortunately, as soon as he had learned to fly, his personality changed, and he no longer demonstrated the qualities of unswerving loyalty and unquestioning obedience Matthew insisted upon in an assistant.

He suspected that the man flying the copter was not of the caliber required in an aide either. Matthew's opinion was confirmed when he retrieved a report from his case and noticed, stowed under his seat, the headphones that should immediately have been offered to him by Greene. At once, he plugged these into the socket on the armrest and placed them over his ears. A burst of static poured through them that made him wrench them off.

Tapping the pilot authoritatively on the shoulder, he pointed at the headset. Grinning, the pilot shook his head, moved his mouthpiece aside, and leaned over to say, "Don't work!"

Matthew's reactions included amazement, anger, frustration, and total disgust with the inefficiency and indifference shown by the inhabitants of this world. People were scattered all over the universe, some of them living in highly sophisticated, totally engineered environments, all scrupulously maintained by Intergal. *He* ended up on an incredibly primitive world with a headset, similar to hundreds he had used before, that failed to work due to what was surely an easily remedied technical difficulty.

Of course, this sort of aircraft was only slightly improved over its ancient counterpart. The old ones had had neither speed nor range and had been limited in the altitudes they could achieve. This particular one, with its incidental malfunctions, was by no means state-of-the-art: it hadn't the power to lift out of the planet's atmosphere, and was excruciatingly noisy.

However, it required very little space to land, could hover, and could set down safely, if necessary, at night unaided by light from the ground. That ability, he reflected, as he studied the map printout on his wrist unit, was a necessary requirement.

He wanted to ask the pilot if flights to the southern continent were frequent. Surely they must be. This planet, north and south, had long been used for troop recruitment, an occupation the so-called sentient world did not seem to obstruct. Ah, and he qualified that as he remembered his notes: It was the young who answered recruitment drafts: those who had not yet been mutated by whatever toxins in their soil produced the glandular deformity and the deposit of "brown fat" that supposedly allowed older members of the population to survive the extreme temperatures.

The nearest city to Harrison's Fjord on the southern continent was Bogota, at the mouth of the Lacrimas River. The sizable peninsula on which the city was situated extruded like a big, clumsy thumb into the sea. He had, of course, scrutinized the maps of this region, now entering its winter season. Most of the population centers—one could hardly call them cities—were situated on the coastal plains near the major rivers: Bogota on the Lacrimas, Kabul on the eastern fork of the New Ganges, and Lhasa on the Sierra Sangre. Another village called Sierra Padre was located farther up the Sierra Sangre at the foot of the Sierra Padre Mountains. A settlement known as Kathmandu was isolated within yet another mountain range, optimistically dubbed the Shambalas.

Kathmandu seemed a likely place to look for culture uncontaminated by the crackpot pseudomystical theories of the natives of the north. Bogota, being the largest and most accessible population center, was the most likely to have been influenced.

For hours after they left the warm harbor of Harrison's Fjord, flanked by the ice-packed coast of the rest of the northern continent, they skimmed the cold gray of the ocean, which didn't particularly depress Matthew, as cold gray was one of his favorite colors. Huge chunks of ice floated in these waters, as large as islands or small continents themselves. Initial reports had suggested that the southern edge of the northern continent had many glaciers, which constantly calved into the unobstructed oceans that girdled the planet.

The sun struck sapphires from the clefts in the ice, and the gray of the clear salt waters was sequined with darting fish. Schools of dolphins followed the copter's shadow across the breast of the sea. Matthew was oblivious to them, as he was to the blowing and sounding of the Petaybean tube whales: so called because their ancestors had been bits of cells frozen and later incubated in test tubes. Brought to maturity in controlled environments, the large, strong mammals had then been released into the planet's newly formed ocean. The whales, like the dolphins, seemed attracted by the novelty of the copter.

At last, toward evening, they were within sight of the southern coast, a sight so spectacular that even Matthew was forced to admire its grandeur.

Though the harbor, like its counterpart at Harrison's Fjord, contained water warmed by the geothermal springs and rivers the planet seemed to have in abundance, the rest of the coastline was glacial. Huge cliffs of ice glittered white and crystal: deepest indigo in the recesses, and a rich bright cobalt where the setting sun struck the crevasses. Glaciers calved, huge chunks splintering off, plummeting into the sea with a roaring crack, surfacing through a rush of displaced waters, displaying new surfaces. On other floating chunks, seals and otters and big tusked walruses basked and swam in the frigid sea.

As the copter drew nearer the southern continent, the sun began setting, burning across the water to recast the scene in shades of mauve and tangerine.

Nearer yet, they saw herds of caribou race across the coastal plains, huge white bears lumbering across the ice or swimming in the lakes that studded the plains like chips of coral.

From those spectacular vistas, the sight of Bogota was a massive letdown.

It contained a double row of barracks-type buildings, no more than a kilometer in length, a landing pad with a pile of fuel cans perilously near, and a number of small hide boats not dissimilar to the ones Matthew had seen at Harrison's Fjord. As they overflew the town, they were close enough to observe those inhabitants who were lounging about. The native costume seemed to consist of cast-off uniform pieces from the company corps. The copter's arrival caused no particular excitement: few heads even turned up to observe its passage.

With great delicacy, the pilot set the copter down right

beside the fuel cans, shut off the engines, and without a word, climbed out and began to refuel. Oddly enough, no one came to check, though Matthew could see people less than a hundred meters away watching the process. While Greene fueled up, Matthew disembarked, demanding a few answers now that the man could not pretend he didn't hear him.

"Shouldn't someone be logging you in or something, Greene?"

"Why? They knew the copter, and they know it's the one I fly. If I had something to deliver here, I'd have flashed my lights and someone would have come to make a pickup."

Matthew digested that explanation—yet another example of the nonchalance and indifference that were so rife on this planet and that *would* be rectified.

"Is this all there is to this town?" He gestured about the landing area and toward the two rows of dwellings.

"Bogota? Yes, sir. Nobody much lives in Bogota."

"Why not?"

"It's unstable, sir. You saw the glaciers. They make sure that the earth *always* moves for you, that's one thing. You get rocked to sleep every night, though some rockings're harder than others. Then there's the bears. They mostly live on fish, but they'll take anything that's handy, including human beings if they're hankerin' for a change of menu."

Braddock, looking nauseated again now that the effect of the pill had worn off, had exited the copter. With an effort, he tried to assume some of his usual assistance duties, his expression carefully neutral. "Do you suggest that we use this place as a base headquarters?"

The pilot scratched his head, pushing his cap forward over his forehead. "Well, this place is as good as any on this continent. It ranks as a depot, not that it has *all* the amenities SpaceBase offered. Mostly it's a drop point to collect recruits and to return soldiers from these parts who are demobbing. I haven't done a lot of flying around here except to Bogota, to tell you the truth, and Sierra Padre.

The warm rivers make the ground swampy in the summer and create powerful turbulence the rest of the year, and you don't go far before you get into the mountains. Sierra Padre is a little bigger, a little more comfortable, and the place a lot of southern folks call home. Of course, you understand, lots of people aren't settled real permanent but move from hunting camps to fish camps and back again, according to the season."

"Thank you, Captain Greene," Matthew said. "In that case, we have no time to lose in reaching Sierra Padre before we run out of daylight. Let us climb back aboard and continue on."

Braddock did not quite stifle a groan, and Matthew gave him a reproving glare. Really, he had thought his chief assistant was made of sterner stuff.

"Well, sir, I gotta tell you," Johnny Greene said. "This is going to get me in trouble back at headquarters. I've got another mission to fly soon's I get back."

"May I remind you that *I* am your mission right now, Captain, and my business has the highest possible priority."

"Yes, sir, so let's get going right now and I'll tuck you in at Sierra Padre before I take off again."

"I was expecting you to stay and act as our transport during this vital research mission, sir."

"My orders were just to fly you here, sir, and return north for my next mission. Tell you what, though. It shouldn't take very long. Why don't you gents settle in at Sierra Padre, get the lay of the land in the snocle, talk to a few folks, and I'll be back in a few days to collect you?"

"I'd prefer you to be more specific than that, Captain."

"Yeah, me too, sir. But everything's pretty unsettled right now. You've got a portable comm unit with you, haven't you?"

"Braddock does. Naturally."

"Then if you don't see me by the time you're ready to go on to one of the other villages, you just ring up to the station and they'll give me a holler or dispatch someone else."

"In case of emergency, I will go to that extreme inconvenience, Captain Greene. However, it is your responsibility and your sole responsibility to see that I have transport to my next destination within three days. If I am at all discommoded by your absence, you will find yourself busted back to flying paper aircraft. Do I make myself clear?"

"Oh, yes, sir, I know how foolish it would be to get crossways of an important man like yourself, sir," Greene said with not quite enough humility to suit Matthew.

Braddock suddenly came to life. "Wait a moment. Greene? What is your first name?"

"Why, it's Johnny, dear heart. What's yours?" Greene replied, batting his eyelashes in a way that was mocking and impertinent in the extreme.

"Sir," Braddock said, turning to Matthew. "Wasn't there a Captain John Greene piloting the copter carrying Dr. Fiske when he crashed in the volcanic blast area?"

Matthew was relieved. His judgment in bringing Braddock was vindicated. The boy might whine and puke, but his mind was unaffected by his physical discomforts. Matthew himself should have referenced the name but had been too preoccupied in gathering new data.

Before he could formulate the questions he wanted to ask, the captain went on.

"Yes, sir, that's me, and to tell you the truth, Dr. Fiske sort of loaned me to you as a courtesy. Normally I'm attached to his exclusive service."

Matthew smiled. "Ah well, then, Captain Greene. Please thank my old friend Whittaker for his kindness and tell him that I wish to deprive him of you for a while longer to assist me with my inquiries. If you'll please drop us at Sierra Padre, we can at least make use of our time there to further our investigations. But make sure that you do return!"

Greene snapped him a salute.

Shush awoke, killing and devouring a vole before she set out on the trail once more, following the spoor of the curlies and the track-cat of Kilcoole.

She was far from her territory, among wild things that

would kill her and eat her as casually as she had killed and eaten the vole, and yet, the farther from the pass she traveled, the better she felt. The very mud and snow beneath her paws seemed to put spring in them, to make her step lighter and her gait swifter.

Shortly after she began walking again, she found the used campsite of the people: cold ashes, churned snow and mud, grasses scattered on the ground from the horse's meals, and a few small bones from the track-cat's. A tentative, fearful sniff relieved her mind that these were rabbit bones, not cat. She sniffed the track-cat's sign and trotted onward.

She thought of Satok, of her massacred race, and of the girl as she walked, but she had to be careful not to drift too long into reverie. Once she noticed barely in time that a wolf was watching her from the bushes. Fortunately, wolves could not climb trees and she could. She slept in a tree that night, and in the morning walked on.

That night, as she stalked a squirrel, she pounced and somersaulted in the air just in time to catch the whiff of the fox a spare few feet away. Her distraction caused the squirrel to bolt for its hole in the tree roots and she bolted after it, squeezing in the tip of her tail just as the fox's nose appeared at the hole.

As she lay there panting, heedless of the squirrel, which had burrowed deeper, she wanted to wail. This was too hard. It was too far. There were too many things that wanted to eat her and she was all alone, and furthermore, she felt as if she just might be going into heat again.

*I am all alone,* she cried, and something said, *But I designed you to be alone.*

*Not all the time,* she said and it said, *No.*

*I am afraid,* she cried. *A man would kill me, beasts would eat me, and the Kilcoole cats are far away and their people are Satok's prey.*

*Did someone speak of the Kilcoole cats?* a voice—a different voice—asked. A big voice, a cat voice, a tom voice, but a big voice. *Who are you, little sister?*

*I am Shush, the last of my race at McGee's Pass,* she said. *Who are you?*

*Nanook. What do you know of the people protected by the Kilcoole cats?*

*I know they strayed into danger. Satok will kill them, as he killed us. He took the girl. He will surely kill the boy or make him submit, as he made all of those under my protection submit.*

*Ah. And the dog? There was a dog? For a dog, she was good.*

*She is dead. Are you—far?* she asked.

*Two days' lope from where we left the boy and girl.*

*I have traveled two days.*

*Your legs are short.*

*I am afraid. I am alone.*

*I am coming,* Nanook's voice said. And as an afterthought it added, *And no, I do not eat my small cousins.*

Bunny and Diego saw the cat tracks in the snow but were too preoccupied to pay them much attention. Both of them had slept badly, but once out of the village, Diego brooded and Bunny couldn't stop talking.

Diego was just attuned enough to her to notice that her hands trembled on the reins. Her face, like his, was scraped and bruised, her mouth swollen so that she kept biting her lip. He didn't know if she had the pounding headache he had. She talked a lot, but she hadn't said anything about a headache, or her aches and pains. Mostly, she was angry, raving about how those people could have let Satok get away with what he had! How had he been able to do that to them, and how could he do that to the planet?

Diego didn't answer. He listened with part of his mind to what she said, and with the other part, he was composing a song. Again, he longed for an instrument, wishing to make a song with angry music which even the biggest drum could not emphasize strongly enough.

When they camped for the night, he began writing his song down, while Bunny looked on curiously, still talking.

Her voice was like rain falling now, or the drone of a ship's engine. He nodded and grunted, but the song was at the front of his consciousness.

> *Buried alive, screaming,*
> *The stone smothered*
> *The roots strangled,*
> *The soil smothered*
> *White death like*
> *Your snow-skin*
> *From one like*
> *But unlike*
> *A son.*

Diego stopped writing. The planet should have a song for that murdered part of it, but this was not complete, not right. It needed a better song than this. He sang it to Bunny and she thought it was good, but then, the critical side of his nature reminded him, she was also proud of her jingle about her snocle license. This song must be the very best that could be sung, for it was of terrible injuries that must be healed.

The next morning, riding toward Harrison's Fjord, they were silent.

*You are not a cub and you cannot live forever with me in the Home,* Coaxtl told Goat-dung.

"I understand why you would not want me," Goat-dung said, "for I am nothing and no one. But if I cannot live with you, then go ahead and eat me now, for I'd rather be eaten by a friend than by strange beasts, and I will not return to Shepherd Howling."

*Did I say that you should, foolish youngling? But there are others in the village at the mouth of this river.*

"They'll make me go back," she said, full of fear, but Coaxtl said she would wait, and if they tried, she would kill them and take her to a farther village.

So there was nothing for it. She submitted to the will of

the cat as she had submitted to the will of others eventually on every occasion but one. Coaxtl walked with her for a way; but on the open plains, where only cold waters fed the river, she lay along Coaxtl's back, hands locked in her mane, knees pressing against the cat's ribs, so that they could cross to cover more quickly.

The sky was still pale pink from the setting sun when they heard the beating heart of one of the company's hummingbird airships. Coaxtl wanted to run away, but the plain was vast and the airship faster even than the big cat's great strides.

Goat-dung watched with awe as the airship approached. She had seen other aircraft in the sky, and the Shepherd had told them those were the Guardian Angels of the Righteous, sent by the company to oversee them. She had seen a hummingbird ship only once before, however, when it delivered supplies to the Vale one hopeless winter when a team of the men had walked into Bogota seeking relief. The Shepherd Howling had agreed to this only reluctantly, for she heard him arguing with his advisers: but they knew they would starve without assistance. When the airship came, it was wonderful. Food, more food than they had had in months, and even warm clothing and toys for the children.

So Goat-dung was not afraid when the airship hung above them, close enough that she could see two men arguing through the glass bubble that formed the hummingbird's single eye.

She climbed off Coaxtl's back, feeling the soft warmth of the cat's fur through the rents in her clothing. Her feet were bound up in uncured rabbit skins now, fur side in; the skins stank, but they kept her feet warm. Stunned with fascination, she watched the airship set down.

"Isn't it wonderful, Coaxtl?" she asked the cat. When there was no reply, she turned to see the cat bounding back across the tundra.

A thought whispered back to her across the distance. *Your own are here. Good hunting and warm sleeping places, youngling.*

"Good hunting and warm sleeping places, Coaxtl," she whispered back, under her breath, but already she was watching the handsome pilot emerge from the aircraft and the tall, thin man with the high forehead and long white tail of hair walking toward her. Another man lingered in a second doorway in the back of the airship.

"Remarkable!" the white-haired man said, staring at her. "Look at her clothing! Why, she should be freezing. And here alone except for a wild animal which would probably have eaten her when hunger overcame it. Amazing! I would have liked a closer look at that cat, though. It seems totally unlike any of the others I've noticed."

The pilot didn't respond to what the elder said but came forward to kneel before her. Before *her* and so unworthy for such an honor! He even looked her in the eye and spoke in a kind voice that almost made her weep.

"You look a long way from home, alannah. Are you lost? Was that big ol' kitty what you folks down here use for a track-cat?"

Goat-dung sank to her knees before him and bowed her head. "Please forgive the companion of this ignorant and despicable child, O Captain of Angels. Coaxtl befriended me out of pity, but now that my own kind are here, she has fled from fear of the righteous. For are not all animals to be meat and fur for the company men?"

"Where did you hear such drivel?" the captain replied in a disgusted tone of voice. Goat-dung did not expect that.

"Did I get it wrong?" she asked fearfully. "Forgive me if I misquoted the Shepherd Howling. I am the stupidest of girls, as has often been said of me."

"If you ask me, you're the luckiest of kids," the pilot said. "And we're lucky to have found you before you froze to death. Now come aboard, darlin', and stop cringin'. Sure, no one will hurt you now." And he looked back at the tall white-haired man with an expression Goat-dung could not see in the descending shadows.

"Of course they won't, my child," the white-haired man said. And while the pilot had quite correctly refrained from touching such filth as she, the white-haired man took her hands in his and raised her in his arms, carrying her to the plane. "You will come with us to Sierra Padre."

"You won't make me go back to the Vale of Tears?"

"Not if that's how they teach you to talk about yourself. Especially if you've run away from all those bruises and cuts I see on you, no, we won't take you back," the pilot said.

"What and where is this Vale of Tears?" the white-haired man asked.

"You won't make me go back there, sir? I don't deserve to. I fled from being the bride to the Shepherd Howling."

"Bride? You're no more than a baby!" The pilot sputtered with outrage.

But the white-haired man said, "We go now to Sierra Padre, where I will begin my work, and you, my dear, will have a hot bath, clean clothing, a decent meal, and a good night's sleep."

"She certainly will," the pilot said. "An old shipmate of mine, Lonciana Ondelacy, lives in Sierra Padre with her kids and grandchildren. Loncie will be glad to take this little one in."

The white-haired man smiled at her, helping her climb into the big plane beside the other man, who did not smile. This reassured her more than anything the pilot had said because, of course, it was only right since she did not deserve to be smiled upon. Then, with a great deal of noise and wind, the Captain of the Angels and the white-haired patriarch sent the hummingbird ship aloft, where, for that night, all was miraculously as wonderful as they had said it would be.

# 10

Marmion, led by Seamus Rourke, flanked by Sally and Millard and followed more slowly by Matthew's five assistants, emerged into early-morning sunlight. Rick O'Shay was the last to leave the cave.

"My word! It is the next day?" Marmion exclaimed. She turned to Seamus, who grinned, a smile that had little to do with the day or anything else immediately obvious to Marmion.

"Sure is, missus."

"But we weren't in there long . . ." Sally began, glancing down at the digital on her wrist. Her eyes widened. "Good heavens."

"The next day?" Ivan grabbed her wrist to peer at her digital before checking his own. The other four men apprehensively conferred over this unexpected loss of time. "But we'll be behind in our work . . ." Ivan wheeled accusingly on Seamus. "You had no right to take us away from our work for a whole day."

"This cave is a mere hour's flight from SpaceBase," Hans said, his expression decidedly aggressive and his anger focused on Seamus Rourke, because he didn't dare accuse Marmion.

"How could we have lost so much time . . . sitting in *mist*?" That aggravated him even more.

"Why, I found it—" Marmion stopped, cocked her head,

and then regarded Sally and Millard. "You know, I'm not sure I *found* anything."

Seamus let out a mighty guffaw. Mischief, as well as satisfaction, twinkled in his eyes.

"You got 'found' anyway, missus. Now, let's not lose more time." He made a whooshing gesture at Rick to start back to the copter.

"How could I get 'found,' Mr. Rourke, when I haven't been lost?" Marmion asked, a quaver in her voice as she allowed Rick and Millard to take her arms as they made their way across the uneven terrain.

"Oh, I 'spect it'll come to you, missus." Seamus chuckled again.

"Mr. Rourke, nothing at all of the nature described by Dr. Metaxos, his son, or even Major Maddock and Dr. Fiske occurred to us," Sally said in an even voice that held just a hint of carefully controlled surprise and disappointment.

Seamus eyed her, his lips curving slightly: she was a very attractive young woman, and he could still appreciate looking.

"Sure hope you wouldn't now the planet's calmed down with no one gouging and blasting holes in it. But you were spoken to," he assured her.

"That's utter nonsense," Hans said. Rick made a noise that sounded like a patronizing rebuke, and Hans whipped around. "I experienced nothing once the mist rose to obscure everything. And then it cleared. You'd have us *believe* that this—this *show* took nearly thirty hours?"

"Seems to have done," Seamus replied affably, helping Marmion up onto the copter's high passenger level. "Think on it awhile. It'll come to you."

"Outrageous," George said, his face contorted into a sneer. "Waste of valuable time."

"I'm not sure how we'll explain our defection to Dr. Luzon," Marcel said dismally, the first sentence Marmion had heard him speak.

"Ah, but you don't have to, my dears," she said, buckling her seat belt. "I shall assume all responsibility for this expedition, and I'm sure such industrious young men as yourselves will be able to complete your assigned tasks well before Dr. Luzon returns."

"Do you mean to imply, ma'am," Hans said, eyeing her suspiciously, "that we should conceal our dereliction of duty from Dr. Luzon?"

"Heavens no, Hans dear," Marmion said soothingly, laying a gentle hand on his arm. "I wouldn't conceal a thing from Matthew Luzon," she added drolly. "It just isn't done! But I shall assure him that I dragooned you, as necessary escorts, on a personal, and possibly dangerous, inspection of the so-called remarkable cave where everyone else seems to have had most incredible experiences." She made a moue of disappointment and turned to Seamus. "Really," she said, and she stretched out the next two words to express her disillusion, "*nothing happened.*"

"We lost thirty hours," Hans said in an implacable and unforgiving tone. "It'll be dark by the time we get back to SpaceBase."

"Well, there'll be a little time before you have to have dinner," Marmion said.

"We'll work tonight," Hans said, making eye contact with his associates. "We'll catch up that way."

"Oddly enough," Millard remarked, "I feel totally refreshed, with an unusual sense of well-being. Anyone else?"

Sally made a small "oh" of surprise. "I do, too. And I don't think I was asleep . . ."

Marmion did not remark on the fact that she, too, felt unusually alert and energetic: as if she could dance all night long and still put in a full day's work tomorrow.

It occurred to her that maybe the planet had a totally unexpected and exploitable facet—for rest cure facilities. However, she intended to go very slowly on that one, since this party seemed to be the only one to have enjoyed that aspect. Had they just been lucky? Had the planet, as Seamus had suggested, settled down after its aberrant behavior? Even so, she felt almost ... almost effervescent. And she hadn't experienced *that* buoyancy in a long, long time.

As soon as Yana saw the little curraghs nearing the wharf, she raced as fast as she dared down the steps to tell Sean the news. Ardis Sounik had confirmed that much of what Johnny Greene had off-loaded was the fuel they would need and Sean's special supplies for his journey. And that Johnny had gone on to Bogota with Luzon, who was up to no good at all. Johnny had hinted broadly that Luzon was bad news. Nanook, who had vanished from the village for some time, suddenly reappeared, fur full of mud and burrs, to bound alongside her. He seemed about to explode with news, too. He licked her hand at one point while she watched the curraghs approach, rubbed his handsome face against her shoulder, and looked deeply into her eyes. She sensed he was trying to talk to her, but she just didn't know how to listen. But, as they descended, all the other cats of the settlement started hurrying in the opposite direction.

"What on earth?" Yana began.

*Bunny,* something said quite clearly in her head.

"Did you speak, Nanook?"

He gave her a resigned look and a sort of growly purr.

"I don't mean to be difficult to communicate with, Nanook. Nod your head if Bunny's safe and coming?"

Nanook solemnly inclined his head.

"That is such a relief." Yana stroked his fine pelt in appreciation. "Maybe one day, we'll hold a meaningful conversation," she added, emboldened by her relief.

*Soon.*

"Oh!"

Just then Sean appeared over the edge of the high harbor wall and she ran into his arms, burbling to tell him that Johnny had managed to leave off fuel here in the fjord. Even with Sean smelling to high heaven of fish oils and brine, it was good to have his arms about her and see his smile of delight at her enthusiastic welcome. Then Nanook, who had sat in dignified patience, obviously spoke to Sean, who smiled broadly and fondled the track-cat's ears.

"Bunny and Diego are on their way here, and Shush, the one cat who survived at McGee's Pass, is just a ways behind them. Nanook rendezvoused with her to reassure her and protect her most of the way, but he left to return to us so we wouldn't worry about the kids anymore. He says the village must be good to Shush. She needs to be safe again."

"She's not the only one. When does he expect them all to arrive, Sean? I've been getting quite worried."

Sean shrugged. "Probably by nightfall." His arm tightened about her. "No point in wasting energy backtracking. Nanook says they're okay."

"Run that past me again, Sean, about *one* cat, *surviving* at McGee's Pass? Only one? What happened to the others? I thought the cats were cared for in all the villages, the way Clodagh looks after the ones in Kilcoole—"

"And they look after her. Yes, that's very serious news to me, too. A village with only one surviving cat is a village in very serious trouble."

"Sean, what did we let those children in for?"

"We'll know soon enough," he said, putting an arm around her shoulders in comfort and reassurance. "The fact that Nanook has stayed here means they're okay, no matter what else. See what I brought you for your dinner, love?" And he held up the pair of rainbow-scaled fish as long as his forearm and considerably thicker.

"Oh, good, Ardis has some potatoes left, and we thawed carrots and onions. Bunny and Diego'll be hungry when they get here."

"Yes, and we, too, for their news."

When Bunny and Diego, who was carefully supporting the wounded Dinah in his arms, arrived at dusk, the evening meal was ready but remained uneaten while more important matters were attended to.

Bunny nodded once at the six place settings at the table. "How did you know we were coming?" she asked. "Oh, I know. Nanook, of course. He started to run past us, stopped long enough for a sniff, and ran away. We didn't see him return though."

"He saw you, though," Sean replied. "He was going to the aid of an orange cat from McGee's Pass. I don't suppose you saw her on the way?"

But Bunny didn't answer; shook her head, preoccupied. Her attention had been captured by watching the movements of Ardis's gentle hand sewing up Dinah's wounds, setting the five broken ribs and the hind leg bone. She splinted the tail, too, but feared that all nerve connections might have been severed. Dinah had managed to convey to Diego that after the man had clubbed her with his staff, he'd caught her by the tail and slammed her against the nearest tree.

Diego had been a thundercloud ready to burst until Ardis had reassured him that, except for the possible damage to her tail, the lead dog would completely recover from her mistreatment. While this was going on, Bunny gave a quick résumé of the situation of the cowed and subjugated folks at McGee's Pass, Satok's activities, and the unthinkable *sealing* of the cave.

"What Bunny doesn't say," Diego began, as Fingaard gently transferred Dinah to a thick blanket near the hearth, "was what that Satok damned near did to her."

"It's what he's done to the planet that's more *awful*," Bunny contradicted him with a fierce look, and tears started in her eyes. "I could escape, but oh, Uncle Sean, he's made it impossible for anyone to *talk* to the planet at McGee's Pass."

"He was going to *rape* you!" Diego said, almost shouting.

"He's already *raped* our planet!" Bunny yelled back, fists on her waist, body inclined angrily toward Diego.

"Bunny! Diego!" Sean said, snapping out their names in a quiet but very firm voice. "Now that Dinah's safe, you can take turns while we all eat, giving us a complete telling of what happened at McGee's Pass."

"Quite right," Ardis said, pushing first one and then the other young person to a seat at the table while Fingaard brought over the baked fish. Yana quickly added the vegetable bowls to the table, and order was restored as appetites were attended to.

"Diego's making a song about it, too," Bunny said.

Diego glared at her, a mix of irritation, pleasure, and artistic indignation. "It's nowhere near ready."

"It'll be some song when it is, I can tell you that," Bunny said, beaming at him.

"We'll listen very closely whenever the song is ready, Diego," Ardis said reassuringly.

"Now, step by step, please," Sean said, bringing them back to the report.

None of the adults interrupted the two youngsters, as they gave a very credible narration of all that had happened, each giving due credit to the other and to Krisuk's efforts. Both Sean and Fingaard had them repeat several points, such as the question of the Petraseal and how far it extended into the cave, and all the details of Satok's background that Bunny had so cleverly wheedled out of him.

"You sly and clever puss," Sean had said, ruffling her hair with affectionate approval. When he saw Diego scowl darkly, he ruffled the boy's, too, laughing when Diego pulled away. "She is my niece, lad. You're lucky I'm willing to share her company with you!"

"Huh?" was Diego's stunned response.

"Now," Fingaard said, taking charge, his roughened scale-scarred finger making circles on the wooden table, "we have an enemy who needs watching. We have a cave that has been damaged. Can this Petraseal be dissolved?"

"Yes, but the chemical compound of such a solvent is not available at SpaceBase," Sean said.

"It'd take barrels of solvent," Diego said, widening his eyes as he estimated the area to be resurrected. "An awful lot."

"Yes," Sean said. "Any solvent strong enough to dissolve

Petraseal might very well be more harmful to Petaybee than the Petraseal is."

"If this has been done at McGee's Pass where the people are just like us, only vulnerable from not having a shanachie for so long," Ardis said, frowning in concern, "can it have been done elsewhere, too? Is it so easy for this Satok to mislead people so they can fail to hear the planet?"

"That thought had also occurred to me," Sean said and sighed heavily. "We came here with a specific purpose . . ."

Fingaard's great hand came down on Sean's shoulder. "There is much we can do now that we know what has happened, my friend, and you can pursue your personal quest which, I have come to feel, is as important as this new problem."

"Then you believed that Aoifa and Mala were right that there'd been an undersea passage to the south from the fjord caves? If they were right, we could establish communications, maybe even a trade route, with the southern continent without company technology for air travel or ice-breaking ships."

Fingaard nodded solemnly several times. "In my father's time creatures emerged from the caves that were born on land, and not undersea, and not here in the north. Mala sent his track-cat back, but she had been badly injured. Only the great loyalty these creatures have for those they love could have kept the beast going until it reached us. We searched, as you know, as far as we could, but the cavern roof had collapsed and our way was blocked." This time his nod was full of sorrowful regret. "But we also saw nothing of Aoifa or her track-cat, Ugraine, so perhaps they were able to go further."

Sean laid his hand on Fingaard's arm, looking up at the large, concerned face. "Now that I've seen the site, I think there's a chance that might have happened. I was going to come here and look before, but the accident took us all by surprise and I was delayed, what with arrangements to be made for Bunka and all—and then, when we held a night chant in their honor in our village, I got a definite sense that both of them were gone. Feeling that, I couldn't bring myself to come. Now that I have seen the tunnel, however, I get a little different sense of things. Someone could have got out, got to the other side. I owe it to myself and to the family to explore that possibility."

They were all startled by an unearthly screeching that penetrated the thick wall of the stone house. It rose and fell, deepened and split into savage howls. Growling deep in his throat, Nanook lifted his head from his paws, and his expression was one of offended dignity and disgust. Sean started to laugh, a tuneful descant to the cacophony outside.

"Why does that awful caterwauling make you *laugh*, Sean Shongili?" Yana demanded. The noise was earsplitting.

Ardis gave a disgusted expression. "The village toms are courting, not that I ever remember them making *that* much noise before."

Wiping tears from his eyes, Sean managed to control himself enough to explain.

"It's Shush." He turned to Bunny and Diego. "The McGee's Pass cat."

"Shush made it here?" Delighted, Bunny started to rise, only to have Sean push her firmly back into her chair.

"Don't interfere with her right now, honey. She wouldn't appreciate it." And he started to rock with laughter once more.

"Sean Shongili, that's not enough of an explanation!" Yana complained.

Unable to speak, Sean waggled his hand at Nanook who, with great condescension, spoke to Bunny. Once she got the message straight, she started to giggle, too.

"Not the pair of you!" Yana said. She felt she could use a laugh right now with the rest of them.

"Shush was the last cat in McGee's Pass," Bunny said, "and there were no toms for her. I think she's making up for a lot of lost opportunities!"

"Do they have to do it here, and now?" Ardis protested.

"Now, lass," Fingaard said, grinning as he pulled his

wife close to him, "you've sounded somewhat like that yourself a time or two when I've returned from a long voyage."

Half-irate, Ardis tried to push her huge spouse away from her, batting vainly at his hands while everyone joined in the laughter. "Never like that, you big oaf!"

One more excruciating cry jarred their eardrums, and then there was blessed silence.

"Well, then," Sean said, "let's turn in and get a good night's sleep. We've an expedition to start . . ." He turned queryingly to Ardis.

"Oh, Johnny brought all the gear you need, and rations for twice the distance," Ardis said, flicking her hand to the outside storage shed. Then she rose, gathering plates up as she did so. Yana and Bunny were instantly on their feet, followed almost immediately by Diego.

The cottage was very shortly occupied by sleepers, so no one noticed the small orange-striped cat who crept in wearily but utterly fulfilled and curled up near the hearth.

Johnny Greene was not at all happy to leave Geedee—how could anyone lumber a child with a disgusting name like Goat-dung—anywhere in the vicinity of Matthew Luzon, though he had perfect faith that she would be safe with Lonciana Ondelacy and her family.

He was especially worried because the child seemed far too content to be in Luzon's presence, looking up eagerly when he spoke and tripping all over herself to answer his every question. Who the frag had ever said that kids could tell scoundrels from saints?

And Luzon, the old hypocrite, was a real smoothie when reassuring the poor frightened and self-deprecating kid, while conveying at the same time how fortunate she was that *he* wanted to talk to her. Frag, she practically apologized for breathing the same air they did.

Johnny hadn't wanted to take Matthew along when he went to look up his old shipmate Loncie, now a grandmother and one of the community leaders of Sierra Padre.

But Matthew had pompously declared that he was determined to do his duty as ranking company official in seeing that the girl had "a suitable placement," and Geedee had looked up at him with wide eyes and clung to his hand.

In the twenty years or so since Loncie had retired and returned to Petaybee, she had acquired quite a bit of weight, an air of authority far exceeding that she had wielded as a chief petty officer, and an incredibly large family. Now almost as round as she was tall, she wore her thick black hair, still only lightly threaded with silver, in an array of braids, secured to her head with an intricately carved and immensely valuable—Johnny saw Matthew looking at the artifact covetously—ivory comb that had not come from any creature supposedly native to this planet.

"Ah, *pobrecita*!" Lonciana cried when she saw the girl. She barely acknowledged Johnny's cautious introduction of Matthew Luzon and his assistant. Instead, she lifted and clasped to an ample bosom the startled, wide-eyed, scrawny waif. "*Qué lástima!* What has life been doing to you?" Her black eyes snapped with anger directed at Matthew.

"Easy, now, Loncie," Johnny said. "We found her on the flats. She says she's from some hellhole called the Vale of Tears."

Loncie sucked her breath in between her teeth and her eyes narrowed angrily.

"We have heard of such a place," she said. "Tsering Gonzales's boy, who was never right in the head, he said he was going there. He had heard of the place from someone who came trading poorly made cloth for supplies—the man had a boy with him. The boy ran away and long after Jetsun left, Tsering heard tales the boy had told the family that took him in. It is a terrible place. They beat and frighten the children with the most outrageous superstitious nonsense and call it religion! Or so I've heard tell."

Matthew Luzon looked as if someone had just given him a gift and opened his mouth to speak, but Loncie had returned to her new charge. "Never mind, *pobrecita*, you are safe here with Lonciana Ondelacy."

Johnny didn't want Loncie to take a wily bastard like Luzon too lightly, and flashed her a rather urgent glance, which she caught and immediately understood. Turning to Luzon, she radiated her own considerable charm.

"Do be seated, most gracious Señor Luzon and rescuer of this little scrap of humanity. Pablo, have you not brought the wine? Carmelita, you and Isabella see to the needs of this little one."

She put the child on her feet and gently pushed her toward two daughters who would undoubtedly rival their mother for size and beauty. They smiled winningly at the child, who was nearly catatonic with such unwarranted treatment.

"And how is the *niña* called, Juanito?" she asked Johnny.

It took him a long moment to answer, but with Loncie looking at him so hard, he had no escape.

"She says her name is Goat-dung!"

"*Ay, de mio!*" And Lonciana's hands went heavenward. "Tsering did say that they name their young in such a way, to shame and humiliate them, but it is beyond my lips to form such a name in front of the innocent ears of my own children."

"But, *mamacita*, we know that goats make dung," Carmelita said, giggling.

"Goats do not make *los niños* wear such names. Pobrecita we will call you, little one. Take her, bathe her, and see what of your sisters' clothing will clad her decently. I will come and see to her injuries while—Pablo, where *is* the wine? Ah, here, and biscuits. Oh, you are so clever, *mi esposo*!" And she beamed on the wiry little man who was entering the room, carrying yet another beautiful artifact to astound Luzon.

This was a silver tray, some of its fine etching cleaned to the copper below the plating, covered with a fine white lace cloth, with a glass decanter and some very plebeian shot glasses of the type to be seen in any Intergal bar.

Señor Pablo, whose last name Johnny didn't catch—it probably wasn't Ondelacy, since that was the name he had known Loncie by when she was a senior chief—was a perfect foil for his wife. He was as quiet as Loncie was verbose, and he showed to Matthew Luzon the deference and respect due to any sneaky and poisonous creature. Pablo gravely insisted that Don Matthew must take the heavy armchair, so incongruous among the rest of the utilitarian furnishings, and gave him first pick of the refreshments.

In his turn, Matthew seemed intrigued by Pablo, who sported a distinguished silvered goatee and sideburns. He was reminded of an extremely valuable painting that he had seen once in a museum on old Terra.

Though Matthew sipped suspiciously at the beverage served him, Johnny enjoyed the resinous flavor that was minor fire in his mouth and left a not-unpleasant aftertaste. The biscuits were lighter than Johnny had expected, and sort of cheesy in flavor, which made sense, since there were goats in a pen in the back of the house.

He saw Luzon's gaze roving around the room, taking in a number of uncommon objects, like the flute and the beribboned guitar hung over a fine white fur, both well above the reach of small hands. Another object, that Johnny at first assumed to be a goatskin drinking bag with various lengths of pipe stuck from it, was actually a musical instrument, too, as Pablo explained when he caught Johnny's curious gaze: the Basque bagpipes.

However, none of them said much, since the noise of Goat-dung's attendants made any conversation difficult, even if Señor Pablo had been so inclined. Braddock looked better after his first sip of the liquor and was casting a judicious eye on the furs that covered the walls and floor. Lonciana kept exclaiming over this and that, arguing over items of clothing and demanding others until Matthew began to wonder just how long it took to clean one scrawny child and dab ointment on a few scratches. He was totally unprepared for Lonciana's dramatic reentrance with the clean and not only neatly but flatteringly clothed child.

Johnny Greene sat bolt upright in his chair as if he were seeing a ghost.

"This *niña*," declared Lonciana, fists planted on her broad hips, "has been constantly beaten with rods. Her ribs have been cracked on several occasions and I distinctly feel the thickening of several bones in both arms and legs where she has had fractures. She has obviously been starved all her life—if she has had the misfortune to live in that Vale of Tears"—Loncie spat to one side—"that is not unlikely."

Washed and attractively clothed, the child looked even more wan and undernourished.

"Now we eat," Lonciana stated. At a clap of her hands, more children appeared from the unseen regions of this incredible house, each bearing elements of the meal and the utensils with which to eat it. Seating La Pobrecita beside her, Lonciana herself fed the child, who did not seem to know what to do with either spoon or fork.

Loncie's maternal presence was too overwhelming not to be threatening to Luzon, who began coaxing the girl into describing her home and her companions.

"Don Matthew, perhaps it is not wise to remind the *niña* of such matters," Pablo ventured deferentially, but Luzon swept aside his objections.

"Nonsense, my dear man. Do you know nothing of psychotherapy? Why, the very best thing for the child is to discuss her traumas and her feelings about them, to speak out fully of everything which disturbed her. Only then can she be purged of her fears. Confrontation is the very best medicine in cases like this."

Lonciana and the daughters who had tended the child were stunned as she fairly blossomed under his interrogation. Black eyes snapped with concern as Luzon deftly elicited information from the girl. On his side of the table, among the Ondelacy boys, Johnny lost his appetite watching Luzon, who, despite all of his protests of horror and sympathy, obviously was being fed exactly the kind of dirt he had hoped to dredge up. The man's ill-concealed relish of the child's story turned Loncie's savory meal into bile in his mouth.

Well, he'd done what he could and found the child safe

harbor. Luzon could question all he wanted, but he wouldn't be able to force the child away from Loncie and her family any more easily than he would be able to force her away from Johnny. Johnny was tempted to pick the kid up and take her back north with him anyway, but he figured he would do better to hightail himself back north and make his report to Dr. Fiske, collect Sean and Yana, and fully cover his own ass. But he did want them to *see* this kid. There was something about her—something he couldn't quite put his finger on. Anyway, if he was to do any real good, he would need reinforcements.

He stood, bowed elaborately to his former chief petty officer, her spouse and brood, gave the child a bit of a salute—which Luzon returned, the ass, with a sharp dismissive one—and returned to his copter. He didn't enjoy flying it half as much on the way back as he expected. Quite aside from the lingering stench of Braddock's puke, it felt contaminated.

Although this southern continent should have been deep into the autumnal season and its ground surfaces well frozen up for smooth snocling, the Big Freeze had not yet occurred, a matter which caused considerable concern among the Sierra Padreans. This bunch were of very mixed ethnic origins; some, like Loncie, were of Central and South American origin, mainly from the Andes, and over time they had mixed with the few volatile high-mountain Basques, the combination tempered by a great many of the imperturbable Sherpas. Pablo, despite his resemblance to one of the characters in a painting by Goya, was half Sherpa, half Basque. While Loncie, as a retired corps member, kept her birth name of Ondelacy, the family name was actually Ghompas.

All of this information Matthew Luzon and Braddock skillfully extracted from the family after the meal was over and Johnny Greene had departed, a very good thing since his presence definitely interfered with the rapport Matthew wished to establish with this family and, in particular, the girl they now called 'Cita.

One thing that particularly excited Matthew was that the girl in no way resembled any of the Ghompas/Ondelacy family. Nor could he see her gray eyes and light hair as placing her among the African or Afghani residents of this sector. No, she belonged to a different ethnic group than he had seen down here thus far, and he was eager to learn if others at the Vale of Tears were as different—both in appearance and outlook—as she seemed to suggest.

He took polite leave of them that night, and spent all the next day, with only Braddock to help him, trying to find alternative air transport. Finally he settled for a snocle. He was warned that, since the thaws of autumn had lasted unusually late this year and winter was not yet fully upon the continent, they might require many detours.

"Planet should be colder in the high country though," granted the man who rented them quite a battered machine. Luzon suspected that the man had no right to have access to one at all and, to add insult to injury, he charged them a large enough deposit to buy a small space station. Matthew smiled sourly but paid, knowing he could easily confiscate the machine if he so desired. But just now he desired to keep a low profile.

In his preparations, he had already gathered that Sierra Padre would be as fruitless as Bogota in his quest for those who didn't speak of "the planet" or "Petaybee" as if it were a friend or neighbor or possibly a close relative. Such superstitious idiocy! He had high hopes for the girl's Shepherd Howling, however, whose nonsense was no less superstitious but in a more useful vein for Matthew's purposes.

Once provisions and other appropriate gear had been acquired and stowed in the machine, Matthew awaited the moment to acquire the final piece in this phase of his investigation.

The girl played right into his hands. While the other children in the huge woman's huge family played at building a snow fort from the new snow of the night before, Goat-dung—he, at least, would give her the proper name bestowed upon her by her culture—sat alone beside a spindly birch next to the pen containing goats. Maybe there was more to her name than just a convenient identity.

Matthew strolled up to her casually, saying, "Goat-dung, I require your assistance."

"Sir, I am told my name is now 'Cita."

"By those who mean it kindly but do not know the significance of your true name, yes. But you and I know that their kindness is nevertheless a falsehood, do we not? You were given your name for a reason."

She dropped those pale calf-eyes of hers and said in a tiny voice, "Yes, sir."

"I wish to speak to this Shepherd Howling."

"I won't go back there!" she said with more spirit than he thought she had left. "I won't!"

"Of course not, of course not, my dear child. I understand your feelings. You are deeply ashamed to have left the community under a cloud, to have been unable to measure up to the simple things your shepherd required of you. But I'm sure he will forgive you and allow you to separate from the community once I explain to him that you are more valuable out here, to me."

"To you, sir?" she asked, the hysteria fading from her voice and being replaced by awe.

"Why, yes," he said. "I need a research assistant who is native to this planet, and who better than yourself? If you work out, I will adopt you as my daughter."

"Your daughter, sir? This unworthy one?"

"Through hard work and appropriate behavior, you may yet become worthy. But first you must be very brave. Come along and I will show you what is required."

She got to her feet and took his hand, with only one backward glance at the house of her erstwhile guardian. He knew very well what he was doing. By replacing the feared figure of the Shepherd Howling in her mind with himself, someone stronger, probably better spoken, and certainly more rational, he placed himself in the role of both master and protector. Oh yes, she would certainly obey him as un-questioningly as she had ever obeyed her—he smiled at the quaint crudity of the primitive notion—betrothed.

On the way back north, Johnny radioed in a coded report to Whittaker Fiske, along with an inquiry about the clouded big cat that had kept Geedee company. It wasn't like any track-cat he'd ever seen. He received a terse acknowledgment. *"Received and acknowledged. I designed no such cat. Ask Shongili. Happy buzzard-watching. W.F."*

When Johnny finally stretched his legs at Harrison's Fjord, Sean, Yana, Bunny, Diego, and Nanook had already started on their journey down the cave that had swallowed up Bunny's parents twelve years before. The presence of Liam Maloney's lead dog sleeping by the fire in the Souniks' house naturally resulted in Johnny being brought up to date on all that had happened at McGee's Pass.

"Satok used Petraseal to block the planet off?" Something very cold descended Johnny's backbone. "Frag it, Fingaard. Do you know how much of that stuff is stocked at SpaceBase? Have you any idea what could happen if anyone, Matthew Luzon in particular, found out what Petraseal can do to our caves?"

Ardis's face was stricken. "The boy, Diego, has made a song of it."

"Well, let's just bloody hope he doesn't sing it."

"He already has. What he had finished of it, at least," Fingaard said in a deep bass whisper.

*"Frag!"* was Johnny's explosive response. He was pensive for a long moment and then, with one blink of his eyes, became the affable, carefree copter pilot they knew so well. "I'd better get back and report in. Gotta get refueled, and then I just gotta come back this weary way again. See ya!" He tipped his peaked cap at Ardis and strode back to the copter, hands in his pockets, whistling.

With Nanook padding along in front of them, occasionally taking a short tangent before coming back, the four of

them made forty klicks down into the cave at Harrison's
Fjord. Within the first hour they had swung away from the
path that led to the fjord's planet place and started descending. The slope was fairly steep at first, but soon began to
have an easier gradient. Once the luminescence lit their
way, they had no need of the artificial hand beams and
carefully stowed them away.

"This isn't at all like the other caves I've been in," Diego
remarked when they reached the easier gradient.

"I doubt you'll find two even vaguely similar," Sean said
with a smile.

"Have you been in all of them?"

"No, I haven't. That'd take a lifetime, I think," Sean replied with a grin. "My grandfather found the first one, more
of a cleft in the rock than a real cave. He knew, of course,
that there were cave systems just under the surface. That's
the way Terraform B works, but his finding the cleft was
pure chance."

"Did it lead into something like this?" Yana asked,
glancing about her with the wonder and sense of welcome
she always felt in a Petaybean cave.

"Not directly, according to granddad's notes, but he
didn't have as much chance to explore as he'd liked, since
he was busy doing what he could to make it easier on the
animals Intergal decided would adapt well to this climate."
Sean gave a snort at Intergal's needless arrogance. "Grandmother located the hot springs at Kilcoole and went looking
for others, with my father strapped to her back to hear him
tell it, and my oldest aunt—the one my sister, Aoifa, was
named for—either on a sled or strapped to a curly-coat's
back. Grandmother really liked a decent hot bath every day
and took one no matter how far she had to tramp to indulge
herself." Sean grinned nostalgically, as he had been a part
of those forays. "I know she taught me how to swim . . ."
He glanced quickly at Yana and winked. "My father and
his two younger brothers found and mapped many of the
caves we now know and use. I think I learned their whereabouts before I learned to spell."

"What happened to all your relatives?" Diego asked, rather amazed that anyone could have so many.

Bunny tried to shush him, but Sean shook his head. "What else? My younger uncles joined Intergal, and my father continued his father's work as I continue his."

"And the other Aoifa?" Diego was persistent.

Sean drew his brows together. "We never did find out. She went off on one of her solo trips—she did a lot of hunting with her track-cats. About a year later, someone found the fur and bones of one of the cats, but we couldn't tell how it had come to die. That was all we ever found of her."

When they made camp for the night, Diego went off into what Bunny was beginning to call his "creative trance." His lips moved now and then and odd sounds blurted out, but he offered no performance. One respected a singer's concentration.

They traveled two more days, steadily downward, past lakes bordered by strange shapes, some like trees dipped in silver or gold, leaves, flowers, and all. Occasionally a mist would rise to accompany them, flowing around their feet as they moved and then, as abruptly as it had risen, disappearing. Twice they had to find their way to the narrowest parts of rushing rivers and, with Sean throwing the hook and line to some high point, swing over to the farther shore.

The fourth day down they came to a thick barrier of fallen stalagmites and stalactites, jumbled willy-nilly on top of each other like unstacked firewood. Sean recognized this from Fingaard's description as the cave-in area. Beyond was a boom and a whooshing that suggested that the sea might have flooded in after the collapse. Sean and Diego tried to work their way over and around the various broken pieces, hacking occasionally at the molded limestone. Only Diego's quick thinking kept Sean, in the lead, from tumbling headlong into the dark waters held back by the obstacles they had managed to pass. For a long moment, while Diego recovered his breath at Sean's near escape from a dunking, Sean looked out across the waters, searching for some glimmer of a distant shore.

They vaguely heard the shrill voices of the women and Nanook's odd snarl.

*"We're all right!"* Sean yelled, cupping his hands, and his cry reverberated. Then he looked chagrined when they both heard the thunder of a rockslide. "Most likely an ice calf," Sean said in a moderate tone. "Let's get back. They're not in trouble, but something's upset them."

They found the others near one of the rock piles at the outer edge of the cave. Yana stood, hands clasped behind her back, looking down, her face bleak.

"Nanook found it," she said, nodding to where Bunny was kneeling over some object. Yana stepped aside so that Sean could see the sobbing girl, who suddenly prostrated herself in a paroxysm of grief to touch with shaking, tear-wet fingers the heel of a booted foot. The sole of another stuck out from under a boulder of ice. Scored across the ice in all directions were the ruts of the claws of Gonish the track-cat who had vainly tried to dig the man out of his tomb. Frozen blood, still red, stained many of the deeper grooves.

Sean knelt beside Bunny, one arm around her as his other hand reached out to touch the boot; he ran his fingers along the sole and what could be seen of the ankle. The leather had long since frozen to the hardness of stone.

Finally, distressed by his silent grieving, Yana touched his shoulder. He looked up at her, tears running down his cheeks.

"We could dig . . ." she began.

Sean shook his head and rose, his arms hanging down by his sides. "He already rests in the planet."

"Which *killed* him," Diego blurted out, and then stepped backward from the look on Sean's face.

Sean sighed deeply, his expression repentant as he stepped forward to touch Diego's arm. "No, it is not a question of 'kill' here."

Bunny rose then, rubbing her wet cheeks against her

arms. Diego immediately went to hold her in a close embrace. She relaxed against him, her body still shaken with sobs.

"I do know that," Diego said over her bent head to Sean. "Bunny's showed me that even though Petaybee can be a hard planet, it's fair. I understand, Bunny, I really do," he said to the top of her head. "When you hear my song, you'll know."

"And mine," Sean said softly.

Diego's eyes widened in respect. "I'd like to hear you sing, sir." Almost absently, he smoothed Bunny's disheveled hair back from her face in a way that touched Yana deeply. Sean didn't miss it, either.

"Uncle," Bunny asked in a very tentative voice, "does that mean . . . my mother . . ."

Sean looked to the big cat, who scratched around the site, sniffing, then brushed hard against Sean's leg and hand.

"Nanook says no," Sean said finally and the track-cat emphasized that with a clear *No* and a sneeze.

Yana held her arms wide in helplessness. "So what do we do now?"

"Well, *I*," Sean said, "go on. It's possible for me. You three go back." He clasped Diego's shoulder firmly when the boy would have argued. "You three can help spread the word of what happened at McGee's Pass. We can't have that happening anywhere else. Or, if it has"—Sean's expression turned even bleaker than it had when he accepted the death of his brother-in-law—"keep the problem from spreading. Yana, could you find out what dissolves Petraseal? Something has to. We've got to clean up McGee's Pass's cave system."

"I'll find someone who knows how, but—" Yana caught back the thought at first, until Sean's querying eyes made her continue. "What if Luzon finds out what Petraseal can do to the planet?"

"All the more reason for us to know how to clean it up, but the people, especially those who are with us already, *must* be warned so they can protect their places. With their lives, if necessary."

"You can count on us, Uncle Sean," Bunny said, standing upright in Diego's embrace, her face stern with resolve.

"I know that. Now, let's eat and get some rest," he said, adroitly guiding everyone away from the ice mausoleum.

Sometime during an uneasy sleep that night, Yana felt Sean's lips on her cheek and forehead, his hands stroking her, pausing on her gravid belly. When she woke the next morning, his clothing, empty of his body, was arranged against her as if he still occupied it.

When the others woke, Yana had had time to bundle up Sean's things so that Diego wouldn't ask unanswerable questions. The boy was appalled enough to think that Sean Shongili had gone on all by himself.

"He's mad. How could he possibly survive in an arctic ocean? I don't understand you, Bunny. How can you just sit there eating breakfast as if this was just another day, when your own uncle—"

"My own uncle has ways not possible for us," she said equably.

"What'd he do? Call a tube whale for a ride?" Diego asked sarcastically.

Yana and Bunny exchanged glances.

"Something like that," Bunny said, gnawing on her jerky meat.

"I've seen him do it," Yana said, seeing that Diego was working himself up into quite a state. "You know he's got a way with animals."

"Yes, but he's left Nanook here."

Nanook gave Diego a long and measuring look and a soft soothing sound started deep in the track-cat's belly, half purr, half reassurance.

"I just don't understand you people!" Diego said, throwing his hands up in the air in resignation.

"You're getting closer, though," Bunny said. She smiled up at him and patted the rock beside her. "Sit and eat.

We've a ways to go today. And you've got to finish your song before we get back to Harrison's Fjord."

"You've one to do, too, you know," he snapped at her.

"Diego!" Yana snapped right back as she would to an insolent trooper.

"Sorry," he muttered, and sat down and gnawed his anger away on his own strip of jerky.

Coaxtl did not entirely desert her youngling. The airship was similar to other machines she had expertly dodged before. They often held people who had proved dangerous to her kind. She followed it on swift paws, venturing perilously near to a human-place, and there, on a hillock overlooking the habitations, she found herself a place where she and the Home seemed as one, and watched and waited.

She did not see where the youngling went, but she saw when the airship flew into the sky again, carrying only one of the men with it.

A night passed, a day, and another night, and still Coaxtl waited, and she saw a land machine that could run very fast, and which she liked no better than the flying kind, scuttle toward a den. A man climbed out of it and she recognized him as the white-tailed one of the bad scent. He walked to a place where young ones were playing and there, so still that even Coaxtl's searching eyes had not spotted her, sat the youngling, small and still as the tree against which she waited while the other human cubs frolicked in the snow.

After a time, the youngling rose and followed the white-tailed one to the land machine, which Coaxtl saw contained another man already and many objects. The machine sped out of the town, past the hillock where Coaxtl waited, and back out toward the plains. Coaxtl knew, without knowing how she knew, that the man was taking the youngling to that place from which she had escaped.

This seemed foolish to Coaxtl. Foolish of the white-tail to take the youngling back to where she obviously did not want to be, and foolish of the girl to go. It did not make sense to Coaxtl why the girl would return to the bad place she had fled. Therefore, since it did not make sense, it could not be true. Therefore, the child did not *wish* to go back. Therefore, the men did not have the youngling's best interests in mind, and such interests were once more protected only by Coaxtl. Therefore, Coaxtl followed, keeping to cover when she could and traveling faster and more quietly than the cloud shadows she resembled.

Luzon headed in the direction of the Vale of Tears, right into the rising sun, which, despite the snow-glare goggles he wore, made driving very difficult.

The girl had been very little help, being too ignorant to know the use of a map. She could simply point out the general direction she had been traveling when he had first seen her with the cat. He hoped she would be of more use later.

The child spoke not at all now, crouching in the pull-down jump seat behind him, her ragged-nailed fingers clutching the safety webbing as if her life depended on its protection. That annoyed Matthew, who considered himself an extremely capable driver. He fixed his gaze on the so-called track he had to follow, while Braddock kept his eyes glued on the compass when the terrain made it necessary to detour about obstacles even the sturdy snocle couldn't run over. Only once did the girl make a sound: a sort of half-stifled cry of relief.

"What was that all about, little one?" he asked, trying to sound as benign as he could.

"Nnnunununn nothing, gracious sir," she said, and he had the vague impression that she had to turn her head back to the front to answer him. He glanced in the mirror but could see nothing but snowy plains and patchily covered mountains behind them.

"It must have been something. You haven't said a word since we left. Are you not happy in my company?"

"You are gracious, sir."

"Then share your thoughts with me."

"Oh, sir, I'm most definitely not worthy to share anything with anyone. It was only that I saw a pretty shadow . . ."

Matthew immediately knew that for a prevarication, as he could see nothing anywhere that might qualify as a "pretty shadow." Because he didn't wish to drive the timorous girl so far into her shell that she would be even less communicative than she was already, he let the matter drop.

It took four days by snocle to reach the Vale. Goat-dung rode in misery and, when she was allowed, in silence. The journey was much for her as sleep had been in the Vale—a respite, a brief time away, but always with the knowledge that she would wake within the Vale.

She was not traveling with Dr. Luzon because of his promises to free her, to adopt her. No, she knew better than to hope for such things, and besides, she was not the sort of person that anyone thought important enough to keep their promises to. She rode with him because she knew, as she had always known, with a dull, dreading certainty, that sooner or later she would wake up, end up, back in the Vale. When she had been with Coaxtl in her Home, she had for a time hoped to be free. With Coaxtl, who was free above all else, it had seemed reasonable to hope for freedom. As soon as she was back among people, even happy, laughing, squabbling people, people who were too ignorant to know that she did not deserve their pity, people who surely lied to pretend they were able to care about her, as soon as she was with them, she knew she was destined to return to the Vale.

And who better than Dr. Luzon, who was like and yet unlike the Shepherd Howling, to take her there? He did not strike her or try to touch her dirty secret places. He did not, in fact, seem interested in her at all. The only harm he did was to batter her ears constantly with questions about the Vale, about the Shepherd, about the Wisdoms and the Great Monster. He battered her about Coaxtl, too, but she would say nothing of the big cat, even to Dr. Luzon.

During the day, mile after mile of snow sped past the

snocle's windbubble—snowy hills, snowy plains, snowy valleys, snowy hills again. They sped past half-frozen rivers and slushy places they had to detour around, through forests and over land too high for forest to grow, past rabbit tracks and moose tracks and the tracks of horses. She wondered if these horses wore horns, like one she had glimpsed long ago. At first, it was exciting to travel over land so fast, but the excitement soon paled when she realized how quickly she was returning to the one place she did not want to be!

Nights were bad because that's when the questions began, so that she had the Shepherd's teachings ringing in her ears as she fell asleep, just as she always had in the Vale.

Only one piece of knowledge made all bearable, something only *she* knew, that just behind the hill, or hunkered down in a nearby bush, or back in the trees, or watching from the rim of a valley, a lone clouded shape vigilantly followed and stood guard at night. And when she woke at night sweating in her new warm winter clothing, she would hear a purr inside her mind, from out of the darkness, and the song of Coaxtl would lull her to sleep again.

> *Sleep, youngling*
> *Sleep and dream*
> *Of when your eyes will open*
> *Sleep, youngling*
> *Sleep and dream*
> *Of the day when your tail will be long*
> *Sleep and dream*
> *Sleep and dream*
> *Safe in the Home you'll be throbbed into slumber*
> *Safe in the Home you'll be crooned to all day*
> *Sleep, youngling*
> *Sleep and dream*
> *At twilight we two will go hunting.*

When this happened, sometimes the bad dreams did not return; sometimes she woke without fearing the daylight.

Such a night had passed before the day when they reached the Vale. Panic rose and choked off her breath as she looked down into the Vale, which now was muddy, but without water, and with a new coat of ice and snow.

She wanted to say "Stop!" to Dr. Luzon, but he would not have listened. Instead, he called to Braddock to drive recklessly down into the Vale, whereupon they were immediately surrounded by the Faithful.

Most of them had never seen a snocle before. Some cried out in alarm, "The Great Monster!"

Others said, "No, an angel of the company."

But when they saw her, people didn't know what to think. Ascencion, whom she saw on the edge of the crowd, gave her a hard look and then turned, to appear a short time later with the Shepherd himself.

The Shepherd looked smaller, somehow, and rather ordinary, not larger than life as he usually appeared. His chin was smooth, to show his purity over other men, who must wear whiskers. His hair was cut short for the same reason, although the women were never, ever to cut theirs unless they were being shamed for some wrong.

He did not, at first, look very friendly to Dr. Luzon, though he retained that air of peaceful detachment and complete calm he carried with him at all times when he wasn't preaching—until he fell into a terrible rage. But now he spoke softly. "We are a solitary and forsaken people, living apart on the hideous monster that is the back of this world. Why have you disturbed us?"

Matthew Luzon said, a slight yearning entering his tone that Goat-dung had not heard there before, "Why, we have come to you for wisdom, of course, good Shepherd. I am Dr. Matthew Luzon, an investigator for the company, and this is my assistant, Braddock Makem. The child you know."

"I know her," the Shepherd said, his calmness turning cold as his eyes touched Goat-dung's face. "She is a traitor who has run from the light. What business has a company investigator got with her or with me?"

"I am a special sort of investigator, Shepherd," Matthew explained. "It is my job to purge the company's holdings of lies that corrupt and mislead the people. Many on this world lie about its nature, seek to make us believe it is not merely a planet, but a sentient organism, whose natural events have intent and intelligence behind them. The girl told me of your teachings. I believe you know the truth and would learn it from you. I would have you testify before the company about this truth, as well."

"The company needs *my* testimony?" the Shepherd asked. Goat-dung would have suspected he'd be delighted. After all, in his teachings, the company was the great force that had changed all of their lives and cast them into anguish at the mercy of the Great Monster. He seemed to be weighing his words when he answered, "This gives me much to ponder. I will do a teaching this evening. You may attend. But there is another matter between us. This girl . . ."

"She told me of your teachings, Shepherd. She's impressed me very much, and I would like to retain her as my research assistant."

"That is impossible. We are betrothed. Tonight will be our deferred wedding night. After the teaching, there will be a feast, and then she shall cleave unto me even as her mother did."

Matthew turned to Goat-dung with a mockery of happy surprise on his face. "Why, Goat-dung! Congratulations."

She hung her head.

Ascencion came forward and took her in charge and led her away to the makeshift tent-shed that was the newly rebuilt wedding hut, while her self-proclaimed rescuer ignored her plight to court her chief tormentor. As she shuffled along behind Ascencion, however, she heard the Shepherd tell Matthew, "After the wedding, she will no longer be Goat-dung. Everyone must address her, as befits my wife, by her new name, Dolores."

Dolores: Full of woe. What could be more appropriate

for her? Goat-dung thought. No, in her mind, she would think of herself as 'Cita.

She allowed herself to be dressed in the ceremonial "Taking Gown," the cloaklike gown that all of the chosen women wore when the Shepherd took them to wife. Once garbed, she was left alone to wait hopelessly for her wedding—until there were shouts from the far end of the Vale and in her mind she heard Coaxtl's voice saying:

*Another one comes! Fear him not but treat him well and care for his wounds. On his safety depends your own and mine, and that of all the people, for the Home loves this one well.*

# 11

Yana, Diego, and Bunny were recovering from their often treacherous uphill climb back to the cave entrance at Harrison's Fjord. Ardis told them they had missed Johnny Greene's return, so they spent two more days anxiously waiting before his copter set down again. They ran out to meet him, ducking under the still-whirling rotors. He looked very tired, as if he hadn't slept in days.

When the noise of the blades stopped, he said, "I know I'm late, but there was something I had to get done, pronto, schnell, fast. And I got news, too." He hauled his backpack from under the pilot's seat. "First let me have a hot bath and get eight hours."

"Where're you fitting a decent meal in?" Ardis asked, scowling at him.

"While I'm bathing, Ardis, love, and anything you have ready'll suit me fine," he said with his charismatic smile. "You're back soon, or did you go?" he asked Yana as she, Diego, and Bunny started back down to the Sounik house. "Oh," he added, noticing the sudden tears form in Bunny's eyes, and he threw a comforting arm about her shoulders.

"My father," Bunny said in a choked voice.

"Cave-in," Yana added.

"My sympathies, Buneka," Johnny said formally.

"It's not as if I *knew* him as a father," she said and gave a little shrug.

"Sean's gone on, hoping to find traces of Aoifa," Yana said.

Then Johnny grinned with pure mischief. "Marmion Algemeine took her folks and the five assistants Matthew made the mistake of leaving behind to the cave where the planet spoke to us after the volcano erupted."

*"What?"*

He grinned again at the astonished chorus that comment elicited. "Yup."

"And?" Diego demanded.

"Well, they were gone thirty hours . . ." Johnny said, and paused, his eyes twinkling as he deliberately lengthened the telling of his story. "And Seamus Rourke and Rick O'Shay said it was one of the nicer visitations they've ever had."

"Yes, but what happened to Luzon's guys? And Marmion? And Sally and . . ."

"Marmion took Millard and Sally. Faber was off doing some other errand," Johnny supplied when Yana faltered. "Seamus swears there's been very subtle changes in all of them. Can't see it myself, but Seamus is more in tune with the planet's ways than I am. Says their hearts are altered even if they don't think their minds have been, and we'll have to wait and see what happens. As far as they're concerned, they spent only a half hour or so in a misty cavern and lost thirty working hours." Johnny's grin was as broad as it could get, his eyes almost lost in the folds of his cheeks. "I'll have to trust him on this one. This is one time the planet's too sly even for me."

"Nothing at all noticeable? They didn't have the dream?" Yana asked. The dream—actually, a sort of experiential emotional history of what the planet had undergone during its relatively short lifetime—that she had shared with Johnny, Sean, the Whittakers, and others shortly before they were rescued would have been quite a revelation for Matthew's physically fit boyos. She would have liked to have heard that they'd got the full treatment so they'd *know* beyond a shadow of a doubt how the planet felt about what was being done to it.

"I wouldn't worry, Yana," Johnny said, and Bunny, still closely embraced, nodded wisely, too.

"I just hope so. Because . . ."

Johnny shook his head, released Bunny, and stopped. "Lemme get a bath, some food, and some sleep, and we'll talk when my head's clearer. Okay?"

So they relented and tried to find other things to do to occupy themselves while Johnny slept, so tired that Ardis swore he didn't move arm or leg from the moment he lay down on the bed.

The curly-coats needed grooming, which took a good hour and a half while Nanook sunned himself on the terrace. That seemed to be the focal point for all the felines of Harrison's Fjord. Even Shush the Survivor was there, the recipient of many rubbings and strokings and lickings.

Yana, easing back muscles for a moment as she was tackling the matted underbelly of her pony, wondered at the attentions Shush was receiving.

"Do they do that to every newcomer?" she asked Bunny.

Shush had put on a good deal of flesh in the scant week she'd been at the fjord and no longer looked like a rack of orange-skinned bones and pathetic eyes.

Bunny looked over and grinned. "Naw, they're educating her. Nanook said something was necessary since the poor cat'd had no one to teach her how to pass on messages. Her mother got killed before she could, so she's being brought up to speed with the rest of Clodagh's cats. And—" Bunny frowned, because there were far more cats there than there should have been. "There must be messages coming in." She put down the body brush she'd been vigorously using on her pony and walked over to Nanook.

"What's up?" she asked, sitting down beside him in a space made available by a resettlement of many orange bodies.

*Liam Maloney is not pleased at what happened to Dinah*, Nanook told her. The cat sat perfectly still and stared into Bunny's eyes through his own wide golden ones, the message rumbling into her mind as all of the more complicated messages did. The cat's vocalizations were limited to the few short human terms within the range of its speech centers. These longer communications needed a bit more concentration, especially with a neophyte recipient such as Bunny or Yana Maddock. With Sean Shongili it was a different matter altogether. Talking to Sean was second nature.

Bunny sighed. "I knew Liam would be upset, but he *does* know she's recovering and is being very well treated?"

Nanook licked a front paw briefly to indicate the affirmative. *He passes on that there is trouble at Deadhorse like what you found at McGee's Pass. Trouble also waits at Wellington and Savoy.*

Bunny thought about that. These were the four towns most remote from Kilcoole, and each of them had been reported by the cats as being in favor of mining. She couldn't help but wonder if each of the towns had also had recent changes in their shanachies. She gave a convulsive shudder. If there were any more like Satok, the trouble was bigger than she'd ever conceived it could be. And if all four of those villages had had their caves coated in Petraseal . . . She shuddered again.

"What else?" she asked, sensing that Nanook was waiting for her to absorb that information.

*Satok has been visiting these other villages. Satok has friends in all of them. The reports, by the way, are from track-cats and feral cats. No more like Shush live in those villages.*

"The hell he has!"

"What's the matter, Bunny?" Yana asked, startled by Bunny's loud, angry outburst.

"But what can we do about it?" Bunny asked quickly, waving to Yana to keep on with what she was doing.

Nanook licked the tip of his tail thoughtfully. *Clodagh has been informed of all. There is more. When the pilot man goes south, we must go with him.*

"Sean's not in danger, is he?"

Nanook blinked. *We go south, too.* Then he stretched his

long body out across the sunwarmed stone of the wall, and Bunny knew he had finished talking to her.

She went back to Darby and picked up where she left off.

"What was that all about?" Yana asked, leaning against Darby's rump.

"Nanook says we'd better go south with Johnny." She added hastily, "No, Nanook doesn't think Sean's in trouble, but he does think we should go south."

Johnny Greene did, too.

"I'd have to go back even if I didn't want to check up on the kid," he said. "Whit wants me to keep an eye on Luzon. Actually, I was supposed to pick him up at Sierra Padre a couple of days ago." Johnny grinned unrepentantly. "Had engine trouble."

Bunny cocked an eyebrow at Johnny.

"Oh, I'll have a *real* one for Dr. Luzon," Johnny said, brushing aside her skeptical reaction. "But I had a sudden premonition, like, and since I've rarely had one that strong before that didn't turn out that I should have listened more closely, this time I did. So I called in a few favors and sorted the problem out. Just in case." Then he grinned with all the abandon of a boy who had just pulled the best practical joke in the world on his worst enemy and there'd be no way of assigning guilt to him.

"What *have* you done, Captain Greene?" Yana asked, resuming her military attitude.

"Nothing, Major sir, to bother your head about." He laid a finger alongside his nose and winked at her. But for all the amusement in his eyes, his expression told her she'd get no more out of him and to let the matter be.

She nodded. "Something which will no doubt please me in days to come?"

"I devoutly hope so, considering the effort I've put into it. Now, since I've had my bath, food, sleep, and more food, let's load up. Nanook wants you south, he gets you south. Ah, and you're coming along with us, are you,

Nanook?" The black and white track-cat had strolled up to the copter and was peering inside it. "He doesn't much like flying, you know," Johnny added. "Looking won't change the flight process, pal."

Nanook crawled under the second row of passenger seats, tucked his tail tight against his body, and laid his head on his paws. His whole attitude was one of patient resignation to an inevitable fate.

"Well, he's stowed. Get yourselves aboard." Johnny gestured for Bunny and Diego to sit over Nanook, while Yana took the other front seat. Then he handed around headphones so they could all communicate during the long journey south.

They knew something was wrong the moment Loncie came to the door.

"Luzon?" Johnny asked simply, and got a stream of Andean invective that was both colorful and inventive, the gist of it being that the son of a scabrous tarantula had stolen La Pobrecita. Pointed inquiry around Sierra Padre by the entire Ondelacy/Ghompas clan had brought forth the information that the vomitus spewings of an excrement-devouring long-extinct reptile which would eat its own mother without shame or serious second contemplation had taken the only snocle in all of Sierra Padre, Lhasa, or any place this side of Bogota, which was, as Juanito knew, a very long journey, especially at this uncertain time of year.

"When did all this happen?" Johnny asked quickly.

"The day after you left, Juanito. I thought she would be safe playing with my own *niños*! I was a fool! A fool!"

Johnny was too angry to say anything more. Mostly he was angry at himself. He should have known Luzon would stop at nothing. At least the man hadn't hurt Loncie or one of her family in the kidnapping—not that they'd ever be able to prove it was a kidnapping. He nearly, but not quite, regretted the two days he had taken to make his private arrangements. One thing was certain: They'd have to move, and move fast, if they were to get the girl away again. This time he was leaving her nowhere near Luzon.

"Didn't she scream? Or—or anything?" Bunny asked, pushing herself out from behind Johnny's back.

"She went willingly, from what my children know of it," Loncie said. "She feared the man, one could see that, but he was the sort she would follow because he is what she is used to, what she has been taught to love. Well, perhaps not love, but someone who acts as she expects people to act. She cannot imagine anything else and so allows him to return her."

"She didn't accept it, though, did she?" Bunny demanded, not just of Loncie but of all the adults and Diego. "She ran away, didn't she? We've got to *help* her!"

Yana put her arm reassuringly around the girl's shoulders. "That's what we're here to do, Rourke. All the lady is saying is that the poor kid had been so brainwashed, she rejected happiness because the concept was so unfamiliar that it was scary."

"Ah!" And Lonciana nodded vigorously. "You have said it. But, come, enter. The evening meal is prepared and you must eat. You will never find this secret place from which she comes in the darkness. Also, you must tell us all that is happening to bring such a planet-defiling dung-sucking leech as this Luzon to our world, and we must sing together."

"Our timing's great, kids," Yana said, trying to inject a little bravado into the currently demoralizing state of affairs. "We may have a song or two to pass along ourselves. Was anyone from this village at Bremport?"

Loncie's eyes brimmed suddenly, and Yana understood the term "dolorous" as she never had before. The woman's chins trembled and her mouth contorted with sudden grief. Yana would have touched her arm, but Pablo was there already, his small frame supporting his wife's larger one like steel scaffolding.

"Our second son, Alejandro."

To Yana's count that made the last of those from

Petaybee who had died in that incident. She heaved a sigh of relief and allowed herself to be escorted into the house.

"Hey, a guitar!" The exclamation burst from Diego's lips and then he flushed, realizing that his excitement was not quite suitable following mention of those who died at Bremport.

"You like guitar?" Lonciana asked, her whole expression brightening.

"Do I like guitar? I've been *trying* to make one." Diego reached into his backpack and brought out the neck he had been so patiently shaping.

*"Qué hombre!"* Lonciana embraced him as if he were a long-lost friend. Diego, momentarily engulfed by her, grinned—more with acceptance of her enthusiasm than embarrassment.

They ate first, of course, and various young Ondelacy-Ghompases were sent to inform the entire village that there would be a special singing this evening: too late to make it a latchkay, but certainly there would be blurry and a bite or two to go down with it.

"I thought blurry was Clodagh's specialty," Yana commented as she washed up before dinner.

Johnny grinned. "The north doesn't have a corner on the market of all good things, Yana. Had you come up from the ranks as I did, instead of training at an officer's academy with so few Petaybean candidates, you'd have learned something of the joys of comparative Petaybean blurry drinking. Every time Loncie returned from leave, she used to bring back a stash: Old Armadillo is what we nicknamed her recipe, because it armors you so well against the slings and arrows of outrageous fortune. The spice she uses gives it a little more kick than the mulled-cider kinda thing you get up north."

Bunny, who was watching Pablo demonstrate to an enraptured Diego first the techniques of playing the guitar and then the sound made by the bagpipes, said, "They have more than a few things down here that we don't have up north."

Lonciana did something with a mess of beans that Yana, sensitive now to such subtleties, would have given her right big toe to discover. It was tasty and filling, satisfying even their hearty appetites.

Immediately afterward, the table was dismantled and taken out of the main room, and chairs, benches, stools, and odd crates were placed about the room. The guitar came off the wall again, and Yana identified one round object with jingling bits fastened in its lip as a tambourine.

Lonciana was busy in the kitchen end of the house, mixing the blurry with the help of her eldest daughters, while Pablo, Johnny, and the older Ondelacy boys began to greet the visitors as they began to pour in.

Once again Yana wondered at the way a small Petaybean house could seem to expand infinitely to contain so many people. Eventually there was only a small space around the high stool that had been placed in the center of the room for the singers—of which Yana was one, and probably the first. Bunny and Johnny both kept her mug as well as Diego's full of blurry once Diego announced that he had his song, too.

Yana missed Sean desperately, but Johnny took her to the stool and settled her on it, taking the mug when she drained the last of the blurry.

"This is Major Yana Maddock, who was at Bremport, and who is now one of us," Johnny began simply. "She has a song for you."

Silence has different qualities, Yana knew, from the absolute one she'd *not* heard on her few space walks to that of expectancy, either a hopeful or happy one, or a mean and miserable show-us-your-stuff kind. This was expectant and almost reverent. That startled her so much that she began to sing to stop what her ears weren't hearing.

After the first few lines got past her teeth, she actually began to enjoy the act of singing, not that she would ever truly enjoy the song that she must sing. Maybe one day soon, as Sean had suggested, she'd find joy in making a song.

*"I was sent here to die, too, here where the snows live,*
*The waters live, the animals and trees live.*
*And you. And now I live."*

The last words came out before she realized she had added them to the song.

Then Lonciana and Pablo made their way to her and took her hands, holding them to their cheeks, their tears moistening the backs of her fingers. Each of the Ondelacy children, smiling shyly with their misty eyes, touched her hands, too.

Other voices lifted in appreciation of her song and she was able to get down off the stool without any help.

Bunny led Diego to the stool. There was a purpose in the young man's eye now, Yana noticed, that hadn't been there before. He was growing into his true manhood, and what had happened at McGee's Pass had tempered him.

"This is Diego Metaxos, who was with me at McGee's Pass and risked his life to save me," Bunny said, giving Diego's hand a squeeze before she released it. "He has a song that all must hear."

Diego tipped his head back, closed his eyes to slits, and rested his hands on his thighs with his feet hooked on the lower stretcher of the stool.

*"Deep is the place of communion*
*Where mist and ice and stone are warm*
*With what is more than friendship,*
*More than father or mother love,*
*With nurturing and understanding.*
*We all treasure this place of communion.*
*It is our place, our place, our place."*

His voice, now firmly baritone, raised to the top of his range and intensified as he repeated the phrase. Then his tone altered to that of a storyteller who is forced to relate truths that disturb him.

*"There are others who do not believe that our place
Is ours and has been since men and women came here.
They were once of us, and knew of communion.
They left and in their years of leaving learned
Much of evil and selfishness and unsharing, uncaring, un-
 kind, self-seeking, self-helping self first and always.
Having knowledge of things that bind and score and cover
They have returned to make evil what was good."*

Again his voice changed, colored with a bitterness that
made Yana twitch uneasily, a bitterness that roused all his
listeners.

*"Why steal what is ours for no purpose but to keep it for
 only one?
Why deprive the many of communion and hope and peace
 in times of worry?
Why bury truth?
Why bury our planet alive!"*

Gasps of horror greeted that phrase, but Diego did not
falter.

*"For it has been buried alive, screaming unheard
At McGee's Pass.
The stone smothered,
The roots strangled,
The soil smothered.
White death like
Your snow-skin
From one like
But unlike
A son.
What son wishes death to his father?
What son demands honor unearned?
Women raped and villages frightened
And deprived of their place of communion
And the gentle mists that heal,*

*The gentle touch that soothes,*
*The spirit that nurtures us. All of us!"*

Diego's song roused the indignation of every listener that evening. Bunny was so proud of his song and his singing she almost vibrated. Then, when he had rested from the exertions of his singing, both young people related what had happened at McGee's Pass, and described Satok's treachery.

Well and truly blurred, Yana was still quite conscious of some of the discussion that went on late into the night, to the accompaniment of guitar, fiddle, flute, tambourine, maracas, and castanets. But she, Loncie, and Johnny—possibly Bunny, too, at one point—had decided that the most important thing they could now do was rescue La Pobrecita from Shepherd Howling.

From Lonciana's description, the man was worse than Satok, but only marginally, if he insisted on marrying a prepubescent child when he already had four or five wives. Yana had been well drilled in leaving alone the customs and mores of indigenous populations, but she was not indigenous, and the whole concept of forced wifehood was abhorrent. That night they pieced together what La Pobrecita had said and came up with a fair idea of where the Vale of Tears might be, judging from where she had been found, how long she said she'd been traveling, and from what direction. By Johnny's reckoning, the place should be a valley set in the Sierra Padres somewhere near the head of the Lacrimas River. Given decent weather, they should have no problem flying right to the place. And if they met Luzon, at least two of them could give chase on the snocub, a two-person snocle that Johnny had fit handily in the cargo net.

# 12

Dr. Whittaker Fiske received the coded messages from Johnny Greene with concern and no little dismay—particularly the second one, the one Johnny sent him after he first returned to the north. He had quickly approved the pilot's scheme and given him all due assistance. By calling in a few personal favors owed the pilot and promising the supply sergeant R&R to the tropical planet of her choice, he had ensured that all Petraseal available at and to SpaceBase had been urgently requisitioned elsewhere. At Johnny's suggestion, the Petraseal cans had been emptied into a single tank for immediate shipment, while the empty containers still labeled "Petraseal" had been filled with the last consignment of white paint, which was rarely used on Petaybee except for camouflage purposes. However, between implementing Johnny's scheme and work at SpaceBase, he had been too fully occupied to be able to return to Clodagh to warn her of the grave implications of what had taken place at McGee's Pass.

He was concerned about how Clodagh would take it. She was an amazing woman, unconventionally beautiful, intelligent, wise, and kind, but she felt everything that happened to Petaybee personally. Maybe if everybody did the same, there wouldn't be any problem, but even after his experience in the cave, he still retained a detachment that kept him from that sort of bond with what he had once thought of as the creation of his family. He did, however, feel a bond with Clodagh—a closer one than he had felt with anyone in a long time—including, maybe especially, his own son.

He walked into Kilcoole the morning after Greene's second transmission. The river was down a bit now that much of the initial thaw had already taken place, but it was still full and fat with water.

He knew Clodagh wasn't at home before he knocked on the door. No cats in the windows, on the rooftop, or perched on the various objects in the yard. He peeked through the open door into the neat, empty house and looked down Kilcoole's one muddy street. The town seemed even more deserted than it had before. He called Clodagh a couple of times, but when he received no answer, he strolled down to Yana Maddock's place. There, at least, her cat Marduk sat on the stoop, and sprang up as if it had been waiting for him. Well, knowing these cats, maybe it had been.

At that point, the door of the house across the street opened and Frank Metaxos poked his prematurely white-haired head out. The man's speech was still a little slow, but he was a far cry from the wreck he had been only a few weeks earlier.

"How's it going, Frank?" Whit asked.

"I hate being stuck here," Frank told him. "You heard anything of my boy?"

"Matter of fact, I did," Whit replied affably. "He's doing fine. Been a great help to everybody. Say, you haven't seen Clodagh, have you?"

"She went out to the springs, I think. Marduk there"—Frank nodded at the cat—"knows the way. Though you'll have to walk. All the curlies are carrying the people to visit the neighbors."

"Visiting the neighbors" was the term the Kilcoole people were using to describe their mission to the other villages. Whit wasn't overly surprised. After all, these people were half-descended from the Irish who had described their own centuries-old guerrilla conflict as "the Troubles" and a massive international war as "the Emergency."

He followed Marduk through knee-high weeds that had been lying in ambush under the snow, waiting for the thaw.

Birds sang and dived overhead, both small, pretty songbirds and swooping, squawking ravens. Small creatures rustled the underbrush; a red fox darted across his path. Marduk scurried up a tree when the fox passed, and hissed and spit at the silvery wake the creature cut in the tall grass.

Whit found Clodagh beside the springs, surrounded by not only her cats but all sorts of animals, including a large, strong curly-coat. They stood, lay, or sat and watched her as she pulled and separated, pulled and separated a profusion of plants growing rampant around the hot-springs banks. Her bountiful wavy black hair was braided and coiled on top of her head; sweat ran down her face and neck as she worked.

"Sláinte, Whittaker," she said without looking up.

"Sláinte yourself, my dear. What the devil are you trying to do?"

"I'm pullin' weeds," she said.

"So I see," he responded dryly. "Are you just pulling these particular weeds around the springs, or did you plan to personally defoliate the entire area between here and Kilcoole?"

She stood up, hands planted on her broad back. "Just these," she said, smiling. "I could use a hand. I'm kinda in a hurry."

"Be glad to. I'm afraid, however, that I've come as the bearer of bad tidings."

"You going to tell me about that guy that sealed up some of the communion places? Silenced the planet and fooled all those people at McGee's Pass and so on?"

"Well, yes."

"Yeah, well, I heard about that."

"You did?" he asked, dumbfounded at first and then shaking his head as understanding set in. "Of course. I suppose your usual informants told you."

"Kinda. It took the cats a long time to find out, because he killed all but one of 'em. But that one got word out to mine and they told me. They say he put some white junk on the inside of the cave that fuses the rock—stuff they use to shore up walls in mines."

"Yes. Petraseal. Johnny Greene also reported that to me. It's very bad news, Clodagh. If our adversaries at Intergal learn that there is something that can defeat your communication with the planet, they're apt to go overboard on using it."

"Yeah," she nodded gravely. "That's what I thought. I was pretty worried about it, too, so I came out here to talk to Petaybee."

"I don't suppose it's very happy about all this."

"It's sure not."

"Did it have any ideas?"

"Well, not in so many words. Except, I just started wondering, what if this stuff doesn't *always* work? What if there's something stronger than it is, that can go through it? And you know, all of a sudden, I looked down and saw where this coo-berry bramble was growin' right up through the floor of the cave, and when I came out here, why I noticed what I hadn't seen before. You know how that is?"

"I do," Whit nodded.

"Anyway, we never had a problem with coo-berries here before. And coo-berries are a problem. Just about impossible to destroy and they'll go through anything. You see what I'm getting at?"

"I think I do. You're sure it'll work?"

She shrugged, then directed him where to pull. The berries had sharp thorns. "After we get a bunch pulled up, we wrap 'em in leaves and our bigger, faster friends here will see that they get delivered." She nodded at the animals.

It was Whit's turn to shrug as he buttoned down his sleeves and started pulling.

Satok had no problem eluding the trackers from McGee's Pass. For one thing, he was wily, with a lot of friends and resources. For another thing, one of those resources was a shuttle hidden in a secret camouflaged shed about a half hour from his house, close enough that he could get to it in a hurry, and far enough away from the center of things that it was unlikely to be found.

He flew first to Deadhorse, then Wellington and Savoy. There former shipmates of his, all of whom he had set up as replacements for the recently expired shanachies, were in various stages of converting the people in the towns to their version of "what the planet wanted."

"I don't see what the problem is," said Reilly, Savoy's new headman, as he sat drinking with Satok. "These people believe anything they're told. Just tell 'em the people at McGee's Pass have gone nuts or something."

"Your problem is you don't think far enough ahead, Reilly," Satok said. "The brats got away. The McGee's Pass people scattered to a lot of places. They know about the cave. Now, the problem is not so much what they think of us as the possibility of competition. Using the Petraseal was my idea. Finding out how to use the Petraseal without the planet freaking us out of our fraggin' minds was *my* idea. I want credit *and* credits. You boys will get yours, as well, of course. But if this committee that's investigating things sees the Petraseal before we claim our finders' fee, Intergal will have everything and there'll be nothing for anybody else."

"So what do you need from us?"

"Ore samples, of course, and a low profile until I can show up with some company bigwig to buy our method." He snapped his fingers for the slattern who was serving the booze to bring another round. This was stronger stuff than the blurry, even considering the effect this stupid planet had of neutralizing intoxicants with every other native beverage or food consumed. Fortunately, Satok had had little else to eat or drink for a couple of days. The girl looked familiar— one of his castoffs, no doubt. Sure had let herself go, though. Moped around with downcast eyes, ugly shapeless clothes, dirty lank hair, sallow skin mottled with bruises.

Some women just had no self-respect. If she'd looked like that when he first came to the village, he'd never have touched her.

"Okay, so when do you need the samples?"

"Now," Satok growled. "Or haven't you been listening? I want the shuttle loaded with the best you've got."

"How do we know you won't just take it and take off?"

"Because there's a lot more to be made here than what we could gouge out of the ground by ourselves. You have to think big. Besides, I'll need some of you along to help me unload."

"So where are you taking this stuff?"

He shrugged. "SpaceBase, for a start."

The cold of the icy waters was more of a shock than usual because Sean had just been so warmly wrapped about Yana. But it was always the first part of him to enter the water that experienced the trauma. Despite the almost stupefying cold, he forced himself to drop into the freezing dark waters. The change occurred more abruptly than ever: self-preservation at its highest level.

Once the waters closed over his altering head, the sounds he hoped to hear pinged back and forth. He sent out his call and felt the stir of water as a tube whale responded. The brush of the huge mammal against him in human form would have been crushing, but the selkie was less vulnerable. Stroking one flipper on the firm flesh of the whale, Sean-Selkie floated forward until he came to the proportionally small whale eye. One flipper-hand reaching as high up on the skull above the eye as possible, Sean communicated his need.

*Do you remember the place before it fell?*

*Yes.*

*Take me to the other side.*

*As you wish.*

Sean-Selkie had time to secure a hold on the side fin before he was propelled forward at amazing speed. For what seemed a very long dark time in this lightless medium,

Sean-Selkie clung there. Finally the tube whale halted, so abruptly that he was sent flipping end over end, past the whale's bright unblinking eye and skidding up the icy slope of a tunnel that gaped open onto the subarctic seas.

*You have been of great assistance and have my gratitude. You are known and your needs considered.*

Then the whale departed, once more singing its weird song, one that Sean-Selkie heard faintly, distantly answered. In that direction the tube whale now swam. Sean-Selkie watched until the churning of its flukes was no longer visible in the dark sea. He climbed up into the maw of this section of the underground link between the continents, with its luminous walls and slightly misted footing.

He had gone no more than a few hundred meters before he knew that both Aoifa and her track-cat had managed to get this far. A neat pile of animal dung, frosted over but identifiable, lay in a little hole, claw marks around it to show that the track-cat had not lost its sense of propriety despite its inability to cover its feces. And four paces beyond the cat's were human excretions. Sean-Selkie sighed with relief and lumbered on up the long slope, through immense caverns and more upward corridors. He saw other signs—fish skeletons—by lakesides and, diving into the same places, found food for himself to keep strong for this long and lonely journey. He saw the crumpled envelopes of travel rations, too.

How far and how long the journey took, Sean-Selkie could not gauge. He traveled more safely and economically as a selkie; having no clothes for his human manifestation was the best reason to continue as he was.

When he eventually emerged into daylight, the sun dazzling him, he had no warning of the danger into which he had blundered. He was always particularly vulnerable as he changed, the transition altering his senses—especially his eyesight and hearing. The first arrow took him in the thigh while it was still elongating from a flipper, still covered with spotted fur; the second would have been fatal but for the fact that a feline knocked him to one side. Snarling, the feline guarded him, facing the ragged humans who surrounded the mouth of the cave, one paw, its claws unsheathed, raised against their advance.

*Thanks, clouded one. I owe you a life.*

*Can you run with me?*

*Must finish transition first. Can't run or swim, not as is, not wounded in the leg. You go. There is a rifle aimed now at you. Go quickly. They think me helpless.*

Giving one last forward leap, which sent the ragged creatures screaming backward though the armed man did not move, the feline whirled and sped back into the cave and disappeared from sight.

"Don't bother with the cat. They're a half credit the dozen. Secure that monster! He mustn't escape!"

So Sean-Selkie, neither man nor seal at this point, endured the indignity of being bound limb to limb and the agony of having the arrow yanked out of his flesh. Even a selkie can faint.

When Sean recovered consciousness, he wished he had not, for he seemed to be lying in a pile of slushy cold water in a dank-smelling and dark place. His enhanced selkie vision told him that he was alone with some bundles and crates, in a tent made of badly cured skins; the air stank of that, as well as of the mold of continued damp. He had been pegged down, and the wound in his haunch ached.

Continuing the transformation to human would not be useful, Sean realized, for his limbs as a seal were thinner and more graceful. The bindings would be tighter on human wrists and ankles. He wallowed in the water beneath him, trying to wet himself enough to encourage the full transformation to seal, despite his wound, but it was useless. The melted slush was too shallow and he remained half-transformed, with his lower legs and his arms those of a man, while most of him remained seal.

Exterior sounds began to filter through to his awakened senses. He could smell fire, a big one, and had a horrible premonition of what a big fire might mean for a captured "monster." He could hear sounds of quite a few people moving about without much energy, and two male voices, which seemed to punctuate the muted noises of the others with orders, too muffled for him to understand.

It was while he was trying to decipher the noise into conversations and understand the orders that he heard other small noises and then felt something sawing at the bindings of his feet.

"I'm cutting you free, monster," a frightened whisper told him above the sawing. "Coaxtl said I must free you. That you are not a true monster but a proper creature, and you can save me. Coaxtl was my friend and kind to me. They are not kind to me here." There was a small hiccup and sob, and suddenly the efforts of the frightened whisperer were rewarded and the thong parted. Fumbling fingers unwrapped the rest of the wet leather from Sean-Selkie's feet. "Please don't eat me, monster. I must help you."

*I won't eat you, little one,* Sean said, for if she had been talking to Coaxtl, whom he had now identified as the clouded leopard that had saved him, she would hear him speak. *I am grateful to Coaxtl. I am also no monster who harms those who rescue him.*

"Shepherd Howling says they are going to roast you in the fire." Another piteous sob broke from the child's lips as she snaked herself along his length to his hands. "And Dr. Luzon is trying to talk him into surrendering you for scientific study. I think that means cutting you up. Dr. Luzon said he would adopt me, but instead, he's given me over to the Shepherd Howling. When Dr. Luzon is gone, I will be punished and then I will be married. If Shepherd Howling prevails, you may be my wedding supper. I would hate to see you suffer. Coaxtl says that if you die, other monsters will avenge you, and the flock would suffer. I know life is supposed to be suffering, but we suffer very much already and I think it is enough. More would be too much."

*Enough is too much,* Sean-Selkie said, trying to assist her sawing efforts by holding his bound wrists as far apart as possible to strain the leather thong. She had to be using the dullest knife in the world to take so long at her job, but he blessed her arrival and her attempts at rescue.

The wrist thong snapped and he inadvertently slapped her face. She gave a little gasp but no more than that, and it occurred to Sean that she was accustomed to blows. The thought infuriated him.

*My apologies, little one, for my clumsiness in striking the one who frees.*

"No apologies are needed for one so unworthy as I, for I am sworn by Coaxtl to rescue you."

The dominant male voices were getting loud, and there seemed to be more noise outside the tent.

*We must leave.*

"This way." She scrambled backward with a speed he was unable to emulate, stiff and sore as he was, with the wound in his haunch hurting even more. But the threat of discovery was a great spur, and blocking the pain in his leg, Sean-Selkie reached the place where she had entered the tent. But his rescuer was a good deal smaller than he. Frantically digging with his hands, he managed to make a large enough opening in the slush to allow him to pass under the edge of the tent. Then, carefully, he reached back inside and, as well as he could, scooped the slush back over the hole.

"Coaxtl waits," the girl said, and rising to a crouch, beckoned him to follow.

*Are there man clothes nearby? The arrow wound will not let me run as quickly as I should.*

"Man clothes?"

*Yes, and the quicker the better, dear child,* Sean-Selkie said, hearing the noises converging on the tent.

"This way."

The child changed direction, and Sean completed the transformation to his human form as he limped as fast as he could after her. The wound hurt more in his human form. At last she stopped and thrust a pile of filthy clothing at him. The pants were for a much shorter man, but the leather jacket and fur jerkin would be sufficient.

The girl had disappeared again. While he was struggling with the clothing, wishing he had something to cover the wound before it turned septic from the dirt impregnated in the pants, she returned and thrust some loose wrappings at him.

"Wrap these about your feet so that—oh! But you have *real* feet. Are you not really a monster?"

"Not really, little one. And as a human I am much safer right now among people who are looking for a monster."

"Oh, but you are not one of us, and everyone would see that you are a stranger."

"At night and in the dark?"

"This night the fire is very bright. Coaxtl said that she would hide you. You are safer with her."

"If I could reach her, yes, but the arrow wound slows me down."

"Yes, of course it would. How stupid of this unworthy one . . . Come with me. There is one place where you will be safe. At least for a little while." She giggled. "And even hot water to clean the wound."

"There is?"

"Yes, I was given hot water in which to bathe myself since I am to be made wife to Shepherd Howling—" Her voice broke.

Rage suffused Sean so that for a moment he couldn't speak; he almost cut off the circulation at his ankles as he wound the foot covering on.

"I must be back there, at my tent. Ascencion said a maiden must be private to bathe on her wedding night."

Poor terrified mite, Sean thought, as he cautiously followed her in a crouch that put more strain on his wound. He could feel fresh blood seeping down his leg. They were, however, going away from the noise and the excited mob about to discover that their quarry had disappeared. When they reached their destination, the child struggled with a tent peg so that Sean would not have to crawl again. He took it from her hand and heaved it loose from the slush, and they both entered easily. Fumbling, he managed to get the peg back into place from the inside.

In the dim light from a small lamp, Sean could see steam still rising from a copper tub, large enough for a good-sized body. He could also look at the pitiful little waif who was going to be forced into an unwanted marriage. Maybe if he could just dress the wound, he'd take her with him to wherever Coaxtl could hide them both.

A savage ululation startled both of them, and the child grew rigid with fear.

"You were just in time, my dear . . . what is your name?"

"I am Goat-dung, lowliest—"

"You are *what*?" Sean exclaimed, quite forgetting that there might be someone beyond the partition. Her wide, frightened eyes regarded him with embarrassment.

"I *am* called—"

"Not by me. Turn your back, little one, while I dress my wound. Then we are both leaving this place, and they will be minus one monster for roasting and one maiden for . . . well. We'll both go."

As he was washing the blood from his leg, he heard a tearing noise and a little hand came from around him, holding out a clean white strip. He turned his head over his shoulder and saw her industriously tearing up what must have been either her wedding dress or, more probably, her nightgown. Maybe both.

"Can you spare several more strips, little one?" he asked.

"All can be yours, man-monster."

Since they were going to escape together, he figured he could risk telling her his name now. "I am called Sean Shongili, little one."

Once he had cleaned the wound in the warm water, he had made two thick pads of the first strips, listening all the time to the frenzied outrage of the disappointed monster-burners. Then he wound more strips until he had a secure bandage on his leg.

Suddenly, the noise changed its direction and came toward them.

"Oh! They will search everywhere for you. That is why you ought to have gone to Coaxtl," she cried.

"Get undressed and into that tub, child," Sean ordered, "and throw your things over the stool against the wall. I can crouch half in and half out, and they won't be looking for me here, now will they?"

Courage the child did not lack, and between them, they arranged her clothing so that its folds afforded shadows where he could hide. Unless someone with very bright lanterns searched the entire little cubicle, he doubted he would be seen.

The child's screech was warning enough, and he huddled even more closely in on himself as the blanket across the opening was thrown open and a variety of bodies stepped in.

"Well, it couldn't have got this far with that wound," said a voice that Sean instantly recognized as Matthew Luzon's. The shock of hearing that voice in this environment kept him frozen motionless.

"It must have had help," snarled an angry voice. "It can't have gnawed through leather like that . . ."

"Ah, but Brother Howling, these monsters are capable of many things mere mortals cannot imagine."

So, Matthew has found a soul mate, Sean thought, and the very kind he could best use against us.

Goat-dung kept on screeching, a sound that occasionally became a gargle as she tried to keep as much of herself beneath the water as possible.

"Be quiet. You are not in danger, Goat-dung. Wait here. The monster has escaped. You are not to move until Ascencion comes for you. Hear me?"

"I hear and obey," the child said in a gargle. Sean heard the blanket being replaced; the intruders made a noisy exit out of the tent, going off in yet another direction.

Before Sean could even make his suggestion, the child was out of the bath and reaching for the scrap of a towel. She had discreetly turned her back on him, which gave him an even better view of the bruising and welts that marked her back from shoulders to buttocks, and even down to the calves of her tiny legs.

He handed her her clothing, and she was dressed and jamming her feet into boots with astonishing speed.

They exited the same way as Howling and Luzon, Goatdung's hand curled trustingly in Sean's. They ran in a crouch, seeking the shadows whenever possible, past the last of the tents that comprised the new locations of the Vale of Tears, and into the night.

Johnny explained as politely as possible that Lonciana could not accompany them to rescue La Pobrecita.

"Then Buneka must, for she will know her," Lonciana said.

"Well, you're not leaving me behind if I have to ride on top," Diego said staunchly. "If Bunny goes, I go, too."

No one even tried to deny him.

Carmelita and her sisters had told Bunny enough about La Pobrecita that Bunny was quite willing to help rescue her.

"Look, worst comes to worst," Bunny said, peering into the copter. "The Major has every reason to be down here, too, checking folks out, same as Matthew Luzon. And if Luzon doesn't help us get 'Cita out of the clutches of that pervert, he certainly won't want all his fine friends knowing he went along with a vile thing like that, now will he?"

Johnny looked at Yana, not as certain as Bunny that Luzon could be shamed into helping free Pobrecita just because she was in a tough spot and it was the right thing to do. From what Johnny had seen, Luzon was unacquainted with shame. Probably Luzon's friends, if he had any, were no more disturbed by doing "vile things" than he was.

"There is a CIS rule about forcing prepubescent children into marriage," Yana said. "Are we sure she *is* prepuberty?" She looked at Lonciana.

"She has no breasts, but that, starved as she was, is not the final test," Lonciana said with a scowl. "But she knows nothing about her courses, though she knows that there is a bleeding sickness and that some girls remain barren. She knows too much of the wrong things, La Pobrecita!"

"Okay, I'm game," Johnny said. "Checking up on Luzon's current whereabouts 'cause he's late to our rendezvous is within the scope of my orders from Dr. Fiske."

Precious time was spent in gathering the ore and loading it onto the shuttle so it could be hauled to SpaceBase. First Satok had to take the shuttle out to each village and set down in a remote area, make contact with the shanachie, and wait for the stuff to be brought and loaded. He certainly couldn't show his face at this stage, since the people of McGee's Pass had been turned against him by those outsider kids and half the village was trailing his ass with murder on their minds. He had to keep alert not only for human trackers but also for any of the spying, slinking felines that he knew carried information back and forth between the villages, though he'd never learned how they did it. Ought to have vivisected one of the sneaky buggers and tried to figure it out, he thought.

He ended up back at Savoy for the last load, and as the faded woman—Luka, that was her name; frag, you'd never know she was the same neat piece he'd first had—loaded the last of the ore on the shuttle, he thought of how much work it would be and announced to Reilly that he was taking her with him. "We'll look like a regular mom-and-pop placer mining team then," he told Reilly. "Besides, I need someone to help me unload the ore and do the grunt work."

"You're welcome to her," Reilly said. "Work's about all she's good for anymore, though she's a lazy slut and never lifts a finger without a beating."

"I'll bear that in mind," Satok told him, as he raised a mock-threatening fist to Luka, who cringed away from him as she obediently climbed into the shuttle.

It took four hours to fly to SpaceBase under ordinary circumstances, and with the craft loaded with ore, it took six. The base, which had always before been open, now boasted a fence and a gate, just beyond the bend in the swollen river that used to be the road to Kilcoole. The shuttle was an unauthorized one, and the ore was too valuable to simply put it within reach of the fingers of any passing soldier, so he set the craft down in the strip between the gate and the woods, where trees and underbrush had been recently cleared and burned—for security reasons, he suspected. The company seemed to be taking these hicks seriously. He left a cowering Luka locked in the shuttle and strode to the gate as if he were a bird colonel, at least.

The MP at the gate took in Satok's furs and leathers and his long hair, his shaman's feathers, and the cat skull, and shook his head while using a firm, sweeping motion of his forearm and index finger to indicate that Satok should go back the way he came.

"No unauthorized personnel allowed on base, sir. Orders of Captain Fiske."

The officious little jerk was more helpful than he meant to be. "Yeah, but that's who I came to see. Captain Fiske. Tell him Lance Corporal James Satok is here to see him about his mining operations." What the hell. He *had* been a lance corporal in the corps once.

"A little old to be a corporal, aren't you?" the kid asked, not bothering to add "sir" this time. "And I'd say you were way out of uniform."

"Is that what you'd say, lad? Is it really?" Satok leaned forward confidentially, his arm resting casually on the window of the gatehouse. "Well, now, that may all be very true, but I was a lance corporal just as you'll soon be if you're smart and don't interfere with me. I've a load of raw ores of just the sort the company has been looking for, and I can tell your Captain Fiske where the company can get more of them here."

"Oh, sure," the kid said with a sneer.

"Hey, if you don't believe me, come and look for yourself."

"I can't leave my post, and if you'd ever been in the corps, you'd know that."

"Son, I was in the corps long enough to know that playing by the rules too strictly can get you in as deep a pile of shit as not playing by them at all. The ore's in my vehicle, just over by the trees there. You can keep one eye on the fraggin' gate all the way. Just come and look and you'll see why you have to tell Fiske I'm here. Look, I might even be able to cut you in . . ."

Without a word, the guard unfastened the door and followed him to the shuttle.

"Now, the ore is back here," Satok said, pointing to the cargo area. The moment the guard turned, he hit him over the head with a thick lump of ore he'd set aside for such a use. Then he stripped him of his uniform and put it on. He also took the badge and weapon, which might come in handy. Throughout all this, Luka said nothing. As soon as Satok had the uniform and the weapon, he shook the boy awake.

"Now then, asswipe. How do I find this Captain Fiske?"

The boy, in thermal underwear only, looked about sixteen and his eyes were a little crossed. "He's not on the base," he said.

Satok turned the boy's weapon on him. "I'm tired of playing games with you, punk. You will answer at length and in depth. Where is Fiske and how do I get to see him?"

"But he ain't here. He's gone to Shannonmouth to meet with the special investigative team from the company. They're probably at the village meeting house."

"You've been so helpful," Satok said. He almost blasted the kid, then thought that if his sellout was going to lead to his being a solid citizen, maybe a fresh homicide wasn't the best way to begin his new life. So he tapped him with another piece of ore, gently but at the physiologically correct point to insure long unconsciousness, and left him in the woods.

Torkel Fiske danced attendance on Marmion de Revers Algemeine, giving her the complete lady-killer treatment, much to her well-concealed amusement. Though he looked much as Whit had looked at his age, and was really quite a charming boy, Marmion decided that he was totally lacking in his father's finesse. There was a somewhat febrile boyish quality about him that was not unappealing. However, it was coupled with a certain calculation and a certain lack of . . . depth? Soul? She wasn't sure.

She had prevailed on him to escort her to Shannonmouth because Sinead Shongili, sister of Sean, and Aisling Senungatuk, sister to Clodagh, were still there and she did want a chance to chat with them, as well as visit another of the small communities. She suspected they would be all much the same, but she couldn't present an in-depth report without some comparison.

There was something to be said about a landscape that was *still* a landscape, fresh-smelling and softly chartreuse as trees and shrubs responded to the precipitated springtime. There wasn't even that much mud on the trail to Shannonmouth: maybe "trace" was the better word, for the way they followed could barely be called a "road."

"Why aren't there connecting *roads* between the communities, Torkel?" she asked as her curly-coat delicately made its way.

Torkel regarded Marmion with something like openmouthed surprise, but the smile that followed gave her an uneasy feeling. "The very thing, Marmion, the very thing. I do believe we have shortchanged the locals by keeping them in virtual isolation." And he continued to smile until the houses of Shannonmouth appeared where the trace became wide enough to be termed a road, muddy and churned as it was, with rough boardwalks and stepping-stones connecting the houses and forming bridges from one side to another.

They could hear the dogs barking long before they caught sight of any humans, though there were curly-coats browsing here and there. Marmion was certain she saw the flick of an orange tail or two disappearing in the underbrush. She must get one of Matthew's boys—they did so like to do graphs and charts and reports—to do a census of the cat population of this planet, if the cats would stay still long enough in one place to have their orange noses counted. And dogs. And curly-coats.

With the animal "early-warning system" in excellent working order, most of the population had turned out by the time the visitors arrived. Marmion was delighted, but Torkel seemed less than pleased, especially as Sinead Shongili stood, feet braced as official welcoming committee, partially eclipsing Aisling Senungatuk.

"Sláinte, all. I do hope you don't mind us coming down here," Marmion said, smiling a greeting first to Sinead and Aisling and passing it around the circle of people. "But Shannonmouth is so close, and Clodagh didn't think you'd mind if we visited. Torkel was kind enough to show me the way, though I think now I could have found it on my own. The cats, you know. They wouldn't have let me make a wrong turn, nor Curly here." She affectionately slapped the pony's neck. Curly's ears twitched back and forth at the sound of her voice, but pricked forward again as it turned to Sinead.

Sinead's lips curved in a smile. "Sláinte, Marmion. You were expected and are welcome." She gave only a curt nod to Torkel. "Dismount here and Robbie'll take care of your curlies." She signed for a gawky youngster to come forward.

When both Marmion and Torkel had swung down onto the boardwalk, Sinead put one hand on Marmion's shoulder.

"This is Marmion de Revers Algemeine, of whom we have spoken, and you all know Captain Fiske," she said, and there was a murmur of sláintes and hesitant smiles. "Come." And with that Sinead turned on her heel and led the way.

Torkel muttered something under his breath about primitive manners and looked pointedly away from the swaying backside of Aisling. The villagers fell in behind the guests.

"Did all the plants survive the journey?" Marmion asked.

"Oh, yes, they did," Aisling said, bubbling with pleasure.

"And Aigur and Sheydil have some for us to take back. It'll be such a marvelous summer for plantings. One of the best we've had."

"To that point," Torkel said, striding to Aisling's side and smiling broadly, "something Dama Algemeine mentioned, you know, I think Intergal really should see to building good roads between villages, and proper greenhouses so you don't have to wait until full spring to have your gardens started."

"Really?" Sinead stopped in her tracks to stare at him. Aisling nearly ran into her. Before she did, Sinead was once more striding forward, or, rather, stretching to meet the next board on the haphazard walkway. "How nice!"

Marmion saw Torkel Fiske flush at such an unenthusiastic reaction to what was, for him, an extraordinary concession. She thought she approved of Sinead's patent skepticism. However, before Torkel could get himself in deeper or prejudice the notion completely, Sinead was marching up the porch steps of a house that had cats sunning themselves all over its patchwork roof of recently replaced shingles, their orange coats an odd contrast to the raw wood. Lounging on the sunny end of the porch were two intertwined track-cats. Marmion saw Torkel give a little shudder. They were large, Marmion realized, but so intelligent. She could see it in the eyes of the one whose head was toward them: open only to slits, but the expression looked deliberate. The cats had probably known when she and Torkel had set out from SpaceBase, she mused.

"You'll be hungry," Sinead said, opening the door into a house that was rather sparsely furnished even by the Petaybean standards Marmion had observed thus far.

Then she saw the huge loom that took up most of the available floor space. Benches and chairs hung from nails on the walls; other things were up off the floor, too, to allow easy access to the loom. A woman was working shuttle and batten with a deftness that made the individual motions a blur—only the *clack-clack* as she changed combinations of harnesses provided any noise. She looked up from her work, nodded, smiled, and continued to concentrate on what she was doing.

"We brought provisions," Marmion said. "Oh! How silly of me not to grab my—"

The door opened again and the gawky youngster lowered the saddlebags to the floor and departed so swiftly that Marmion had to shout her thanks to the closing door. She then glanced apprehensively at the intent weaver to be sure she hadn't distracted the woman.

Sinead smiled. "That was good of you, but I think our larder can stand two extra mouths tonight."

"But I insist that you have the use of our supplies, Sinead. Clodagh said you were probably out of five-spice and—oh, what *was* the name of the other seasoning?" Marmion made for the saddlebags and began pulling out the bottles and sacks, and the dried foods that Clodagh had told her would be acceptable to any host. When she added the five-kilo sack of sugar, she said meekly, "I take so much sugar in my tea that I insist you have this. I promise not to use it all up, because there'll be berries to conserve so very soon now."

"That is very welcome indeed, dama," the weaver said. "For we'll have a fine crop, and soon, and there's nothing like a bit of jam to make pan bread a real treat."

"Aigur, this is the dama I told you about, and Captain Torkel Fiske."

Marmion's quick mind mused over the implication that no one had talked about Torkel at all, but then, her appearance would be more unusual than his. Still, she could see by the twitch of his lips that he caught the subtle insult. Really, the Shongilis were a delight, Marmion thought. A pity to have to spoil them. For that matter, why should they be spoiled? They were marvelous just as they were.

Tea was brewed and drunk, sweetened by Marmion's gift. Marmion brought Aigur's cup to her loom so that she could have a closer look at the intricate pattern. She couldn't resist fingering the texture and exclaimed at its softness.

"Curly-coat," Aigur told her

"It's such an amazing pattern. Some special order?"

"My daughter's marrying and this will be for their wedding bed," Aigur said proudly.

"Oh, it is stunning, but—" Marmion cut off the rest of her intended remark about how much weaving of this beauty and intricacy would bring in the sophisticated shops of her usual environment. "—such a labor of love," she concluded, smiling.

The problem with coming from her usual ambience to this one was that even the most mundane items were unusual, from and of this world, and *that* was where they should stay. She should not contribute to the despoiling of Petaybee. She was becoming more and more certain of that.

"As I said, Sinead," Torkel was saying, "we should really look into a network of roads between settlements, particularly over the passes."

"Oh?" Sinead raised her eyebrows in polite surprise. "Then Intergal *has* come up with an all-weather surface that can survive the temperature, wind-chill factors, permafrost sinkholes, and ice intrusion?"

Torkel ducked his head, smoothing his hair. "We will. We will. It's only a matter of time, Sinead, but a road system would certainly help."

"SpaceBase folks, perhaps, while you're 'investigating' Petaybee, but snocles in the winter suit us fine and can go many places you couldn't put a road that'd last a year or two, and the curly-coats manage slush, mud, and summer hard tracks. No, Captain Fiske, though we will all appreciate the thought, I don't think any road works are necessary. 'Sides which we don't have the personnel you'd need to construct them."

"The company has enough manpower and machinery for that and all it takes is convincing the board to spend the money to solve the surfacing problem, Sinead," Torkel repeated, and Marmion thought his voice just a trifle sharp. "Meanwhile, you wouldn't say no to teachers, and schools, and libraries, and viewers."

Aisling's mouth made a perfect O. "Oh, books would be marvelous, and schools for the children."

"They learn what they need to learn from their parents about how to live here," Sinead said bluntly.

"There is such a wide world out there," Marmion put in. Surely knowing more about the inhabited galaxy wouldn't really harm the children; it would merely give them other interests than the limited ones of this planet, however beautiful and diverse.

"Which they see soon enough if they join the company," Sinead finished blightingly.

"But, Sinead, there's more in books about how to do *our* things differently. And more stories . . ."

"And old songs from many ethnic traditions," Marmion put in. "And different instruments to play on . . ."

"We could sure use a few more decent fiddles," Aigur remarked, and then continued hesitantly, "and I'd like to know how to read and write. That way I'd be able to figure out some of the old patterns my great-great brought with her."

"Schools, teachers, reading, writing, arithmetic," Torkel said emphatically. "We've not paid sufficient attention to *your* needs." And he bowed smilingly at Aigur, whose eyes still shone with the prospect of being able to read.

Aisling leaned across the table and appealingly touched her partner's arm. "That would be good to know, Sinead dear. For everyone, and not having to join the company to get the learning."

"You must ask Clodagh," Marmion said firmly. She ignored the look Torkel shot her.

Sinead gave Marmion a long searching look. "We all admire and respect Clodagh, make no mistake, but something like this is decided by all the shanachies, not just one."

It was Marmion's turn to lean with an air of gentle petition to Sinead. "It is, however, a way of spreading this news to all the other villages for them to make up their minds, isn't it?" Marmion didn't smile at Sinead, but let her eyes dance with challenge.

To her surprise, Sinead threw back her head and laughed out loud, shaking her head and refusing to explain.

"Schools and elementary education, and power stations, too," Torkel went on, slowly building his case.

"Power stations?" Sinead was immediately antagonistic. "What for? To break down in a blizzard, to crash down on our homes in the high winds?"

"We've more sophisticated power sources than pylons, my dear," Torkel began.

"I'm not your dear, and we'd have no use for such power."

Torkel gave back as good as she gave, with raised eyebrows and a mocking expression. "No use for lighting that doesn't stink like sour milk? No use for power tools that cut your workload, could drive the harnesses of that big loom and save Aigur hours, heat your houses, water, so you could have a hot bath in your own home without having to trudge two miles to the volcanic springs?"

A silence fell in the room—even the cats on the roof ceased to move about—for one long moment while Sinead, face utterly expressionless, regarded Torkel. Marmion took good note of the shock, surprise, and consternation on the other two faces. Then suddenly Sinead shrugged, grinned, and made a good attempt to toss off her reaction.

"The hot springs are sort of social, Captain, and we don't have the need for power tools as you do at SpaceBase. Too expensive for us to buy, even with what trade items we have, but the matter is something for the villages to decide for themselves, the way we always decide what is good for us, and for our planet."

The sound of an airshuttle overflying the village distracted everyone.

"What the . . ." Torkel was on his feet and to the nearest window, craning his neck to get a view of what he knew had to be an unauthorized flight. Sounded like a light shuttle, too, and there shouldn't have been *any* of that type vehicle down here.

" 'Scuse me," he called over his shoulder and was out the door before he heard a response.

He caught a good glimpse of the battered rear end of the craft and its trajectory. Frag it! The loon was landing just outside Shannonmouth. As he plowed a direct course across the mud road, ignoring the boardwalks, he also caught just a flick or two of orange tails. Turning to look back over his shoulder, he saw that there wasn't a single cat on any of the roofs. The next thing he knew, he had tripped over a rock in the mud and measured his length in the thick gooey mud.

This did nothing to improve his humor. He got to his feet, scraping off as much as he could with his bare hands, then with a branch he savagely broke from a shrub, and finally with handfuls of moss from the trunks of trees. In a way, he realized, the accident had just helped him frame what he would say to the misbegotten asshole flyboy who had illegal possession of an illegal-size vehicle and— He stopped dead at the clearing where the craft had landed, and at the man sauntering across the bracken toward him, unshaven, despite the clean guard uniform he wore and the badge that identified him as SpaceBase personnel.

"Captain Torkel Fiske?" the man asked, and the voice somehow set off a memory in Torkel's mind: the voice, the stance, the swaggering insolence of a man in a common soldier's uniform.

"What in hell do you think you're doing, soldier? In an illegal vehicle, and here at a village site against the strictest orders . . ."

"Take it easy, Captain, I've got something on board this shuttle that you've been after for a long time."

"I doubt it," Torkel said. Then, before he could continue to outline the penalties and fines the man had already accrued against specific regulations, he saw a slatternly female figure appearing to lean casually against the frame. "What the frag!"

"Oh, I don't mean her," the man said, dismissing the

woman with a wave of his hand, "but I've heard you can't find ore on this planet, not no way and nohow."

Torkel had started moving toward the man and the shuttle again for the purpose of ending this farce when the man's taunting offer made him falter a stride or two. If he'd found ore on this bleeding planet . . .

"*You* have?" Torkel moved forward again, aware that his unkempt state was being observed by the man, who was now grinning. "Don't—mention—it," Torkel warned, with a pause between each word.

"Why should I care if you tripped and fell in the mud?" the man said, shrugging his shoulders and lifting his hands high, but he had the wisdom to remove the smile as Torkel approached him.

"You are . . ." Fiske paused for the man to identify himself.

"Satok . . . shanachie of McGee's Pass." The man narrowed his eyes at Torkel, immediately resuming his cocky manner. Then he pulled out a fold of the clean uniform he was wearing by way of explanation for his present garb. "Needed to find out where you were. You're a hard man to contact."

"The ore, man . . ."

"Trouble's been, you Intergal guys been going about your searching all wrong, and looking in the wrong places."

"Oh, have we?"

Satok gestured for the girl to back out of the way to let Torkel enter.

The shuttle was in no better condition inside, but the moment Torkel saw the crates of varied shapes and colors netted safely away from the piloting area, he ignored everything else. He had studied just enough geology to be able to recognize the variety of ores *known* to be available on Petaybee, even if none had actually been found here. He touched greeny copper-bearing rock, grayish tin, copper-red-orange germanium; he saw the gold vein through rock, and even emeralds embedded in clay.

"I can't deny you've found a variety of very interesting

items, Satok," he said with a nonchalance that was far from the exultant surge that he was experiencing at the sight of what they had spent years trying to locate on this iceball. "Small as this cargo is . . ."

"This cargo's a very small portion of what's easily available—if you know where and how to look for it."

"And you do?" Torkel challenged him.

Satok contented himself with a smug smile. "I can show you enough lode-bearing sites to make your eyes bug out."

Torkel jerked his head at the girl, wondering if Satok should be so blatant. Satok merely shrugged. Then his expression changed so abruptly that Torkel drew back in surprise; as Satok was raising a weapon, Torkel was already reaching for his own sidearm, but Satok was not shooting at him. He was aiming out the shuttle door at small darting orange figures, and firing until the clip was empty.

"Hate them bloody orange mothers!" His face was a rictus of an intense hatred. He calmly slammed another magazine into the hand weapon, and then gave a surprised exclamation. "What the . . ."

Torkel looked around to see the slatternly girl racing toward the cover of the trees, her sobs trailing back like the sounds of a lost soul, a tail protruding from one side of her body. But there were no corpses of orange cats on the ground—and that surprised Torkel as much as it did Satok.

"Frag it, I can't have missed!" Satok was shouting as he stared about. He jumped to the ground to peer under the shuttle's slanting prow.

"Forget them, Satok. They're unimportant."

"Yeah?" Satok snarled. His loss of poise gave Torkel a chance to seize control of the situation.

"Yeah! I want to see more of this sort of stuff," he told Satok. "And I want to see it as fast as you can get me to these mother lodes you rave about. But, first, I've got to go back to the village for a moment . . ." And Torkel cursed the necessity. He pegged Satok as an opportunist and unreliable. But if he'd come to find Torkel Fiske, he must also know that Torkel was the best officer at SpaceBase to deal with.

"Yeah, yeah, I guess so. But do we have a deal?" The man's eyes glittered with greedy anticipation.

Torkel assumed a casual pose. "That depends on how accessible this ore is."

"Far more accessible than you've any idea, Captain dear," Satok replied with the oily smile Torkel would have liked to wipe off his face.

"If that's the case, you may be sure that Intergal will be appreciative."

"As always?" The sneer was back as Satok leaned against the doorframe.

"Why don't you accompany me to town?" Torkel began, adding quickly when he saw the apprehension flash in Satok's eyes, "There's woods enough to hide you from prying eyes while I make my farewells . . . And there's no one to hear us talk out here." He gestured at the open clearing, the forests deserted even by small animals after the arrival of the shuttle.

Satok punched the button to close the shuttle door and gestured ironically for Torkel to lead the way.

During their walk, Satok mentioned that there were sixteen different locations where ore had been collected, claiming that all the deposits were extremely rich and, furthermore, were so accessible that the company had simply overlooked them time and time again. The man wouldn't be more specific, but the hold full of ore was proof in itself. Torkel was both delighted and infuriated. If the deposits had all been there, and so accessible, why had the best geological teams of Intergal failed where this miserable excuse for a man succeeded?

He left Satok on the edge of the village while he went on, resuming his attempt to brush the mud off his clothing as he walked. This time Torkel took the boardwalks, which were noticeably empty of pedestrians, and the long way around to Aigur's house. The damned cats were back, he noticed. As well he'd left Satok screened from the village and the tempting display of orange cats, or the man's hatred of the beasts might have overcome any sense he had.

Torkel noticed a mud scraper on the first step of the house and dutifully used it on his shoes. He heard some odd scurryings inside the house, and it seemed to him that he also heard a faint hissing overhead. Too late now. He rapped on the door: courtesy was always appreciated.

When the door opened to him, he wasn't so sure about that from the stony looks he received.

"I'm extremely sorry, Marmion, but an emergency's come up and the shuttle has come to collect me," he said with a disarming smile. "I really hate to abandon you like this." He turned to Aisling, and only then noticed that Marmion and the large woman were the only two in the place.

"Oh dear," Marmion said, "I had hoped to have longer . . ."

"I don't see why you can't, dear lady," Torkel said, smiling at Aisling. "Is it possible Sinead could guide Madame Algemeine back to SpaceBase, or would it upset her schedule too much?"

"Oh, and isn't it a shame, with you in a hurry, and Sinead not here to ask, but sure I couldn't speak for her and me, I'm hopeless in the out-of-doors," Aisling said, gushily, twitching her fingers through the fabric of her voluminous dress. "She won't be that long, and you've hardly had a chance to finish your coffee. Let me just heat it up a bit for you." She had already taken the cup and was lifting the kettle lid to check the water. "Ah, and that will be more pleasant to drink . . ."

"Really—" Torkel held up his hand, trying to forestall the courtesy. "I absolutely must return immediately to the shuttle and—"

"Good heavens, Torkel, did you fall in the mud?" Marmion asked. "Is there a brush about, Aisling?" She'd taken up a kitchen towel and was advancing on him. "A stiff one, so we can get the rest of this off. You don't want to ruin your reputation by appearing back at SpaceBase looking like something a cat dragged in, do you, Torkel?"

Torkel tried to reassure her that he could change the moment he returned, and anyway, it had dried out and wasn't a problem, but this did not suit Marmion de Revers Algemeine. Controlling his temper, Torkel was forced to submit to their ministrations. He hoped that Satok didn't take it into his head to disappear.

It took a long time to get him neat enough for Marmion's satisfaction, and by that time Sinead had returned from her errand. Immediately, she agreed that she and Aisling had better return to Kilcoole and could certainly guide Marmion back to the SpaceBase.

Torkel was nearly quivering with rage and frustration by the time he was allowed to leave. As if to deliberately delay him further, Marmion thought of a message she'd better send to keep others from worrying about her. It took time to find paper and a stub of a pencil Aigur used for making pattern drawings, but in the end, with the note in his cleanly brushed pocket, he was allowed to leave.

"Where the frag have you been?" Satok demanded. "I didn't expect you to take the rest of the day to get back to me." His hirsute face turned even slyer than before. "You didn't make some private deal for yourself in there with the company on a private comm unit, did you?"

"Don't be stupid," Torkel snapped, striking out toward the clearing and the shuttle. They walked in tense silence for the twenty minutes or so it took to reach the shuttle. Torkel banged the Open button, then swung into the shuttle and took the passenger seat while Satok closed the door and assumed the pilot's place. They took off and headed northward.

Back in Aigur's cabin, Marmion looked sadly down at the limp body of the orange cat. Her throat was tight; she really wanted to weep at the sight of the beautiful intelligent little animal laid low by such a savage attack. A track-cat was gently licking the graze wound across the smaller creature's spine. She and Aisling had shielded the cats from Torkel's view by hiding them behind the covered loom frame, but now the big cat tended its smaller cousin while the girl who had first brought it to Aigur's house looked on agitatedly.

"Can't we do more for the poor thing?" she asked, wringing hands covered with rock dust and bleeding from scrapes and scratches.

"Now, now, the cat's already getting the best treatment possible, really, Luka," Sinead told her. Sinead's hands, like Aigur's, were covered with dust, scrapes, and bruises. She'd had to keep them in her pocket while Torkel was present. "Takes a lot to kill one of these cats, and the others all escaped without injury."

"But will this one be all right?" Luka sobbed. "Satok killed all there were in McGee's Pass, you know."

"We'll know if the spine has been damaged when it regains consciousness, but I don't think Patchog would be cleansing the wound if he didn't think the cat had a chance."

Marmion watched the exchange with interest. Shortly after Torkel had left to investigate the arrival of the shuttle, Luka had arrived, bearing the cat's limp body in her arms and crying. Entrusting the cat to Aisling's tender ministrations, she had turned away from Marmion to whisper urgently with Sinead and Aigur.

Immediately Sinead had turned to Marmion. "There's something we have to do now. I can't tell you what or why, but Aisling will stay with you and help you, if you'll agree to detain Fiske and any guest he might have with him when he returns for as long as you possibly can."

"But why can't you tell me?" Marmion had asked, a little offended.

Sinead gave her a warning look, which told Marmion enough right there. This was not something that they didn't want her to know, but something that, for the sake of her position, she should not want to know. She had nodded agreement and quickly helped Aisling conceal the cats as the other women disappeared into the village.

Now Torkel and his companion had gone, leaving Luka, who had been weeping for many reasons, only one of them the injury to the cat. She seemed ashamed and frightened, chagrined and relieved, and wept with all of these emotions, stopping finally as her tears fell on Marmion's soothing hand. She looked at that elegant hand on her filthy, torn dress and then up at the kindliness in the beautiful face.

She looked to Sinead and the others. Sinead, searching Marmion's face, nodded sharply.

"All right, ma'am, I'll tell you now," Luka said. A sly smile curved her mouth until the recently cut lip made her wince. She snuffled, wiped her nose on the back of her hand, and then began to explain what facts she knew, repeating, evidently verbatim, conversations she had overheard.

She spoke of a man who had been one of the outcasts of Petaybee, who had never known what even Marmie had experienced in the cave, who had joined the company after turning against his own planet, and joined pirates after turning against the company, as well. Luka herself had been dazzled by him when he first came to McGee's Pass, claiming he was there to help them over the grief following their great tragedy. "That was before I knew he was after causin' it himself, ma'am. He as much as killed the McConachies, he did, and convinced us all, the devil, that the planet had turned against us. All the time he was takin' from the sacred place, though I didn't know how or why until I was well away from there, I swear I didn't. When I started gettin' suspicious and would have returned to my own people, he gave me to one of his bloody accomplices, as if I was a sack of beans, and that man told all in the village that I my own self was a reject, one Petaybee cast out and made mad. All the time they were takin' stuff out of the planet, and I learned that they was killin' it in bits, so that it couldn't harm them when they took from it. But I heard him say that when the little girl from Kilcoole came and he was found out, that now was the time to sell out to the company, and he brought everything to show yer man the captain. So I got the notion, even then, that maybe when the captain looked, what was in the shuttle wouldn't be of any interest to him, but would have changed to common rock. Sinead and Aigur here helped me, as did others in this town. But I fear we were too late, for the captain already saw the real stuff."

"Which you didn't," Sinead said. "So all you have is hearsay from us."

Marmion nodded wisely. "I see."

"But I'm that worried about what they'll do now, ma'am," Luka said. "For that evil man knows where more's to be found, and if the captain believes him . . ."

Marmion nodded, waving her understanding with elegant fingertips while her mind was already leaping ahead on the problem. Fiske in unwitting collusion with pirates? How far was he prepared to go for these little mining projects? She almost wished she didn't know as much as she did now, because the whole issue brought her into something of a conflict of interests. She felt great sympathy for the Petaybeans, but realized that her position as a nonpartisan investigator for the commission was already severely compromised.

"Ah well," she said. "The exchange was, of course, a very clever idea, although naturally I would have been forced to forbid it, had I known. Did Aisling and I give you enough time?"

Sinead snorted at the very notion that she couldn't organize a simple exchange like that, even if it had taken every available villager and every rock they could find in the clearing.

"I think we better start back now, dama," Sinead said.

"I would be honored if you would call me Marmion, as my friends do," she told Sinead, including Aisling, Luka, and Aigur in her glance.

Sinead gave her a thoughtful glance and for one dreadful moment, Marmion thought perhaps that she might not live up to the criterion Sinead Shongili expected of "friends." Her smile was much like her brother's and oddly shy, as if she did not give her friendship that often.

"Then we are honored ... Marmion. May we stop at Kilcoole first, though?"

"Of course, I was going to suggest that. Clodagh and Whit will have to be informed ... unless," Marmion added, smiling ruefully at the still able-bodied orange cats who had slipped in to join the big cat in its attentions to their fallen brother, "they already *know*."

"Some, but not all," Sinead replied with a smile, as she and Aisling began to pack up their belongings.

At first light, the weather did not look too encouraging, but Yana gave Johnny an appealing look as he turned from the window, and he threw up his hands in surrender.

"Might be damned bumpy," he told her.

"I'd risk more than that," Yana told him.

"Me, too," Bunny added. Diego only gave a sharp nod of his head.

Loncie insisted on packing them some food, which Johnny said he'd replenish on his next trip north.

"Ay, *de me*, and someone will go hungry here in the meantime? Off with you, *amigo*, and do not concern yourself with such details at a time like this. *Find* La Pobrecita, and *that* is more than enough."

When they were strapped into their seats, with Nanook crouched again in the rear, enduring his discomfort valiantly, Johnny took off. Once on a southeasterly course, he handed Yana an aerial map.

"I want you to double-check something for me. It seems to me the Lacrimas River runs pretty straight from the mouth, which is almost directly opposite Harrison's Fjord. Am I right?"

"I see what you're getting at," Yana said, unfolding the chart and giving it a shake as she searched it. "You think that the undersea tunnel might come up near the Vale of Tears?"

"Well, it's more of a possibility than you might think," Johnny said, not sure enough to mention *why* he thought it a possibility, even as he mentally matched the face of 'Cita with Bunny sitting behind him.

He shook his head. Shongilis all had unusual bone structure, so, unless Granddaddy Shongili had warmed a few beds he hadn't dared mention to his possessive wife, Johnny could think of only one logical conclusion.

Yana perused the map and gave a yelp of triumph as she found the two relative points; then, with a worried frown, she said, "Johnny, there's two thousand miles between the two continents!"

"Uncle Sean thought there'd be that at least," Bunny said, releasing her seat belt to lean over Yana's shoulder.

*"Belt up!"* Johnny said in a roar that reverberated in the small cabin and made Nanook snarl. "Sorry."

Yana passed the map over her shoulder to Bunny.

"We made it in about a hundred and fifty miles to the cave-in . . ." Bunny began, her voice trailing off. "That isn't very far . . . considering . . ." Her voice went on, slightly muffled as she bent down to Nanook's head. "You did say Uncle Sean was alive, didn't you?"

Nanook sneezed, and Bunny sighed, not completely reassured.

They traveled a long way in silence broken by Diego, who whistled odd little snatches of tunes and muttered to himself. The others respected that he might be working on a new song. Bunny looked out her window at the endless snow, shaded blues and grays and occasionally lavenders in the shadows. She could see the distant jagged teeth of spiky upthrusts and wondered which set of them rose above the Vale of Tears.

Then, just as they were approaching the general location of the Vale of Tears, they saw the glow of a huge campfire, sparks rising high above it. Bunny shouted unintelligibly, grabbing Johnny by the shoulder and pointing downward; at the same time, Nanook made a sudden attempt to squirm out from under the seat. Johnny issued loud orders for everyone to keep their places and shut their faces. Following Bunny's screeched directions, he circled the copter to starboard. Below, it was possible to see the three figures stumbling and falling down a hill, actually rolling in one case, leaving a pattern of bloody circles on the snow. One of the figures was feline. Nanook let out an ear-piercing yowl, a sound Bunny had never before heard a track-cat utter.

To her astonished gaze, the cat on the ground looked up, and she could see its jaws opening as if to give voice to a similar cry.

"Tighten your fragging seat belts, all of you," Johnny cried. His warning was unnecessary: his passengers could feel the turbulence he was fighting as he tried to land.

He was making a low pass to examine the dangerously uneven terrain below when Yana pointed to the bleeding man lying on the ground and cried out, "That's Sean down there!"

"And La Pobrecita with him," Johnny said. "I've still got to have a reasonably flat space to put this bird down without splintering a skid. Bear with me."

Using the three figures as the center, Johnny circled until he spotted a suitably level place. As soon as he landed, Yana, medikit in one hand and a bundle of extra winter clothing in the other, was out of the plane, Bunny and Nanook right behind her. Just as Johnny was about to follow, Diego pulled at his shoulder and pointed to the top of the rise and the swarm of folks coming over it, brandishing an odd assortment of armaments.

Johnny motioned for Diego to take the LD-404 down from its brackets over the entrance to the cargo bay as he checked that he had clips for his hand weapon and the spare automatic he hauled out from under his seat. Then the pilot and Diego followed the women and the track-cat.

Yana was kneeling beside Sean, wrapping him in the winter clothing and tending his wound. Bunny assisted in the medical chores, searching for the items in the medikit Yana demanded. The track-cats stood about six meters from each other, sniffing, tails twitching amiably enough. The child, in a fur jacket much too large for her, was huddled against the clouded cat, wide eyes in a frightened white face.

Diego caught Johnny's arm, staring a question at him as he pointed his free hand at the child. Johnny grinned and nodded, and then turned to watch the progress of the mob slipping and sliding down the hill toward them.

" 'Cita, Señor Luzon is as bad a man in his own way as Shepherd Howling," Johnny said in a gentle voice, bending down to the child. "Loncie was real upset to see you got talked into going with him. So we came to take you away, back to your own people."

"This unworthy one has no people," 'Cita said, getting an even firmer grip on Coaxtl's fur.

"That's where you're wrong, kiddo," Johnny said. "Bunny, come here. *Now*, pronto!"

Both Yana and Bunny looked around, their faces showing disgruntlement at being interrupted. Both stared, and Bunny's mouth dropped wide open.

"You must be—you can't be anything else . . ." Bunny's hand wandered to her cheek, her nose, her lips.

"Your mother made it through, niece of mine," Sean said, nodding solemnly, looking from Bunny's face to the thin gaunt one of a child who was so obviously a blood relative.

"But I am Goa—"

"Don't you dare use that name for yourself, Pobrecita," Johnny said, angrily shaking his finger at her. "Buneka Rourke, this is your sister, though I think we can find a better *proper* name for her than 'Cita, or Niña, don't you think?"

"A sister!" And Bunny was folding the startled child into her arms. "A sister of my very own! Everyone I know has at least a sister or a brother, and all I've ever had were cousins . . ."

"And uncles and aunts," Sean prompted through gritted

teeth as Yana yanked the bandage to make sure it was firm about the jagged arrow wound.

"Hey, we got trouble," Diego said, staring up the hill. "If that isn't Matthew Luzon, my name's not Diego Metaxos, and I do know my own name!"

"And the good and reverent Shepherd Howling, too, I'll wager," Johnny added, noticing the man in flowing robes beside the Intergal vice-chairman.

"Oh, he's come for me. He'll make me marry him . . ."

*"Marry him!"* burst from five throats.

"Not while *we* live!" Johnny said in a voice that sounded much like the snarls issuing from both track-cats. "Bunny, get your sister into the copter and stay there!"

"She's my sister and I've the right—"

"Go," Sean said and pointed to the copter. "Lock the doors."

"There's a box of flares, Bunny. Get 'em out, and if you see me circle my hand, aim 'em at that crowd."

"Gotcha!" And, lifting her sister into her arms, Bunny sprinted back to the safety of the copter. Push come to shove, she'd fly it out of there herself—she'd watched Johnny often enough to understand the principles of the yoke and the gearing. No one was going to get *her* little sister, not when she'd just found her.

Johnny handed Yana the automatic and the clips, slapping Sean's hand away when he tried to get the weapon.

"You handle the cats, Sean. That is, if the clouded one will take orders like Nanook will," Johnny suggested.

Both cats growled low in their bellies, making their necks vibrate as they took positions on either side of Sean Shongili.

The crowd's noise had died to a murmur. Matthew and Shepherd Howling led the pack by several strides.

"Well, Dr. Luzon, you've led me quite a hunt," Johnny called when the men were near enough to hear him.

"While you, Captain Greene, did not reappear as you promised."

"Oh, I reappeared, Dr. Luzon, just as I said I would, but

you'd taken off in old Scobie's beat-up snocle. My compliments on your driving to get that snow bucket this far."

Shepherd Howling raised one arm, his robe falling back over his bony wrist, pointing to the copter. "The child Goat-dung is one of my flock and is about to become one with me, to the salvation of her humanity. You must return her to my protection. I don't care what error you infidels fall into or what the Great Monster does to you, but she must be returned to me, and the monster who abducted her, as well."

"Well, now, sir, I can't rightly do that," Johnny said.

"Watch who you're calling a monster, you abomination," Sean snarled. "This child is my niece, and she is and will remain with her closest relative. I, her uncle, and male guardian, did not condone and *will not* condone a marriage for the child to anyone."

Shepherd Howling looked from Sean's face to the wound on Sean's leg, and back to his face again, his eyes widening with horror. "You! You were the monster! The seal man! Then the girl—she, too, is a monster."

"Monster?" Yana challenged, inserting herself between the injured Sean and the self-proclaimed Shepherd. "I only see one monster here, and it isn't Dr. Shongili. Do you always throw lethal weapons at visitors, Mr. Howling?"

"He was no visitor when we first saw him," Shepherd Howling blathered. "He looked like a seal at first and then started—growing. And he came from the underworld via the portal from which all of the damnable abominations of this planet emanate!"

"Nonsense," Yana snapped. "He was exploring an underground passage where his pregnant sister and brother-in-law disappeared many years ago. You're making up this incredible story to prevent further inquiry into your own abominable activities."

"I very much doubt that," Matthew Luzon said, smiling unctuously. "When I arrived, all of the Shepherd's flock were exclaiming about the monster they had found and were preparing to burn it over an open fire. I didn't see the beast myself, but I was naturally trying to prevail upon the Shepherd to allow me to study it rather than destroy it, to take it back to the laboratory and run some tests. Since Dr. Shongili's wound corresponds with that of the beast, I'd say he has some explaining to do."

"I'd say you had more, Dr. Luzon," Yana said in a voice so cold it made Johnny shiver, "for I'm reasonably certain you would know the paragraphs in Collective Interplanetary Societies' regulations—which apply to Intergal as well as the rest of inhabited space—about forced or child marriages."

"But, Major Maddock, all during her return trip to her home here in the Vale of Tears, Goat-dung—"

"Phah!" Sean exploded.

"The child," Matthew went on, "told me how happy she was to be coming home to such an auspicious marriage."

"How many wives have you at the moment, Shepherd Howling?" Yana demanded.

" 'Cita mentioned five," Sean said icily. "Also against the customs of this planet which do not, to the best of my knowledge, sanction polygamy."

"Now now, Dr. Shongili. We mustn't be ethnocentric," Matthew said with his smile still in place. "We must allow religious communities their own mores and folkways and rites, however strange they may seem to us."

"Not with *my* niece," Sean said.

"And how can you *prove* that you are her uncle?" Matthew demanded.

"Hell, man, that's so obvious, it's the stupidest question you've asked so far," Diego Metaxos said, sputtering in his rage and turning the LD-404 in the Shepherd's—and Matthew Luzon's—direction.

"Young man," Matthew began, "you are in grave danger of—"

"Let's save the talk for a more appropriate time," Yana said, noticing Sean beginning to sway with fatigue and pain. "Captain Greene came to collect you, Dr. Luzon, so we'll do just that and leave these people to sort their sordid little folkways by themselves in whatever way they care to, so long as it doesn't involve Dr. Shongili or his niece or any of the rest of us, for that matter."

Matthew Luzon turned his back on her to appeal to the Shepherd, who was swelling with righteous indignation and anger. "Shepherd, you can see what the investigation is up against. These people all justify each other's views, and no dissenting voice is allowed to be heard. If only you would appoint an apostle to lead your people while you come with me and speak to the commission on your views of the effects this planet has on people, justice would be far better served . . ."

The Shepherd's eyes widened with interest, and he nodded as Matthew spoke.

Johnny Greene cut them off short. "If you think I'm bringing that one back in the same plane with that little girl, Dr. Luzon, I'd think again very carefully," Johnny said. "Not to mention the fact that we'd be grossly overloaded for the fuel I have on board."

"You can refuel at Bogota, man," Matthew snapped back, "and you know it as well as I do."

"I have a wounded man, Dr. Luzon, which requires me to take the straightest route back north." Johnny jerked his head at Yana and Diego to help Sean back to the copter. "So this captain limits his passengers to those in jeopardy and those he originally ferried over. You, of course, are one, sir, but I can't authorize another passenger. So if you don't care to join this flight, Dr. Luzon, I'll be happy to request that other transport collect you, and your guest, ASAP!"

"Why, you . . ." Luzon's eyes sparked with suppressed anger.

"Captain Greene, sir, yes, sir, attached to the exclusive service of Dr. Whittaker Fiske, sir." Johnny held the eye contact.

Suddenly, suspiciously, Luzon capitulated, saying in a deceptively pleasant tone of voice, "Then, as soon as you are airborne, you will contact SpaceBase and request the immediate departure of a copter to collect myself, my assistant, and my guest. Is that plain? Any delay in the dispatch of that request will be a matter of record and dealt with appropriately. Do I make myself clear to you, Captain Greene, in the service—for the time being, that is—of Dr. Fiske?"

"Plain as day, sir. Thank you, sir. Good day, sir. And to you, sir," Johnny said, snapping salutes at both Luzon and the astonished Shepherd Howling.

Then with a smart about-face, he leapt over a hillock and proceeded as fast as the terrain permitted back to the copter.

He took off, aware of the moans of Coaxtl, who had never endured such an experience, and the purring reassurances of Nanook, who found himself suddenly braver about flying.

No sooner was Johnny in the air than he switched channels on the comm unit, grinning as he did so. "Hey, there MoonBase, this is Bravo-Jig-Foxtrot four-two-nine-one, Captain Johnny Greene, calling in for the immediate—I repeat—the immediate dispatch of a copter to these coordinates—" He read them out. "—to collect Intergal Vice-Chairman Matthew Luzon, assistant, and guest passenger. This is top priority. Please log in request immediately as of 1940.34.30."

"You got yourself in Luzon's bad books, honey?" asked a female voice.

"Me, MoonBase? Not me," Johnny replied in his most ingenuous tone. "Is that Neva Marie's voice in my ears?"

"The very one."

"Well, listen up, Neva Marie, because Luzon is in urgent need of transport, and I cannot seem to make contact with either SpaceBase or any airborne copters planetside. So cut loose one of those light shuttles and let one of your bush-pilots have some fun. Landing's dicey, so tell him to be careful where he sets down. Oh, and off the record, bring a real strong deodorizer!"

"Beg pardon?"

Johnny repeated his last remark and grinned at Yana over his shoulder. "You got this request logged in proper and on the dot?"

"Like you said—and the off the record is *off* the record."

"Neva Marie, I owe you."

A low chuckle preceded the sign-off as the dispatch officer purred, "I'll give a good deal of thought to that, Johnny. Over and out. Shuttle pilot scrambling as of right now. 1943.30.02."

"Won't he get back to SpaceBase faster than we will?" Bunny asked anxiously from the snocub, where she had strapped herself and her sister in. That way, Sean had room to stretch out his injured leg while Yana cushioned his upper body against hers. Diego sat up front with Johnny.

"Possibly," Johnny replied carelessly. "The important aspect is that the request was logged in as we were taking off. And I *know* for a fact that all the SpaceBase copters are being used by Luzon's men for 'field research.' " He chuckled to himself and then raised his voice. "Bunny, how's your sister traveling back there?"

"Fine, Johnny, just fine! I'm thinking what name we should give her."

"Why not give her your mother's, Bunka?" Sean asked in a low tone that hid much of the fatigue he was feeling from all save Yana. She could feel his body spasming and shivering from his recent ordeal and clasped him more tightly to her. "Your dad had his way with yours."

"Aoifa Rourke!" Bunny savored the name, which she pronounced properly as "Eeefa." "Your name, your real name, your heart's name, is Aoifa, 'Cita. But, if you feel safer, we will only call you 'Cita."

There was a sleepy mumble, and very shortly there was silence from all Johnny's passengers, though Diego's lips moved frequently, soundlessly.

# 13

Johnny landed his passengers at Kilcoole; then, once he and Diego had carried Sean into Clodagh's house, he flew on to report to Whittaker Fiske at SpaceBase.

"That's very interesting, son," his boss said when Johnny had completed the debriefing. "Found the lost Rourke child and brought Shongili back, too. You didn't happen to spot Torkel anywhere down there, did you?"

"No, sir, I didn't." Johnny kept private his notion that the presence of Captain Torkel Fiske would have been one burden too many. "Is he with one of the other investigative teams?"

Whit shook his head and then dismissed that problem with a wave of his hand.

They both looked up at the unmistakable rumble of a shuttle coming in to land.

"Cut it fine, didn't you, son?" Whit grinned as he rose. "I'd best go out and see what I can do to pacify Matthew."

"Sir, I had wounded . . ."

Whittaker Fiske nodded vigorously, raising his hand to reassure his copter pilot. "You did exactly as you should. And so did Major Maddock. The very idea of polygamy, especially for a religious purpose, with a prepubescent child is revolting in this day and age. *And* specifically against the Collective Interplanetary Societies' Bill of Individual Rights. Better get that copter serviced, son. I want it kept ready to scramble."

Johnny raised his eyebrows, hoping for a little off-the-record advice, but Whittaker's expression suggested that he tend to his current orders.

Contrary to Whittaker's expectations, he received neither call nor visit from Matthew Luzon, nor was there a complaint officially logged in against Captain John Greene. Nor, during that day, was there any message from his son or a whisper concerning his whereabouts. Only the matter of a concussed guard found at one of the side access gates to SpaceBase.

Torkel Fiske was angry enough, but Satok was livid with rage, kicking at the crates, splintering half a dozen, and paying no attention to the rocks that bounced down on his boots, as if he welcomed the pain. Torkel also listened to the invective Satok cast on the head of that slatternly Luka and what he intended to do to her when he found her again. From the brief glimpses he'd had of the girl, Torkel could not quite believe that she had had the intelligence, much less the strength, to remove all the genuine ore samples, which Torkel had himself handled and seen, in the time they'd been absent from the shuttle.

Without proof of the find, however, the commission would pay scant attention to Satok and might reach their decision before the man could gather more samples. There were other ways to assert company control of this planet, of course—the company-built and maintained roads, power plants, hospitals, and schools Torkel suggested to Marmion. All in the name of taking care of the colonists, of course. If they were better treated, more civilized, they'd be more cooperative. Especially when the planet was overrun with corps troops—not originally from Petaybee: he'd make sure of that this time—doing the building and maintaining. Especially if company doctors also made sure that the physiological aberrations peculiar to Petaybeans were studied and eliminated, and if birth control was strictly monitored so that the Petaybeans at no time grew too numerous to control. Company teachers would slant their curriculum to insure the loyalty of their students, and company communications systems would insure that inhabitants, both original and new to the planet, accepted the company agenda and kept the company side of any dispute foremost in their minds at all times. And if they didn't, troops could travel by company roads to make sure people remembered their manners.

And the planet? The living planet? Within himself, Torkel didn't sneer at the idea. Petaybee was sentient. He knew it. He had felt it, seen it, heard it himself. But that didn't mean he liked it. That Satok had stolen ores from the body of the beast itself impressed Torkel no end—but only if the man could *show* the lodes. All they had in the shuttle were common rocks and dust. The ore was no better than the fairy gold of Grandmother Fiske's bedtime stories.

He would have preferred to play with his coin collection or dissect a roundworm before bedtime, but Grandmother Fiske, who, he supposed, was responsible for the weird streak in his father, was a great believer in the twentieth-century philosopher Joseph Campbell. She thought that children needed myths and fairy tales to inform their lives. She had never understood him, Grandma Fiske. Torkel was an explorer, a womanizer, and a developer precisely because he loathed mysteries. He liked everything well explained.

And now he and Satok both would have some explaining to do if they were going to convince the company commission that Petaybee contained secrets valuable enough for them to make the necessary investments to civilize and control the planet. At the moment, all he had to show was one green hunk of copper-bearing rock and one small gold nugget that had rolled out of the crates into a dark corner.

"That was a good trick," he told the still-fuming Satok. "I don't know how you treated these rocks to make them appear to be the ores I thought they were, but in this state they'll never convince the commission." He knew as well as Satok that the ores had been replaced by Luka and those Kilcoole women, if not by a conspiracy of the whole village of Shannonmouth, but he wanted to force Satok to reveal more. As long as the man kept his secrets to himself, they were of no use to Torkel or the company.

"There's more where those came from," Satok growled.

"And where, exactly, is that? McGee's Pass?" The man had said he was shanachie there, so Torkel's guess wasn't that wild. Space probes had shown some ores in that general area.

But Satok shook his head. "Nah, that vein's played out for now. But I got other sources. Only thing is, and the reason I decided to cut the company in, I need supplies. For my method."

"Like what?"

Satok grinned for the first time since they'd discovered Luka's treachery. "That's right, Cap'n. When I tell you what I use, you think you're gonna have some ideas about my method. And you will have. Only thing is, it's somethin' you've been using all along. What I need the most is Petraseal. You get some of these boys to load up the shuttle with Petraseal, and I'll get you some more ore samples within a couple of days."

"I go with you and you show me," Torkel said, negotiating, "and I'll get you all the Petraseal you want."

But the hairy bastard had the gall to shake his head. "No way. Not till I have a contract with the company patenting my methods and with full claim to my sites."

"You can't get that without proof," Torkel said.

"Well, without my help, man, you can't get samples of ores you need for proof the planet's worth something to Intergal, so I guess if you don't get me my supplies, we're both out of luck."

"All right," Torkel said on a long exasperated sigh. "I'll release you the Petraseal. But go get those samples ASAP, okay? I'm not sure how long the commission is going to take to come to their conclusions."

"Then have your boys start loadin' my shuttle. Oh, and fuel 'er up while you're at it, will you?"

Torkel agreed, still seeming reluctant for the sake of verisimilitude. Actually, he would go along whether Satok agreed or not. He could easily plant a bug and track the man to his mine. He could even invite the commission along to see the results of the new mining operation first-hand, and learn something of Satok's secret process while they were at it.

Birds—songbirds, ravens, ducks, geese, hawks, and herons—brought them, as did relays of rabbits, foxes, wolves, feral cats, tame cats, track-cats, bears, and squirrels. Each bird, each animal, carried in its mouth a cutting, a root, a shoot, of coo-berry bramble. The birds flew directly to the farthest points, to Deadhorse, Savoy, Wellington, Portage, Mirror Lake, Harrison's Fjord, and McGee's Pass. Following the cats' directions, they dropped the shoots near the planet's portals, the places where humankind could commune with Petaybee. The largest deliveries went to the places where the planet was at its most open and vulnerable, and could be most easily looted. All of these places were caves, and around the entrance of each cave and on the ground above the entrance, and all along the length of the cave, the shoots and roots and cuttings were dropped by birds and buried by the other animals, the badgers, the squirrels, the rabbits, and the foxes. Every quarter of an hour or so for two days, fresh bits of coo-berry bush arrived, supplied by the tireless efforts of Clodagh, Whittaker Fiske, and assistants from the town and the surrounding forests and tundras of Kilcoole.

In most places, the increased and highly specialized activity of the animals was little more than a curiosity. In some places, no one even noticed what was going on. At McGee's Pass, Krisuk Connelly and his family, who had been keeping watch on Satok's old house, noted the odd influx of animals and, between deliveries, sneaked in to see what they could possibly be doing.

The coo-berry plant was one of the planet's great puzzlements. Most things on Petaybee were good for many things: medicine, food, shelter, warmth. Coo-berries had never been much good for anything. They were poisonous if you ate more than a handful, and the ailment that might have been devised by the planet to cure it had yet to be discovered. The thorns were sharp and stingy, the leaves were sticky, and the blossoms were as small, and rare, as the coo-berry itself. Once they got a start on any little dab of dirt, the damned bushes were almost impossible to kill. Worse, they grew so fast you could watch them grow, which was what Krisuk spent two days doing: watching the infestation of coo-berry. While the birds were still ferrying shoots in daily, bushes sprang up from the first plantings and grew waist high overnight, their roots spreading out to cover the field between the town and Satok's house and climbing up the house's stone exterior and covering the outbuildings.

When that happened, Krisuk called the whole village to come and see. His mother's mouth was set in a bitter line and her dry eyes watched the incursion despairingly. *"Now,"* she said, *"now* Petaybee *is* punishing us. For ever listening to Satok. For letting him harm it."

Matthew Luzon resisted the urge to hold his nose. Really! The things he did for the company in the name of humanity. To say the least, Brother Howling smelled extremely gamy. Even Braddock was tempted to open the helicopter's door to escape the stench and showed signs of wanting to divest himself of his most recent meal over the ice-speckled sea.

At least the headphones in this helicopter worked properly, and Matthew could occupy himself by listening to the pilot's transmissions and the messages received from SpaceBase and MoonBase.

As they approached land again at Harrison's Fjord, a crackling message came in from MoonBase.

"Captain Torkel Fiske requests that all council members get in touch with him immediately. He is currently tracking the activities of the shanachie of McGee's Pass."

Matthew needed to hear no more. McGee's Pass was on

the way back to SpaceBase from Harrison's Fjord, and a break from his present company would be most welcome.

"Take us directly to McGee's Pass, pilot," he ordered, and the man gave him a thumbs-up signal and headed up the coast.

As they approached the pass, Matthew saw that the village was built on an incline, gradually scaling the foothills leading up to the pass itself.

"Well, for frag's sake!" The pilot cursed as he flew beyond the village over a field heavily overgrown with vines stretching from the houses all the way to a stone farmstead about half a mile distant. "What the frag have they done to the fraggin' helipad?"

"Set it down anywhere, man!" Matthew commanded. "The plants'll cushion the skids."

The pilot sounded doubtful as he said, "Well, okay. You're the boss, Dr. Luzon."

Finally, someone who did as he was told, Matthew thought with relief.

The pilot landed, crushing a good half meter into the surrounding vegetation. When he made no move to leave the aircraft, Matthew impatiently tore open the door and leaped out, and instantly regretted it.

His legs caught fire all the way to his crotch, and thousands of tiny needles stung through his pants, boots, and undergarments to tear at his flesh with each tiny movement.

In fact, he didn't even have to move. The wind from the copter rotors drove the plants all around him. Involuntarily, he screamed. Braddock jumped down to help him, and he, too, began to scream.

The Shepherd Howling stood in the doorway, one hand uplifted, his mouth moving and his other hand pointing.

"What?" Luzon managed to ask as the chopper engines stopped.

"The Great Monster has thee in its grasp!" Shepherd Howling cried. "Beware!"

"For pity's sake, man, it's no great monster, just some sort of vine!" Matthew screeched. "Help!"

A young man sitting atop a rock that was a virtual island in the sea of stinging brambles called out, "Can I help you, sir?"

"Get us out of here!" Matthew demanded.

"Ah. Your aircraft will be the safest place for that, sir. I suggest you get back in it before the vines overgrow it."

"What? No plant can grow that fast!" Braddock replied, doubting his own words as he unsuccessfully tried to disentangle the vines from his legs.

"The Great Monster is devious and wily and tireless in clutching for the souls and bodies of virtuous men!" Shepherd Howling declaimed.

"Indeed!" Matthew snapped at him. He turned to the boy. "If I wished to return to the helicopter I would never have landed here, young man. Please assist us out of these weeds and take us to your shanachie and Captain Fiske at once."

"Never heard of no Captain Fiske," the boy called back lazily, obviously enjoying their situation, "and we run the shanachie off."

"Did you?" Matthew stood among the stinging brambles and digested that.

"You heard him, sir. Let's get out of here," Braddock whined.

But any inclination Matthew might have had to do just that had vanished with the boy's words. "Now why did you do that, son?"

"He was a wicked man, sir. Tryin' to make us think the planet wanted one thing when it wanted the other."

"I'd very much like to talk to you about that, son. Please get us out of here." Matthew, despite the stings, turned on the force of his not inconsiderable charisma.

The boy shrugged and disappeared. Matthew and Braddock shoved Shepherd Howling back and sat in the copter while a crew of villagers arrived with various stones and pieces of board to make a path for them. Matthew was somewhat surprised that they hadn't brought machetes or sickles to hack the weeds down. Before he could ask about that, the boy ran across the stones and grabbed him by the arm.

"You'd best hurry, sir, or the coo-brambles will be a-growin' over these, too, like."

"You will be rewarded by the company, my son," Shepherd Howling said, pushing Matthew aside to sprint over the stones with the agility of a mountain goat. The speed with which he took advantage of the temporary path and his nimbleness in avoiding questing bramble tendrils caused Matthew to reevaluate the man's degree of insanity.

Matthew followed quickly, Braddock somewhat more reluctantly. The pilot opted to remain with his ship.

With the boy leading them, Shepherd Howling on his heels, and Matthew followed more slowly by Braddock, they reached the nearest of the hovels. There they were joined by a man and woman and a pack of whooping children. The rest of the village crowded in after them.

Shepherd Howling slowed to hover noisomely by Matthew. "This is possibly a wholesome place, Brother Luzon. None of the orange minions of the underworld one sees in many of the heathen towns are visible. And nowhere did I see the monster's yawning maw waiting to be fed by the ignorance of the unenlightened."

"That is good news," Matthew said tersely, and turned to their adolescent guide. He was far more interested in what the villagers had to say.

"Now, my boy, you must explain something to me, for I am a bit confused. I was supposed to meet Captain Fiske and the shanachie of this village here. Now you tell me you've banished the shanachie. Being a stranger to this planet, but one very interested in your customs, have I indeed been brought to McGee's Pass?"

"That's where you are, sir," said the woman of the house, undoubtedly the boy's mother, pushing herself to the front. "And the best way to explain, sir, is by singing you the song we made."

Groaning inwardly at the prospect of another of the

Petaybean songs, Matthew arranged his features in an engaging and interested smile.

"We sing it together," explained the man who seemed to be the woman's husband and the boy's father. "Because it happened to us all."

"We were all duped, he means," the boy said.

A little girl said, "All but Krisuk. He wasn't fooled."

"Please sing," Matthew said, trying to cut to the performance if he *had* to hear it to learn what they were talking about.

"You start, Krisuk," the mother said.

The boy stood stock-still, arms at his sides, not a foot from Matthew, and began to chant in an eerie singsong style:

> *"One day the roof of the world fell*
> *It killed our friends, our cousins*
> *It killed the heir to its wisdom*
> *For days we dug, too numb to cry.*
> *Our world had ended.*
> *Aijija!"*

The other villagers joined in, some crying loudly, some mumbling, all reciting the nonsense words at the end of the verses as if they were expletives.

> *"A stranger came among us to dig*
> *He came among us, he said, to teach.*
> *Sure he was.*
> *Strong he was.*
> *He knew what to do.*
> *He knew where to dig.*
> *The world still spoke to him,*
> *He said.*
> *Aiji!*

*He said if we followed him we could win back the world*
*He said if my sister lay with him she would be one with*
  *creation*

*She went with him*
*He said if we gave him the best pups of the litter*
*His team would carry the spirit of our village to the world's*
*   corners*
*And it would know us once more*
*We gave him the pups*
*He said that the planet's orange feet carried tales against*
*   us to other villages*
*He said if we were to heal, the feet must be killed.*
*This, to our shame, we allowed."*

And here, quite alarmingly, people began to tear their hair. All of the villagers sang the next verse loudly and lamentingly.

*"To our shame we didn't hide them*
*To our shame we didn't feed them*
*To our shame we heard his blows*
*To our shame we heard their cries*
*To our shame we did nothing*
*Until only Shush*
*Shush the silent and swift*
*Survived. Shush who led us back into the world*
*Shush who brought our neighbors to us*
*Shush who left us at last*
*Footless in a world*
*Whose voice had been strangled*
*Whose tongue had been blown away*
*By the one we called*
*Satok, shanachie.*

*Where is our sister now?*
*Gone to a bad man in a distant village.*
*Where are our best pups?*
*Starved and broken in spirit.*
*Where are our cats, the world's orange feet?*
*No longer walking, bones except for Shush*
*And when our world speaks to us again as we have*

*Hoped and dreamed?*
*It screams.*
*Aijija."*


"Oh, dear," Matthew said when they had finished. "And all this because of your shanachie, eh?"

"Yes, sir," the boy said. "He took all of our best for himself and betrayed everyone."

Matthew could scarcely keep from rubbing his hands together with glee. "Oh, that's terrible. Terrible indeed. Right, Brother Howling?"

Howling's lips twitched with a smile. "That's what comes of trafficking with monsters."

"You can say that again, mister," the woman said. "Can you stay and eat, sir?" she asked Matthew, but he waved a negative.

"I'm sorry, dear lady, but your story distresses me so much that I really think our best course is to resume our journey and seek to bring justice to you and people like you who are taken in by those who would mislead you. I hope I can count on you to repeat your song before the council when I call on you?" he added, addressing the boy, who had sung every word in a voice unexpectedly good, loud, and clear.

"I'd be honored, sir," the boy said, although he sounded puzzled and wary.

The villagers had to throw fresh stepping-stones and logs over the brambles for Matthew's party to return to the helicopter. Even then, the pilot had to climb out and hack at the vines with a machete before he could free the copter's skids. The vines were tight against the belly of the ship, strands attempting to encircle the narrow stern. Matthew thought that such fast-growing vegetation would also bear scrutiny. George, he rather thought, had some botanical knowledge. He'd send him to get a sample—if one could be contained long enough.

\* \* \*

Satok landed the shuttle, loaded with barrels of Petraseal, at Savoy. His three assistant "shanachies" were still there, drinking and talking.

"Where's Luka?" Reilly asked.

"Ran off," Satok replied. "Don't worry. I'll get her back, and when I do, I'll make her sorry she was ever born. The fraggin' bitch stole the ore samples and put rocks in their place."

"So you didn't get to make a deal with the company?"

"Course I did! Guy named Fiske saw them first before Luka switched 'em, but he wants to have genuine samples to show off."

"It was hard enough getting together what we did without you letting it get snitched," Reilly complained. He liked easier work than mining.

"Hold it! All we gotta prove is that there is genuine ore available. We'll use the one here, and who's to know if we don't tell 'em, huh? Fiske gave me some more Petraseal, so Reilly and I will mine the earlier veins while you two paint us a path back."

"Shit! I hate doing that," Soyuk grumbled. "Damn caves give me the creeps."

"Stop bellyachin'," Satok told him. "If we make this deal with the company, you'll have enough money to go off-planet permanently."

They climbed onto the Petraseal-laden shuttle and flew to the cave mouth, which was inconveniently distant from the village. In Satok's absence, the location had grown even more inconvenient.

"Where the hell did these weeds come from?" he demanded, astounded by the sea of tangling vines choking the cave mouth and cloaking the cliff and mountain meadow where they usually landed.

Reilly shrugged. "I dunno. They weren't here a coupla weeks back, but the season's gone nuts. We can torch 'em?"

"Not enough time. The fraggin' cave would fill with smoke and we'd never get at the ore."

"We could try the site back at my place," Soyuk suggested.

"No, hell, we'll hack 'em back and splash 'em with Petraseal as we go. We only need to get inside the cave."

The stalks were amazingly tough and the stinging vines clung to the men with fierce tenacity, but they hacked and splashed until they reached the entrance of the cave.

"Just hack this crap away from the front here, and it'll all be clear back where the Petraseal is, boys," Satok directed.

The way was not as clear as he had hoped. They had to make several trips to lug the vats of Petraseal into the cave. Left on his own while the others pumped the Petraseal in, Satok wondered how the weeds had managed to penetrate right through the ceiling of the cave. Had the latest tremors shaken a hole in the roof? Roots and tendrils of vines drooped from the ceiling.

When Soyuk, Clancy, and Reilly returned, he sent the first two on ahead to paint where they could excavate, and told Reilly to start patching farther back in the cave. In order to listen for Fiske's copter, Satok took the area nearest the entrance—he wanted to make sure the captain didn't see too much of the operation.

He hacked and daubed and hacked and daubed. The interior of the cave, now insulated by the cover of vines, seemed hotter than it ever had before. The light grew dimmer and greener as he worked, almost as if he were working underwater.

He thought at one point he heard some scuffling, and the others seemed noisier than they had been for a while, hollering and swearing as they worked. Getting stung, no doubt, he thought with a grin, but that noise was soon masked by the steady chop and daub of his own work. The beat of his own heart, the rasp of his own breath, was all he heard.

In this new rhythmic silence, he worked and sweated, the faint drip of his perspiration landing on the cavern floor the only other sound he heard as he strained to listen for the engines of Fiske's copter.

He didn't notice when he first heard the slithering sound, a soft rustle followed by a dry whispering crackling noise, as if paper had fallen—or leaves.

Then it came to him, just as he felt something slide across the toe of his boot and curl to brush his pant leg, that he had heard *nothing* from the others for some time. The thought crossed his mind just before the thorns bit into his leg as the vine tendril tightened.

"Reilly!" he hollered. "Soyuk!"

For an answer, another rustle, another slither. It was darker now, and as he turned toward the doorway, he saw that a thick net of greenery had replaced what they had hacked away a bare hour before. More alarmingly, some of the greenery bore splashes of white. He tried to kick off the vines clinging to him, but succeeded only in embedding the thorns deeper into his ankles. Feeling an edge of panic, he switched on the flashlight he'd brought along.

It seemed to attract the plants, as if they couldn't tell the difference between the light and sun. First roots, then more tendrils dropped from the roof, opening leaves as they slid.

This shouldn't be happening, Satok thought. This couldn't be happening! The Petraseal should have impeded any new growth, reduced it to dust. Where he had painted so industriously, he now realized that the Petraseal was marbled with cracks, fine in places, broadening in others to allow the plants to burgeon forth. Even the swath he had just painted had opened to emit tendrils.

And all of them seemed to be sliding toward him. From its sheath on his belt, he took his machete and hacked himself free, running to the rear of the cave as fast as he could without tripping over the vines.

He found Reilly first, hanging upside down by his ankles, which were pinned to the upper part of the wall. The vines twined down his legs and wrapped his arms tightly to his sides. His machete lay useless on the floor. The end of the vine—or maybe the first part to catch him—had wrapped around his neck five or six times, very tightly. Tender green shoots grew out of his mouth, nose, and ears.

Satok wasted no more time looking for Soyuk or Clancy. He didn't even worry about why the Petraseal hadn't worked. He jumped, hopped, and ran for the entrance, hacking and slicing.

He went at such a speed that he dropped his flashlight. That's why he didn't see the root looping down from the ceiling, to lash itself around his throat while another knocked him to the floor.

He didn't scream for long as the stinging, snatching vines overwhelmed him. As the sound died in his throat, he seemed to hear from the cave a low grumbling hum. As oxygen was cut off from his brain and optic nerve and his sight failed, the light from the setting sun pierced the leaves, lighting the greenery in the cave's entrance like the watchful eyes of a thousand gloating cats.

Marmion and her entourage had returned to Kilcoole, bringing with them Luka and an injured cat for the attention of Kilcoole's fat witch doctor, leaving Rick O'Shay's bird available to fly Torkel to Savoy to meet Satok.

Torkel was not actually rubbing his hands together with glee, but he felt like it. O'Shay had received a radio message that Matthew Luzon, his assistant, and an unspecified passenger had just cleared the coast at Harrison's Fjord. Torkel considered Luzon his staunchest ally, and he quickly sent a message asking Matthew to meet him and the McGee's Pass shanachie at Savoy.

"Hope they got that clear, Captain," O'Shay said, shaking his head. "Terrible amount of static lately."

When they circled the Savoy settlement, Torkel thought nothing of the brambles growing some distance outside the town until he saw the gleam of metal beneath them. Even then he thought it was some piece of cast-off machinery a local had allowed the vines to overgrow.

When he inquired in the village for the shanachie, he was

told that the man had been conferring with his fellow shanachies for days and yesterday had made a visit to the cave and had not yet returned.

"Important gennelmen such as yourself should be sittin' and restin' and havin' a cuppa, and not go worryin' after the shanachies. Sure they was all together and they'll be after makin' powerful decisions and discussions and suchlike out to the cave. I shouldn't like to be the one to interrupt them." This advice came from a middle-aged woman in raggedy clothes.

Why did Torkel get the feeling that there was something spurious about her rustic humility? Perhaps it was because he had lately had occasion to hear many Petaybeans speak. They seemed to use that broad colorful accent only when addressing company officials.

So he was uncharacteristically curt with her as he said, "Take me to this cave at once. Shanachie Satok's business is with me and I've come to meet him."

"Ah, well, sir, I'm too old a woman to take you on that sort of a hike, sure I am. But my son now, he'd be after takin' ya on his way up to the fields with the sheep like."

"Then let *him* take us, but let's *go*," Torkel snapped.

A boy appeared abruptly, a human island in a white woolly sea. He shook his head when Torkel wanted to use the copter to get them there. "Coo-berries'll take that, too. C'mon!"

It irritated Torkel no end that Rick O'Shay had the time to relax, drink tea, and exchange gossip with the woman while he traipsed after the boy. About a mile from the end of the village, the boy started swinging in a wide arc around the lake of weeds.

"Just where is this cave, son?" Torkel asked him, panting slightly at the uphill climb. He'd have to get back into working out again at the station.

"Over there, sir, but you won't want to go there, sir. Only shanachies go there."

"Are all you people nuts? I already told your mother I

have business with the shanachies. Now then, how do we get through this shrubbery and into the cave?"

"Ah, sure and I couldn't be doin' that, sir. Coo-berries is dead poison to sheep, and they've not sense enough to keep from eatin' them. Worse, I'd never get the stickers and thorns out of the wool."

"Then don't *take* the sheep, son. Did that ever occur to you?"

"But like, what would I do with 'em then, sir?"

Torkel was about to make a suggestion when he heard the engine of another copter. Seeing it overfly their position and head for the village, he abandoned the boy and sprinted back down the hill to intercept it.

He arrived winded, back where he'd started from, in time to see the pilot shut down the copter and jump down, followed by the imposing figure of Vice-Chairman Matthew Luzon; one of his entourage, who looked a bit pale; and an individual dressed in ragged leather and fur. As Torkel approached, his nose twitched at the rancid stench that exuded from the creature.

"Dr. Luzon, thank you for coming. I'm afraid there's been a bit of a delay, however."

Luzon smiled knowingly. "Ah, yes, the vines. I encountered the same problem when I serendipitously ended up at McGee's Pass on my way to meet you. It's a small problem, but a bit tricky, Captain. You simply enlist the aid of the villagers to throw boards and stones on top of the weeds to form a path. We found that worked fine when we landed in the middle of a patch ourselves."

"You went to the cave at McGee's Pass?"

"Cave? Ah, was that what the locals were singing about? No, we didn't examine the cave. When we discovered that you were, in fact, here, we came as soon as that . . . ah . . . song was over. I did, however, make a quite satisfying discovery during our brief stay which I'll discuss with you later. Now then, where's this fellow we were supposed to meet?"

"He's in the cave," Torkel said. "Beyond the weeds. Though I'm damned if I know how he got through."

"Easy enough if you think about it," Matthew said superciliously. He turned to the villagers who had gathered to watch the company men confer. "I want a work party to gather boards, stones, sheets of plasglas, anything that can be thrown across the weeds for a path. Now, step quickly, will you! We must reach the cave."

"Sure, carryin' enough things to get back there, that's a week's work you're talkin' about, sir," said a local man with the broad weathered face of an Eskirish cross, scratching his head at the prospect.

"We've used all that sort of stuff we had building bridges across the streams when they flooded," the woman said. "There's not a scrap left hereabouts."

"Then we'll send back to SpaceBase," Torkel said with a curt nod to O'Shay. "You radio for a team."

O'Shay got on the radio, and in a moment he emerged and said, "None of the other copters are at SpaceBase, sir, or even available later today."

"Then one of you fly back and pick up help and material," Torkel said, vastly annoyed at all of the delays and rather surprised that Satok, who'd had twenty-four or more hours to work ore, had not been on hand to guide them.

"It will have to be your pilot, Captain Fiske," Luzon said. "I require the full-time services of my own."

Torkel nodded to O'Shay, who climbed back aboard and restarted his engine. By now it was well into the afternoon.

"Why do you suppose we haven't heard from your shanachie?" Torkel demanded of the woman as the noise of the copter faded in the distance.

"Cave's a powerful ways back, sir."

"How *did* he and the others get there, then?" Torkel demanded. "We could try the same thing."

"Ah, sure, sir, shanachies has their ways as wouldn't be known to others."

Matthew Luzon nodded to Braddock, who hastily made a note of that remark.

"Yet more misguided souls in league with the Great Monster," wailed the unwashed man.

"Ah, Captain Fiske, this is a particularly valuable . . . acquaintance. From the southern continent. Brother Howling, meet Captain Torkel Fiske, who has spearheaded the effort to have this planet fully investigated. Captain Fiske, the Shepherd Howling, a major spiritual leader from the Vale of Tears. A most influential man."

Torkel gave the scruffy man an impatient look and limited his response to a mumbled "Delighted."

While they accepted the dubious hospitality of the village, Torkel gave the commissioner the details of his meeting with Satok and the ore samples he had himself handled and identified. To his relief, Luzon did not appear at all skeptical about the authenticity of the ores. He knew the planet was ore-rich: every space probe had verified that, even pinpointing the exact sites from space. Finding the precise locations on the surface had proved to be impossible.

Howling had apparently been listening carefully and now he nodded wisely. "The monster is treacherous. Perfectly capable of transforming gold into stone, winter into summer, harmless plants into murderous serpentine weapons. Time and again I have warned my flock they must rise up and subdue the monster with no hint of capitulation, but they were weak and faltering."

Torkel glanced at Luzon, appreciating what merit the lunatic could provide in discrediting the Kilcoole interpretation of the planet's behavior. He smiled at Luzon. "We need a few more new . . . acquaintances like this good and wise Brother Howling, don't we?"

Matthew wore a smug expression while Brother Howling said gravely, "Thank you, my son."

Matthew mentioned to Torkel, in an amused tone, what the villagers had sung of Satok at McGee's Pass.

"We've constantly been given the impression here that shanachies are universally respected and their views reflect those of their communities. At McGee's Pass, this was not so."

"I see. Discrediting what we have been told of the whole system. Yes, definitely, Dr. Luzon, we will need to have testimony from McGee's Pass at the hearing. And Brother Howling here, too, will represent a unique viewpoint at odds with the Kilcoole party line."

"My thoughts, exactly. Although Brother Howling also falls into the error of believing this planet to be sentient, his view is that the planet, far from being a benefactor and friend, is in fact a great monster. He believes that the colonists were brought here by the company as banishment for misbehavior elsewhere and that one day, if they do well and obey his teachings, the company will redeem them."

"Verily, have I said it thusly, my brethren," Shepherd Howling said. "I have done the company's work on this forsaken rock, Brother Matthew, that I and my family may be delivered from the monster and into the grace of the company once more. I will commune with the planet here, if you will excuse me."

His absence was welcome on several counts: the obviously fresher air, and the chance for Torkel and Luzon to make plans based on their respective discoveries. Torkel listened intently to Luzon as the man talked of similar investigations he had conducted into the folkways of various planets and systems and how he had corrected mistaken concepts and behaviors. The dialogue was briefly interrupted when a bewildered and bruised Shepherd Howling was herded back at the end of their hostess's broom.

"With all respect, gentlemen, you keep this maniac away from my little girl or I'll geld him!" the woman said and stomped away.

"Sit in the sun, Brother Howling," Luzon suggested, pointing to a half-broken bench against the outside wall—downwind of them.

All the while, Torkel kept expecting Satok to arrive to guide them to the rich ore faces as he'd promised. But several hours went by with no sign of the man. Finally the sound of helicopter engines once more routed the four men from their chairs.

Two helicopters approached the village. Torkel figured one would have men and one equipment to rid the area of the bushes, but when the passengers disembarked, he was annoyed to see that there were no figures in fatigues emerging, except the pilots, O'Shay and Greene. No one useful at all, in fact. Marmion and her entourage had come, along with George and Ivan from Luzon's group. And to his further irritation, he watched as Clodagh Senungatuk was courteously helped to descend by O'Shay from his copter.

"You're on report, O'Shay, for disobeying orders," he told the pilot.

"Oh, please don't punish the dear boy, Captain Fiske," said Marmion, with a flourish of fashionable fabric scarf and a charming moue. "It's all my fault really. Captain Greene returned from the southern continent with Yana Maddock, Dr. Shongili, and those sweet youngsters, plus another little girl Dr. Shongili says is the sister of his other niece—"

"Goat-dung!" Shepherd Howling said. "She is mine. She is to be my wife."

"Oh, surely not," Marmion said, smiling brightly at him. "The girl's less than twelve years old. But, at any rate, our teams were in need of one of Clodagh's hearty meals and we sat listening to Yana and Sean tell us the *most* fantastic adventures—ah, but I needn't tell you, need I, Matthew? You were present for some of them."

Luzon inclined his head, his eyes half-hooded and dangerous.

"Well, Johnny Greene heard Captain O'Shay's message about the weeds here, and then Clodagh said that a work party wouldn't do much good and might even be in danger. But that she knew something that *would* work." Marmion paused, as if expecting approval, her eyes all wide and innocent. "*Et voilà!* We have come to offer assistance."

Before anyone could say anything else she added ingenuously, "Also, Matthew, your young friends were absolutely *pining* for you, and I simply had to help reunite you, isn't that so, boys?"

Luzon's muscular assistants nodded—rather miserably, Torkel thought.

While everyone was standing around thinking of a response to Marmion's gabble, Clodagh Senungatuk started walking out of the village.

"Where the devil do you think you're going?" Torkel demanded.

"To make a path to the cave," she said simply, and kept walking.

By the time she had gone five more steps, Torkel recovered from his surprise enough to tell her that she wouldn't be able to penetrate such a hedge of weed, and where were the boards and other spanning materials he had sent for? She gave no answer, plodding up the track toward the cave. The other new arrivals followed, plus half the village, which seemed to consider this expedition fine entertainment.

At the edge of the vast jungle of waist-high vines, which seemed even more impenetrable since Torkel's first look at them, Clodagh paused. She bent down and gently touched the center of one of the leaves.

"So what are you doing? Asking it nicely?" Torkel demanded.

"Lookin' at this white stuff. Wondering why somebody tried to *paint* the bushes. This is the only thing that works." She drew out a large clear flask filled with a greenish liquid, uncorked it carefully, and then inserted a sprinkler head of home manufacture. She shook the bottle a bit in front and to each side of her.

Instantly the vines retracted as if they had been mowed with a scythe, and as she moved forward, Marmion fell in step behind her, followed by Sally Point-Jefferson, who had had the good sense to put on heavy boots.

Marmion turned around and said, "Quickly, boys. I don't know how long the effect lasts. Clodagh's very mysterious about it."

They followed with alacrity. Torkel felt like a fool, trailing behind the big woman as she doused her concoction to the right, the center, and the left, like some ancient prelate dispensing holy water or preparing a pontiff's path with incense.

When they reached a wall of greenery where the vines from the meadow above the cave spilled down over into the field, she increased the area and parabola of her casting, widening the path. The vines drew back like curtains, and Torkel saw the entrance to a largish cave.

"Better use lights," Clodagh said, though she imperturbably stepped into the dimness, Marmion behind her.

"Oh!" Marmion said. "What ever has happened here?"

"Somebody tried to kill this place," Clodagh said. "But Petaybee fights back." She indicated the streamers of vines and roots extending from the ceiling.

She proceeded until, farther inside the cave, she stepped cautiously around what looked like a green hillock.

"Ah! Here, Captain," she said to Torkel, sprinkling the hillock so that the vines gradually shrank away to show the body they had encased. "Is this yer man here that you were looking for?"

The popped eyes, protruding tongue, and cyanosed face were nevertheless identifiable as those of the former shanachie. The bloodied grooves tightly scored about his neck gave ample proof of the agency that had killed him.

"He said he had a surefire mining method," Torkel said. "Something to do with Petraseal."

Faber knocked on a piece of the roof that had remained vineless thus far. "This is Petraseal all right, but this on the cracks—" He ran his fingers over it and shone his flashlight beam on the result and on what had covered the ends of the withered vines. "Look. It's not even white. It's pale lime green and it's not Petraseal, Captain Fiske. This is exterior wall paint, and not a real high quality at that."

Shepherd Howling, visibly shaking, suddenly sprang at Matthew Luzon as if attacking him. "Get me out of here!

I must escape the Great Monster before it devours us all as it devoured that man."

"Uh, Dr. Luzon," one of the assistants called nervously. "Can you come back here?" He had followed Clodagh, who was continuing to sprinkle, undeterred by her grisly discovery, farther into the cave. "We've got three more corpses."

"I demand that this woman be held for questioning and that the bottle containing her weed-killing solution be seized and analyzed," Matthew Luzon said.

Marmion Algemeine, still unhappily abstracted by the grotesque deaths of the four men, regarded Matthew with stupefaction.

"Held for questioning? Whatever for?" she demanded. "Clodagh *helped*! Without her we'd never have found those poor men."

Matthew didn't exactly say "aha!" but a malicious light did glitter in his eye as he said, in a quiet voice, "And how exactly did she know that these particular vines would need her particular remedy? And how did she just happen to have it available?"

"And I," Torkel said sternly, "only requested materials and manpower to reach the cave."

Marmion was not to be confounded. "Why, I would suppose that plants as aggressive as these might be a fairly common nuisance. Is that how you knew, Clodagh?"

Clodagh shrugged but didn't defend herself.

A woman from Savoy spoke up quickly. "And how wouldn't she know that? Sure, coo-berries has never been this bad before. It's that hard to root them out wherever they grow, but they never *strangled* anybody before this. Still, it's been an uncommon early spring, and everything is growin' the like of which I've never seen before in all my life."

"So you would say, would you, madam," Matthew said, "that the weather was unusual and the plants are unusual? Tell me, if what Ms. Senungatuk used on the coo-berries was an ordinary remedy for their sting, why didn't the rest of you use them?"

"Sure, why should we?" she asked. "Coo-berries wasn't botherin' us any, were they? And only 'cos you come, did we know they was up at the cave. And another thing," she went on, winding up to unburden all her complaints, "back before Shanachie Reilly arrived, people used to come here for latchkays and have a chat with the planet, like. Only then Reilly gave us to understand that a lot of our problems, the floods, the avalanche, the quakes, were on accounta we were too pig-ignorant to understand properly what it was the planet was sayin' to us. After the time lightnin' struck the meeting hall and burned up all them people, just before Reilly came to us, we let him do the talkin' and I would say things have been pretty peaceful since." She paused and said, "But for all that many folk thought Reilly knew best, he never did learn the remedies like Kilcoole's Clodagh. Our old healer died two winters back and we've been wanting to get someone new trained up, 'cos I've known about *her* since we was both younglings. Village even had a promising girl child ready to go 'prentice herself to Clodagh, iffen Clodagh Senungatuk'd have her, but Reilly wouldn't allow it."

"Thank you, madam, for the testimonial," Matthew said. "We'll let you know if you'll be needed to repeat your statement at the hearing. Meanwhile, I must insist Ms. Senungatuk be placed into company custody and her flask seized for analysis, along with the contents of the barrels the deceased had with them in the cave. Autopsies must be performed on the bodies and the entire area sealed."

"No worries on that score, sir," Ivan told him. They were standing just outside the field of coo-berries, and Ivan's nod indicated the place where Clodagh's path had been. It was once more covered with twining brambles.

Two weeks later, the investigation was finished and all the data collected had been entered by Luzon's overworked computer men and hard copies made for presentation.

First, however, at Shepherd Howling's insistence, he was sent off-planet on the same shuttle that carried the bodies. He couldn't have been on the MoonBase for more than an hour before angry messages arrived from first MoonBase command, then the hospital facility on Bethany Station, which indicated that the Shepherd was urgently proselytizing on a broad scale for converts to his just cause of trying to raise an army to fight the monster, which must be overcome before the planet could be truly holy. He had a real knack for spouting his cant to the already disaffected, the misfits, and those in the lower ranks who were more easily swayed by his rhetoric. Within the first three days, he came close to single-handedly instigating a mutiny.

Such complaints made Matthew thankful that the man was out of the way so that he would not be part of the group greeting the remaining commissioners. They were soon to arrive on the planet's somewhat seismic-shaken surface to read and evaluate the information prior to the final hearing. He wished there had been someplace he could have immured Marmion Algemeine and her assistants, but her absence would have caused embarrassing questions even if he had thought of a way to rid her, however temporarily, of her three constant attendants.

Torkel Fiske was invaluable in helping Matthew and his committee. It was he who suggested that they should also interview newly arrived colonists in the most recently formed villages far from the influence of such people as Shongili and the Senungatuk woman, or even families such as the brood that had entertained Matthew in the south.

The new people, it was hoped, would be more objective and scientific in their outlook. When Matthew noted that the influx had come from the Mariana Islands and the Scottish highlands, where large deposits of deutronium and molybdenum had recently been located, and some resettled from the disastrous colonies of Bremer, he was equally ready to cancel that idea if the initial interviews proved negative. He resolved to read each of the collected reports before permitting them to be admitted as evidence. Meanwhile, his assistants and Marmion's vied with each other to be the first to record the testimonies of people from the villages of the four murdered shanachies.

Matthew himself had made a special, personal effort to reach Goat-dung and persuade her to tell the truth about her part in the sudden disappearance of "the monster" who had been injured by members of Howling's community—an injury rather too similar to the one from which Shongili was recovering. Matthew also had placed a strong letter of reprimand in the file of Captain John Greene, who had certainly exceeded his authority by removing the girl from Matthew's custody at a critical time.

Now no one seemed to know where either the girl or Shongili was. Shongili's mannish sister and her girlfriend were also nowhere to be found. Through Marmion's influence, Clodagh Senungatuk, much to Matthew's dismay, remained in her own home, under nominal "house arrest," and still ran the village. And the whole planet, as far as he knew—including Whittaker Fiske, who actually seemed to have the poor taste to be besotted with the fat cow—paused to gossip to her through her windows. Unstoppably, of course, those damned cats went in and out as they pleased. Discreet efforts to capture any of them—either by the lure of choice cuts of meat or by chasing them with otherwise savage canines—had met with abysmal failure. They had spurned the food and terrified any dog set on their spoors.

He had tried to insist that Shongili and Clodagh both be sent off-planet in detention cells pending the hearing. Whittaker Fiske and Marmion Algemeine had immediately blocked that, just as they'd quashed the offworld reassignments he tried to engineer for captains Greene and O'Shay.

He let himself be consoled by the fact that it was only a matter of time for all their little petty tricks to come tumbling down about their ears. Once he presented his evidence at the hearing and it was seen how these two-bit shamanistic charlatans were preying on the people's fears and hopes to influence them against the company, Shongili and Clodagh and all their helpers would be evicted from their cushy company homes and Maddock, Greene, and O'Shay would be busted back to KP duty.

The workload was overwhelming. While he seemed able to gain momentum in his search for truth, his assistants, who had previously seemed so promising, had grown unaccountably bumbling and incompetent. Their reports did not have bottom-line conclusions that satisfied his requirements. And then the computers kept developing breakdowns and suffering from sporadic erasures.

The locals, including company troops, were hostile; the working conditions were appallingly primitive, and the weather—how he *loathed* wild weather—was unspeakable. Lashing rains and electrical storms alternated with spitting snow and heat far above the comfort zone. The SpaceBase facility was constantly quaking with unexpected convulsions on land that had originally been tested as geologically stable. Matthew longed for the sane and sanitary shipboard ambience, one engineered for human comfort by rational minds such as his own. No mold grew there, as it did on the walls of his lavatory despite the repeated scrubbings of some low-ranking corpsman. No thunderclaps disrupted his concentration, and despite the fact that one was always moving in space, one never experienced sensations of bobbing like bubbles in a test tube as buildings bounced.

To make matters worse, another volcano erupted, ten klicks to the northwest, sending ash into every crack and crevice. This emergence occurred in a meadow, near nothing else, and didn't even cause copters to falter overflying it. However, a seaquake of 9.3 on the Richter scale had a midocean epicenter that caused tsunamis in every direction and quite devastated the small facility at Bogota.

The company would simply have to face facts. This planet was not working out. The terraforming was faulty, the terrain had not fully stabilized, the whole place should be evacuated, scraped clean, and either abandoned or reformed with more modern techniques. *That* would put an end to all this talk of sentience and settlements.

# 14

Yana couldn't shake a sense of foreboding, something she would not give voice to, even to Sean. At least his wound was closing with extraordinary rapidity, thanks to a poultice and Clodagh's expert attention. That bit of doctoring had happened before Matthew Luzon's asinine notion of putting Clodagh under "house arrest." That wasn't as bad as Luzon's original orders to send both off-planet. Sean had been immediately hidden in Bunny's snocle, which had been decommissioned for the "summer" and stored in Adak O'Connor's garage. Clodagh had shrugged off the threat and maintained it wouldn't come to that. Which it hadn't, with the forceful help of Marmion and Whittaker Fiske. Only someone totally ignorant of the situation on Petaybee, as most of the company brass were, or someone so hostile as to be beyond reason, as Luzon was, would think that putting Clodagh and Sean in any sort of detention made sense.

Yana couldn't quite believe, or hope, that Luzon had failed to realize the function of the cats in Clodagh's—and the planet's—communications network. Torkel knew. She wondered why he didn't try to round up the cats and put them under house arrest, as well. It would have been just about as ridiculous.

When they knew the order was for house arrest rather than transfer off-planet, Sean, with his customary imperturbability, emerged from hiding like a bear from hibernation and smilingly chose Yana's as the "house to be arrested in." She was glad to have him near for several reasons. Although the wound *was* healing so well, the arrow had torn muscles and almost severed one tendon. She could keep an eye on it and him better if she didn't have to worry about concealment. She knew it was unrealistic to think she could single-handedly protect him from the company if they tried to take him, but she would do what she could. And now that she was well again, she could do quite a bit. With her years of training and experience, she was not without resources. And quite aside from that, it just helped having him there. He calmed her. Here *his* world was on trial and *he* was able, with a look, a smile, or a joke, to soothe *her* fears.

She needed that. Even with the "off-planet threat" dissolved, tension vibrated in the air like off-key music whether it was in sympathy with Clodagh, or apprehension of what the Powers That Be would try to do to them *next*.

Not that everything in Kilcoole came to a standstill: everyone carried on, gardening and planting all hours of the lengthening days. But the smart ones were frightened, as they should be, with Matthew Luzon coming on so strong. At least that loony, Howling, had been shipped out, which gave the planet one score against the Powers That Be, as the locals called the company in all its omniscience. She wondered if the MoonBase had smelled him coming. She'd had the first laugh in days when Adak reported that Howling had the base command howling complaints.

Adak said he had ears the size of flapjacks from listening in on his radio, trying to make sense of orders misheard through the static. He usually brought a summary of what he had heard to Yana so that she could convey the information to Clodagh. Like everybody else, she just went to the windows and chatted. If the guard was new, and didn't know her—as the guards often were, since Torkel was obviously afraid Clodagh would bewitch her jailers as he seemed to feel she had his father—Yana cleverly disguised herself as what she had been, a major in the company corps, collected a smart salute from the trooper on duty, and walked into the house. This worked only if the guard hadn't already been posted on *her* house to guard Sean, but she slipped past all of them an amazing number of times just by putting her hair up in a fatigue cap when she wanted to be a ranking officer, and throwing one of Aisling's handwoven blanket jackets over her uniform and letting her hair down when she didn't. Nevertheless, she had to keep a fairly low profile when she did this, lest Torkel or one of the other brass who knew her catch on and prohibit her specifically from visiting Clodagh. They hadn't thought of it yet, which was not an oversight that Yana would have permitted had the mission been under *her* command, but fortunately, it wasn't. Whittaker Fiske visited Clodagh often, openly and casually. The first time Yana had walked into the house to see him sitting at Clodagh's table having tea, she had been wary, until his wink reassured her. "We would appreciate a knock next time though, Major," he said, squeezing Clodagh's hand. Clodagh had surprised Yana by responding with an actual blush and a mischievous bawdy chuckle.

But Yana was at home, in mufti with her hair streaming, talking to Sean, when Adak, who was also still officially a company corps employee, knocked briefly and entered without waiting for permission. Sean, who had been slowly walking around the room to supple up his abused leg muscles, stopped just short of the abruptly opened door. Yana had been listing the issues and arguments concerning them that were likely to come up at the hearing, and practicing succinct answers. That always impressed committees: this witness had all facts in order and did not hesitate in answering.

"Sean, oops, sorry, Yana, the static's getting worse but the committee's ship has landed. That Luzon fella was transmitting orders to the crew for the last couple of hours about how the committee was supposed to be taken to *his* boardroom for a private briefing first, but somehow"— Adak gave a good imitation of an ingenuous shrug for a fifty-five-year-old man—"Dr. Fiske and Dama Algemeine found out and beat him to the landing pad."

"Sure, now, and wasn't that lucky for us?" Sean mused, slyly deepening the faint trace of Irish lilt in his voice and lifting his left eyebrow in an amused, quizzical way. "Did these same mysterious circumstances that alerted Whit and Marmion also warn Clodagh?"

"Didn't need to," Adak said. "The cats were already on the job. Leastwise, that clouded one padded by me on my way here and leapt right in the window neat as you please, and that black and white fella, who lies on the roof and snarls at the guards when they get too close, slithered in after her." Adak grinned maliciously.

"Well, then, since the cursor's up on Matthew's screen, let's hope all this waiting's over," Sean said, and gave a convulsive shrug of his shoulders, one of the few manifestations of his own anxiety Yana had observed. He shot a wry grin in her direction. "So the waiting's over now, love, and the dance begins. Ready?"

She nodded solemnly and held up the coffeepot. "Have time for a cup, Adak?"

"Sure do, Yana," Adak said, closing the door behind him.

He strode over to the table, which had been enlarged from a small square to a large circle, with one section covered by Yana's notes and pad and a long-handled wooden spoon that Sean was whittling. Sean had needed some occupation while he was recuperating: Yana now had four chairs instead of one. She'd helped, but she'd done more watching of his clever hands than working.

Yana put three cups and some of the sweet biscuits Sean had made on the table. Sean joined them; as usual, turning his chair round so he could lean his arms across the back of it. *That* chair he had made to his own specifications.

"There was also some report," Adak went on, "came in for that fella with all funny words . . ."

"Ah, the analysis," Yana said, leaning forward hopefully. "Can you remember any of the words?"

"Of course I can. Who do you think teaches the youngsters the corpsglory songs and the company manualsongs to keep them from harm when they're first spaced? My memory's good as Clodagh's." He gazed roofward, eyes almost turned completely up, mouth open, and then recited: "Plant juices of an unknown alkalinity of unusual strength and a small amount of an unidentifiable animal protein. The combination is unusual and most likely derived from indigenous elements not yet included in botanical or biological records, which are unusually brief for Planet Terraform B. On the subject of the so-called coo-berry bramble thorn plant, the vegetation showed virulent growth even under controlled laboratory conditions. It secretes acid from leaf surface, thorn, and stem of such potency that it permeated Petraseal, as suspected, and etched deeply into every metal sample presented. Coo-berry sample destroyed before its mass imploded the triple plasglas container. Antidote is still undergoing testing. Could be useful against other alien plant-forms of similar toxicity and rapid growth. Request quantity and availability of ingredients." Adak dropped his head, and his eyes returned to a normal position in their sockets.

"Well done, Adak," Sean said with a laugh, and gave the old radio operator a friendly clout on his arm.

"And they want to set up a school so's we can learn reading and writing," Adak muttered scornfully. "What's wrong with training a memory to remember what it's heard 'steada having to look it up in books allatime?" He took a long swig of the coffee, smacking his lips. "Mind you, more of *this* on a regular basis wouldn't be hard to take."

"You have to be careful what you *accept* from the company," Yana said urgently, extending her hand across the table toward Adak. "Teaching the people to read and write again is essential if we're to keep the buzzards off this planet indefinitely, but we have to choose our own material."

"Don't need to tell *me* that, Yana. It's the younger kids need the caution."

Yes, that was the problem, Yana thought. It was the kids who would only see the advantages of the perks Torkel was so eager to load on them. Krisuk, who had never had much and wanted to make something of himself. And those like Luka, who had been abused all her life. She gave a wry grin. Not Bunny, she thought, nor even 'Cita, who still thinks three meals a day is sinful.

They had sent the girl with Bunny, who wouldn't let her sister out of her sight, and Aisling and Sinead to Sinead's old cabin, deep in the woods. Diego sneaked out at night, Dinah limping along in escort, to bring supplies and news. 'Cita seemed to go into shock when she was told that Shepherd Howling had left the planet. Diego had reported that the day after she seemed to relax for the first time and had spontaneous questions for him: Was Coaxtl all right? And was Sean healing, and what was happening to all those left at the Vale of Tears without leadership? Diego said he'd have to find out. Which reminded Yana to ask Adak.

"Well, I got the odd word or two from Loncie that when they'd gone out to collect Scobie's snocle, some woman—Ash-sen-see-on," he said, stumbling over the name, "was more or less in charge. But she was gettin' a lot of argument from folks who said the Shepherd didn't like women bosses."

"Out of the deep freeze and into the permafrost," Sean groaned.

"That was before the tsunami, a' course," Adak added. "Some of the people left of the Bogota group might resettle in the Vale. I hear it's freezing up proper again now."

Then all three fell silent, each wondering privately if there would be resettling along the lines that had worked so well for Petaybee so far.

"Any more surveys on that equatorial island chain that's emerging?" Sean asked, the light of mischief dancing in his silver-gray eyes.

Yana wondered briefly if he'd *known* that would happen.

"Ah, yes," Adak drawled, grinning to show all his even strong white teeth. "There's copters up, and Johnny and

Rick and that other bozo flitting down, doing runs. Right smart-sized islands blossomin' like fireweed, and where it's warm, too. Don't 'spect that was in anybody's plans, now was it?" Adak looked sharply into Sean's face, which wore a bland expression, except for the twinkle in his eyes.

"Well, with volcanoes emerging here in the north, it's possible that there'd be a reaction elsewhere. Though speaking scientifically, the odds *are* low of so much crustal activity occurring."

"But Petaybee *is* an unusual planet," Yana said equably, her expression matching Sean's, "so we can expect just about anything!"

"Shouldn't wonder. Won't, either," Adak said, and drained the last of the coffee. Rising, he gave a quaint little bow in Yana's direction, grinned at Sean, and then paused at the door. "What should I be listenin' for now, Shongili?"

"The names of our latest visitors."

In point of fact, it wasn't Adak who brought Yana and Sean that news but Marmion Algemeine, her poise shaken, and Whittaker Fiske, looking glum.

"It couldn't have been a worse selection, really, it couldn't," Marmion said, making for one of the chairs at Yana's table as if her legs would support her no further. With an agitated flourish of one hand, she went on. "I've got my aides checking every man jack of them. And it *is* every man, too. I was so hoping Metuska Karianovic of KCCE would elect to come, but she's off having some sort of rejuv treatment. Wouldn't you just know!"

"Who did come?" Yana asked as she poured coffee all around.

"Mostly Matthew's palsies," Marmion said with a raising of her arched eyebrows. She pouted her lips. "Though Chas came: Charles Thraves-Tung. He's always reasonable, I'll say that for him. And he does *think*. He'll appreciate a reasoned argument, which is more than I can say for Bal Emir Jostique." She gave a little shudder of revulsion. "Greasy old man. He'd *enjoy* having prepubescent girls as wives: as many as he could get."

"He has 'em already, doesn't he?" Whittaker said, regarding her with mild surprise.

"He'll *never* have enough, but even *he* has to wait until they're fourteen!" She gave another little spasm of her elegant shoulders, clad today in a soft, dull brown leather. She raised her hand to tick off names. "So we've you, me, Chas Tung against Matthew, Bal, that old bag of bones Nexim Roberts Shi-Tu, with Farringer Ball on the monitor, acting as chair again."

Whittaker raised his eyebrows. "Do you *know* that Chas is with us?"

"How could I? You saw how Matthew scrambled his broad young men between us and the new arrivals so we didn't have a chance to say more than 'hello, safe trip' before Matthew whisked them away on his 'survey tour'? Nor was there room for one of us to go or send someone."

Whittaker gave a bark of laughter. "I wouldn't have wanted to go on that trip! And I don't think Matthew won any points by insisting on flying them over the equator. Turbulence was fierce, and neither Nexie nor Bal like their innards disturbed any more than the indigestion their fancy foods give them. Speaking of which, did you notice what was being unloaded from the shuttle for their delectation?"

Marmion made a grimace, which then became a hopeful grin. "Yes, and the chefs who'd know what to do with such provender. Take no offense, Sean, Yana, because I *have* enjoyed the unusual tastes and texture that only Petaybee can provide, but I'm likely to be the only one, bar Whit here, who would. Terribly spoiled the others are as far as their palates are concerned." Then she frowned again. "Did you notice, too, Whit, that *all* Matthew's boys look absolutely pooped? He's had them running around night and day. Poor Braddock Makem looks transparent. Does he never let people have time off?"

"Where're yours, Marmie?" Whit asked, cocking an eyebrow at her.

She winked. "I don't work them half as hard, but they find out twice as much. And," she said on a sigh, "we'll need every smitch of help we can find with Farringer the tiebreaker."

Adak burst through the door. "He's dead!"

"Who's dead?" everyone demanded simultaneously.

"That smelly Shanachie Howler!"

"Of what?" Sean asked.

"Smelling himself in a MoonBase cubicle, probably!" Yana quipped.

"Nah! Not a bit of it." Adak shook his head and waved his hands in his excitement. "Get this! He was done in by the same thing as killed Lavelle!"

Yana locked eyes with Sean.

"There's more, too!" Adak was almost spitting in his effort to get the second message out. "Satok had ..." He turned his eyes to the roof again and recited, "An atrophied node in the cerebellum, only four hundred twenty-three grams of brown fat, and all his vitals was poisoned. Soyuk Ishunt, Clancy Nyangatuk, and Reilly also had atrophied nodes and poisoned organs."

"Was the node in Howling's case mentioned?" Sean asked.

Adak looked down, wrinkling his leathery brown face in deep thought. "Hmmmm ... think it was, but it wasn't atrophied none." He took another breath. "And they're sending some special medical equipment down. CAT scanner."

Yana couldn't help inhaling at that news and glanced at Sean for reassurance. He cocked an eyebrow in response, but his unworried attitude and relaxed posture still did not relieve her fears that his shape-changing abilities would somehow be revealed by scanning.

On the other hand, Marmion burst out laughing. "One thing sure," she managed to gasp out, "there isn't one built to accommodate Clodagh Senungatuk!"

That observation did provoke chuckles, and the tension in the room went down a few notches.

"But that's probably the only good thought I can express," Marmion went on, "as Nexie's a biochemist and has"—she paused, her expression darkening—" 'other methods' more intrusive and certainly unpleasant."

"We'll see about *that*," Whittaker said, his eyes narrowing. "Neither Clodagh Senungatuk nor Sean Shongili have committed any crimes against Intergal regulations. Even this house arrest is farcical. Intergal cannot subvert CIS civil rights except in circumstances of armed conflict, and Clodagh's squirt bottle doesn't appear on any list of weaponry I've ever seen, modern or ancient. Adak, you still got the secured channel?"

"Ah, hmm, well . . ." Adak looked wildly around the room at everyone except Sean, but somehow saw the brief nod.

"C'mon then," Whittaker said, urging Adak to the door and laying an arm across the man's shoulders as they departed. "Be back in a nano."

Marmion looked considerably more cheerful. "Let's hope he can get a message through all the static to the proper authorities. At first, I thought the pilots were just saying that to be obstructive. But it's real now. Do you know what's causing so much interference, Sean?"

"Sure," he replied good-naturedly. "Atmospheric anomalies and the stratospheric turbulences caused by the crustal activity with some vigorous sunspots." Then he paused and creased his brows a little. "Coaxtl told Nanook that the 'home was changing.' According to Bunny, Coaxtl also told that to 'Cita when she was in her charge. But none of the track-cats, nor Clodagh's, for that matter, are the least bit worried."

"They never are," Marmion said wryly.

"Oh, they have been," Sean replied in mild reproof.

Marmion leaned forward, resting one hand lightly on his forearm. "How does she—"

She broke off at the sound of footsteps on the stairs. Whittaker and Adak returned, neither looking very pleased. Whittaker almost slammed the door.

"Could barely get the call letters out clear enough to be recognized," Whittaker said, frowning with frustration.

"Message was short and maybe too sweet for the kind of action we might need to have available. Got hold of Johnny, too, and asked him to send next time he's above turbulence. Damned planet's messing us all up, and we're the ones trying to *help*!" He turned on Sean, who seemed unaffected by the communications failure. "Boy, how long can you live on a space station with no immunity?"

"Four, five days."

Yana felt her heart skip a beat and surreptitiously placed one hand over her still-flat belly. How could he announce his life expectancy so calmly?

"Clodagh?"

"Same, but it won't come to that, Whit. Believe me."

Dr. Whittaker Fiske cocked his head toward his right shoulder, planted both fists on the belt that circled his thin waist, and demanded, "If I could believe you, Dr Shongili, I'd sleep a lot easier, and so would all your friends."

"Believe me, and that's bankable!"

"It is?" Marmion perked up, her fiscal senses alerted.

"Look." Sean splayed one hand, folding a finger down for each point he made. "We've got to prove the planet is sentient? We can and we will! We've got to prove that it's in the company's interest to let the settlements remain because they can prove economically profitable, though not necessarily as predicted from the original surveys. We've got to prove that our ways"—and he gestured to Adak, Yana, who managed a little smile at the compliment, and out the window toward Clodagh's house—"protect an environmental entity from abuse and misuse in the best interests of itself and the company which awakened it." He nodded at Whittaker. "We also have to prove that the charges of malfeasance, misconduct, insubordination, and fraud, which Matthew Luzon's about to level against some of us and/or the entire population, are as ludicrous as Shepherd Howling."

"And smell just as bad," Adak added with a sharp nod of his head.

*"Sacre bleu!"* Marmion exclaimed. "We're not asking

for much, are we?" Then, sighing, she shook her head slowly from side to side. "We got a lot of heavy metal men against us in that crew Matthew's brought down."

"But they're on *our* turf," Sean said with one of his most charismatic and enigmatic smiles.

"And Matthew's doing his best to predispose them against Marmie and me because we've been so obviously 'taken in' "—Whittaker made the bracket signs with his hands—"by the natives."

"Indigenous personnel, Whit, please," Marmion said in mock petulant correction. "However, I can prove readily enough that I haven't lost my wits or been mesmerized by local shamans." She rose. "I shall demonstrate *that* this evening." She gave a little chuckle. "I happen to know that Bal and Nexie lost a few trillions on an enterprise which I"—and she placed one hand with elegant grace on her chest—"had the good sense to forgo. So we'll leave you." She linked arms with Whittaker and led him out of the house. Just at the door she paused and looked back over her shoulder at Sean, her lovely eyes anxious. "You're positive, Sean, that neither you nor Clodagh are in danger of being removed from this planet?"

He nodded, smiling. "Positive!"

When the door closed on the two, Yana and Adak turned on Sean.

"Positive?"

"Positive!" he said, but his mouth had a particularly grim set as he said it.

# 15

To her amazement, Marmion de Revers Algemeine found that her taste had altered during her weeks on Petaybee. The elaborate and extensive array of courses set before the committee members at dinner that evening—an evening fortunately free of tremors, shudders, or shakes—did not suit her palate, much less her mood. She really *did* prefer the simpler, sharper tastes of Petaybean foods: a rabbit stew would have been far more satisfying than the overly subtle coulis, sauces, and dressings that accompanied each dish. She saw Whittaker making as slow a progress through the banquet as herself, but at least she could cry off on the grounds of watching her diet.

Matthew and Torkel cleared every plate, bowl, and platter set before them, but Marmion slyly noticed that like her own three aides, some of Matthew's pretty boys were less than enthusiastic about the rich food. Chas, Bal, and Nexim had no problems, though twice Bal called the head steward over to make muttered complaints and reject a dish after one bite. Maybe his new stomach was developing the same ulcers the old ones had, Marmion thought to herself. A body could have certain dispositions no matter how many parts of it were replaced with functional substitutes.

She did have a chance to obsequiously inquire of Nexie's latest investment projects. That gave her a chance to make a passing reference to the Omnicora Steel Venture, which she had decided was not properly based to make any sort of a profit back on the original investment. She had raised her voice just enough for Matthew to overhear her comments. That would remind him, too, that she had lost none of her acumen. She discussed with Bal the possibility of investing in one of his schemes, which she had recently investigated, though she pointed out one or two organizational problems that should be addressed before she could consider the project. By the fleeting expression on Bal Emir Jostique's face, she had hit the very weak points he must have discovered. That should take care of *that*, then, if Matthew chose to call her gullible.

She was exhausted with smiling and waxing charming by the time she and Sally could leave the "gentlemen" to whatever it was gentlemen insisted on doing without female company in this stratum of interplanetary society.

"Any luck, dear?" she asked Sally as they both made for their quarters in the wing of the livid yellow building.

"We may need more than luck, dama," Sally said with a sigh. "Dr. Luzon has got some twists that a Spican contortionist would envy."

"Ah, but we knew he would."

"My report's on your desk, but I really think, ma'am, you need a good night's sleep more. Bad news keeps."

"Thank you, dear. I'll take your advice only if you'll take it yourself."

Sally sighed, for the first time since the start of the tedious dinner party allowing her own fatigue to show, and nodded. "I think I'd best if I'm to be sharp up to the mark tomorrow for you. At least, we have all our *facts* in hard copy and not innuendos."

"Sleep well, then."

Others did not. And, later, both Faber and Millard, who had stayed on as courtesy required, admitted that they had not seen the discreet accord that must have been reached during that interval by Matthew, Torkel Fiske, Bal Emir, and Nexim Shi-Tu. They knew that the four must have made a deal during that time, because not even Luzon would have dared to take the draconian measures that followed without the support of Fiske and the other two board members. Marmion blamed herself for having taunted Bal, but she had been pursuing another course of action entirely.

At midnight, the several shuttles that had brought the other commissioners from their separate capitals silently lifted from SpaceBase on their assigned missions. None of the crew or troopers had ever heard of Petaybee before, though what they'd seen of it hadn't impressed them at all. They'd had no rest or more than a hasty meal of hard rations while they erected the detention cells that had been sent along at Luzon's request.

As soon as the soundproofed, windowless two-by-one-meter cells had been erected in one of the empty storage facilities, the shuttles took off for their destinations. Squads had trank guns and orders to use them if any of the detainees resisted arrest. They were also ordered to secure local felines, with a bonus for each one caught.

"Whaddaya think they want cats for?" muttered one enlisted man, only to be sharply reprimanded by his troop leader: "If *they* want cats, they get 'em."

The shuttles separated to pick up their passengers at the Vale of Tears. Ascencion was collected, and Lonciana and her husband were dragged out of their beds and barely given a chance to clothe themselves. Loncie protested as loudly and vehemently against such an unwarranted intrusion as only a former chief petty officer could, demanding to see the detention order, while Pablo gave quick and decisive household instructions to Carmelita. At Kabul, Shanachie Chau Xing was collected; at Portage, one of the newer settlements, an irate McDouall swore eloquently that, if this was the sort of cooperation Intergal wanted on Petaybee, they'd had the last of his! At Savoy, they made three pickups: Luka, the outspoken woman, and the man, identified as Eamon Shishmareff, who had been so uncooperative in helping Luzon and Torkel Fiske get across the coo-berry forestation. Fingaard and Ardis Sounik were collected from Harrison's Fjord. It was there that a trooper got a lucky shot into an orange cat and, throwing the stunned carcass over his shoulder, grinned at the thought of the bonus he'd get.

"You *shot* Shush?" The Harrison's Fjord woman was too indignant to be cowed by the huge trooper.

"Jeez, lady, I just tranked him," the trooper said, backing a step away from the woman, who was nearly as tall as he. But he didn't interfere when she removed the limp cat from his shoulder; she cuddled it in her arms on the way back to SpaceBase and glared at him the entire trip.

Another shuttle picked up the Connellys—father, mother, and Krisuk—at McGee's Pass; Liam Maloney, still visiting at Deadhorse Pass; and then the shanachies of Little Dublin, New Barrow, and Mirror Lake. The third started at Tanana Bay, went on to Shannonmouth, where they collected Aigur and Sheydil, and got to Kilcoole before the fastest cat had had a chance to get halfway there.

Since Adak was among the first taken and the cats had scattered when pursued, Clodagh, Aisling, Sinead, 'Cita, Yana, and Sean were caught unprepared.

"Major Maddock, to you, Lieutenant," Yana had protested furiously, wrapping the bed quilt around her while Sean swung his feet over the side of the bed and unconcernedly pulled on his pants and boots. "Now get out of here while we dress."

"Orders, ma'am, not to let you out of my sight."

"About face, Lieutenant, and I'm not kidding!"

"Neither am I," he said, shifting his weapon threateningly. But to avoid her scathing glance, he stared straight forward, as if at attention.

"Okay then, fine, have it your way, you prurient bastard," Yana said. She stood up and dropped the quilt, straight and proud in her nakedness and inordinately relieved that she was now accustomed enough to the Petaybean temperatures that her flesh did not rise up in embarrassing bumps. Sean moved between her and the offending soldier, but she was not mollified.

"We'll meet again, Lieutenant, under other circumstances," she said softly, and had the pleasure of seeing him flush.

Sean did nothing but stand, leaning slightly in favor of his good leg, between her and the guard, but only when she had pulled on the dress uniform she had folded so carefully in the back of the small clothespress did he drop back beside her to clasp her hand. Then, silently, they were escorted outside.

Outside, the predawn morning was brooding, fog sitting on the sun to keep it from rising to brighten the sky. Suddenly, from the edges of the buildings visible, a black and white bolt flew past.

"No, Nanook!" Sean shouted, and as the troopers, all eager to claim the cat bonus, turned to find their target, they were rewarded with a snarl of such malice that, hardened though this squad was by encounters on many strange planets with many strange beasts, they looked anxious.

The lieutenant recovered first and detailed half his squad to fan out and see if they couldn't get a shot at the creature. Out of the corner of her eye, Yana saw the slight smile on Sean's face. No one was likely to catch Nanook. Coaxtl? She would have been at Sinead's, guarding her person, 'Cita. Yana fretted over that as they passively followed their guards to the shuttle. She could also sense that everyone in the village was awake and watching. That was all they could do with such a superior force.

When Yana saw the range of her fellow captives, her heart sank. Clodagh was as composed as usual, even though she was surrounded by nets of her potions and salves and medications. Hadn't witch-hunts gone out three centuries ago? Yana wondered numbly. Sinead looked furious, lips tightly compressed, while tears ran down Aisling's face, making her oddly more appealing than ridiculous. 'Cita was terrified and clung to Bunny, who had taken her cue from Clodagh and was holding her head proud. Adak looked frightened, as frightened as probably everyone else felt. He had always been the one in the know, the community's link with the base, as well as being a responsible company employee. Now he was just another ip, an "inconvenient person," as Bunny called herself and her fellow Petaybeans. Poor Adak seemed to shrink in on himself when he saw first Yana and then Sean pushed into the shuttle. Then he seemed to gather himself and twitched his shoulders to sit more erect on the hard metal seat.

As Yana was pushed down, she wondered if Diego, Frank, and Whittaker—naw, they wouldn't *dare* remand a company director, would they?—were missing from the roll of those Matthew considered dangerous dissidents. Then a large male body crowded in between herself and Sean. Looking around, she saw that every Petaybean was separated from another by a trooper—a big, heavily armed trooper.

She grinned broadly. What a backhanded compliment.

"Wipe that grin off your face," the nameless lieutenant ordered.

"Son, I outrank you and I've five times as many first-drop bars as you do," Yana said, sounding quietly amused but putting commander-steel in her voice and narrowing her eyes at him. "You can barge into my private quarters and arrest me without due process, but by all that's holy, don't you dare try to deny me the right to react to this whole ridiculous operation!"

The lieutenant, all too aware that she had outfaced him once before and determined not to let her get under his skin again, laughed. "Nothing's ridiculous about this operation and you'd better start believing it now . . . Major!"

"You mean, it isn't ridiculous that it took two squads of heavily armed non-Petaybean troopers transferred from Omnicron Three, Plexus-Four, and Space Station One-Thirty-One to arrest unarmed citizens of a backward, low-tech world?"

With a snarl, the lieutenant had gone as far as drawing his hand back when a voice from the cockpit abruptly ordered him forward.

Yana was proud that she had not so much as tensed to take the imminent blow and that her smile had stayed in place. No one spoke, of course, neither Petaybean nor alien trooper, but 'Cita and Aisling stopped weeping, and Clodagh's lips turned up just that little bit.

The moment the shuttle took off, Yana's courage seemed to leak out of her and fear pressed against her guts. She noticed that Clodagh's smile vanished and her lips were set. Bunny, too, looked more apprehensive. It wasn't until the shuttle landed a familiarly short distance away, where the heavy fog was pierced by a great quantity of bright lights of the kind employed only at SpaceBase, that her courage returned. Ah, but she was once more in touch with the planet. Somehow, some way, as yet inexplicable, the planet *was* aware: and Yana saw that Clodagh's smile had returned.

Yana's apprehensions returned, doubled, the moment they were marched out of the shuttle, which had landed right by an anonymous block of temporary housing. Though it was hard to see more than a few feet beyond her, Yana could tell from the only glance she had time for that they were at the far end of SpaceBase. It wasn't that large a facility by company standards, but being at the far end would place them at an awkwardly long distance from the administrative area and any help from Marmion Algemeine or Whittaker Fiske, if he was still at large.

Inside the building, bare corridors were brightly lit, and lined with doors, depressingly close together. That made this, she thought glumly, a temporary detention center: small cells, no amenities, and no communication between the reluctant residents.

A sergeant with a clipboard merely pointed a stylus to the right and they were led that way. Yana was thrust in the second room, and the door closed behind her with the odd thunk of a noise-proofed construction. A single strip of bright lighting, a blanket, a toilet, and a washbasin completed the furnishings. The temperature would have been chilly to those accustomed to space stations, but Yana was comfortable in it. Score one! She used the toilet, washed her face with her hands, and dried herself on one edge of her blanket. She took off her boots, tunic, and pants and laid them neatly on the rough carpet, then rolled up in the blanket and told herself to go back to sleep.

# 16

"It's a cat, common domestic Terran-type feline, female, weighing just above a kilo, which makes it somewhat larger," the veterinary surgeon said after doing every test he could think of on the limp orange-striped body that had been brought in. "Scanner shows no unusual organs, average brain size, average everything, except a dense fur of several layers, probably a requirement to survive in the temperatures you say exist in winter on this planet. It does have large ears, with more fur growing across—doubtless to prevent snow getting in—and a phenomenal length of whiskers. It does have heavily callused paw pads, with hair growing between the toes, and a long-haired tail, but I've never seen a healthier animal. And I can't find *anything* out of the ordinary about it, given its environment. For instance, the hair between the paws would make it easier to travel over snow."

"You have the report?" Ivan asked. The vet tapped one key of his handheld pad, and a narrow, long sheet inched its way out of the paper slot. He handed it to Ivan. "Thank you."

"What do I do with that cat?"

Ivan hesitated. He knew what Matthew had ordered, but what had the cat done to him? "Keep it under observation. Maybe awake, it will show some deviations."

The vet shrugged and gave a small snort. "Cats are deviant, and devious, by nature. Exactly *what* sort of aberrant behavior is this one supposed to exhibit when conscious? I mean, give me a clue to know what to watch out for."

"Maybe one isn't enough," Ivan muttered under his breath, then added louder, "No other squad caught one?"

"No other's been brought in to me." The vet stifled a yawn.

Another was brought in two hours later, only it wasn't a cat: it was a crossbreed feline that the vet couldn't find mention of in his files. It was nearly the size of the lions that had once roved Africa, had a thick coat of dense fur with a clouded-spot design, had the fangs and retractable claws of a tiger, and had to be tranked again before the vet and the four troopers struggling with the half-aware creature could put it under the scan.

Awed by its size, beauty, and uniqueness, the vet, when Matthew Luzon himself came for his report, could only verify that this was an unusual breed of feline.

"In what way?" Matthew asked with an edge to his voice that put the vet on the alert.

"Size, color, density of fur, condition, in that most feral animals are less well nourished," he answered, shrugging.

"No unusual organs? The size of the brain?"

"Normal for the size of the skull certainly." Suddenly the vet decided not to mention that that was the one particular in which the animal varied from any other specimen in the genus: its skull was larger, to accommodate the larger brain.

"Destroy it," Matthew said. "And do an autopsy. I'm looking for a scientific explanation of the so-called communication link these creatures have with the humans here. Implants, maybe."

"Sir, for that sort of information wouldn't behavioral observation be more—"

"Destroy it! Do I have to give orders twice?"

"No, sir." The vet wheeled around and made a show of filling a syringe and plunging the sterile water into the back of the neck. There were certain orders he would not obey, not with the oath he had taken as a young idealist who planned to catalog marvelous new alien life-forms. "Takes about twenty minutes, sir, with an animal this size."

But Matthew Luzon had already left the surgery and the vet wondered where the hell he could safely dispose of a sleeping animal this size without being noticed. He was still running through alternatives a half hour later when a major, with two soldiers, one a massive man and the other a mere slip of a lad, appeared at the door, saying they had orders to collect a dead animal. Reluctantly, he showed them the unconscious beast and desperately hoped that the second trank would wear off soon enough that the creature could escape being buried alive. Sometimes the favors one tried to do could boomerang.

He was very unhappy with what had seemed like a routine mission. None of the animals that had passed through his facility that day had been unusual except for their obvious adaptations to the climatic conditions of this peculiar place—although the purpose of that extra bony layer on the nose of the curly-coated stallion still puzzled him. The interior nasal flap was listed as a characteristic of the breed and kept icy winds from penetrating to their lungs. And now Luzon was intimating that the creatures might be— well, psychic! He never willingly destroyed an animal wantonly, and certainly not a psychic one!

Utterly depressed, he went to the cubicle allotted to him and tried to sleep. He woke up, even more depressed, for his dream had been about a clouded leopard running across a snowy waste, its effortless stride as graceful as it was powerful.

Awake, Coaxtl found, one had a dreadful thirst. One's body was slightly sore with pricks, scrapings, and bruisings, and one's senses were dull. Rolling over, one ducked one's head because of the low bushes under which one lay. A sniff brought no useful information as to one's location. The pursuers, men who rattled as they ran and shouted, were gone, though Coaxtl seemed to remember them being close enough to pounce. No mind. Now they were gone.

Unfortunately, the youngling was gone as well, still, and if Coaxtl had escaped the men, they had triumphed in preventing Coaxtl from finding the youngling.

Coaxtl had seen the little female forced into a huge bird machine, bigger than the terrible creature that had carried Coaxtl, the youngling, the seal-man, and his mate to this land where the youngling was to live with her kin. Where the black-and-white Nanook had been interested in one as a mate. Nanook had had much to tell Coaxtl, who had listened with growing wonder. More than "Home" was changing, it would seem. "Home" had indeed altered, if one could be so robbed of sense and then dumped unceremoniously under a thicket.

There was, however, some snow still left in the center of the shrubbery, and Coaxtl licked at it. The cool silvery water relieved the nasty, stinging taste and dryness in one's mouth, while the cold snow and the water seeping into one's fur revived one further.

Food would be a good thing. One lifted one's head and sniffed, sneezed. Too many humans, too many bad smells. Nothing appetizing nearby. Through the wind and the distant man-made noises came the rush of water. Water always held fish, and fish were edible. Yes, one could quite easily snag many fish on clever, swift claws and relieve one's hunger. Then one could plan what to do next. Finding Nanook would be best. This was his territory. He would know where to seek the youngling.

As dawn broke over the low hills and the new volcano, Coaxtl scooped the fourth large fish from the icy river waters, then continued standing, motionless until more unsuspecting aquatic shapes passed nearby. Coaxtl had eaten well by the time the sun was up.

Marmion did sleep well, but more because of Sean's infallible confidence than Sally's reassurance about demonstrable facts. When she woke the next morning, she was more than ready for the battle about to ensue.

She was not ready for Sally bursting into her room, her eyes wide with fright.

"They did it. Gathered up every one of the people Luzon calls 'renegades and traitors,' using the commissioners' shuttles and troops we didn't even suspect were on board them," she said in a spurt. "They've got them in detention cells on the far side of the field."

"Whittaker?" Marmion experienced an unusual pang of fear. Had she outsmarted herself last night? Whittaker would never have gone along with that sort of a ploy.

"No, he's free, and so are Frank and Diego Metaxos, and I told Faber to stay with them. Millard's dogging Whittaker, who is furious!"

Marmion bit her lower lip, ranging through alternative plans. "Who, exactly, did they seize in such a highly irregular procedure?"

"Only half the damned planet, including the wildlife," Sally said. By the time she had completed the list, Marmion found herself grinding her teeth.

She launched herself out of her bed toward the bathroom. "Get me my usual, and buckets of coffee, and what channel are we using this morning on our personal units?"

Sally gave her the frequency. "And I'm making your breakfast with my own hands," she said as she departed.

That made Marmion pause at the threshold of her bath. Surely Matthew . . . No, he wouldn't, but Bal wouldn't be beyond it. The ploy of detaining the persons the commission would call before them was a matter she *could*—and *would*—protest, since none of them could be proven guilty of any action against Intergal, unless a passive resistance was now considered a crime. All the *active* resistance had come from the planet. And Intergal doubted that this world had a mind of its own! She allowed herself a rather ruthless smile, one that had many times alarmed business colleagues who opposed her, as the hot shower water completed the process of waking her up. She was already clothed and discreetly made up by the time Sally arrived with a laden tray.

"Place is in an uproar, dama," Sally reported, her usually

cheery demeanor rather forced today. "All of Matthew's lovelies running about with streamers of hard copy, all of which seems to upset them for some reason. I saw Braddock Makem taking one of the others to task for coming up with results that were the opposite of what Luzon had ordered. Couldn't find out much more. The place is as well guarded as a first-touchdown camp, and more troops were shuttled in from, I think, the CISS *Prometheus*."

Marmion paused in the act of pouring her first, badly needed cup of coffee. She stared at Sally, aghast. "They've called in a CISS cruiser? But they're not authorized to call in CIS until this matter has gone through committee and up the chain of command. Otherwise, of course, I'd have preempted them and already called in CIS myself."

"You might remember, dama, that the captain of the *Prometheus* is a nephew of Vice-Chairman Luzon."

"Scuttled, are we?" Challenge only made Marmion sharper. "We'll just *see* about this!"

"I must also inform you, dama—" Sally's face was sad and angry. "I heard that a large clouded feline was seen being wheeled into the veterinary surgery early this morning."

"Ah, not Coaxtl!" Marmion took a deep breath and, eyes glittering, added fiercely, "It's bad enough that the humans of this world have to be mauled and pushed around like pawns, but when the beautiful animals are . . . Well, there's a thing or two Patrick Matthew Olingarch-Luzon will not want to hear as public gossip back at Space Station One-Thirty-One!" She downed the coffee in one gulp, poured another cup, and then went to the work desk and her terminal.

# 17

Yana was roughly aroused by an imperative hard shaking and looked up to see two of the Omnicron troopers, truncheons in their hands. One of them gestured for her to get up. When she went toward her clothes, they each caught an elbow. She shrugged, as much as she could in their grip, and did her best to match their long strides down the hall to the end and an open door, through which she was pushed with sufficient strength to propel her several meters into the room. The smell and the appurtenances told her it was medical. A male orderly swung through the open door on the right, a paper shift in his hands. He gave it to her and gestured to the screen.

She took it with a flicker of a smile. The silent treatment continued as she stepped out from behind the screen and was marched, strong fingers gripping her elbow, through the open door.

CAT scan, she thought as she saw the huge cylinder, and she nearly burst out laughing, remembering Marmion's observation that Clodagh would never fit in that, though the circumference of the equipment was wide enough for most human bodies.

She endured the prodding and probing, took the jars and produced the specimens, and had rather a lot of blood samples taken. She was crowned with the metal band of one of the more sophisticated brain-function devices she'd ever seen and sat through that while her reflexes were tested and she was pricked with more needles and had patches slapped on and pulled off. The doctor who performed the gynecological examination did a double take when he realized she was pregnant—at her age!—but murmured automatic reassurances that the fetus seemed to be in good shape. She was put up on a treadmill; and as it moved, she had to run faster and faster to keep from falling. When they stopped that test, she was barely puffing—and rather pleased that she was so fit. She waited passively, while the various medics had a huddle. The oldest of them, and he couldn't be more than her own age, finally gestured to the orderly and she was taken back to collect her underwear and then marched back to her cell.

She reckoned the examination had taken approximately an hour. As she put her underwear back on, she grinned, thinking of the CAT scan and the treadmill, which wouldn't accommodate either Clodagh or Aisling. She put the medical gown on again, rolled up in the blanket, and tried to get more sleep. She hoped the others, no doubt undergoing the same procedures, weren't unnerved by the silent treatment, which was supposed to demoralize the recipient. She wondered who else had been grabbed in the midnight snatches and finally fell asleep listing them in her head.

An earsplitting siren hooted her awake and she dressed quickly, not wishing to be caught again. A ration bar and a plastic cup of water were delivered by a silent guard while another watched, idly tapping his left hand with the truncheon. She said nothing as she accepted the food. She did, however, sniff the water before taking a sip to roll around in her mouth; but it was good Petaybee water, and the ration bar was standard Intergal in its original wrapping, complete with bar-coding. To her practiced eye, she read an expired date, but that oddly reassured her that nothing had been "treated."

She was sitting cross-legged, doing some relaxation exercises, when she felt the rumble under her buttocks: faint but definitely a seismic tremor.

"Good ol' Petaybee, you're not letting them get away with this, are you!"

"No talking!" The command was issued from a hidden speaker.

Yana reprimanded herself for not thinking to look for a bug, but of course they'd be listening in on all their prisoners, testing the efficacy of the silent treatment on the various personalities.

"Whatever!" she murmured, just to be contrary.

Commissioner Matthew Luzon had been awakened at two o'clock by Braddock as the first of the medical reports was presented. They proceeded to spew out of the remote printer in his office at regular intervals. He noted that Major Yanaba Maddock was two months pregnant and wondered just how he could use that fact to best advantage. He ignored the fact that she was in excellent physical health, no sign of the lung-tissue damage that had discharged her from active service. That was a harder issue to make viable to his needs.

Sean Shongili, too, was in excellent physical shape. The scan showed the largest of the cerebral nodes yet noticed, also, the largest brown fat concentration and an enlarged pancreas. His toes and fingers were abnormally long but could not be considered either an adaptation or a mutation; the slight increase in digital webbing was odd, but not entirely exceptional. They had been unable to get clear readings of his internal organs—the medic claimed that slight earth tremors prevented him from being able to calibrate the machine properly the whole time Shongili was being tested—but these were evidently functioning normally according to other forms of testing.

Matthew, who knew what he had seen at the Vale of Tears, had his suspicions about the internal organs, but realized he might have to win his case before he could take Shongili off-planet where sufficiently extensive invasive tests could be performed. He knew the man was not normal, but none of the tests he could legally conduct here provided enough data. Just little things: a slight anomaly in configuration noted that Shongili's torso was inappropriately longer than his legs. If his leg bones had grown in proportion to his body, he would have been several inches taller. This was not considered unduly important, but his unusual lung capacity was, along with a high metabolic rate while his blood pressure was on the low side of normal.

They had been unable to scan the woman, Clodagh Senungatuk, and had barely managed to fit her sister, Aisling, in the device. While obese in medical terms, the women were also in excellent health and, since Aisling Senungatuk had a well-developed node and five hundred grams of brown fat, it could be concluded that her unscannable elder sister was similarly endowed.

Analysis was continuing on the various liquids and powders found in Clodagh Senungatuk's house, but so far they tested as herbal, with some minerals, mineral salts, and occasional animal-protein additives. Nothing toxic or poisonous had yet been found. When questioned on the usage of various items, the subject had answered willingly and at some length, describing preparation when asked and the places where she obtained the ingredients. The biochemists in charge of this aspect of the investigation were clearly impressed by the almost sophisticated pharmaceuticals available in such a primitive society. In the course of questioning her, it was learned that Senungatuk's great-grandparents had been the resident biochemists during the initial seeding of flora and fauna on Terraform B, working with the elder Dr. Shongili. Senungatuk had an exceptional memory and, although she reeled off by rote long passages of biochemical procedures, she obviously *understood* the material she recited.

Matthew Luzon excised that section from the report. In fact, if the medical procedures hadn't also been intended to demoralize the renegades, he would have stopped the examinations as a waste of time. The "splendid physical health" was not at issue and was not to last long in the conditions to which he intended to send them all—if what Maddock had told Torkel was true: and Shepherd Howling's unexpected demise upheld his theory. He was rubbing his hands together in pleasure when he felt the rumbling under his feet. That gave him a moment's pause. But only a moment. Seismic activity was no proof of sentience, as Whittaker and some others claimed. It only proved that the Terraform B program had developed unforeseen problems. On the other hand, he now had plenty of proof of subversion and sabotage among the inhabitants *and* a premeditated homicide in the deaths of the four shanachies. He also had proof that the belief in the sentience of this rock was not at all universal.

"Braddock," he called. The young man appeared immediately. "Find out how widespread this seismic activity is and how long it will last. I don't want it affecting the conference time slot."

Braddock gave him a startled look, then said an obedient "Yes, sir" and ducked away.

Matthew then turned to some of the other reports his minions had been organizing. The demographics were not what he had anticipated. The first settlers had been from mixed Eskimo-Irish, Scandinavians, Sherpans, Andean Indians, Slavs, Somalis, Afghans, and a handful or two of other inconvenient people who had had to be removed. Most of those he considered "renegades" were Eskirish, a really absurd combination in terms of melding violence and resourcefulness. Whatever had the original Intergal committee been thinking of to allow such interbreeding!

The most recent colonists, whom he had hoped would be untouched by the local superstitions, so resented their resettlement that they had been remarkably uncooperative. They would prove hostile witnesses even if they hadn't fallen under the mass hallucination that the planet was self-aware. They were not interested in working in mines, even at the wages Matthew, in the name of Intergal, had offered: they were interested in either getting off Petaybee or, failing that, in surviving the next year. He must find out why George, Ivan, and Hans had completely ignored the possibilities in that wish. Not like them to miss an opportunity. If he'd had a little more time, he might have used the wedge to his advantage. He did have a Scotsman on hand, antagonistic or not, and Ascencion—now that she had been thoroughly bathed and properly clothed—as witnesses that not all settlements believed as the people of Kilcoole did. But the time spent gathering most of these reports had been wasted. He tossed them aside and picked up the files dealing with the four recently deceased shanachies.

This was more like it. Each of them, Satok, Reilly, Soyuk, Clancy, and Shepherd Howling, had been leaders of their communities and actively trying to find the ores that Intergal knew lay below the surface of the planet. Torkel could verify that Satok had showed him rich samples. Satok had also found an ingenious way to neutralize the "mesmeritic" effect of the caves by the use of Petraseal, before his work had been sabatoged by what Matthew suspected was the deliberate planting of coo-brambles, which had not only broken through the Petraseal, but had murdered Satok as well. Clearly an attempt to discredit the technique, as well as silence its innovator.

Not that that murder had worked! Matthew grinned. That woman would be punished. And it had only proved that the metals were there, in these so-called "communion" caves. Of course, it was entirely typical of primitive peoples, or regressed ones, to designate valuable areas as somehow "taboo" to scientific study and use. But such thinking was backward and counterproductive on a company facility such as this planet. Part of Matthew's mission was to expose such cultural backwardnesses for what they were and suggest reform programs to reeducate the natives while helping the company make maximum use of the resources.

Usually he felt no personal involvement whatsoever, merely a sense of satisfaction at a mission well done. But Petaybee—Terraform B—irritated him. If he had any influence at all, and he did have—a nephew captaining the CISS *Prometheus* specifically—no matter what any one of these primitives said or did or claimed that the planet said or did, it would be mined of every ounce worth even a half credit.

He'd sent Torkel Fiske to find at least one vein of ore—anything would do, copper, iron, manganese, silver, gold, platinum, germanium—in the underground passages to prove that the indigenous people had deliberately kept Intergal scientists and engineers from locating the ores; that there had been a long-standing passive resistance and discreet sabotage to prevent Intergal from reaping the financial rewards of its investment in the terraforming process. He had also sent a team to Shannonmouth with metal detectors to find where the traitors had hidden the ores they had clandestinely taken from Satok's shuttle. He would heavily emphasize how long these Petaybeans had been bilking Intergal of its rightful gains.

That sort of accusation would strike a punitive chord in the minds of men like Bal Jostique and Nexim Shi-Tu, and quite likely affect Chas's known softheartedness. Marmie's little supercilious smirk last night over their bad investment had not endeared her to Bal and Nexim.

His nephew was standing by in the CISS *Prometheus*. All the troops on SpaceBase now were strangers to this planet and incorruptible, and the Petaybee-born troops that Torkel had unwittingly ordered in before had been rounded up and confined to barracks. The two arrogant copter pilots were incarcerated as well for their obstructionism and would face a court-martial for their crafty dodges. The only drawback to his revenge on O'Shay and Greene was that they wouldn't suffer from immune deficiencies as much as the other Petaybeans soon to be removed from their "beloved" planet.

Marmion, too, felt the rumbling through the thick carpet and smiled. Just what could the planet do to impress the unimpressible, who had seen it all, done it all? Only they hadn't, had they? She gave a light laugh, although she could not ignore the cramping of her stomach muscles as the time for the meeting approached.

# 18

The committee convened at 10:00 promptly. Matthew
had had even smaller, padded detention cells set up in an
annex by the temporary boardroom. All prisoners were
present and accounted for, although the sergeant in charge
had reported that the medics had insisted that the child,
Goat-dung, be placed with her sister or they wouldn't take
responsibility for her sanity when it came time for her to be
questioned. Matthew shrugged that off. An eleven-year-old
was not necessary, not really. The testimony of Shepherd
Howling's senior wife, Ascencion, would be more than sufficient.

He looked about for Torkel, who had had time enough to
locate at least one viable ore site. Not seeing the captain
among those in the anteroom, he told Ivan to locate the
man and have him come, with or without samples. As a
well-respected officer of Intergal, Fiske's word would be
sufficient.

As he entered the committee room, Chas, Bal, and
Nexim were standing by the windows, watching the thick
mist left over from the night rolling across the cracked con-
crete landing field of SpaceBase. Matthew frowned. The
met report had been that the fog would burn off and that
they would have clear weather and temperatures slightly
above normal for Petaybee this time of year—still too
bloody cold, in Luzon's opinion, for civilized people—but
nothing had been said about ground fog continuing right

into the day. With an unusual burst of imaginativeness, he realized that he considered this fog to be unnatural, sneaking and insidious in the way it moved, stifling in the way it muffled sound and prevented a clear field of vision.

Shaking off such thoughts, he grabbed Braddock, walking a pace behind him, arms full of notes and documentation, and told him in a low voice to close the blinds. He didn't want any distractions during the proceedings.

Marmion arrived at the dot of the appointed hour, smiling charmingly to everyone, with just that tall bitch of hers in attendance. She looked pleased about something. Well, that would change! And swiftly, Matthew thought with great satisfaction. As chairperson of this commission, her ladyship grandly invited all to be seated.

The blankness of the main screen altered swiftly to an image of the secretary-general of Intergal, Farringer Ball, seated at his desk, tapping the end of a stylus on the finely grained wood surface.

"Well, let's not dally. I've other matters to attend this morning." A spray of "snow" across the screen coincided with a rumbling that all could feel, judging by their reactions, as Matthew did, through the soles of their feet and the vibration of their chairs. "What the—I'm losing reception. Get your technicians to stabilize it!"

Matthew signaled for George to do so. "Local interference, Farringer, nothing to worry about. This *is*, as you know, a very primitive planet and the equipment all but obsolete. Generally adequate enough for the purpose, especially considering the time and investment already expended on this wretched place."

"Let's cut to the bone: Can this planet be made profitable?"

"Yes, actually it can," Marmion said, pouncing in ahead of Matthew. "As chairperson of this committee, in case you'd forgotten, I have no doubts about that, Farrie." She gave him her saccharine smile.

"You've found the ores then?" Secretary-General Ball asked hopefully.

"Petaybee is more important to Intergal for a heretofore unexplored source of *renewable* wealth," Marmion said firmly, "that will require no further capital expenditure while it offers gainful employment to permit the indigenous a decent standard of living as well as a profit for Intergal, and will attract no retaliation from the sentient being who *is* the planet."

"Oh, come now, Marmion, you can't prove that," Matthew said scornfully, "and you know you can't."

"The pharmaceutical wealth of Petaybee?" She raised her eyebrows in surprise. "Why, the reports from your own team of biochemists are quite clear on that point, Matthew. This planet is a treasure trove of diverse and easily harvested medical components."

Seething, Matthew managed a weak smile. *How* had Marmion Algemeine got hold of those reports? He had told the head of the team to release information to no one but himself. But then, his team had seriously let him down, their performance declining ever since he had left them alone while he flew to the southern continent. Usually they and their computers were masterful at manipulating statistics to show the results he desired. Since his return, almost every report he looked at reflected data supporting conclusions the opposite of those he wished drawn. More than Petaybean heads would roll when this conference was over. And where the hell was Torkel Fiske?

"Pharmaceuticals? What pharmaceuticals?" Farringer Ball demanded, looking decidedly interested.

Matthew inwardly writhed. Everyone knew that the secretary-general experimented in consciousness stimulations and was still searching for longer-lasting mood adjusters with no side effects.

"Yes, Farrie, some really marvelous concoctions and remedies, guaranteed pure and free of toxic additives and remarkably no discernible side effects," Marmion went on. "Preparations which, if merchandised properly—that Nova Bene Drug Company you've an interest in," she added, hesitating only briefly over that allusion, "could promote them in an interplanetary campaign—will substantially reduce the debt incurred by the earlier, and unacceptable, purpose of Intergal on this planet. Indeed, we have every reason to believe the planet will assist us in this venture, provided harvesting is carried out in a responsible and prudent manner."

"As it assisted the murders of four shanachies who had discovered the vast metal and mineral wealth of this rockball?" Matthew asked.

"Murders? What murders?" Farringer looked from one to the other.

"Five, in fact," Matthew said challengingly, "since the shanachie of the Vale of Tears was so convinced that he would be the next victim that I naturally afforded him asylum on MoonBase."

"Five? Four? He's dead, too? Of what?" Farringer Ball was again confused.

"He unfortunately succumbed to a virulent respiratory infection three days ago," Matthew said quickly, and then pointed behind him, in the direction of the detention cells, "but his death, as well as the murders of the four shanachies, is directly attributable to the concerted program of sabotage, misdirection, and treason perpetrated by the leaders of this conspiracy against Intergal."

"Who?" the secretary-general asked, more confused by Matthew's rhetoric than ever.

"By the woman, Clodagh Senungatuk—"

"The Kilcoole biochemist and healer of considerable expertise," Whittaker Fiske interposed amiably.

"Who, before witnesses, admitted to knowing the toxic quality of the plant which was instrumental in the deaths of the four shanachies!" Matthew snapped back, trying to keep his growing frustration under control. "And the so-called doctor Sean Shongili, the reputed genetic scientist who has, in fact, aided and abetted Senungatuk in her program of sabotage, subversion, and the estrangement of the population from their natural protectors, Intergal!"

"What a load of cod's wallop!" Whittaker said, shaking

his head and raising his eyes skyward at Matthew's accusations.

"Not only that," Matthew went on, "I find that Captain Torkel Fiske's request for a court-martial of Major Yanaba Maddock, *formerly* an agent of Intergal, has adequate grounds on charges of treason and counterespionage. She's in league with Senungatuk and Shongili and, furthermore, two months pregnant by someone or other!" He said the last four words scathingly.

"I thought Major Maddock was discharged to this planet in a terminally disabled physical condition," Chas Tung said as he peered at his own notepad. "She's certainly well over the customary age to conceive a child." He looked around for an explanation.

"Which is more proof that the healing powers of this planet's pharmaceutical wealth are most unusual," Whittaker Fiske said, chortling, "and worth a packet to Intergal."

"Rubbish! Ridiculous!" Matthew replied. "The true value of this planet is, after evacuating the immigrant population, the minerals and resources Intergal has invested in during its development and has every right to ship from it, until it is nothing but the core of ice and rock it was when the company first set eyes on it. Once we have extracted what is rightfully ours, we can leave it all by itself again."

"Ha!" Whittaker jabbed a finger at Matthew. "You said it yourself. You believe it's sentient, too. 'Leave it all by itself!' See, Luzon admits sentience."

"I admit nothing of the sort! Rock can't have sentience! That can't be proved."

Everything on the table began to rattle; on the screen, Farringer Ball's livid, baffled countenance dissolved and reformed several times.

"It just was proved by that tremor, Luzon," Whittaker Fiske said.

"The esteemed doctor has lost his esteemed mind, sir, you see?" Matthew crowed over Fiske's softer voice. "He now interprets every perfectly natural phenomenon as some sort of statement by the ground he walks upon."

Fiske didn't even change expressions as he continued, when Matthew ran out of breath. "Furthermore"—Fiske pointed to a thin mist oozing through the seams of the building, floor, walls, and ceiling—"you may be about to partake of the 'mass hallucination,' as my dear son called it, as proof positive of our claims of sentience."

"What's hap'ing . . . there?" the secretary-general demanded, the "snow" and static interfering on both sides. "How . . . I possibly un . . . stand what's going on when I . . . even . . . clearly. Luz . . . what's . . . matter?"

Matthew was irritated not only by the poor reception but also by the mist seeping in under the doors and the supposedly tightly sealed window fittings. He was further distracted by the note handed him by Braddock that told him that Torkel was unable to locate SpaceBase in the thick mist and his pilot, one of the *Prometheus*'s flight lieutenants, would not risk his craft and his passengers when he couldn't see where to land.

The secretary-general banged a gavel fiercely. "Fix that . . . screen. Stop . . . fusing issues. Marm . . . on, can you clar . . . matters?"

"I have, Farrie. And we're working on the reception here. The technician should have things cleared up in a moment. Please raise your hand if you can't hear me. The planet's worth more as a pharmaceutical source, renewable *in perpetuity*, than as another strip-mining operation," she said. "I have had cooperation from all sides and professions on this planet. The indigenous population are hardy, industrious, resourceful people—they have to be to survive in what is a harsh environment. But for four generations they have coped and provided Intergal with strong, healthy recruits who have been a credit to the service and their planet. They have sabotaged nothing, even though the company has given them precious little assistance. This planet, however, registered a complaint which Whittaker Fiske and Torkel, if he'd admit it, have heard, and this committee is in response to that complaint. Petaybee, the planet, has refused to be exploited in a brutal and ecologically senseless fashion. Its complaint is not only valid but points us in the more feasible and useful direction of considering alternative sources of profit. Why ruin a world for crass metal when its wealth in renewable products is by far greater and longer lasting? I have myself experienced the total communication with it that Whittaker here and most of the population have enjoyed, and hallucination it is not, as Whittaker has already testified."

At that point, the door opened, admitting an Omnicron officer who, despite Matthew's scowl, presented him with a large green rock, veined deeply in orange, and a note.

"Aha!" Matthew sprang to his feet, flourishing the rock toward the screen. "The ore samples that were removed from Satok's craft have been found by metal detector in the woods at Shannonmouth, where they were illegally removed from his vessel and hidden: yet another example of the sabotage that is almost planetwide. This is high-grade copper, according to this quick assay."

"Copper? Is that the best you can do, Matthew? Copper?" Nexim Shi-Tu demanded. "Not gold, or platinum . . ."

"Lieutenant, did you see any gold or platinum among the samples?" Matthew asked, his eyes gimleting the Omnicron man.

"Sir, I wouldn't know either in the raw state. I was told to bring this to you because it's the purest of the lot we found."

"Pure copper is not to be sneezed at," Marmion said without a trace of sarcasm, "but hardly in the same category as a respiratory remedy that cures damaged lung tissue, now is it?" A technician bent and spoke to her and she said to the screen, which was still fuzzy but not so noisy, "Is that better now, Farrie?"

"Yes, I believe it is. Continue."

"D'you have something for immaculate conceptions, too?" Bal asked slyly.

"By whom is Major Yanaba Maddock pregnant, Marmion?"

She shrugged. "Let's not digress from the purpose of this commission, gentlemen. Major Maddock's personal life is not at issue in this hearing and should not be at issue in any other hearing as long as she has obeyed her orders."

"*Aha!*" And Matthew once more jumped to his feet. "That's just it. She hasn't obeyed orders."

"But she did," Marmion replied firmly. "As she was instructed by Colonel Giancarlo, she became a part of the society of Kilcoole and set about learning as much as she could about Petaybee. She learned a great deal, although it was not, perhaps, what her superiors had expected her to discover."

"Where is she?" Farringer Ball asked, looking around the room. "She was the uniformed one from our first conference, wasn't she?"

"I believe she has been detained on Vice-Chairman Luzon's orders," Marmion said, turning to Matthew with a suddenly implacable expression on her composed, elegant face, "another breach of the civil rights of Intergal officers. And that's for the record, Farringer," she added sternly. "Even an Intergal commissioner cannot go about denying officers their civil rights."

"Of course I had her detained," Matthew almost shouted back, "as an unrepentant renegade ally of the Kilcoole group. As a matter of course, I had medical tests run on all the renegades—"

"Why?" Whittaker cracked that one word out. "What right had you to impose a restriction on any one of the citizens of this world? I've told you once and I'll keep on telling you: *They* are not sabotaging Intergal. Intergal is sabotaging itself on Petaybee."

"Oh, come now!" Matthew said, his voice dripping with scorn and the indignation that, rather to his surprise, he found he was actually shaking with. Or *was* that indignation causing him to shake? It seemed to be shaking everyone else, too, and the table, as well.

Fiske was continuing, heedlessly. "By denying the demonstrable proof that the pharmaceutical wealth will be a long-term and highly profitable use of Petaybee. So what did your needless medical tests prove?" Typical of the man, he had no sooner asked the question than he answered it himself. "Not a damn thing except they're the healthiest bunch of people your tame medical staff has seen in a hunk of years. So they've a few spare parts that help them adapt to Petaybee's climate. So what? Nothing mysterious."

"Vice-Chairman Luzon has been so busy he hasn't seen the obvious, Farrie," Marmion said with a hint of sympathy for the misguided Luzon. "I'm sure we can come to some arrangement to extract some ores when they don't involve disturbing invasions of Petaybee's integrity. Open-pit mining is as disfiguring as deep-pit mining is—is—"

"You're saying the damned planet *feels* mining operations?" Farringer Ball demanded, staring with round eyes at Marmion.

"Just as much as you'd feel a bone drill for a marrow sample: an archaic example, but then most mining methods verge on the archaic, as well as the destructive," Marmion remarked. "Certainly it's like peeling skin from an appendage, or suffering first-degree burns, and even you can appreciate how painful that would be."

"Marmion de Revers Algemeine," Farringer Ball began at his most pompous, "do you actually subscribe to the theory that this planet is sentient?"

"I most certainly do. And so do Sally Point-Jefferson, Millard Ephiasos, and Faber Nike, and you know very well, Farrie, that none of them are the least susceptible to 'illusions' or 'hallucinations,' not with the reports they have submitted to you on various occasions which I need not specifically mention."

Matthew interrupted with a contemptuous gesture and his silkiest tone. "Madame Algemeine is a beautiful, intelligent woman, quite talented at making money, well adapted to survive under civilized circumstances, but she is used to dealing with people of the same sensibility. Here, I fear that she has fallen under the influence of the same primitive passions that claimed the major's good sense and caused her to cast disrepute on her previously outstanding military record. A lady of such refinement as our chairperson . . ." Matthew shrugged, but was gratified by the rising color flooding across the delicate flesh on Marmion's aristocratic cheekbones and slender neck. "In the best interest of Intergal, I'm requesting—no, *demanding*—a purge of all residents on this colony planet due to their almost unanimous obstructive behavior, the deliberate sabotage of Intergal expeditions, and subversions too numerous to list. And I charge Major Yanaba Maddock with treasonable activities; captains O'Shay and Greene for deliberate acts of sabotage and treason to this investigation; Dr. Sean Shongili for willful acts, including homicide, against the best interests of Intergal, whom he has contracted to serve; Clodagh Senungatuk for—" He paused to look down at his list.

"Oh, great stars in the sky, Matthew," Marmion said, with a laugh, "how many people *did* you steal away from their homes in the middle of the night to remand on such ridiculous, trumped-up charges?"

"Don't laugh too soon, Marmion," Matthew said severely. "Not when community leaders have been slain to prevent them from disclosing local lodes to Intergal officials."

Unfortunately, his long list had given Marmion time to recover her composure and her rather deplorable sense of humor. "And please remember to indict whoever it was you allege seduced me to primitive passions, Matthew." She twinkled at him in a childish way, then added disparagingly, "*Do* be sensible, Matthew, and face the facts you've helped gather. The autopsy reports clearly state death by misadventure—"

"A highly toxic plant was purposefully *allowed* to infest the ore locations—"

"To spring up overnight? That's quite a green thumb, Matthew!" Marmion snapped back. "How can *anyone*, other than by actual planting and nourishing over a considerable period of time, tell a plant where to grow? Besides which, you've been so busy quizzing innocent folk about all kinds of misdemeanors that you never took a look at the records of four of those 'murdered' men. James Satok, James Unidak Reilly, Clancy Nyungaruk, and Soyuk Ishunt were dishonorably discharged from Intergal for fraud and black-market activities involving Intergal supplies."

"No such report reached my desk," Matthew said, turning to Braddock. The younger man shrugged, but his startled face expressed guilt and chagrin. "Moreover, I have proof positive that that highly toxic coo-berry bramble thorn was deliberately placed in the caves at four or more different settlements to prevent entry and discovery of rich ore-bearing seams!"

"Wait a minute!" Farringer Ball said, banging a fist on the table. "All this is beside the point, Matthew. Especially if Marmion says we can harvest pharmaceuticals and get at least some ores . . . which ones, Marmion?"

"That is to be decided," Marmion replied, "but drills, excessive use of explosives—"

"Secretary-General Ball!" Matthew all but roared. "You cannot *believe* the aberrant notion put forth by Chairperson Algemeine that this planet is sentient?"

"No, I believe in cutting losses and getting what we can out of a place that's causing far more fuss than it's worth," Farringer replied.

"It's a ball of rock, an inanimate object . . ." Matthew was pounding the table with one fist and almost bouncing on his feet in his protest.

Suddenly he was catapulted onto the table, facedown, his nose spurting blood, as seismic activity produced a havoc that had everyone in the room either grabbing their chairs to stay in them or being bounced about the committee room. Grinding sounds were so loud that people clapped hands to their ears, as the building shook and more mist poured in from the cracked seams of floor, walls, and ceilings.

"Under the table!" Whittaker Fiske shouted, practically dragging Marmion after him as the two of them, closely followed by the other committee members, hogged the most sturdily built piece of furniture in the room. Before Matthew could join them, they were joined by Marmion's overqualified secretary, and there was literally no room for another body to squeeze in. Or so he thought, until he spied one far corner unoccupied and dove for it, only to be knocked away by Braddock Makem, the sniveling coward.

"Get out of there at once, Braddock!" Matthew commanded, or he meant to sound commanding. He was appalled at how his normally controlled decibels elevated into panicky-sounding squeals. "Where's your sense of priorities? *I'm* the commissioner here."

The guards stationed in the room and others—he wasn't sure who—seemed to be trying to beat in the door, or break out a window, permitting the mist to flow more freely through the shambles of a committee room. A loud crash suggested that the main screen had fallen victim to the earthquake.

Matthew heard someone screeching for help and to his chagrin realized the voice was his own. Never mind. This was an emergency and he had been deserted by his colleagues. No time for niceties. *"Help!"* he screamed again.

"Try apologizing to the planet, Matthew!" Marmion bellowed over the crashings, splinterings, bangings, and other sounds of rending wood, plastic, and plaster. Ha! Easy enough for her to taunt him when she was protected by the table.

*"Tell it you believe, Matthew!"* Whittaker Fiske hollered as well. It was the last thing Matthew heard as the entire building convulsed; he felt wetness warm the crotch of his trousers and slide down his leg, and, as the sound of the tumult was drowned out by a roar that came from within his own head and the snow from the comm screen seemed to be affecting his eyesight, he followed his own urine onto the floor.

Whittaker Fiske nearly choked because he had been trying to yell to Luzon and laugh at the same time. The floor abruptly canted to the far end of the committee room. The table and those it sheltered were willy-nilly propelled downhill. Whittaker, one arm crooked around the table leg nearest him, managed to grab hold of Marmion, who caught Sally by the shoulder. Bal, Chas, and Nexim helplessly slid downward. Losing his footing, Luzon was rolled lengthwise against the table's sturdy legs and caught there. A tangle of uniformed limbs pressed him even harder against the table legs, and he began shouting warnings and dire imprecations against those who had him unwillingly pinned against the furniture.

The grinding noises increased, drowning out all other sounds, and then, with a mighty swooshing sound, the walls and roof of the commissioners' room collapsed over the table, which stolidly bore the extra weight, though some of the surface veneer audibly cracked.

The ensuing silence, as the swirling mist settled on everyone, was almost worse than the horrific bombardment of noise had been. Then a breeze, most peculiarly scented with floral aromas, wafted through the damaged room, settling the dust caused by the building's collapse and dispersing the mist.

"Marmion?" Whittaker asked, shaking his head to clear it from both the tumbling he had endured and the residue of the mist.

"I'm fine, shaken, but not bruised, thanks to your quick grab," she said, though her skirt was ripped and her blouse torn. "Sally?"

"Okay, I think!"

Whittaker completed the roll call; the names he called out were answered by either groans or curses.

"Matthew?" Whittaker asked with some anxiety. It would be awfully awkward if the planet had inadvertently caused the death of Vice-Chairman Matthew Luzon. That could be considered vengeful, not that he didn't deserve it with his notion of removing all the Petaybeans and cutting the planet into bits.

"He's alive, sir, but unconscious," a deep male voice said. "I think it's all over and—oh, my God!"

"What? What's the matter?" Marmion asked, duly concerned by the awe and respect in that slowly enunciated epithet. She looked about her for a way out from under the table, but the walls and roof seemed to have collapsed to cover everything except for the spot kept open by Matthew's unconscious body.

She moved that way, gesturing for Whittaker and Sally to follow her. There was just enough room for them to crawl under the table top and over the limp Matthew, whose aroma was decidedly *not* floral, where he had been caught, chest and thighs, by the two table legs. Hands helped them to stand in a relatively free space, crowded though it was by uniformed bodies and the splintered remnants of the original door into the room. Oddly enough, that wall was standing.

Then Marmion turned in the direction the officer was staring.

"My *word*!" Her jaw dropped as she gazed out at the massive rock structure that had been punched through the surface that had once been the landing field of SpaceBase. "No, it's not quite a ziggurat," she murmured to herself, trying to remember where she had seen a very similar formation, like building blocks, or stepping-stones in some unfathomable pattern, rising high above them. Yet even as her amazed eyes took in the scope of the elevated area, she could see how one could fairly easily climb to the top, if one were daring. Once the last of the mists had cleared, what a splendid view one would have, too, to see what Petaybee had done to prove Matthew's assumption wrong.

People were emerging from upended and broken buildings all around this extrusion, dust-covered, quite likely amazed to have escaped with their lives.

"Is anyone hurt down here?" a familiar voice called from the corridor.

"Yana! Yanaba Maddock, is Clodagh with you? I think Matthew may be hurt," Marmion called back.

"Luzon?" There was a definite edge to Yana's tone, but then Marmion scarcely blamed her. "Is anyone else hurt?"

"I—I don't think so," Marmion said, twisting around to see Chas Tung, Bal Jostique, and Nexim Shi-Tu getting to their feet and dusting themselves off. Then they, too, caught sight of what had been elevated on the landing field and just stared at it.

Do them good, Marmion thought, for doubting!

"Are you all right? And everyone with you?" Marmion called.

Then Yana poked her head through the door while Sean carefully broke off the splintered wood of the doorframe before it could do any harm.

"Clodagh's still counting noses, but we had the benefit of padded cells during the rough bit," Yana said with an irrepressible grin, "and the door locks released when the power went off." She gave a snort at the inadequacy of the security as she clambered over the door and knelt beside Matthew, feeling the pulse at his throat. "Well, he's alive—but you're bleeding, soldier. And Sergeant, that looks like a broken arm to me. Sit down here, against the wall. If it hasn't fallen before, it won't come down now. Ah, Bunny, find some water and see if you can find a medic running around loose."

"The usual medical facility is just down that corridor and to your right," Whittaker said. "I'll show you." He stepped over the remaining doorframe to lead Bunny—and also to add his authority to any request she'd make of dazed or possibly reluctant personnel to assist her.

# 19

It took the rest of that day to assess damages, but these were actually rather limited, despite the wreckage of the conference wing and its temporary detention cells. The ones on the far end of the field had also been demolished, but there had been no loss of life and only a few minor broken limbs, lacerations, and bruises. There were plenty of outraged dignities and addled wits. Some of the Omnicron and the other imported soldiers spoke of hearing a voice in the mist, though they hadn't a clue what it was saying, other than somehow reassuring them.

Halfway through Johnny Greene's and Rick O'Shay's attempts to reestablish communications with the MoonBase, a disheveled and enraged Torkel Fiske arrived on foot with the copter pilot, both of them lugging jury-rigged backpacks full of ore samples. He insisted on seeing Matthew Luzon, and "don't give me any excuses," so he was duly shown the bandaged but still unconscious commissioner.

"Massive bruising on the chest," the almost apologetic medic told him, "and he's got two broken legs."

"Who did that? I don't see any of you wearing bandages," Torkel said, belligerently glaring around at those who were working in the temporary incident room set up in one of the half-empty warehouses on the perimeter of SpaceBase.

"I *told* Matthew to get under the table," Whittaker cheerfully lied, "but he never did pay a blind bit of attention to

302

sensible suggestions. Ask Captain Urambul over there! He was one of the bunch that rammed into Matthew."

Torkel's accusatory stare relaxed slightly when he took in the huge frame of the Omnicron captain and the others in his group. They did, at least, have some noticeable face and hand cuts, and probably some bruises they would ignore. The captain was speaking into a handheld, evidently repeating everything he said, for he wore a resigned look of strained patience.

"At what point in the meeting did the earthquake happen, Dad?" Torkel asked, his manner and tone far less belligerent.

"About the time Matthew was banging the table and insisting the planet couldn't be sentient," Marmion said. "Oh, by the way, Whit, Coaxtl was released from durance vile by Frank Metaxos, Diego, and Faber, dressed up in uniforms and looking very officious. The poor vet turned Coaxtl over without a word, and she was last seen by Liam Maloney swiping fish out of the river at dawn."

"Thank God for that!"

"Coaxtl?" Torkel looked from one to another in puzzlement.

"Yes, of course, Coaxtl was one of the plotters Matthew wished to indict," Marmion said in the tone one used when speaking to someone of deficient intelligence. "Along with a little bitty skinny pregnant orange kitty cat. Quite subversive for felines, or so Matthew was going to try to prove."

"Dr. Fiske?" Braddock Makem said with considerably more vibrancy in his voice than he had ever used in addressing his employer. "That earthquake was local, the epicenter the exact center of the landing field. Only those three small aftershocks, and no more expected."

"Thank you, Makem," Whittaker said, smiling. "Now, Torkel, where did you find the samples you brought back with you?"

"In one of the passages of the cavern we were all rescued from after your shuttle came down," he said, and a look of disgust passed over his face. He made a fist. "We were right there, not more than ten meters from one of the biggest veins of pure gold I have ever seen, and these Petaybeans—"

"I've had enough of that from you, Torkel, to last the rest of our mutual existence," Whittaker said, abandoning his homespun manner and straightening up so abruptly that Torkel backed off a step in surprise at his father's sudden authoritative manner. "Company policy has shifted from exploitation of the mineral wealth of this planet to its pharmaceutical—"

"And renewable," Marmion interposed, touching Whittaker's arm in reminder.

"And renewable pharmaceutical wealth."

"Its *what?*"

Torkel glared at his father, who stared him down, and then glanced about the room to spot any Petaybean on whom he could vent his frustrated anger.

"*Colonel* Yanaba Maddock and Dr. Sean Shongili," his father began, noticing his discomfort, "will share a joint governorship of the planet Petaybee, under the auspices of Intergal and Nova Bene Drugs to develop a local industry of fine Petaybean pharmaceuticals—"

"Ah, just a moment if you please," said a light baritone voice.

Everyone turned to see the man who had discreetly appeared amidst them in the temporary incident room. He was wearing the distinctive gray and silver-trimmed uniform of a high-ranking official of the Collective Interplanetary Societies.

"I've just managed to land here, via the *Prometheus*, on a matter of gravest urgency," he began. "Oh," he added, smiling apologetically, "my name is Phon Tho Anaciliact. I seem to have come at a bad moment. I understand there has been a hearing under way today to determine the findings of an investigative committee. Who is the chairman of that committee?"

"I am." Marmion creased her brows slightly in surprise. "Madame, excuse me if I seem to overrule your authority, but I have taken it upon myself to investigate circumstances here. I have been hospitalized at the Intergal Infirmary Station for a virus I contracted on my last assignment in the Fuegan Galaxy. While at the hospital, I could not help but overhear a denizen of this planet, supposedly a witness for this committee, I learned upon inquiry, demand his conjugal rites with someone he referred to as an "ungrateful child." He claimed that she had been seduced away from him and his family of other wives by some monstrous sentient life-form that apparently lives within this world. As you can imagine, much of what he had to say deeply disturbed me, and so I prevailed upon the captain of the *Prometheus*, who was bound for orbit here, to transport me, as well. I'm sure Intergal is aware that while they may govern humanoid life in accordance with CIS regulations—which this witness apparently was *not* following—on their incorporated worlds, new life-forms are specifically the concern of the CIS. They are, in fact, specifically the concern of my department and myself."

Torkel looked about to explode, Whittaker's face was wreathed in smiles, and Braddock Makem almost fainted.

"Not a monstrous sentient life-*form*, Messer Anaciliact, but most certainly a sentient being." Marmion corrected him with a smile, hardly daring to believe the good luck that had brought not only CIS, but Phon Tho in particular, to them at this time. And they had Matthew and his nephew to thank for the man's prompt arrival! It was a mercy to Matthew that he wasn't here. The knowledge would probably seriously impede his recovery. She continued, "The sentience is *not* a monstrous one. That was a perception entertained only by the witness and the people he forcibly influenced. He was the monster."

"I shouldn't doubt that a bit," Anaciliact said, remembering vividly his distaste for the witness in question. "I stand corrected."

"You also stand on this supposed sentient being," Torkel snapped, jabbing his index finger at the floor.

The dark arching eyebrows in Anaciliact's duskycomplected face rose high in his forehead. "Do I take it you mean the *planet* is sentient?"

"It most certainly is," Whittaker and Marmion said in firm chorus. Then Marmion, seeing Yana and Sean close by, gestured urgently for them to come to her.

"And this is the finding of the committee?"

"Most decidedly," Bal Jostique said, with a nervous glance at the piled stone skyscrapers looming where Intergal's runway and the streets and buildings of SpaceBase had been.

"We were interrupted before formal adjournment, messer," Chas amended, "but I think if you check with Farringer Ball you will find that Intergal has decided to . . ."

Anaciliact held up his hand, his expression counseling silence. "Intergal has overstepped its bounds in deciding anything without consultation with CIS. And your statement, Dr. Fiske, that two persons have been appointed governors of this . . . living body . . . is totally out of order. No sentient creature may be coerced, only negotiated with."

"That's been my argument all along," Yana said, having been close enough to hear the last statement.

"The problem has been trying to get Intergal to accept that this planet is sentient," Sean Shongili said, standing close enough to Yana to hold one of her hands discreetly behind him. "Now that we have reestablished contact with the secretary-general of Intergal, Farringer Ball, he seems to be willing to believe the proof." He gestured in the direction of the singularly elevated field.

"That is as well, I suppose," Anaciliact said suavely, "for the . . . ah . . . extrusion seems to have limited itself in a most unusual fashion and in the most clear terms that it wishes this facility evacuated. So that I may commune with the sentience, I will also require the removal of even the indigenous personnel—"

He was interrupted by a rumbling that seemed to make the solid floor underfoot ripple from one end to the other.

"Messer Anaciliact," Marmion said, waggling a finger at

him, "I believe the planet just said 'No.' It likes the people who live here; it protects them in ways that cause them to die very quickly when removed from its custody."

The CIS representative's expression had altered as he staggered to keep his balance. "It cannot so quickly perceive—"

Another rumble, quicker, so that it appeared to be more emphatic.

"We weren't supposed to get any aftershocks," Braddock Makem murmured, thoroughly dismayed.

"Messer Anaciliact," Sean began, smiling and with a little conciliatory bow, "I think it would be best if we took you to one of those special places where the planet communicates with us in its unique fashion. I believe it is quite ready to discuss the terms of its . . . use as a habitation and the uses to which its gifts may be put."

"Don't, I beseech you, Messer Anaciliact," Torkel said, on the point of grabbing the hands of the CIS representative, who deftly avoided him, "go into one of those misty caves! It's all hallucinogenic. You'll believe anything."

"Captain . . ."

"Fiske, Torkel Fiske." The man's handsome features were contorted with the urgency of his entreaty. "You'll end up like *them*!" He gestured toward his father, Yana, Marmion, and Sean.

"My dear Captain Fiske, I am conditioned to reject any hallucinogenics and drugs, and trained to perceive illusions or spells of any nature," Anaciliact replied with imperturbable and gentle reassurance. "I assure you I am well able to probe the substance of sentience in all forms of creatures, to the exact degree of self-awareness and percipience. Now, if we may just proceed to wherever it is I may start my investigations?"

"This way," Sean said, gesturing toward the door through which the CIS investigator had recently entered. "It's a short distance from here but I believe—ah, Johnny, did your copter survive?"

"It did, Sean." Johnny eyed Sean's companion. "And it's even fueled and ready to go."

"Yana, where's Clodagh?" Sean asked, looking around the busy incident room. Then he noticed orange cats prowling discreetly or observing from the tops of piled cartons. "Never mind. She'll be there."

When they reached the outskirts of Kilcoole and Johnny circled the copter to land it close to the warm springs, Coaxtl and Nanook bounded out of the forest to await their descent.

They sat back on their haunches when they saw Phon Tho Anaciliact step down. He turned, slightly startled, then bowed with a touch of reverence in the motion.

"You are messengers?" he asked.

*Occasionally that is our function,* Nanook said. *But we do as we please.*

"As your breed always has," Phon Tho said with another respectful bow.

*You may follow us. The way has been cleared.*

"Sean, the coo-berry . . ." Yana said as she saw Phon Tho following the track-cats toward the warm springs.

"Why did you think Clodagh, Sinead, Bunny, and Diego skived out of SpaceBase as fast as they could?" he asked her, taking her hand as he landed lightly on his feet beside her. "Coming, Johnny?"

"Sure am!" Johnny had helped Marmion, Whittaker, and Sally descend from the other side of the packed copter and now they all followed the leaders.

Dried stalks lined the path, but not a single live coo-berry tendril remained. Some might have been killed by Clodagh's antidote, Yana thought, but the rest seemed to have simply . . . been swallowed up by the planet's crust. Oh well. Anywhere else that would have been incredible, but as always, Petaybee played by its own rules.

The track-cats deftly trotted across the stepping-stones to enter the gap between cliff side and cascade, the CIS arbitrator not a step behind them as they disappeared into the Kilcoole access area.

Mist was already forming by the time all had gathered, for Clodagh, Sinead, Aisling, Bunny, and Diego were waiting in the cave, having cleared the way. Clodagh smiled and gestured for Phon Tho to seat himself nearby, and he immediately assumed the very difficult lotus meditation position, back erect, hands with thumbs and index fingers meeting. Marmion settled herself with Sally and Whittaker. Sean and Yana seated themselves so that they faced Phon Tho.

That gentleman had a good long look at the wondrous colors and forms that were shortly obscured by the thickening mist. A slight smile curved his finely molded lips, and then he closed his eyes.

Sean and Yana, shoulders and thighs touching, experienced an overwhelming sensation of relief and total relaxation, of reassurance and goodwill: a sense of great achievement, although relief was the dominant feeling.

When the mist dissolved at last, leaving the lambent glow of the rocks in their splendidly delicate colorations visible, the relief still remained. Then all the participants turned their attention to Phon Tho Anaciliact.

He rose from his lotus position with the special gracefulness of someone well accustomed to such a maneuver and smiled at them.

"This planet is self-aware in a manner I have never before encountered. It is an entity, a being with consciousness, and as such deserves the protection which is my prerogative. While it insists that it is no longer indentured to Intergal, it honors the obligation of life and will redeem itself in due course." Then he turned to Clodagh. "You are named as one minister to its needs, and you, Sean Shongili, are another." Then he looked curiously around, first at Sinead, then Bunny, until his glance settled on Yana. "Ah, yes, it is you, Colonel Yanaba Maddock, whom I take with me to the headquarters of CIS to verify certain particulars in my report. As soon as communications are repaired, I shall give an interim report to my superiors, but in the meantime, I am authorized to evict the incumbent authority as inimical to the Subject Sentience. You who have lived long on Petaybee are requested to remain. I fear there may be some hardships yet for you to undergo until a proper authority can be framed to deal with such an unusual Sentience and the needs of its inhabitants." His lips curved with wry humor. "But you are welcome, it would seem," he said, smiling at Clodagh, Sinead, Aisling, Whittaker, Johnny, and Sean, "for without you, the Sentience would never have become truly aware of its potential."

"And just what is that potential, Messer Anaciliact?" Marmion asked with one of her more radiant smiles.

He gave a shrug, opening his hands. "It is—boundless, it is—unchartable, it is—unfathomable, it is—"

Yana's pent-up nerves of the last few weeks released in a short guffaw. "I think what Messer Anaciliact is trying to say is, 'whatever.' "

The Sentience gave a tremor that might have been a laugh but certainly concluded the current interview.

"What songs we'll make of this, huh, Bunny?" Diego whispered as people turned to file reverently from the cavern. Bunny smiled in agreement, just as a peculiar echo rang through the cavern. It repeated not the last words of Diego's sentence, nor the first word, but the middle ones. As they turned to listen, the cavern played rainbows on its reflective surfaces and the echo sang back to them, in a voice neither Diego's nor Bunny's nor that of any human being they knew, "Songs we'll make, songs we'll make . . ."

Coming to bookstores everywhere in July 1995.
Published in hardcover by Del Rey Books.

# POWER PLAY

by Anne McCaffrey
and Elizabeth Ann Scarborough

Read on for a sneak preview
of this exciting new science-fiction adventure. . .

# 1

Yanaba Maddock and Sean Shongili held hands in a darkness illuminated only by the glowing eyes of hundreds of animals and the flames of hundreds of candles. The drumming had stopped now, replaced by the sweet slapping of sliding water, the beat of many hearts, and the breathing of many creatures. One pulse was louder than all the drums had been, one breath a wind that guttered and flared the candles with each respiration.

"So how do we do it here?" Yana whispered nervously to the father of her unborn child. "Does the planet give me away or what?"

Sean smiled and winked. "No one has that right but you, love. Let's just say that the planet acts as witness and honorary best being."

"... *best being* ..." an echo sang from the cavern walls. "... best being ..."

He stopped walking and she stopped beside him. All she knew was that they were getting married, Petaybean-style.

She'd been so busy with her new duties as Petaybee's administrator over the last two months that she hadn't had enough time to inquire as fully as she would have liked into the rituals or folkways of the Petaybean marriage ceremony before it was upon her. Sean's neice, Bunny Rourke, one of her chief informants on matters Petaybean, had told her that it was a special sort of latchkay with a night chant at the hot springs. Yana had attended the breakup latchkay when she first arrived. This occasion differed in that the night chant was at the beginning of the latchkay instead of at the end. As at all latchkays, there would be much singing; however, there would probably be more at this particular one. Sean and Yana were each to prepare a song for each other. Songs were how Petaybeans celebrated or commemorated all their most noteworthy experiences. The mode was mostly either a rhyme scheme to some ancient Irish air, or a free-verse poem, chanted Inuit style to the accompaniment of a drum. Yana, whose heart was full but whose mind was too crowded with administrative details while her body was having to make physical accommodations to her pregnancy, had finally created her song. Other than that, she simply hoped that things would go well and allowed herself to be led through the proceedings by the people she had trusted with her life more than once.

Two hours earlier, Kilcoole's premier couturier, Aisling Senungatuk, had arrived with the gown she had created for Yana—rabbit hides crocheted together with woolen yarn in a long, paneled design with a flared skirt, scooped neck, and long sleeves. The crocheted lace inserts were heavily decorated with beads made from scavenged wire and the little pebbles found in certain Petaybean streams. Tumbled, polished, and drilled, the stones were lovely and translucent. The gown was yellow, the Petaybean wedding color, Aisling explained, "because most of the plants make yellow dye." The rabbits were contributed from the collecting places of all of the hunters in the village. Sean's vest was a darker shade of the yellow, trimmed with beaver fur and blue and white beads.

Now the light motes formed a circle around the two, and Clodagh Senungatuk, Aisling's sister and the village's healer, stepped into the center with Sean and Yana. Yana noted with some amusement that as many of Clodagh's orange-striped cats as could crowd around her feet did so, their eyes eerie and iridescent in the candle glow.

"Sean Shongili and Yanaba Maddock, we've come here because we understand you got somethin' to say to all of your friends and kin here where the planet hears you best, is that right?"

"It is," Sean said. "I have a song to sing for you all."

"Sing for us," soft voices said from the shadows, accompanied by an underlying rumble of throaty feline purrs, the whicker of the curly-coats, and the affirmative yips of the dogs.

"Sing," the echo said.

Yana had no idea how many bodies were clustered into the cave that day. The line seemed to stretch clear back to the village and included every man, woman, and child, horse, cat, the larger track-cats, and even everybody's dog teams. And she could have sworn that she saw wild game emerge from the brush and join in the procession just before Clodagh led them into the darkness of the cave behind the hot-springs waterfall.

Sean cleared his throat. The candle flame shadowed

the chiseled planes of his face and softened the outlines of his mouth as he began to chant.

*"Yanaba, she met the enemy*
*Coming to us, she met friends as well*
*And honored them.*
*She met me, and I met love.*
*Aijija*

*With her friends, here around her*
*With her lover, I who take her hand*
*For these people and this world embracing us*
*She met the enemy again and again*
*It is in her name to do so.*
*Aijija*

*Yanaba, who knows my aspects*
*Yanaba, who has my heart*
*Yanaba, who honors my world and my people*
*Yanaba, who carries our future in her body*
*Yanaba, you are already part of my life*
*Yanaba, you already possess my heart*
*I tell you this here, with our world as witness*
*I want you with me forever.*
*Aiji."*

Yana's mouth went suddenly dry. Something soft and furry rubbed against her bare ankles. Her stomach gave a heave and she wondered if the baby could be moving so soon, pushing her to speak. She took Sean's hands as much for support as encouragement and clung to them so tightly that she was afraid she'd leave bruises. But he returned the strong grip, and that gave her the courage she needed. Suddenly light-headed, she felt as if she needed to hold on to him to keep from floating to the top of the cave.

> *"Sean Shongili, my truest friend and love.*
> *Here I am, a woman whose only song*
> *Was of war and death.*
> *How can I sing what I feel for you?*
> *You gave me life when I was dying*
> *A home when I had known none in*
> *Many years of wandering*
> *A family when all of mine is dead*
> *A life to bear*
> *When I thought I could give only death*
> *You showed me a new world and*
> *Invited me to make it my own.*
>
> *"And I do.*
> *In old songs by better singers*
> *They say, 'You are all the world to me.'*
> *I say so, too.*
> *Sean Shongili, you are all the world to me*
> *And the world to me is you.*
> *I love you. Take me as I take you.*
> *As they used to say on earth, 'I do.' "*

Sean took her in his arms then and kissed her, letting his body rest against her belly, which, although still not too obvious, was growing fuller and rounder by the day.

Then Clodagh clapped her hands and everyone dispersed, leaving Yana and Sean alone in the cave, but not in darkness. As the candles departed, a warm soft glow pulsed throughout the cavern, and he eased her to the rock, which seemed to melt into a comfortable bed as she and Sean made love. They always enjoyed that occupation, but here, now, in the cave, where the planet was also part of their communion, she felt as if she had never before been so consumed by the passion that always fired up between them in the act of love. Sean felt it, too, for his hands were tender, possessive in a fashion she would once have resented, exciting in ways she had never experienced. The climax was so extraordinary that she wept and knew, from the wetness of the cheek he pressed hard against hers, that he also had been rocked by the intensity of their consummation. For a moment, she thought she had died.

This time they did not sleep afterward; nor did they dress before leaving the cave to join the throng waiting outside at the thermal pools.

Cheers and laughter greeted them. Overhead the stars and moons, real and man-made, lit the sky, while the candles planted along the sides of the pool garlanded it with ribbons of light. The big cats sported rather clumsily in the water while the dogs fetched various things thrown by their masters. The smaller cats sat disdainfully on the edge of the pool. Yana laughed when one of the curly-coats took a running jump and dived into the pool, making a whale-sized wave that swamped the shore and wet several disgusted felines, who began furiously to lick themselves dry.

Then Sean pushed her in, and a moment later, a seal appeared among the splashing, laughing, naked company. This activity continued till daylight and was the merriest, raunchiest festivity she had ever attended. Periodically, someone would hoist himself out of the water and run bare-assed to the baskets beyond the candles to fetch something to cram into his mouth before diving back into the pool.

At daylight, everyone went ashore, dressed, and walked limply home except Sean and Yana, who rode double on one of the curlies, following Bunny and the village girls, who strewed flower petals and seeds on the path before them.

"I'm starving," Yana muttered up into Sean's chin.

He nuzzled the top of her head. "Good, you'll like this part then. The feast was prepared before we left. But don't eat so much you'll be too full to dance with me afterward."

"*Dance?* You have to be joking! My legs feel like noodles. Umm, noodles. Do you suppose Clodagh made hers? The ones with the smoked fish and dried tomato sauce?"

"I have it on good authority that she did. Is all you think of your stomach?"

"I'm eating for two!"

"So you are. Forgive me," he said, lifting her down from the curly-coat's back.

During the feasting, she had an ample chance to rest and gaze into Sean's eyes and messily feed him and be fed by him, also part of the wedding protocol. The food was arrayed in the middle of the meeting house, and Sean and Yana and the other adults sat on benches along the wall, while Bunny led the youngsters of Kilcoole in offering them food.

Meanwhile, everyone occupied themselves by singing

319

the songs *they* had written for Sean and Yana. Bunny sang of her first meeting with Yana and their wild ride down the river. Sean's sister, Sinead, told how she knew Yana would be one of them from the time she went on her first hunt. Adak sang of the hiding of Sean in the snocle shed with Yana, making frequent clandestine trips which the Powers That Be did not know anything about.

Even Steve Margolies, now residing in Kilcoole with his partner, Frank Metaxos, and Frank's son Diego, sang of how Yana and Sean had reunited him with his family.

Yana's neighbor across the street had a hilarious pantomime song about Yana throwing Colonel Giancarlo out of her cabin with the burned fish. That was one of the few songs rhymed and sung to an old Irish air instead of chanted to drums. Clodagh said she believed the tune went originally to a song called "The Charladies' Ball."

As the other young people began to clear away the empty serving plates, Diego took his newly crafted guitar and joined the drummers, Old Man Mulligan on his whistle, and Mary Yulikilik on her handmade concertina. All together, they wheezed up a quite respectable dance tune.

Sean took Yana's hands in his, led her out on the floor, and then swung himself opposite her at the top of the cleared hall. Two by two, the others followed: Dr. Whittaker Fiske, who had returned especially to dance at the wedding, partnered Clodagh, followed by Sinead with Aisling, Moira and Seamus, Bunny and her sister 'Cita, Frank Metaxos and Steve Margolies; Liam Maloney and Bunny's cousin Nula completed the reel line. Captain Johnny Greene, who had extended his

```
SALE              7111 1 00010 28877
MEMBER       0120 09/01/95  02:29 PM


MEMBER NO.            0013
1  9780345387806
  POWER LINES - A. MCC          5.59N
QTY 1

         GST 7%                  0.39
    TOTAL                       $5.98
              CASH               6.00
              CHANGE             0.02
```

* GST: R138910161
* QST: 8507-1038

```
***************************************
* NO REFUND OR EXCHANGE ON SOFTWARE,  *
* CD'S, TAPES, VIDEOS, RIBBONS AND    *
* TONER IF THE ORIGINAL PACKAGING HAS *
* BEEN OPENED.                        *
***************************************
```

OLDE BIZ   LITERALLY BLOWS YOUR MIND

shore leave for the occasion, had Captain Neva Marie Rhys-Hall from SpaceBase as his partner for the dance in another reel line, while his fellow copter pilot, Rick O'Shay, gallantly led old Kitty Intiak onto the floor. Orange cats tiptoed daintily to the food that had been put on the side for them, while the dogs went home to their kennels to eagerly await scraps from the feast. Track-cats lounged by the doors and on top of the roof, and the curlies grazed in the last of the green fields left by the unusually long, warm summer, now turning to fall.

Somewhere in the middle of the third dance, Terce, who was minding the snocle shed, came in and tapped Adak on the shoulder; Adak, in turn, tapped Johnny on the shoulder and whispered something in his ear. The men left, accompanied by Captain Rhys-Hall, and returned in time to rescue Yana from a fifth dance.

Marmion de Revers Algemeine and two company corpsmen in dress white uniforms were with them.

Yana and Sean stopped dancing to greet their friend. Marmion was elegant as usual, in a royal blue tunic with a purple underdress, the top heavily embroidered in jade and silver, matching her earrings and rings.

"Marmie! How wonderful that you could come!" Yana cried. Marmion kissed both her cheeks, then Sean's.

"Yes, and in addition to your wedding present, I'm afraid I've come to take you away from all this. The CIS court is reconvening a week from now and your testimony will be necessary to augment Commissioner Phon Tho Anaciliact's decision on Petaybee. I thought you'd want to do it yourself, since going off-planet would be lethal to native Petaybeans." She glanced down briefly at

Yana's middle and a look of consternation flowed over her classic features. "Oh, my. Time flies, doesn't it?"

Yana smiled. "It does indeed. But I see no reason . . ."

"I don't think it's wise for you to go off-planet this far into your pregnancy, Yana," Sean said, his hand on her shoulder tightening protectively.

But others in the room had joined them by now. Clodagh and Whit Fiske greeted Marmie with busses on the cheeks, and Bunny pushed her way through to them, trailed closely by Diego, who had stopped playing and slung his guitar across his back as soon as he saw the newcomers arrive.

"How long does she need to be gone, Marmie?" Clodagh asked.

"Not long, I should think. Counting the journey, two weeks your time, three at the most."

"Huh," Clodagh said. "I'd never last that long. Sean neither."

"I mean to be there, too, Yana," Marmion said, "though as an Intergal board member, my testimony is assumed to be biased and self-serving in one of those peculiarly bureaucratic fashions that people can't really explain anyhow. It's too bad there's no qualified native Petaybean to testify."

"I qualify, and I think I could go, too," Bunny said, pulling at her sleeve. "I'm young enough to go off-planet without any ill effects, and I know everything that's happened. I could sing them the song I made about it. Though Diego's songs are better."

"If you're going, I'm going," Diego said. "Now's my chance to show you all those technical things you keep telling me couldn't possibly work! Besides, I wouldn't want your head getting turned by all those guys in uniform. And I could see my mom," he added with a glance at Marmion, as if the more conventional reason might sway her where his desire to be with Bunny might not.

"Still, we need Colonel Maddock—or is it Shongili now?" Marmie asked with a twinkle.

"I think for courtroom purposes I'd better remain Maddock for the time being," Yana said.

"Yana, you're four months pregnant," Sean said. "With *my* child." The emphasis, Yana knew, was not merely possessive. Because of Sean's dual nature as man and seal, he was concerned about just how many of his traits his children would inherit and how deeply an off-planet experience would affect them.

"Many women are on duty right up until delivery now, Sean," she said, dropping her hand to his arm and giving it a reassuring squeeze. "And you heard Marmie, it will only be three weeks. If I have Bunny along—"

Clodagh touched Sean's hand, "It should be okay that long, Sean. And Petaybee needs her to do this."

"I suppose so. I only wish I could accompany her."

"I'd take good care of her, Uncle Sean. You know I would," Bunny said, throwing her arms around his waist.

"And I'd take care of both of them, Dr. Shongili," Diego said, with a challenging look at Marmion.

Marmion smiled at him, then turned back to Yana. "With you as adult guardian, I see no problem with Bunny and Diego accompanying you, Yana. In fact, I'm sure the CIS Anaciliact would appreciate all the support he can get. I don't suppose little 'Cita . . ."

But Sean denied that choice with a firm shake of his

head. "After all she's been through, she's much too fragile in my opinion. 'Cita stays here. Besides, Coaxtl frets herself into molting mountains of hair if the girl is out of sight for any extended period."

"I can tell what needs to be told, to anyone who asks," Bunny said at her staunchest.

"Sean," Yana said, turning to look into his dear, worried face. "Duty does have a way of calling regardless of personal convenience, love."

"I wouldn't stop you from doing what you think you need to do, even if I thought I could get away with it, Yana." His grin was slightly strained and anxious, and so were his eyes. "But be careful."

Yana understood his concern, maybe more than just "understood" after their union in the cave, and she deeply regretted the necessity of leaving her new husband so precipitously. She consoled herself with the knowledge that what they had between them would keep, on the ice and in the heat, come what may.

Two hours later the envoys were ready to depart.

Clodagh gave each of them an almost ritualistic kiss and embrace, putting a little leather bag on a thong around each of their necks.

"What's this?" Yana asked.

"It's dirt," Clodagh said simply.

"Dirt?"

"Yes. Petaybee wants you to have something to remember it by. The dirt's from the cave."

Not long before, Yana would have been stymied by such a statement, but now she squeezed Clodagh warmly in an embrace of her own. "This makes me feel a lot better."

324

Then Sean clasped her in a farewell embrace and she, Bunny, and Diego boarded the company shuttle that would take them to Marmion's executive spaceliner, waiting in orbit. In Yana's carryall was Sean's wedding vest, to sleep with, and a hastily made town recording to Petaybean relatives in company service. Bunny carried a frozen fish for her cousin Charlie from his parents and a basket of pemmican from the wedding feast for homesick Petaybeans. Diego carried letters from his father to his mother, and a basket of his favorite Petaybean foods, plus nutrients to keep himself and Bunny healthy on the journey.

Once aboard the spaceliner, Sally Point-Jefferson, Marmion's aide, carefully placed Charlie's fish in the freezer. Bunny remained glued to the viewscreen, watching Petaybee disappear into a tiny point of light in the vastness of black space. She bent and unbent her fingers against the port in farewell as her home disappeared altogether.